THE BERLIN CROSSING

KEVIN BROPHY

headline
review

First published in Great Britain in 2012
by HEADLINE REVIEW
An imprint of HEADLINE PUBLISHING GROUP

First published in paperback in 2012
by HEADLINE REVIEW
An imprint of HEADLINE PUBLISHING GROUP

1

Cataloguing in Publication Data is available from the British Library

ISBN 978 0 7553 8086 2

Typeset in Giovanni book by Avon DataSet Ltd,
Bidford-on-Avon, Warwickshire

Printed and bound by
CPI Group (UK) Ltd, Croydon, CR0 4YY

Headline's policy is to use papers that are natural, renewable and
recyclable products and made from wood grown in sustainable forests.
The logging and manufacturing processes are expected to conform
to the environmental regulations of the country of origin.

HEADLINE PUBLISHING GROUP
An Hachette UK Company
338 Euston Road
London NW1 3BH

www.headline.co.uk
www.hachette.co.uk

'EMOTIONAL CONVICTION AND DETAILS OF LIFE UNDER COMMUNISM... BROPHY ULTIMATELY OFFERS HIS OWN DISTINCTIVE OPTIMISM IN THE HINT OF HOPE AND RECONCILIATION' *METRO*

'THIS IS A BRILLIANT EVOCATION OF THE EARLY 90S WHEN GERMANY BECAME A CHANGED COUNTRY WITH THE FALL OF THE BERLIN WALL' *PETERBOROUGH EVENING TELEGRAPH*

'A TERRIFIC STORY... WITH DEPTH AND INTRIGUE... I LOVED IT. THOROUGHLY RECOMMENDED' WWW.THEBOOKBAG.CO.UK

'*THE BERLIN CROSSING*'S GREAT STRENGTH IS ITS UNDERSTANDING OF TANGLED LOYALTIES TO FAMILY AND COUNTRY... BROPHY IS A TALENTED WRITER' WWW.BOOKMUNCH.WORDPRESS.COM

'A DIFFERENT AND REFRESHING PERSPECTIVE... *THE BERLIN CROSSING* IS A NOVEL OF LOVE, SACRIFICE AND OF AWAKENING... AS WELL AS THE CLEVER PLOTTING AND STRUCTURING, THE CHARACTERISATION IS STRONG... [A] THOUGHT-PROVOKING AND EVOCATIVE BOOK' WWW.2606BOOKS.BLOGSPOT.COM

'MICHAEL RITTER IS A FASCINATING CHARACTER FOR HIS TAKE ON THE EAST GERMAN EXPERIENCE... BROPHY HAS DELIVERED AN INTRIGUING NOVEL ABOUT IDENTITY' DECLAN BURKE, WWW.CRIMEALWAYSPAYS.COM

KEVIN BROPHY has told the story of his childhood in the Army Barracks in Galway, Ireland, in the memoir *Walking the Line*. Educated locally, he later obtained an MA at Leeds University. In 2009 he was Writer-in-Residence to the city of Langenfeld (NRW) in Germany. He has taught in England, Ireland, Poland and Germany.

for Elisabeth Wölk

Acknowledgements

I'm a pen-and-paper writer. Throughout the various computer versions of this book, I was guided and helped by my daughter, Georgia Brophy; typesetter, Helen Geary; my elevenses buddy, Paddy Lydon; my neighbour, Lorcán Mannion; my colleague at Lodz University, Andrew Tomlinson. My thanks to all.

I'm happy to acknowledge, with gratitude, the friendship and support of my writing guru, Christopher Murray, through all my endeavours.

Lastly, and certainly not least: my characters and I negotiated this Berlin crossing with the help of two consummate professionals – my editor at Headline, Claire Baldwin, and my patient agent, Caroline Montgomery. Sincere thanks to both.

What need you, being come to sense
But fumble in a greasy till
And add the halfpence to the pence . . .

W. B. Yeats, *September 1913*

Prologue

December 1962, The Berlin Wall

The vast sea of lights on the Western side drew your eyes from the grey darkness of the Wall. You tried to keep warm in the high watchtower, tried to keep your eyes on the killing zone below, but the Western lights were too bright, too warm. An ocean of lights, red and orange and green and gold, shimmering in the snow, across the night.

Across the Wall.

Corporal Hans Keiler tried to wriggle his toes inside his rubber-soled boots. His wife had knitted him extra-thick socks for his nights in the watchtower above the Wall. The socks kept his feet from freezing. His wife's back was warmer, in their narrow bed. *Night duty.* Still, the pay was better, it would pay for a bigger bed, a new table, maybe a sofa. Greta knew how to warm a man on a sofa, not just in bed.

Enough of that. Wriggle your toes. Blow on your fingers. Flex those fingers around your rifle. Remind yourself that it was your expert shot that got you this assignment on the Wall. *If it moves, shoot.*

Corporal Hans Keiler shivered – and not from the cold. He'd never trained his weapon on anything other than a cardboard target or a plywood silhouette swinging on a cable at the end of a shooting range. He'd never looked down his rifle sights at a man or woman.

His friend Jurgen, runner-up in the regimental shooting competition, had never been the same since he'd shot that student in broad daylight a month before. A big, genial farm boy from south of Rostock, always ready for an unmalicious laugh, that was Jurgen. Until he'd trained his sights on that idiot student who thought he could sprint his way across the zone in the middle of a quiet afternoon. One shot, that was all it took, and the fellow dropped in the middle of the zone. Hardly twitched; Jurgen just clipped him in the back, right through the heart.

Jurgen won a citation, was awarded a bonus, honoured at morning parade. But he never did Wall duty again.

The last Corporal Keiler had heard, Jurgen was spouting rubbish in a loony bin outside Magdeburg.

Concentrate. Shut your eyes to those seductive lights to the West. Follow the path of the searchlight as it orbits the killing zone of the Wall. Concentrate on your field of fire.

And hope you have another incident-free shift.

He narrowed his eyes, squinted through the falling snow. Heavier now, big soft flakes floating in the translucent beam.

A sound below him, slight, a rustle in the night.

The beam paused, lingered on the forbidden space, was swung back by the operator.

A figure caught in the lights, rising to his knees. Corporal Keiler watched the figure stand upright, tall, a peaked cap above a young face, stubbled.

Halt! The command barked in the night. Another spotlight, the fellow transfixed between the crossbeams.

A siren screamed.

Lights flashing now on the Western side, voices raised.

Corporal Keiler went through the motions. Weapon to his shoulder. Marksman's eye trained on the figure in the lights. So young, younger than me, Keiler thought, in the split second before he pulled the trigger.

The figure in the lights blinked, took a step towards the West.

The bullet caught him in the shoulder, spun him round to face East Berlin.

The second shot was better, lower.

The fellow was dead before he hit the grey surface of the killing ground.

He fell on his back and the snow fell on the flowers of blood blooming on his chest, on the peaked cap lying beside his outstretched hand.

Corporal Keiler shivered, knew he'd have to deliver a lengthy report to his commander. He knew he wouldn't mention the smile, the damnedest thing, he could swear to it: the fellow seemed to smile as his body fell to the ground amid the falling snow.

BOOK 1

BRANDENBURG

1993

One

Frau Winkler said that, yes, she knew I had an appointment with the Director but that she'd check, anyway, just to make sure He (you could hear the capital letter in her voice) was not engaged. I was afforded a full view of the shapely Winkler figure sheathed in a taut, black skirt that seemed designed more for display than modesty, as our new school secretary got out from behind her new desk and knocked on the Director's office door. I'd overheard staffroom whispers about the Director's more detailed knowledge of Frau Winkler but I kept my own counsel on such musings. Old habits die hard – never more so than in these post-Reunification days.

Frau Winkler opened the door and as it closed behind her I was left to study the immaculate emptiness of our secretary's desktop. Only the new Siemens phone, all buttons and lights, was permitted to stand on the veneered surface. It was all part of the new *Wessie* outlook – all clean lines and no clutter. Especially in our hearts and minds, which obviously needed sanitizing, delousing and Western streamlining.

When Frau Winkler re-emerged from the Director's office, her well-chiselled, mid-forties face gave no indication as to whether her nether (or upper) landscape had enjoyed any brief exploration. She stood aside to usher me into the Presence; I caught the scent of something cool and musky and was reminded that I hadn't had sex for over a year now, since Stefanie had asked me to leave and I'd gone back to my mother's flat near the railway station—

'Herr Doktor Ritter!' The Director's voice was fulsome. 'How good of you to come!'

I didn't point out that I had no choice, that the victors wrote the history books.

'You wished to see me, Herr Direktor,' I said as we shook hands.

Dr Wilhelm Frick motioned for me to be seated. My chair left me looking slightly upwards at our new Director, across the vastness of his desk. Like Frau Winkler's in the outer office – and like all the other furniture in both offices – it was new. While the Director busied himself with a yellow-bound plastic folder – I could read my name on the taped tag – I took a quick look around. Not a trace of the old Director's office – nor indeed of the old Director himself – remained. Martin Stork, the Director who had run the school even when I had been a student here, had been swept away, along with his old metal desk and matching grey cabinets, in the great *Wessie* tide of Reunification. I'd sensed Martin's imminent departure on the last day of summer term – the diffident handshake had been uncharacteristic, unlike the firm grasp which had always marked our holiday partings and our start-of-term renewals. We'd never been friends, Martin Stork and I – in the GDR even the coin of friendship had to be tested between your teeth before being put under the microscope – but we had both known that our loyalties belonged to the same flag. On that blistering July day when we had wished each other an enjoyable summer break, I think we'd both known that Martin Stork's tenure as Director of Brandenburg Gymnasium No. 1 was coming to an end. The city of Brandenburg, like all the other towns and cities of the old German Democratic Republic, was already showing the results of West Germany's Chancellor, Helmut Kohl's promise to make the fields of the East bloom again with flowers: carpetbaggers from the West were sprouting everywhere in the East, their purses and pockets gaping open for whatever windfalls they could engineer for themselves. Their cars were beguilingly monstrous, their accents disconcertingly strange, as they sat in our seats and took over the running of our lives.

Just as Dr Wilhelm Frick was now running mine.

'The Social Review Committee has been studying your case, Herr Doktor Ritter.'

The Director paused, making space for me to comment, perhaps, on the wondrous nature of the Social Review Committee, but I had no intention of making it easy for the balding bastard. The full-colour, framed photograph of Cologne Cathedral on the wall above the Director's head just about summed up the absurdity of the fellow's appointment: what did we want, here in the heart of the old East, with a Director who took off for Cologne every Friday at noon and did not see fit to return to his desk in Brandenburg until mid-afternoon on Monday? Was it for this that Martin Stork had been found wanting? Was it for this I sat in silence opposite this balding, bespectacled interloper who couldn't even be bothered to set up a home in our city? *To facilitate this shit who spent four nights a week in our newest hotel while he presided over a long-established secondary school that many of us were devoted to?*

'Yours is a most interesting background, Herr Doktor.' The Director fingered a page from the yellow plastic file. 'Most interesting indeed.'

'I'm a schoolteacher, like a lot of other Germans. It's neither unusual nor exceptionally interesting.'

'But what's interesting is that you're a teacher of *English*.'

'It's what I studied.'

'It's a bit more than that – it's what you were *allowed* to study.'

'So what? Everybody had to get permission to do whatever course they wanted to do.'

'Don't be disingenuous, Herr Doktor.' Behind the spectacle lenses the pale eyes were flinty. 'In the GDR, English was the voice of America, the language of the enemy. Only the chosen few, the *trusted* few, were allowed to study the vernacular of the capitalist world – only those who could be depended upon not to succumb to the terrible evils and temptations of capitalism.'

I met his gaze. 'You haven't got much idea of how we did things here,' I said. 'I applied to do English at Rostock University and I was offered a place there. But you know all this,' I added, pointing at the yellow file.

'I also know that only card-carrying Party members were allowed to study English.'

'That's more than I know – and anyway I've never concealed the fact that I was a member of the Party.'

'You've never advertised it either.'

'Do you flash your card everywhere you go?' I retorted hotly. 'Social Democrat or Christian Democrat? Or does it make no difference, just Tweedledum and Tweedledee?'

For what seemed like minutes the anger was palpable, simmering above the leather-topped desk.

'You should realize, Herr Doktor Ritter,' he said at last, 'that offensive remarks are not helpful to your situation.'

'And what *is* my situation?' I demanded.

'The Social Review Committee has studied your background and has made its recommendation. You were an outstanding student at Rostock –' another page in the file was fingered – 'becoming a very active and successful Chairman of the

International Student Friendship Society. In that capacity you were the face of the university to all visiting students, mostly postgrads from communist and socialist states who arrived to study German in Rostock. A few such students came from the UK and these were paid particular attention by the Stasi, with a view to recruiting them for intelligence activities—'

'That's nonsense!' But Frick's words stung. In my time at Rostock I had chosen not to wonder about these approaches to British postgrads.

'Please don't interrupt. The Committee is in no doubt that these International Friendship Societies were used in all GDR universities as recruiting grounds for spies and informers. There is no evidence that you yourself were involved in such recruitment activities—'

'That's a relief!'

'Neither is there any evidence that you were *not* a party to such activities.'

'Strange,' I said quietly, 'in the GDR we operated on the principle that a man was innocent until proven guilty.'

Dr Frick stared at me.

'You people!' He turned back to the file. 'When you finished your degree, you were chosen, perhaps –' an eyebrow raised – 'perhaps even *ordered* to continue on to doctoral studies in English.'

'Why are you going over all this? It's all just ancient history.'

'It's not so ancient but it *is* history. It's history that shows you to have enjoyed privileges only available to the elite.'

'Even before I'd finished my PhD I was back in this school as a teacher and I've been here ever since. I just hadn't realized that being a schoolmaster was a privilege of the elite.'

'I'll grant you that,' the Director said. 'You may not know that your old department at Rostock wanted you back to teach there and –' he shuffled among the papers – 'the Head of English at Leipzig University also wanted you to work there.'

He saw the astonishment on my face.

'Your old Director, Herr Stork, didn't want you to go – said you were a first-rate teacher who got on well with the students and that in time you would make a first-rate Director of Brandenburg Gymnasium No. 1.'

To cover my confusion I looked away from him. Through the tall window of the Director's office I could see the Director's BMW, all gleaming West German confidence, tucked into its own special parking spot. Frau Winkler's red Golf nestled in its shadow. Beyond them stretched an array of cars never seen in the Brandenburg I had grown up in – Volkswagens, Toyotas, Fiats, Fords and every car make you could think of – a roll-call of the triumph of capitalism. At the end of the line of cars stood my own green Trabi. Martin Stork would have understood why I refused to let the old car go, even in these days of plenty, but old Martin was gone and I knew I was about to follow him into the wilderness of former card-carrying Party members.

'Ironically, Herr Doktor, it is Herr Stork's enthusiastic endorsement that finally makes it impossible for you to continue at my school.'

My school: this place that we had laboured to build was now the property of a BMW-driving Johnny-come-lately from Cologne.

'So now it's clear that I can't do my job, is it?'

'You don't need me to remind you that education is about more than classroom performance and examination results. Education is about young hearts and minds – about opening those hearts and minds, and shaping them to contribute to the good of society.'

'And just what do you think we were doing here all those years before you arrived with your liberation flags?' I couldn't keep the bitterness out of my voice.

'It seems to me, Herr Doktor Ritter,' he said flatly, 'that you were closing minds and hearts, just as you were closing borders – and your own people were prepared to die trying to cross them.'

His words were the smug boast of the conqueror; there was no easy reply to them. When Stefanie used to hurl the same words at me across the no-man's-land of our sitting room, I used to tell her that all those who fled, or tried to flee, to the utopia of the West, would find only a fool's paradise. What kind of society could be founded on a vision of endless supplies of washing machines and Levi jeans? At least the world we had striven for included a job for everybody.

I didn't bother to reply to the Director's goading. All of a sudden I was tired – tired of the long struggle against the tide; tired of life without Steffi, tired of wondering how long I might last under the new regime at Brandenburg Gymnasium No. 1. A great many of my old colleagues had already been cast into the limbo of unemployment where, it seemed, I was about to join them.

I turned my gaze from the window to the Director. Keep your mouth shut, I told myself, don't give the bastard the satisfaction of hearing the fear in your voice.

'The School Board,' he began, 'has accepted the recommendation of the Social Review Committee that it is no longer safe, prudent or acceptable to allow you to continue as a member of our staff and your appointment is therefore terminated –' he paused, staring across the desk at me – 'with immediate effect.'

'Immediate?' I couldn't help myself: the word, creaky with fear, scrambled from my mouth.

'Your replacement arrives tomorrow.'

'From Cologne, or Dusseldorf, or Hamburg, or some other home of the free?'

'Your sarcasm ill becomes you, Herr Doktor. You refuse to believe that the world has moved on, just as you refuse to get rid of that foul-smelling Trabant – God knows, you are now being paid enough to afford something better.'

'Maybe it's just as well I didn't buy into our great new consumer society,' I said, 'since I'm about to join the army of the GDR unemployed.'

'Of course, your literary skills will stand you in a good stead, Herr Doktor.' He took my book from a drawer, threw it on the desk in front of me. *'Workers' Dawn* indeed!' His voice dripped sarcasm. *'Stories of the Proletariat* by Michael Ritter! Truly a great dawn, one that inspired your countrymen to flee in their thousands.'

I could have struck him for that. The little book of stories – about men and women and children who had overcome varying personal difficulties to work effectively for their homeland – meant as much to me as my PhD from Rostock University. It was a handsome book, hardback, with a dust jacket that showed a young worker in dungarees, blue cloth cap tilted nonchalantly on his curly head, facing optimistically into a rising sun. My dungareed worker looked – like me – not to a land of bananas and Deutschmarks but to a country where every working man and woman was a contributing hero. Even my mother had admired it. My mother's dislike of our rulers in East Berlin was unspoken, but for all its muteness it was palpable in our silences and our occasional arguments; in the same way, her pleasure in my own achievements was rarely expressed – no matter how much my adolescent self longed to hear it. My book in her hands was one of the rare occasions when her mask slipped. 'It's lovely,' my mother said. *'Gut gemacht*, Michi.' *Gut gemacht*. Well done.

My misfortune was that, just a few months after the publication of *Workers' Dawn*, the Berlin Wall had fallen and, with it, my homeland. Yes, I *could* have struck him. It wouldn't have made any difference to my future employment prospects, which were already nil.

I didn't. I took the book in my hands, turned it over. It still gave me a tingle, to see my name on the front, my passport-size photo on the back.

'You couldn't understand,' I said. 'We weren't in it for what we could get out of it. We *did* dream of a . . .' I wanted to say 'dawn' but it would have seemed both pretentious and defeated in the presence of this interloper who wasn't bothering to conceal his delight in firing me.

'You'll be paid for the rest of the school year,' Frick was saying, 'a very generous settlement, I'm sure you'll agree.'

And after that, I thought, what then? A thirty-year-old Doctor of English Literature wasn't the hottest property in the great new reunited Germany, especially one who carried the guilt of loyalty to the state he had grown up in.

The Director seemed to be reading my thoughts.

'You shouldn't have any problems, not with your English-language qualifications – not like your old colleagues who taught Russian.'

Like Fritzi, I thought, and Ursula: the Wall comes down, the Russians go home and, before you know it, Russian language and literature are as redundant as poor Fritzi and Ursula.

'English is all the rage now,' the Director said. 'New schools are starting up everywhere. You won't have any problem finding work.'

'It's a racket,' I told him, 'and you know it as well as I do. Bonn is pouring millions into our cities but they're sending their own cronies over here to collect the loot. Most of these so-called language schools are being set up by chancers who don't know the first thing about English. Their only reason for coming to the East is to cash in on the fat contracts that are on offer – and they certainly don't pay their teachers much.'

The Director shrugged. 'Every society has individuals who exploit the system for their own advantage – you, above all, should know that.'

Why me 'above all'? I had done my job, I had believed in the ideals of the GDR, nothing more, nothing less. *From each, according to his ability; to each, according to his need*. But I lacked the will, the energy, to debate it with him. The society I had believed in had been betrayed and the Director and his like had possession of the high ground. The photograph of the twin peaks of the distant Cologne Cathedral was the proof of that particular unpalatable pudding.

I stood up. 'I have a class in a few minutes,' I said. 'I must go.'

'That won't be necessary. It's the last class of the day.'

'But—'

'It won't be necessary,' the Director repeated. 'I have made arrangements.'

'But my students—'

'I think it's best this way.'

'I might infect them in some way, is that it? After all this time I don't even get the chance to say goodbye to my students? Is it OK if I go back to the staffroom to collect my stuff – or is that also against the new rules?'

'I think you'll find that Frau Winkler has emptied your locker and has all your belongings waiting for you in her office.' He smiled thinly at me. 'Frau Winkler naturally has a master key to all the new lockers, for both staff and students.'

The new lockers, the white metal ones that had arrived the

previous year, the same day as the Coca-Cola machines that now stood sentinel on the main school corridors.

'Fuck you,' I swore. 'I'm going to the staffroom to say goodbye to my colleagues.'

I slammed the door as I left. Frau Winkler's red mouth was open as I grabbed the two cardboard cartons from her desk and kicked the door of her office shut behind me. I dumped the pair of cartons at the foot of the central staircase and marched up to the first floor.

When I pushed open the staffroom door, I was confronted only by people who were strangers to me. The new Home Economics teacher. The new Business Studies teacher. The new Economics – or was it Sociology? – teacher. Their unfamiliar faces stared expectantly at me, standing in the doorway, breathing heavily.

'Herr Doktor?' It was the plump Home Economics lady who spoke. 'Is everything all right?'

I looked at the three of them around the small table, strangers from another time and place, and knew I no longer belonged there. I closed the door without answering and went downstairs to collect my belongings.

Two

You couldn't hurry a Trabi. Push it, curse it, force the accelerator pedal to the floor and the two-stroke engine pouted, sulked and refused to budge. You had to nurse it, gentle the choke, fiddle with the accelerator and let her move in her own time, belching clouds of petrol and oil behind her box-like rump. No, you couldn't push a Trabi around but that didn't matter much on the narrow cobbled roads of Brandenburg. The road makers of the West had already invaded my home town, bringing us the democratic blessing of new tarmac surfaces and traffic lights where nobody needed or heeded them but there wasn't much they could do about our narrow streets, overhung with old gothic houses which seemed to bend towards each other in some arcane ritual of mutual obeisance. Sometimes you'd think the old houses must tumble upon each other – or on the long-serving tram which clacked its noisy way along the centre of the street. Get stuck behind a tram on the narrow street which snaked its way along the spine of our town and you just followed in its wake, stopping and starting, dropping off and collecting passengers on its unhurried way. Our new masters in Bonn – soon to be transplanted to more luxurious quarters in Berlin – no doubt had plans for our narrow streets, just as they had plans for fellows like me who didn't fit in with their brave new vision of a consumer-driven society.

And as I nursed the old Trabi out of my old school for the last time, I nursed my wounded bitterness in the clattering comfort of its noisy engine. Just who did Dr Wilhelm Frick think he was, to despise me for my loyalty to a fallen flag? Must I, like so many of my former countrymen, dispose of my Trabi just as I had disposed of my country – or as others had disposed of it for me? True, my part-time job at the Police Academy had enabled me to jump the long waiting list for our national motor car but that was no crime: allegiance brought its own rewards. Dr bloody Frick and his fellow carpetbaggers were the living proof of that. Nearly every block and building in Brandenburg was under new ownership and – if the tide of rumours held even a grain of truth – the bricks and mortar of our town had been bought for a proverbial song.

And now Michael Ritter, PhD, could sing his own proverbial song for his supper. But what proverb, I mused, the engine idling noisily as I waited for the tram to pass and let me cross the Hauptstrasse, could comfort me? *Faraway hills are green:* but which hills, far or near, would welcome a former Party member? *The early bird catches the worm*: but I was the worm, swallowed whole by the invading bird. Or better still, *It's an ill wind that blows no good:* the country that had shaped me had blown apart in the storm – and the Fricks of the West had swooped like vultures to gorge on the carcass.

Watch the mixed metaphors, I told myself, easing over the tramlines into Kurstrasse. I used to tell my English students the same thing – that, and a lot of other things – but that was no longer my concern. Nor was the identity of my successor, that unknown teacher who, from tomorrow morning, would be taking over my classes. And yes, I liked my job, I liked my students, and I'd miss them, especially the group of seniors that I had taken to the brink of the final examination, the *Abitur*. As of tomorrow morning, that responsibility was someone else's.

As of now, Michael Ritter, I reminded myself. All things change. Look at the shops on the street. The pharmacy. The supermarket. The banks. The video store. Even Beate Uhse with its garish window full of scarlet knickers and lacy bras. All things change. Like the Soviet war cemetery at the end of the street, once abloom with flowers but now the litter-laden, syringe-strewn hangout of the winos and addicts who have mushroomed in our reunified streets.

All things change, I reminded myself again, as I swung left, heading towards the railway station and, opposite it, the block of flats where I lived with my mother.

Or maybe I should say: where my mother lived and where, in my thirtieth year, I had gone back to live with her.

Or: where my mother was dying and I was waiting for her to die.

I owed her that much, to wait with her for the end. We'd had a difficult relationship: from my earliest days I'd been confused by my mother's wildly swinging moods – there were days when she clung to me, as if my going out of the door of our apartment to school must wound her, like a knife to her heart, but there were other days when that same knife was pointed at me, as if she could not bear to look at me even for another moment. It's not easy, when you're eight or nine years old and you don't know which mother will come home after work, the doting mum who smothers you with kisses or the alter ego whose baleful eyes and words leave you in no doubt that your very existence is an affront to her.

And yet, I thought, easing the Trabi across the canal bridge between the shiny invaders, we had never given up on each other. I'd tried to let go in my first years at Rostock – and maybe my mother had tried too: a whole term would pass without so much as a line from either side and I'd haul my books and bags home reluctantly for each vacation and we'd resume our erratic pas de deux in the fourth-floor apartment opposite the railway station. Just the two of us, smiling and snarling at each other like a pair of puppets doomed forever to dance to their own discordant music. Just the two of us, like it had always been.

Now the nurse came, twice daily, morning and evening, with her syringes and phials of relief. These mornings I was waiting for her, my mother's moaning a grief too great as the night-time injection wore off and the pain took hold of her skeletal body. More, I urged the nurse, why must she suffer so, and the nurse, bleary-eyed at six thirty in the morning, ignored my entreaty and whispered women's words to my mother as she lifted her gently and soothed her ashen face with a damp flannel. She couldn't stay, the nurse whispered to me, the new Agency Controller had just issued all the nurses with new schedules, new timetables. 'You know how it is now,' she said sleepily. Because of my mother's condition, the nurse's visit could be extended to fourteen minutes. Yes, I knew how it was. Targets must be achieved; my mother's dying needs had to be disposed of in fourteen minutes.

The apartment block rose up in front of me. Six storeys of grey cement, peeling windows and six metal doors fronting on to a cracked strip of pathway and a balding patch of lawn. A central corridor ran the length of each floor, with flats to the front and the rear. For the last month or so my mother had been unable to sit up and watch the trains coming and going, great red beasts bound for Magdeburg or Berlin or points further afield. Now she lay on her nest of plumped-up pillows, mostly sleeping until the pain stirred her, and I wondered if she could hear the trains below us, rattling their way on iron rails to places that she would never see.

I could hear her raspy breathing the moment I stepped on to

our fourth-floor corridor. The door to our apartment was slightly ajar: Frau Mertens, our neighbour across the corridor, must be with my mother.

When I eased the door fully open, I could see Frau Mertens through the open doorway of my mother's bedroom. Her bulky body slowly turned from my mother's bed; I felt her eyes upon me, taking in the pair of cartons I was carrying, my old satchel on top of them. She levered her heavy body from the chair and plodded towards me, flat-footed in bedroom slippers.

'She's having a hard time of it, God help her,' she whispered. Frau Mertens was a Pole; God was a frequent figure in her conversation.

'At least she's sleeping.'

'She is, thank God.'

'It's good of you to come,' I said. 'I don't know how I'd manage without your help.'

'Isn't that what neighbours are for? Especially now, the way things are.'

I didn't remind her that she'd been one of the mob lighting candles in St Katherine's, aping the devianto in Leipzig, praying for deliverance from the snares of the GDR. Anyway, Frau Mertens had her own troubles now, with the new Management Committee (i.e. the new owners of our block) advising her that her apartment was too large for one person and that, if she refused to move to a smaller home, 'her position and tenancy, including rent, would have to be reviewed'.

'Even so, Frau Mertens,' I said, 'I'm very grateful – without you . . .' I shrugged. We both knew the truth of my words.

'You're home early.' Her small eyes darted to my cartons of books; there was a question mark in her voice.

'Change of plan,' I said off-handedly, recognizing in her words the other Frau Mertens, the one who had made her husband's life a misery, while he smoked and coughed his way to death on cheap tobacco, the woman you knew was listening behind her closed door to your every move as a pimpled adolescent, the one who'd reported nearly every one of her neighbours to the Stasi (as a 'competent' person, I'd seen the file of letters before the Wall came down) – and then the one who'd jumped on the candle-burning bandwagon in the pews of St Katherine's.

And yet Frau Mertens was not all of a piece: the care and attention she lavished upon my mother were both heartfelt and real.

'I'll sit with her now,' I said. 'You go home and rest.'

'There'll be time enough for rest, all in God's own time.' She looked back at my mother, her thin chest rising and falling in time with the wheezy breathing. 'I didn't always understand your mother, Michael, but God knows she always did her best for you.'

'I didn't always understand her myself.'

She smiled at that, her doughy features transformed almost into girlishness, and I felt her pudgy hand on my arm.

'I have a stew made, Michael, I'll bring you in a bit later on.'

'No, it's too much trouble—'

'What trouble is it? Now go and sit with her – she was rambling a lot in her sleep, Michael this and Michael that – I don't think your mother has long to go now and you should be with her.'

I couldn't speak, her words welling inside me in depths I had no wish to plumb. I watched Frau Mertens leave, black from head to toe in her widow's weeds, her squat body shuffling snail-like along the lino-covered floor, and it was not darkness that left the room but a sense of light, the half-caught cadence of a waltz.

I fixed myself a cup of instant coffee after Frau Mertens left: that at least had improved under the new regime and, as the Director had pointed out to me, my revised salary was ample for the new goods that filled our newly appointed stores. 'You have bananas now,' our conquering fellow countrymen reminded us: hunker down and peel the goodies we bring you. Like good little chimps.

'How can you be so blind?' my mother would rail, in the months after the mob stormed the Brandenburg Gate and stuck yellow flowers into the soldiers' rifles. 'Can't you see, Michi, that the world is changing, that we're free to live our own lives at last?'

'Yes, free to live the lives dictated to us by Reagan and Thatcher, and the rest—'

'Michi, you're such a fool! Can't you see the truth about the kind of life we've had here for the last forty years!'

On and on. Sniper fire across the breakfast table. Artillery salvoes on the bitter evenings when I came in from work. I didn't understand it. My mother had never offered a political opinion until the Wall came down.

When Kohl declared reunification there was a shift in her position. The field was hers, the banners of the enemy not merely fallen but obliterated from the record. The only records that mattered now were the files from the Rathaus basement, the thousands of letters that sometimes showed no more than the settling of neighbourly scores, the venting of personal spleens, but which, in essence, were the vernacular and documented history of a society under siege. Under the new dispensation, concerned citizens were shown in their allegedly true colours as traitors, oppressors, saboteurs. Traitors to what? To whom? They acted in the best interests of the country that nurtured them, fed them, educated them. As I had done. Director Frick and his ilk could point a finger, could accuse me of silence or even complicity and I could answer, truthfully, that sometimes for the greater good, you had to close your eyes and hold your nose.

'At least,' my mother said, on the first anniversary of the fall of the Wall, 'at least keep your opinions to yourself. You'll get yourself into trouble, sounding off the way you do.'

'So dissent is a dirty word now, is it? I thought dissent was a cornerstone of the great democracies of the West!'

'They'll get rid of you if you shoot your mouth off like that at school. You know they'll find you in the files,' my mother said. 'For all I know, not just here in Brandenburg but even in Berlin.' The stream of names from the Stasi headquarters was threatening to become a torrent: if it went on, there'd be no honest citizen left to pass judgement on the rest of us . . . Although the *Wessies* would always be there to help us see the error of our ways.

'What can they do?' I snorted. 'Shoot me? Send me to Siberia?'

'They can take your job away from you.'

'So I'll get another.'

I remembered the look she gave me: we both know, her eyes said, that you're bluffing.

Steffi didn't even argue about it: she just told me that she was divorcing me and that she wanted me out of the flat.

It didn't, at first, seem such a big deal, going back to my mother's; I'd been in the habit of calling in on her most evenings. The move just meant that the skirmishes between my mother and myself had time to burgeon into proper battles.

I held her hand throughout the afternoon. A withered hand, black and blue from the umpteen needles that fed her the morphine. The fingers slightly askew: I'd asked but she'd never told me how they'd been broken. Sometimes I stroked her hand, felt the fleshless mortality of the wounded fingers, remembered, as through a mist, the touch of her hands in my hair, long ago, in the days of boyhood. In the same room. In another country.

The trains came and went. Whistles from Hanover, echoes

from Rostock. Other places, cities on station boards. They were beyond her now, beyond the reach of her dying hands, her obstinate will. I sat beside her deathbed and remembered her fierce pride in me, in my achievements at school, the cheap silver football cups and medals that still shone, polished, on the ancient sideboard.

And yet, after the Wall came down, her attitude towards me seemed almost schizophrenic. Once I had overheard her boasting to Frau Mertens about my appointment as a teacher in the very school I myself had attended; later she became openly critical of the life that had led me there, my attachment to Party and country. We were growing apart. I knew, holding her poor punctured hand, that soon we would reach the last parting.

It came sooner than any of us expected. Maybe it was the returning pain that roused her, the morphine's edge blunting; maybe it was the four o'clock from Berlin, pausing briefly on its way westward to Magdeburg. Or maybe it was just the knuckle of death at the door of my mother's heart reminding her that it was time to look her last on the life she had lived, time for farewells.

I was leaning over her, wiping the spittle that leaked from the corners of her mouth, when she woke. The blue eyes blinked; she frowned in pain. And then, for the first time in weeks, a smile lit up the hollows of her ravaged face – the kind of smile, however momentary, that reminded you of the girl she had been, the young woman in the photograph on the sideboard, big-eyed and blonde and staring confidently out at the world.

'Roland.' At least I thought that's the name she whispered.

'Mutti, it's me, Michael.' I fastened her hand in mine.

'Roland.' Did I dream the answering pressure on my hand? And who was Roland anyway?

'Mutti, it's me. It's Michael, Mutti.'

Outside, the train roused itself, lumbering into life. I turned towards the sound. I was not dreaming the renewed pressure on my hand.

'Don't go, Roland, don't go.'

I could see the panic now in my mother's eyes; I could sense it in her clutching fingers.

'It's Michi, Mutti,' I said again. 'It's Michael and I'm not leaving you. I'm staying with you.'

The hollow eyes swivelled; I watched her scan the room, the familiar objects, the dressing table with the big mirror and her comb and brush and jar of skin cream, the dressing gown hanging from the back of the door, the old wardrobe, the wicker bucket chair that she had salvaged from god knows where. I sensed her touching them with her eyes, measuring each item, discovering herself again in days that were gone.

And in the day that was here.

'Michael—'

'It's OK, Mutti, don't try to talk.' I looked at the red alarm clock on the dressing table. 'The nurse will be here soon—'

'I don't want the nurse, Michi.' A strength in the voice that surprised me, like the strength in her fingers clutching at mine. The pain, I thought, energized by the pain.

'Rest,' I told her. 'Just rest, Mutti.'

'It's dark, Michi, light the lamp.'

When I switched on the bedside light, the furrows in her face were deeper, the dark below the saucer eyes darker.

'Is that better, Mutti?'

'Leave it on.' The eyes pleading with me. 'Don't turn the light off again, Michael.'

'Hush, Mutti, I'm not going to turn the light off.'

A small smile on the ravaged face as though she could read my mind: soon, now, the light will go out anyway.

'Michael.'

'I'm here, Mother.'

'Promise me – go to see . . .' A racking bout of coughing. I was afraid to raise her on the pillows. I waited for the spasm to end and wiped the cold sweat from her face.

'Promise me . . .'

'Please, Mutti, rest yourself.'

'Promise me you'll go to see him.' The fingers tighter now, the faded blue eyes darkening.

'Who, Mutti? See who?'

'Pastor Bruck.' I had to strain to catch her words. 'Pastor Bruck in Bad Saarow. Promise me you'll go . . .'

'I promise, Mutti, now rest, just rest.'

'He'll tell you . . .' Was that a smile or a grimace on her face? 'He'll tell you about your father . . .' The words in a rush now, a race against the dying light. 'I should have told you when it was safe – after the Wall – Pastor Bruck will tell you about your father . . . about Roland . . .'

The rattle then, the rattle of death. I had read of it in novels but the long, shuddering roll of it frightened me. A long, gasping noise from her, a last gentler trembling of the cancer-ridden body. Her head turned slightly, her mouth dribbled on the pillows; the stain stared back at me like a question mark.

My father was a name on my birth certificate: Johannes Vos, dead before I was born. I'd never suffered from any curiosity about my unknown father and my mother had always deflected or rebuffed the few half-hearted questions I had ventured about him. So who the hell was Roland – and who was Pastor Bruck?

I don't know how long it was before the nurse arrived: I stirred to feel her hand on mine, releasing my fingers from my mother's frozen grasp. Frau Mertens came in then; I watched her bless herself, throw the window open wide and cover the dressing-table mirror with a towel.

Go for a walk, Frau Mertens told me, or maybe I could make some tea. She was gentle about it, ushering me out of the bedroom. From behind the closed door I could hear the soft murmur of their voices, as they set about washing my mother's body.

Three

Nothing is written in the pages of my small pocket diary for the weeks after my mother's death. Days, weeks, drifted by; a continuum without markers, undivided by the mundane, trivial appointments and outings that mark our lives. I slept, I ate, I walked. Life became existence. A beer, a coffee, a nap, a newspaper – nothing mattered, everything the same. Those pages of my diary are as blank as my mind: nothing happened, nothing recorded. As if it were I and not my mother who had exited life.

I let Frau Mertens take charge of the funeral. My widowed neighbour seemed pleased to take on the business; I saw no reason to interfere.

In the cemetery overlooking the River Havel, Steffi stood beside me at the graveside and whispered, 'I never knew your mother was a Catholic.'

I looked at the priest, sprinkling holy water from a brass urn on to the coffin. I shrugged. The service was Frau Mertens' idea; her eyes were closed, her dry lips moving, as she prayed on the other side of my mother's grave. Frau Mertens looked at peace, as though she had found her place in life.

I wondered, idly, while the priest droned on, about my mother's place, in death. Her mother, my grandmother, had not survived the war; her father had died in the last frantic days on the Baltic Coast, as the German army tried, in vain, to escape the rampaging Soviet forces. My mother had been raised in an orphanage in Chemnitz (renamed Karl-Marx-Stadt in the GDR but now once again known by its old name in our brave new world); after school she had been sent to work in a printing works before being assigned to a similar job in Brandenburg. And then there was me, and the flat on the fourth floor, and the closed-doors life we lived together. And now my mother had her patch of ground on the bank of the Havel, and the low stone that, in good time, like a dutiful German son, I would raise over her: *Petra Ritter, 1943–1993.*

My mother had lived for fifty years and what I knew about her could be written in a handful of words and a couple of dates. A chill wind gusted in across the river and I looked from the grave to Steffi, slim and lovely in the navy, knee-length suit, and I knew my own loss: there was no one to fight with, now, and anyway the war itself had been lost . . .

Even the streets of Brandenburg seemed lost to me. Only bread and beer, the merest basics, brought me into the shops; otherwise I shunned the town, as though I might be picked up by the agents of the new invaders. Once, stepping out of the supermarket, my loaf and *Wurst* under my arm, I almost collided with a couple of my old students, and I grunted a kind of greeting as I hurried away from their smiles, their hellos, the question in their fresh teenage faces. They reminded me too much of what I had no wish to remember.

So I snapped open the cans of beer, drank the cool liquid and tasted nothing. Sat at the open window of the flat and neither saw nor heard the passing trains. Pulled the Trabi in on the dirt road beside the lake and opened another beer. The white swans glided by on the rippling waters; the fading grasses stirred in the November wind. When Frau Mertens asked, on the stairs that evening, if I'd had a nice drive, I struggled to remember where I'd been.

I caught the look she gave me, saw the concern in her eyes. The moment passed, as we stood facing each other on the stone steps. Don't ask, I thought, and she didn't. It was the way we lived, the way we had survived. Frau Mertens understood, even if my mother had always seemed uncomfortable with the way you had to respect one another's space.

Frau Mertens had always accorded me a certain deference. Especially when I was appointed to the town's Education Committee, soon after I'd joined the staff of Gymnasium No.1. Maybe she guessed that, as an up-and-coming young member of the Party, I'd be given sight of letters from my fourth-floor neighbour in our apartment block. Her deference had been unnecessary: what did I care about the neighbour overhead who was forever listening in to the American station, AFN? Why should I give a damn about the fellow on the ground floor who played rock music on his record player until after midnight? Besides, her prying, spying eyes notwithstanding, I had never disliked Frau Mertens.

Now she wanted to know if I'd like her to clear out my mother's wardrobe.

'It's been over a month now, Michi.'

'Tomorrow,' I said, 'and thank you.'

'I won't disturb anything personal.'

'Do as you wish with the stuff. If there's anything you like—'

She blushed; I thought I might have offended her.

'I'm really grateful to you, Frau Mertens. I hope you can find something to keep as a memento, that's what I meant.'

She thanked me, continued downstairs with her two sacks of rubbish.

What could she possibly find of value in my mother's things? Old clothes, cheap shoes. Jewellery of glass and paste and plastic. A few paperback books. A handful of photos in a cardboard box with dark red roses on the lid. Nothing much to mark a life lived.

And a few words coughed on her deathbed.

Your father. Pastor Bruck. Bad Saarow.

I realized, shutting the door of the flat behind me, that, ever since my mother's death, I had been trying to lock these words out of my mind. These words that belonged in the darkness, in the narrow pit where my mother lay. Across the river, beyond the town. Not here in this fourth-floor flat, where no father had ever walked, had ever breathed. Or had ever been breathed of.

Now some spectre ghosted from the grave by the river and padded with silent steps across the water, across the sleepers and tracks of the railway, and insinuated himself into the fourth-floor flat. Into my mind. Into my life.

Well, he could just spirit himself back to wherever he had come from. And he could go fuck himself along the way.

For the umpteenth night in a row I couldn't sleep. About three in the morning I called Directory Enquiries, the great new we-never-sleep service that had reached out to us across no-man's-land as part of our new and wonderful reunified country. The voice said, we can't help, there's no listing for that name.

At eight o'clock I was behind the wheel of my old Trabi, polluting the atmosphere, coughing my way past the winter trees and the naked fields to Bad Saarow.

Four

Bad Saarow. A T-junction south-east of Berlin, a stone's throw from the Polish border. The Romans had settled here, lured by the spa, the thermal spring that gave the place its name. In the Weimar days, after the shame of Versailles, artists and writers and film-makers had clustered here: the thermal waters soothed them, the light was good, the great lake was a place to swim and frolic and dream. The Nazis had replaced them: nightmares roamed where dreams had blossomed.

Bad Saarow: a place without a centre, a crisscross of roads between the lake and the woods, around the railway station and the spa baths. I had been there once, during my years at the university in Rostock. When Dieter had invited me to spend the weekend at his family's place, halfway through our third year in college, I'd been nervous: I'd never been to the home of a senior Party official – a senior officer in economic and strategic planning at the ministry in Berlin. Groundless fears: Dieter's parents had put me completely at ease in the weekend villa on the lakeshore, had encouraged me to come again to enjoy the lake, the launch; their home was always open, they said, to any friend of Dieter's.

I pulled in at the wooden kiosk near the railway station. The small hatch was surrounded by magazines and newspapers, the new glories of tits and football, the staple fare of *Bild* and *Express*

35

and the rest of the 'free press' from the moralizing West. I watched the steam from my coffee swirl in the November morning above the high metal table on the pavement and wondered what Dieter's father would make of our new homeland, the new Bad Saarow. I'd lost touch; Dieter had left after graduation to join his parents in Damascus, where his father was by then heading up a new development unit in the Syrian capital.

There would be no place for him in the new Bad Saarow. Dieter's family was just one more casualty of the fall of the Wall; unremembered statistics, not even blips on the graphs and tables of our new prosperity. Like the shiny new tiled front on the station; like the huge noticeboard which announced that work would shortly begin on the redevelopment of the spa – whirlpools and swirlpools, water slides and water rides, all the glories of the new dawn that would bring Berliners by the trainload to this quiet backwater where I was supposed to be searching for a Pastor Bruck.

No, the fellow in the kiosk didn't know any Pastor Bruck but then, adjusting the New York Yankees baseball cap on his small head, he hadn't lived here for very long. There was a whole biography in his few words, in his accent, but I thanked him anyway, before dumping my empty plastic cup in the rubbish bin and getting back into my car. I felt his eyes on the Trabi as I pulled away from the kerb.

Hardly knowing what I was looking for, I drove slowly along the empty, quiet road. The large, detached houses that lined both sides of the street looked deserted: rumour had it that these were now the property of money men in Berlin and Munich – and even further afield. The spiked metal fences warned you off the lush lawns and gardens; the closed-circuit TV cameras drove home the message. Once these palatial lakeside homes had been the reward of the servants of our state, their place of retreat from the heat of the day; now they were the addenda of the wealthy, the playthings of rich, absentee financiers and traders . . . and my mother and her deluded accomplices had burned their midnight candles to deliver us into this . . . paradise?

A gardener in overalls paused from his raking of leaves to watch me chug by. He didn't return my small wave but bent again to his leaves; maybe the cameras were for him too – and you didn't find work nowadays at every crossroads. Our days of full employment were gone for ever.

Between the houses, behind the leafless trees, I caught glimpses of the lake. I remembered Dieter at the wheel of the powerboat, the sailor's cap jaunty above his laughing face. When we tied up, exhilarated, he pointed out to me a lone sculler on the lake, tiny in the distance; she was, he said, one of our international scullers, preparing for the next Olympics. Now, it seemed, even our sports achievements were to be mocked, as though our past too was there only to be plundered and stolen from us. The morning was sharp and bright, the air clear and brittle, but I could taste sourness on my tongue.

And then, just as I was approaching the sign pointing to the new beer garden and marina, I caught a glimpse of a grey spire rising above the trees on the other side of the road. There was no traffic sign to indicate the turning to the left but the narrow road, curving among the trees, looked newly paved. The grassy margins on either side were freshly trimmed; even the trees seemed to have been cut back in an attempt to let the light shine through in the crisp November morning. The spire I had spotted from the road was no longer visible, however, blocked out by the screen of trees that shadowed the road, not much more than a lane; for a moment I wondered if I had been mistaken. A wild-goose chase anyway, I told myself; what did it matter if this rustic path led exactly nowhere?

Thump-thump. Hammering, loud in the wooded stillness, clearly audible above the Trabi's bronchial labouring. Again, *thump-thump*, a softness in the hammering, like wood on wood.

The fellow doing the hammering was before me now, shirt-sleeved, the long-handled mallet easy in his big hands as he stood to watch my arrival. In front of him a newly erected white picket fence, a few metres behind him a small stone-built church building, slate-roofed, above it the tapering steeple that had drawn me into this clearing in the woods. I felt his eyes upon me as I drew the Trabi to a halt beside the rusty gates; noticed his frank inspection of the Brandenburg plate. He was shorter than me, probably older, but he didn't look like the kind of fellow you'd want to have a falling-out with.

I smiled as I stepped towards him but he was having none of it, his face as closed as the rusty gate between us.

'Good morning.'

He nodded by way of reply. Carefully leaned the mallet against one of the stakes he had driven into the hard earth just inside the fence. When he folded his arms his biceps bulged, muscular and blue-veined.

'*Nur eine Frage, bitte,*' I said. A question. Please.

Another nod from the shaven head. A tiny diamond stud in his right earlobe. The wooden signboard that would sit on the supports he was erecting lay beside him on the ground, gold lettering on a solid blue background. The angle made it difficult to read.

'I'm looking for a pastor who lives in Bad Saarow.'

'You're in the right place.' The rough accent of these parts. But maybe a hint of humour in the sarcasm. 'Did you have a particular pastor in mind or will any old one do?'

I tried to smile. Tried to read the upside-down board on the ground. *Evangelische Kirche*, in capitals, the times of services underneath. A name across the bottom of the board.

'I don't know if he's an evangelical minister,' I said, making another attempt at a smile. 'I just saw the church spire from the road and thought I'd drive in to ask.'

'And who's asking?'

Christ, what's wrong with this fellow? I'm not trying to steal the poor box here, just making an inquiry.

'Michael Ritter, from Brandenburg.' Craning my neck, trying to read the name at the bottom of the board.

'You're a long way from home, Herr Ritter.'

'Even in a Trabi it only takes an hour.' *Rev. Dr Something.*

'Don't see many of them on the road now. Most folk were glad to get rid of them.'

I shrugged. 'I have a sentimental attachment to the brand.' A mistake: at my words his face seemed to close even more.

'You're hankering for the good old days, Herr Ritter, is that the way?'

'Not really . . .' Discomfited by his hostility but moving sideways along the fence, not bothering now to hide my attempt to read the name on the bottom of the board.

'*Reverend Doktor Theophilus Bruck.*' My words unnaturally loud in the morning air, my arm pointing at the board on the ground. 'The very man I'm looking for! I can't believe this!'

I stopped, feeling slightly embarrassed by the edge of excitement in my voice.

My companion said nothing. I watched him take a packet of West from his jeans pocket. He took a long time over it – easing the cigarette out of the red packet, the brief sizzle of the match, the first sucking pull, the slow exhalation through thin lips. I held his gaze through the grey cigarette smoke.

'It's quite a coincidence,' I said. 'Finding Pastor Bruck just like this.'

'Yes, I'm sure it is, a *real* coincidence.'

I frowned at him. Wondering if I were imagining the suspicion in his voice.

'I told you, I saw the church spire – I just came in on spec—'

'Yeah, and I'm Joe Stalin's godson.'

The edge in his voice sharper now, my own confusion deepening.

'What's the matter with you? I just stopped to ask about the pastor. Why are you behaving like this?'

'Why am I behaving like this?' Pulling furiously on the cigarette, as though he could suck venom from it. 'Why am I behaving like this? You drop out of the sky with your fucking questions and your fucking Trabi – your fucking "sentimental attachment" – and you wonder why I'm behaving like this? I can smell the stink off you, pal, you and your kind have been coming around here for so long now with your threats and your questions that I'd know your kind in my sleep. But it seems you haven't heard the news, my Trabi-loving pal – the Wall's been down for over three years now and you no longer have the right . . .' He threw the cigarette on the earth, ground it beneath his boot heel. 'It's over, pal,' he said softly, 'it's been over for years now and Pastor Bruck doesn't have to listen to your lot's questions any more, so why don't you just fuck off back wherever you came from.'

At least he hadn't picked up the mallet again. All the same, it seemed prudent not to antagonize the fellow any further.

'I'm sorry if I've somehow offended you,' I said, 'but I'm just a schoolteacher from Brandenburg, and I want to see Pastor Bruck about a personal matter. If you won't tell me where he lives, I'll just ask someone else.'

'I know your kind – you've been hounding Pastor Bruck all his life. You just can't get it into your head that the world has moved on and left you fuckers behind. D'you think I could've done this a few years ago?' His jerky gesture took in the new fence, the freshly oiled church door, the new church noticeboard lying on the ground. 'Do you?'

Pointless to debate the issue with this fellow. If I had any sense I'd get in the Trabi and get the hell out of this nothing place. Still, I wasn't going to be faced down.

'Thanks for your help.'

I took a step back and did what I should have done first: take a good look around. The little church, though obviously old, maybe nineteenth century, had a reborn look about it – new roof, new door, probably new windows in teak frames. Like the fellow said, you couldn't have done this a few years back. The stone walls around the church widened backwards in a triangular shape; behind the church itself I could see, on either side, the dark grey tombstones of a churchyard.

And further back, beyond the back wall of the little graveyard, I could just glimpse, through the encircling trees, the glint of sunlight on glass. Windows, a low-rise house or hut.

I noticed the path that led from the church gate to the entrance, then round the church, heading towards the graveyard.

I put my hand on the rusty gate.

'Where do you think *you're* going?' The mallet in his hands now.

'It's a public place, isn't it?' I held his stare. 'I'm going to take a look around.'

'The church is not open today.'

'Then I'll just look in the graveyard.'

'It's closed too.'

'Maybe I'll just ask in that house.' I nodded towards the cottage in the trees. 'They might be able to tell me where Pastor Bruck lives.'

'What do you want to see the pastor for?'

'That's my business, not yours.'

'If it's the pastor's business,' he said, 'then it's mine.'

'It's none of your business,' I said slowly. Mallet or no mallet, this fellow had nothing to do with my mother's gasping words.

'I think you'd better fuck off right now and leave the pastor alone.'

'What's the matter, Thomas?'

He was tall and bony, dressed in clerical grey, his long face pale under a bald and shiny pate. He was slightly stooped, his knobby fingers curled around the black metal handle of the half-open church door. I thought, looking at his stooped figure, that he might fall down if he let go of the door handle.

'Is everything OK, Thomas?' His Adam's apple bobbed against the loose dog collar; from such a skeletal body the deep voice was incongruous.

'There's no problem, Father.' The mallet man spoke without turning round. 'This gentleman stopped for directions but he's leaving now.'

I turned towards the cleric.

'I'm looking for Pastor Bruck.' To my own ears my voice sounded unnaturally shrill. 'I've come from Brandenburg to see him.'

'For goodness sake, why didn't you say so?' Words of impatience but neither impatience nor irritation in the tone of voice, in the facial expression. A lined face, a face in its seventies, furrowed by more than years. 'Come along inside, where we can talk.'

'Father, I've told you this gentleman is leaving—'

'Thomas, don't be ridiculous. The chap's come from Brandenburg to see me.'

'He's trouble, Father. Believe me, I can tell.'

The old man looked from his son to me, then back again.

'You shouldn't worry, Thomas.' His voice gentle. 'Those days are gone. Gone for ever.'

'There's plenty would like to bring them back again, Father.'

Father and son looked at each other; watching them, I felt as though I were a spectator at an oft-played scene.

'You worry too much, Thomas.'

'And you don't worry enough, Father.' There was no mistaking the anger in the younger man's voice. 'You never did.'

'Thomas, Thomas! What way is this to welcome a caller to our door? Whatever will Herr . . .' He turned to me. 'Herr?'

'Ritter,' I said. 'Michael Ritter, from Brandenburg.'

Not a flicker of recognition in the grey eyes.

'Would you like to see our church, Herr Ritter?' His stooped posture was, or so it seemed, even more bent; the bony, outstretched hand was pointing at the church door. 'It's been renovated, thanks to my son.'

'No thanks to fellows like this, Father.'

'Thomas—'

'All right, Father. But there's no heat in there and you'll catch your death, parading around like this on a cold morning without an overcoat.' The anger gone from the younger man's voice, replaced by a kind of solicitous tetchiness, like a fussy mother clucking over a wayward adolescent.

'Thomas, I assure you I am wearing a long-sleeved undershirt.' A hint of a smile on the pale, craggy face. 'And look, I am wearing my woollen pullover.' A childish tug at the grey pullover. 'My son fusses, Herr Ritter, but his father is a tough old bird.'

I tried to smile but the younger man's hostility still bristled in the morning air.

'So, you'd like to see our church, Herr Ritter,' he said again.

'Yes, Pastor Bruck,' I lied again, and we stepped inside the old building.

43

The interior of the church was as run-of-the-mill as its outside. Cream walls, tall gothic windows, rows of dark pews. The pews new, the cream walls freshly painted.

Pastor Bruck noticed that my eyes were drawn to the single stained-glass window, halfway along the right-hand wall. All the other windows were of plain, clear glass.

'A sort of miracle, Herr Ritter.' A hint of amusement in the priest's voice. 'That window somehow survived everything – the war and everything else. After the war this building was used as a store for a while – lumber, soldiers' stuff, some of it just junk that the army didn't know what to do with. After some years they left it empty, they didn't interfere too much when I tried to make it into a church again.' He smiled his pale, almost spooky smile at me, at the window. 'I couldn't do much. I had no money and no materials. Sometimes faith needs a little help. But that one window remained unbroken. I used to look at it and say there must be a reason for that.' We both stared at it in silence. A nothing window, nondescript as everything else here: coloured squares of glass, blue and red and purple and orange, seemingly dropped at random in their metal casings. 'I still don't know the reason it survived,' Pastor Bruck was saying.

'Maybe there is no reason,' I ventured.

'Maybe it's a symbol, Herr Ritter.'

I knew I shouldn't ask, knew what the answer would be.

'Of what?'

'Of our own survival. Of the need to go on. Of the need to struggle.'

'For some the struggle is over now.' Staring into the grey eyes, angry with myself for starting this, for baring more than was necessary. 'For others the question is whether there's any point in struggling at all.'

'If we're sure of the rightness of our cause, then we have a duty to fight for it, Herr Ritter.'

'Try telling that to the Board of my school, Pastor Bruck.'

We'd been making our stop-start way along the central aisle of the church; now we stood in front of the altar table. A simple affair of four marble posts, covered by a green velour cloth with gold tassels and gilt lettering: *My Lord And My God*.

The sudden, deepening silence that followed my words seemed to emanate from the altar. Or maybe from the regret that welled within me. I hadn't wanted to give myself away, to show my loss to this grey cleric in this church. He and his kind had won, his miserable stained glass was a symbol not of survival but of loss. I could feel the hate welling inside me, inside the regret, boiling over it, swallowing the regret, swallowing me. I hated this grey cleric, this grey stone building.

'Wait, Herr Ritter, please.'

The pastor's hand was on my arm; I hardly knew that I had turned away from him.

'Please.'

The grey eyes locked on mine. A kind of pleading in them. And knowledge. The knowledge of loss, maybe hopelessness.

'Sit a moment.' He motioned me towards a pew, waited, watching, while I sat, as though I were an invalid.

'My son and I have not been very welcoming, Herr Ritter, and you must forgive us. In the past,' the faint smile again, 'we didn't welcome the kind of visitors who called at our door. Nowadays we get callers at the weekend, mostly kind folk who have given to our rebuilding fund. Sometimes they come to see how we're spending their money, sometimes they're just full of curiosity about how we're making out in *Dunkeldeutschland*.' Dark Germany: a phrase the Western newspapers used: I hated it. The pastor went on, smiling, 'But we don't get many visitors from Brandenburg, early on a frosty Wednesday morning.'

I had come to ask a question, full of doubts about my own sanity in doing so. Yet, doubting and disbelieving, I heard myself recounting my recent past to this backwater pastor. He was what I had once heard Frau Mertens, recalling her childhood in Poland, describe to my mother as a 'listening priest'; there were two kinds, Frau Mertens had said, the kind that knew nothing but thought they knew everything and just kept talking at you, and the kind that knew something but wanted to know more and just listened a lot.

Pastor Bruck was surely one of the listeners. He prompted me a little but for the most part he just listened to my story. Of my school, my job. And back to my studies in Rostock. And further back to my days in the Freie Deutsche Jugend. And forward again to my weekend with Dieter's family at their villa in this very place, in Bad Saarow. And so to my school job. And November 1989. And the streets of the East blooming with Helmut Kohl's flowers and, most recently, my dismissal for my undesirable past.

To this day I don't know why I should have told all these things to somebody I had never met before. Maybe it was the womblike, tomblike building I found myself in. Or the weeks of silence, of isolation, since my mother had died. Or a delayed reaction to her death. Whatever. The fact remains that I laid out the bones of my life, as I had never done before, in front of this dog-collared officer of an organization which trafficked in lies and superstition.

When I had finished, my own breathing, shallow and raspy, sounded loud in the silence of the small church. I sat in the dark pew with bowed head, my hands covering my face, as though to hide from the grey eyes. From the loin-clothed figure on the crucifix behind the altar. From the inscription: *My Lord And My God*. Maybe from myself.

'We all have a past, Herr Ritter.'

It's not the past, I wanted to say, it's this fucking present that's the problem.

'All of us have to live with what we have done and what we have failed to do.'

His words horrified me. Did this fellow think I had come here searching for forgiveness?

'Is that why you've come looking for me, Herr Ritter? So that you might be forgiven?'

'What?'

'Is that why you have come here?'

I could hardly remember why I had come. It didn't matter: I got no chance to answer.

'Who cares why he's here?' It was Thomas, standing in the aisle beside his father. I hadn't heard him come into the church, didn't know how long he'd been there or what he'd heard.

'He's one of the bastards who made our lives a misery.' Fury unleashed in the growled words. 'He's one of those bastards who broke down our door in the middle of the night and then broke your back—'

'Thomas, please.'

'Why do you listen to these bastards, Father? You heard him – Party card and Education Committee member . . .'

I saw the clenching of the fist, saw the muscled arm being raised.

'Thomas, don't.'

I tried to get my head out of the way but I was stuck in the confined space of the pew. Thomas's fist caught me on the side of the head; I heard Pastor Bruck's beseeching cry of alarm as I fell and my head struck the stone floor and there was a ringing in my ears as the darkness enveloped me.

Five

A voice in my ears, soft but insistent.

'Herr Ritter! Herr Ritter!'

The voice faint, but coming closer.

'Herr Ritter!'

A gentle tapping on my face, fingers on my cheek, cold fingers but soft, unlike the hard wood pushing against my spine. I blinked my eyes open. The high, vaulted ceiling of the church focused into vision as I went on blinking. The ringing in my ears was gone but my head hurt as though it had been kicked.

'Herr Ritter, can you hear me? Say something.'

Pastor Bruck was kneeling on the stone floor beside the pew on which I lay stretched. Close to, his face looked older, the skin almost transparent, like old hide stretched in the wind. The grey eyes under the high bony forehead were wide with concern.

'I hear you, Pastor Bruck.'

'Thank God.'

I tried to lift my head but his bony hand pushed against me.

'Gently, Herr Ritter, you're bleeding.' His hand around mine, guiding it to my forehead. 'Press on this.'

I felt the cloth under my fingers and instinctively lifted it to look. A white handkerchief, stained with the darkness of blood. Pastor Bruck took my hand again.

'It's better if you hold it against the wound,' he said, 'and try to sit up slowly.'

I lifted my head, put my hand on the edge of the seat, levered myself slowly up into a sitting position. The pews had been pushed apart; Pastor Bruck looked up at me from his kneeling position on the stone floor. I looked from him to his suit jacket on the seat beside me, where my head had been resting. And then I looked around, slowly, pushing the handkerchief against the cut over my left eye, as though the stained cloth could stop both the flow of blood and the banging inside my head. And then I looked around again. Just to be sure.

'Thomas is not here, Herr Ritter. I told him to leave us.'

I said nothing

'He gets upset, Herr Ritter. I apologize for him.'

'He's a fucking animal.'

Pastor Bruck looked at me, saying nothing, but his pale, cheesecloth skin grew darker – with shame, with anger, perhaps both. I flinched before the grey, staring eyes.

'Perhaps we should go outside, Herr Ritter.' A shrug of the wide, thin shoulders in the grey clerical shirt. 'We have no heating in the church yet, it's probably better for you to be outside.'

'That's what your son said to you, Pastor Bruck, when he was fussing about you.'

'Yes,' the priest said. 'My son fusses about me, Herr Ritter, it's true. He has seen much, maybe too much, things that a boy shouldn't have to see.' The church door groaned as he pushed and held it open for me. I blinked in the pale, wintry sunlight. The mallet and noticeboard lay on the ground but of Thomas Bruck there was no sign. 'Thomas finds it difficult to believe that the old days are gone, he's afraid that someone is going to come and . . .' he spread his arms, encompassing the old stone building and the churchyard, 'and take all this away from us, Herr Ritter.'

'That's not very likely, is it, Pastor Bruck?' I couldn't keep the sourness out of my voice.

'That's what I tell him.' He stopped and laid his bony hand on my arm. 'I know that's not what *you* want, Herr Ritter, but I have to speak the truth as I see it.'

'And *my* truth? Is there no room for *my* truth in this new world?'

'The old question, Herr Ritter.' The smile almost sorrowful. '*What is truth?* And two thousand years after Pilate, we still cannot answer it.'

A flurry of wind shook the bare branches above us. Fallen leaves rustling on the narrow pathway that wound among the graves.

'Look at these stones, Herr Ritter.' He gestured towards the tombstones that surrounded us. Blackened with the years, the lettering unreadable, most of them leaned every which way like drunken layabouts. 'There are few new stones or new graves here.'

I shrugged. 'People had given up.' I didn't wish to be rude to this old priest, limping against the tide in this backwater cemetery.

'Perhaps they had given up on faith, Herr Ritter. Maybe that's why almost all those who died in the last twenty or thirty years are buried in the municipal cemetery on the other side of the town. But maybe their families were afraid also. Those who chose to have their loved ones buried here – and there *were* a few – almost always encountered difficulties later. A son or daughter couldn't get to university. The Trabi the family had been patiently waiting for, all those years,' once more, that wintry smile, 'was suddenly and mysteriously no longer available. You know the sort of thing, Herr Ritter.'

'Like being fired from your job, Pastor Bruck.'

'Believe me,' the pastor said, 'I know how you feel.'

In the silence that fell upon us, a rook cawed, long and raucous, and we both turned towards the sound. There was no sign of the bird but for moments we stood there in silence, looking and listening, as though the leafless trees might speak to us.

'Herr Ritter.' There was a different tone in the pastor's voice as he turned towards me on the earthen path – softer, but more businesslike also. 'I don't know what you need from me. You have not told me why you are here.'

'My mother,' I said. 'She died recently. Just before she died she told me to speak to Pastor Bruck in Bad Saarow about—'

I couldn't get the words out: the whole idea seemed dafter by the minute.

'About what, Herr Ritter?'

'About my father. It's ridiculous. I never had a father . . .' I turned away to hide my embarrassment.

'We all have a father, Herr Ritter.' The voice gentle behind me. 'Every one of us.'

'I mean . . .' I shrugged, facing the priest again.

'I know what you mean. It was just you and your mother.'

'Yes, it was just me and my mother.'

'And her name was?'

'Petra,' I said. 'Petra Ritter. Raised in an orphanage in Karl-Marx-Stadt. Lived and died in Brandenburg. No known relatives. Just Petra Ritter and Michael, her only son, standing before you in a graveyard in Bad Saarow, unemployed, without prospects and spouting this incredible nonsense to you.' I turned away, disgusted with myself and my gibberish.

'Petra Ritter.' The priest's words came at me from behind like a frightened whisper. 'Petra Ritter, from Brandenburg.'

I turned to him, frowning.

'You knew my mother?'

'How old are you, Herr Ritter?' he asked, ignoring my question.

'Thirty – so what? Did you know my mother?'

'You were born in nineteen sixty-three?'

'Yes, but why?'

He was staring at the faded gravestones but his eyes were elsewhere, focused on some greater distance.

'Have you a photo, Herr Ritter? A photo of your mother?'

I felt afraid now, of what I couldn't say. Of the blank look in Pastor Bruck's grey eyes, of the old gravestones leaning in upon me, of the small black and white snapshot that I was taking from my wallet and handing to the priest.

I watched as the priest first glanced, almost casually, at the photograph. The picture had been taken on my thirteenth birthday, the first day I had worn my blue Deutsche Jugend shirt and cap; I could remember Frau Mertens' enthusiasm with the old box camera – and my mother's reluctance, as though she could not bear to be photographed beside her lanky son.

'Forget the stupid uniform, Frau Ritter.' Frau Mertens' voice a mixture of laughter and sternness. 'Just think of it as a picture of your son on his birthday.'

And now, all these years later, the fading cardboard image in the skeletal fingers of this ageing priest among the faded gravestones of a cemetery in Bad Saarow; my dead mother and my distant boyhood being scrutinized by those pale grey eyes in that transparent face. Something – shock, recognition, alarm – dawned in the grey eyes. Pastor Bruck held the photo at arm's length, eyes narrowed.

He glanced at me as he fumbled in his jacket pocket. An old brown metal spectacles case in his left hand, the photo in his right. Confusion in his expression. I took the spectacles case from him and snapped it open. The glasses I handed to him were a reminder of our lost world: round, brown-rimmed, heavy.

Now he drew the photograph close to him and there was no doubting the recognition in those old eyes. And more than recognition – fear, alarm, sadness, perhaps anger, I couldn't be sure. What I was sure of, standing there in that decayed graveyard, was that this priest had known my mother.

'You knew her,' I said. 'You knew my mother, Pastor Bruck, didn't you?'

He handed me the photograph. His Adam's apple bobbed in the grizzled neck. I caught at his sleeve with one hand, waved the snapshot in his face with the other.

'Tell me what you know about my mother!'

The priest seemed to quail before me; I realized I was shouting.

'Please,' I said in a softer voice.

The grey eyes darker now, dark with some unwanted memory.

'Who are you?' he asked.

'I'm Michael Ritter, the only son of Petra Ritter, from Brandenburg.'

'How do I know? How can I tell? Maybe it's some stupid trick, after all these years—'

'I told you, Pastor Bruck. My mother was dying, she said to ask you about my father—'

'*Don't you raise your voice to my father.*'

The pastor's son was standing beside me on the narrow path.

'I want you to leave now, Herr Ritter.'

'But—'

'No buts, Herr Ritter. Get out of here *now* or you may not be in a condition to leave at all.'

I looked at Thomas Bruck, wondered briefly how such a bull-like figure could be the offspring of this cadaverous priest.

'I'm talking to your father,' I protested.

'You've just finished talking to him, Herr Ritter.'

'That's for him to say.' I turned to Pastor Bruck.

Tiredness in the old face, the tiredness of centuries.

'Go now, Herr Ritter,' the pastor said.

'Please—'

'You heard my father,' Thomas said. There was menace in his voice, in his expression, but it was his father's face that stilled me – I could read in that haunted face a loss that echoed my own.

'OK.' I tried to keep the sullenness out of my voice as I turned away. 'OK. Thank you anyway.'

I was rounding the corner of the church on the footpath when I heard the pastor's voice again.

'We'll talk another time, Herr Ritter.'

I turned eagerly. 'When, Pastor Bruck, when?'

He was leaning against his son; I thought of a tall old tree, dying, being held up by a shorter, sturdier neighbour in the forest. He opened his mouth to speak but no words came.

'When my father decides, Herr Ritter.' Thomas drew his father closer to him as he spoke.

'I'll leave you my phone number.'

I felt their eyes upon me as I scribbled my name and number on a scrap of paper and handed it to Thomas. I walked back to the Trabi in a deepening silence. The cawing crow was gone, the trees were still in a windless day. I could hear my own heart pounding and an odd voice in my head, a strange and unbidden voice, asking an unfamiliar question: what must it feel like to have a father to put your arm around?

Six

'No,' Frau Mertens said. 'Your mother never mentioned anything to me about your father.' Standing beside me in the small kitchen area, she smelled of carbolic soap mixed with baking and cooking. 'I suppose it's losing your mother has made you think of – of such a thing.'

I wouldn't – couldn't – tell her about my visit to Pastor Bruck's church in Bad Saarow. Frau Mertens' day turned upon the routines and rituals of morning Mass and regularly cooked meals – the plate of freshly baked apple strudel on the kitchen worktop was what had brought her across the corridor – but her daily excursions to the Catholic church would not, I felt, make her any more sympathetic to my church visit earlier that day. For all her piety, I was pretty sure that my neighbour's god was a god of the practical, a down-to-earth deity who traded in certainties, not doubts or fantasies.

'You're on your own too much, Michael.' The small eyes in the round, doughy face narrowed in concern. 'It's all right for a woman like me but a young man like yourself – maybe you should go to the West like the rest of them – they all say there're plenty of jobs in Frankfurt and Dusseldorf and . . . and . . .' Her chins wobbled as she paused for breath. 'You know what I mean, Michael, there's nothing for you here. And you're a good-looking man too, Michael . . .' The round face lit up in a smile, her pudgy fingers briefly touched mine. 'You'll meet nobody in this place, Michael, but over there those *Wessie* girls will be queuing up to get a look at you.'

I muttered something non-committal and thanked her again for the strudel.

'A dish of *apfelstrudel* won't give you back your life, Michael. Think about what I said.' She turned away and I walked with her to the door of her flat. 'It's not easy being alone, Michael, nobody knows that better than me, but you're young enough to do something about it.' She smiled, another crumpling of the round face. 'You're an orphan now, Michael, and you have to be your own father and mother.'

The door closed behind her and I wondered at her words, wondered why I had never noticed her wisdom before.

From beyond the flat came the railway noises. An engine shunting. A whistle blowing. Trains shunting and whistling their way to the cities and jobs Frau Mertens had spoken of.

And the girls, the women. Driving the streets of the town, my eyes would be drawn to some shapely figure, swinging in tight jeans along the pavement, and I'd take a look in the rear-view mirror as I passed, but nothing stirred in me, not in my head, not in my groin. Not since the day the Director had fired me. And not much before that either, when Steffi had ordered me out. There had been a hurried encounter with a checkout lady from the supermarket a few weeks after Steffi, a brisk opening of buttons and zips, the rasping sound of Velcro parting and an equally brisk fuck in the checkout lady's marital bed before she told me to go, her postman husband could arrive any minute.

Standing at the window, looking out at the station across the road, I shut my eyes and tried to remember something – anything – of the checkout girl. Young, in her twenties. Dark red hair. Her black lacy knickers on the floor beside the bed.

Nothing more. Not even a name.

A miracle I could even recall Steffi's name. And yet in the not-so-long-ago she and I had seemed almost to share a single soul.

I opened my eyes. The railway station was still there, hulking in the darkening light. Maybe Frau Mertens had the right idea. A ticket to the West. To the bright lights that my sometime fellow citizens had dreamed of. The freedom of bananas and shiny automobiles. And girls who would breathe life into your listless limbs and make you forget about Bad Saarow and the country you had lost.

The knock on the door brought me back to the flat, the thin brown carpet, the lumpy sofa.

I thought it must be Frau Mertens, maybe she'd left something more than her words behind.

It wasn't Frau Mertens.

It was Steffi. Steffi in ankle-high boots and a tailored denim coat that hung open to her knees. Steffi in a tightly fitting lemon top and short navy skirt. Her blond hair cropped like a choirboy's, the fringe almost reaching to her ice-blue eyes.

'I came to see if you were OK.'

The red bee-stung lips shiny with lipstick, the mouth pouting as it always did.

I drew her to me, bending over her mouth.

'Wait.' She closed the door, reached behind her to switch off the light.

She didn't resist when I drew her to me again. Under the short skirt her buttocks were firm in my hands. My fingers reached inside the soft stuff of her knickers. She gasped.

'Not here.'

She pushed me away, then led me through the open doorway of the bedroom. She laid the denim coat neatly across the back of the chair beside my bed and pulled the lemon-coloured top over her head.

It was a quick coupling. It could have been the checkout lady. Maybe, for Steffi, it was the same, maybe I could have been anybody too. She and I had made love to each other a hundred times but, as we fucked each other in the narrow bed that I had slept in for most of my life, there was no sense of belonging, no sense of being home or coming home, and afterwards we lay in each other's arms like uneasy strangers. No longer a single soul, just two separate strangers.

'I'll have to go.' In the unlit room her voice sounded lost.

'Wait a while.'

'Frank will be back soon. He was in Berlin today.' Frank had taken my place in Steffi's flat and Steffi's life. He travelled for some software outfit.

'He doesn't like it if I'm not there when he gets back.'

She got dressed without turning on the light. A slither of silk and lace on skin. I watched her bend over the small mirror on top of the chest of drawers and fix her mouth with the red lipstick. A flick of her fingers through the cropped hair and she was ready.

'I just wanted to make sure you were OK, Michael.'

The words whispered, the door closing behind her. The bedroom heavy with the scent of her perfume. Why had Steffi come? Why had she come to bed with me?

Nothing made sense any more. Nothing except this childhood flat, these pathetic sticks of furniture I had lived with all my life. The rhythmic noises of the railway station, the whistling of the trains.

And even that had changed: now shiny new trains in sparkling new livery sped west to once-forbidden destinations.

I breathed in the woman smell of Steffi. The small alarm clock beside the bed said 5.45. Frank would probably be home soon:

maybe Steffi would shower before he got home. Maybe Frank didn't give a damn if Steffi took it into her head to fuck her ex-husband. Maybe that was the way you needed to think in our brave, new, democratic world. Anyway, who was I to talk?

I fell asleep.

The telephone woke me. The darkness was deeper when I opened my eyes. I could taste and smell Steffi on my breath. I made no move to get out of the crumpled bed but the phone didn't stop ringing.

It went on ringing as I swung my legs out of the bed and walked, barefoot and naked, to the living room. When I picked up the phone, the dark, bulky furniture seemed to relax back into the shadows.

'Ritter.' My own voice sounded strange to me, as though Steffi's tongue were still trawling inside my mouth.

'Herr Ritter.' The voice deep and hard: it was like listening to his relentless malleting of the wooden stakes inside the church gate. 'This is Thomas.' A pause between the blows. 'Pastor Bruck's son.'

'Good evening, Herr Bruck.'

My greeting was not returned.

'I am phoning only because my father asked me to.' Another pause, then the mallet raised for another blow. 'My father will meet you tomorrow evening, after the evening prayer service. Come to the church about six thirty.'

'Thank you—'

'Don't thank *me*, Herr Ritter. If I had my way, my father would have nothing to do with people like you.'

'Even so, I'm grateful.'

The silence was so long that I thought he'd hung up.

'Twenty or thirty years ago they broke my father's back, Herr

Ritter. Now he wears a steel brace so he can walk but he still feels pain every day of his life. If you cause my father any grief, Herr Ritter, believe me, *you* are the one who will feel the pain.'

'All I want from your father is some personal information.'

'That's what they told him when they broke his back, Herr Ritter.'

'Please, this is just a personal matter.'

Pastor Bruck's son didn't hear me: this time he *had* hung up.

Seven

Tall rectangles of light spilled out of the windows of the church into the dark, wintry evening. The yellow light looked warm and inviting, but I had never been to a church service in my life and I wasn't about to start now. I turned the ignition key and pushed the accelerator pedal to the floor as the engine spluttered into life, and there was a momentary burst of smelly heat in the interior of the car. I clapped my gloved hands together, glanced at my watch. It was after six thirty: Pastor Bruck must be reciting extra prayers tonight. Maybe he was praying for an increase in his congregation. Two cars, a Volkswagen Beetle and an old Citroen station wagon, were parked on the roadway between me and the church gate. And, in the light of the lamp above the church door, I could see an old-fashioned bicycle leaning against the wall, its saddle covered by a navy blue beret. The cars and the bicycle had been there when I'd pulled in just after six. Two cars and a bike: it hardly seemed enough to warrant a prayer service.

I turned off the engine. The heat was fading as the smell of petrol intensified. I could pick up an old Beetle like the one beside me for a few hundred Deutschmarks but somebody had to keep the faith. Like Pastor Bruck and his handful of fellow worshippers. Maybe, after all, we had something in common.

The church door swung slowly open. An elderly couple

emerged; silver hair peeking out from under her dark hat, her hand holding firmly to her husband's arm as they made their way carefully to the station wagon. He helped her into the car; the soft thud of the door sounded loud in the darkness. Then car lights sweeping the road and the church wall, the crunch of tyres as the old man laboriously turned the car in a series of stop-start manoeuvres. When he was ready for departure, he halted, window down, to speak to the other two who had come out of the church: a schoolmistressy type fixing herself and her bicycle, a stooped farmer type standing at the door of the mud-caked Beetle. Voices in the darkness, safe home, see you on Sunday. The Beetle door closed, opened, slammed firmly shut the second time. Headlights briefly filling my car; I blinked against the passing light. The middle-aged lady on the bicycle examined me carefully as she slowly pedalled past.

Silence settled back on itself. The church waited in the darkness. The church door swung open again and Pastor Bruck stood there in the falling light, peering into the darkness. I got out of the car and went to meet him. Above the black cassock the bony face seemed paler than before.

'Thank you for seeing me, Pastor Bruck,' I said.

'I prayed about it – I didn't know what to do. Sometimes it's better to leave the past alone.' For a moment the sunken eyes met mine, then he looked away. 'Maybe you won't thank me later, Herr Ritter.'

He didn't wait for an answer but set about locking up the church. He pushed home the heavy bolt on the inside of the main door and closed the padlock on it.

'Unfortunately we've had some visitors who are not very fond of what we do here.' A wintry smile, a shrug. 'It's the way of the world.'

He walked ahead of me up the aisle. A slow walk but ramrod

straight. I thought of the words his son had spat down the phone. *Who* had broken his back? And *why*?

I almost stumbled into him at the low railing in front of the altar. For a moment or two the priest stood there, head bowed, hands joined. A page from a picture book of superstitious practices, a shaman in his temple. Yet mine was the faith that was mocked and discarded. He led me across the polished wooden floor and into a small room just off the altar. I watched him press switches on a board inside the door. Darkness marched towards us from the back of the church until the only light was the lamp burning in a hanging bowl above the altar. It was spooky, looking out at that space, full of gloom.

'I've asked my son to wait in the house,' Pastor Bruck said. 'We can talk here in the sacristy.'

Pastor Bruck closed the door to the altar and motioned me towards the two stools beside the small plug-in radiator. The sacristy was an odd mix: religion, dressing room, kitchen. A large wooden crucifix with a delph Christ hung above the wide chest of drawers; another smaller crucifix stood on top of the dark chest. A cassock and a plain white surplice on hangers were hooked to the back of the door; a wall cupboard and a stainless-steel sink completed the minimalist furniture of the small room.

I sat on the stool beside the radiator. There wasn't much heat; it felt like sitting in a bus shelter.

Pastor Bruck looked at me almost apologetically.

'We rely on donations, Herr Ritter. We have to be careful with our bills.'

He moved his stool closer to me. He looked even straighter sitting on the small stool. The brace, I thought. The brace and the pain. Every day, his son had said.

'My mother,' I said.

'Your mother. Petra Ritter.'

'Yes, Petra Ritter.'

'Please, show me the photograph again.'

Once more the priest looked at the small picture of my mother and me. An image from a lost time. A fair-haired young woman who seemed almost to be trying not to smile, a serious-faced youngster trying to live up to the cap and uniform of his Socialist Boy Scouts. The wheezy breathing of Pastor Bruck and the irregular clicking noise of the small electric heater. And my own heartbeat, loud in my head, waiting for this old fellow to speak of my past.

'I knew her,' he said at last, 'but how can I know who you are, Herr Ritter?'

'She was my mother.' I stared at the priest, confused. I hadn't expected this. 'I'm her son.'

'So you say.'

I took my wallet from my inside pocket and drew out my shiny new Bundesrepublik ID card. He was turning the laminated card over in his long bony fingers when I handed him my old GDR driving licence.

The thin lips curled, a hint of a smile.

'Two cards, two countries,' he said.

'One person,' I said, 'only one.'

'And which country do you belong to, Herr Ritter?'

I shrugged. 'I have no choice about that. I'm here because my mother sent me, Pastor Bruck. That's all I know.'

'And you are Petra Ritter's son.' He looked at the photograph. 'I can see it in the face, in the eyes. The same look of – of stubbornness, a refusal to be told what to do. Does that ring a bell, Herr Ritter?'

My mother's lonely-furrow obduracy came back to me. Her manifold refusals. To join our apartment block committee. To join the Workers Committee at the factory. Or the Parents Committee at my primary school. Or to go on the North Sea holiday with the rest of her factory colleagues. Her face set, one 'no' after another.

'That sounds like my mother,' I said.

'And yourself?' The priest was smiling.

I shrugged again. I wasn't about to reveal to this priest any more personal stuff. I had said too much on my first visit.

'My father,' I said. 'My mother sent me here to ask about my father.'

'You never had a father at home?' Gentleness in the wheeziness.

'It was just my mother and me, just the two of us.'

'So why now, Herr Ritter? Why try to find your father now? What good can it do you? You and your mother shared a life, she brought you up on her own and I'm sure she was proud of you. You did your best, you told me you have a doctorate from Rostock University, any mother would be proud of your achievement. What good can it do you now to seek out knowledge that might upset you, even do you harm?'

'My mother wanted me to know.'

'Your mother was dying, Herr Ritter. I've seen a lot of people die. Sometimes they want to change things just *because* they're dying. They ask for things they'd run a mile from if they thought they could go on living.' The priest edged his stool closer to mine. 'Despite what you read in storybooks, Herr Ritter, the words of the dying have no special value – they're just the words of people who know they haven't long to live. They have no special wisdom, believe me.'

'Still, she sent me to you—'

'And I'm saying to you to think of yourself. All we have is today, the past is over and done with.'

'So everybody keeps telling me.' I could tell from the look he gave me that he knew what I meant but he let it go.

'So why go chasing a father now, Herr Ritter?'

And in that barely heated sacristy in Bad Saarow, under the grey gaze of a priest I hardly knew, I found myself confronting the many ghosts of my absent father. School prize days, certificate days, days when my classmates gloried – and, as teenagers, squirmed – in the presence of their fathers. Fathers on the touchline at football games, loud with encouragement and remonstration. Fathers in summer allotments, smoking in shirtsleeves, hailing one another across the makeshift fences. And the way they'd sometimes call me into the allotment huts with their own children for a lemonade and a sandwich and I'd try not to see the wariness in their expressions, the words held back, constrained in the presence of this serious schoolboy with the non-participating mother and the dead father.

Maybe the priest read the struggle in my expression.

'I just want to know.' It sounded lame, even to myself. 'I'm thirty and I just want to know.'

Pastor Bruck studied my ID card for a moment.

'You were born in August nineteen sixty-three, Herr Ritter,' he said, fingering the card.

'So I'm told. I don't remember any of it.'

Pastor Bruck chose to ignore my flippancy.

'I knew your mother for a short while in the winter of nineteen sixty-two, Herr Ritter.'

'I suppose . . .' I hesitated, 'I was on the way then.'

'In November and December of nineteen sixty-two your mother was . . .' it was the pastor's turn to hesitate, 'a slim and lovely young woman. And brave too.'

'Brave?'

'Yes, brave and beautiful.'

'She sent me here – you must have known my father?'

The priest seemed to slump on the stool; maybe the metal

brace was failing in its job of keeping him upright.

'I knew the young man she loved at that time – the young man who loved her.'

He looked away from me. He closed his eyes, wrapped his arms around himself as though to protect himself against something other than the damp cold of the sacristy.

'Please,' I said.

When he opened his eyes, I could see the struggle in him.

'In that winter of nineteen sixty-two, the world was a different place. It was a dangerous world. In Berlin they had just built the Wall, every day we could see army trucks and tanks on the roads. Many of us feared there might be war, the Americans and the British were rumoured to be building up their armies in the West. Rumours, always rumours. And the Russians were here – officers, colonels, generals, being driven in and out of Berlin, on the boats in the lake – and the sky was full of planes, Herr Ritter, even here in this quiet place, in Bad Saarow.' He paused. I could see the shadow in his face, the remembered fear, but I wanted to get the old man back to the point.

'What's all that got to do with my father, Pastor Bruck?'

'It was in that dangerous time that Petra Ritter met a young man in Berlin. God help us, I was responsible for their meeting. It wasn't what I wanted, I was just trying to help a young fellow in serious trouble but then, I suppose, things happened, the way they do between a young woman and a young man.'

'What young man? Tell me.'

'The young man was a foreigner, Herr Ritter, he was on the run from the police – and God knows who else. Like I said, the roads were thick with the military anyway and you couldn't tell if they were on manoeuvres or hunting your . . .' He spread his hands, looked up at the wall as though enlightenment might descend from the crucifix.

'Or hunting my father,' I finished for him.

'Yes,' Pastor Bruck said, 'or hunting the man who probably was your father.'

'And they caught him?'

The priest's pale face became whiter than ever. Eyes closed, the skin stretched like brittle paper across the skeletal cheekbones.

'They always caught their quarry, Herr Ritter.'

Quarry. A beast fleeing across the snow-covered fields somewhere beyond the sacristy. Men and dogs in loud pursuit, the squeal of pain, blood on the snow.

'But why? What had the man done?'

'It didn't matter. He was guilty of whatever they said he was guilty of.'

'And this man, this man they were hunting – what was his name?

'Roland.' The eyes closed, remembering. 'His name was Roland.'

'What . . . what was he like?'

'He was young, Herr Ritter, younger than you are now. He was young, and he was brave and he was lost.'

'And he came here to meet my mother?'

The priest smiled at that. 'Maybe that was the *real* reason he came, Herr Ritter. Maybe that was the real God-sent reason that brought him here, so that he and your mother could meet. But in terms of this earthly kingdom, no, Roland didn't come here to meet Petra Ritter.' He moved his stool a little; the metal stool leg squealed against the wooden floor. 'Roland was sent here by others, on a mission, they would have said, but really, to carry out an impossible task.'

'I don't understand.'

'Which of us did understand, Herr Ritter?' He stood up suddenly, agitated, his long frame filling the small room. 'The world we lived in seemed beyond understanding. That young man was lost from the moment he stumbled into this crazy world of ours – I imagine that your mother was the only thing in it that made any kind of sense to him.'

'I wish it made sense to me, Pastor Bruck.' I struggled for words. 'Where is this man – this Roland? If he was my father, why did I never see him? Why did my mother never speak of him?'

'For the same reason, Herr Ritter, that I never spoke of him, never until this night. It was too dangerous. One life had been lost, wasn't that enough?'

I knew the meaning of his words, I knew the question I wanted to ask. I couldn't ask it. In my heart I already knew the answer.

I felt the priest's hand on my shoulder.

'It's not easy,' he said. 'You've just lost your mother, now you lose your father in the moment of finding him.'

'Some of us,' I said, looking directly at him, 'have lost a country.'

It was impossible to contemplate: how could the country I loved have taken from me the father I never knew?

'And some of us cannot share your grief about that, Herr Ritter.' The mildness of tone took the sting out of the rebuke. 'Come, I'll show you.'

I stood up, buttoning my coat.

'Show me what?'

'You want to learn about Roland – about your father?'

I nodded.

'Then come with me.'

The cold night air filled the sacristy when he opened the door. Pastor Bruck waited until I had negotiated the stone steps that led down from the sacristy before switching off the lights. I watched while he locked the door with a black iron key and then, in the darkness, I followed him on the dirt path among the graves.

The pastor's son must have been watching out for us: the door of the cottage at the end of the churchyard swung open and Thomas Bruck stood there in the lighted doorway. By way of greeting he gave me a malevolent glare; in silence he switched on the flashlight he was carrying and led the way along the side of the little cottage into a small fenced-off back garden. Thomas unlatched a low, wooden gate in the fence and went on into a bare open space; fifty or sixty metres beyond lay the dark bulk of the pine forest.

Even in the dark, Thomas's step was sure. He flashed his torch along the bare earth until the beam fastened on a small wooden cross. The tiny cross bore neither name nor date; in the dim light of the torch it looked lost, orphaned.

Nobody spoke. Just three overcoated men standing in silence around a bare wooden cross in the darkness of Bad Saarow.

Pastor Bruck took a smaller torch from his pocket and switched it on. I blinked as he flashed it towards me; I saw Thomas blink too as the beam fell for a moment on him.

'Thomas.' There was a note of pleading in the pastor's voice.

His son made no attempt to hide his anger. For a long moment he glared at his father but then he shrugged and stooped over the earth beside the wooden cross.

In the weak light of the torches I had not noticed that the earth here was disturbed, newly turned. Nor had I noticed the mound of fresh earth just beyond the beam of torchlight.

'Help me.' Thomas Bruck was looking at me with undisguised loathing.

I knelt beside him.

'There,' he said, pointing to my right.

Thomas was lifting an earth-covered board about the size of a door. I moved away from him and scrabbled with my fingers in the earth until I located the other end of the board. Together, still on our knees, we raised it from the ground and laid it against the mound of freshly dug soil.

Beneath the board was a shallow grave. I caught my breath, the smell of the soil as strong as dung. Above my own breathing I could hear the hoarse whisper of other times, other lives, insistent in this open trench. Pastor Bruck, standing above us, played the beams of both torches into the dark hole in the ground. Incongruous in the grave, a white plastic bag lay folded in the wet earth. Thomas took the bag from the grave, handed it to his father. The bag was folded a couple of times around something rectangular, like a small box, maybe a book.

'We opened the grave earlier today.' Pastor Bruck looked at me, then at Thomas. My eyes were becoming accustomed to the darkness: I could see the pity in the priest's face. 'Thomas opened it, Herr Ritter.'

'Thank you,' I said. It didn't take much to work out whose remains lay here in this unmarked spot.

Thomas Bruck didn't answer me, his expression grim as ever. Maybe he was still thinking about the brace on his father's back.

'This is yours, Herr Ritter.' Pastor Bruck handed me the plastic bag.

I took it gingerly. I pressed it between my fingers. Softish, like paper, or cloth. But solid.

'What is it?'

'I don't know,' Pastor Bruck said. 'Your mother gave it to me the last time I saw her.' A weary smile. 'Not like this,' pointing to the plastic bag in my hands. 'She gave me a cardboard box, for safe keeping, she said.' He stopped, looking beyond us to the shadowy trees. 'It was too dangerous for your mother to keep, I suppose; she had you by then, she had someone else to worry about.'

'And who was going to worry about you?' Thomas interrupted. 'Tell me that, who?'

'Thomas, Thomas.'

His son snorted. In one movement he stooped, grabbed the board from the ground and hurled it into the open grave. Without another word he stormed off. We could hear the cottage door slam shut behind him.

'I'm sorry,' I said. 'I seem to have a gift for upsetting your son.'

'It's not you, Herr Ritter, just all that has gone before.'

For a moment we both stared in silence at the mud-covered board leaning askew in the shallow grave.

'My son was seven years old when they came, Herr Ritter. Three of them, in the dark, a freezing night. They drove the van into the church grounds, took it in as far as they could. They man-handled the box out of the van on to a trolley and forced my son to wheel it here between the graves. The trolley fell over once, they made jokes that it might break open and what would Thomas do then? They picked this spot, Herr Ritter, and the three of them stood here smoking while Thomas and I dug the grave. They mocked him, made fun of the way he was digging, said a girl could dig better.' He bowed his head. I waited while he visibly pulled himself together. 'It wasn't deep enough, Herr Ritter, but they said it was deep enough for what was going into it and anyway they were too cold, they said, standing around in a graveyard. They almost threw the box – the coffin – down there but they waited until Thomas had filled it in again. They warned us to say nothing, Herr Ritter, to put no name or mark on the spot.'

Something was bothering me.

'But how did you know it was . . . Roland?'

'When the box – coffin – fell off the trolley. They prised the lid off with a crowbar, just a little, but enough for me to see his face.'

I stooped to pick up the board that Thomas had flung into the grave and manoeuvred it to cover the gaping hole.

I didn't want to look at the pastor.

'I don't understand, Pastor Bruck.' I picked up the plastic bag, slimy from the wet earth. 'How did this come to be in the grave?'

'I put it there, Herr Ritter.' The beam of the torch traversed the nameless grave. 'Well, Thomas did. Your mother gave it to me some time after – after that night.' A stomping of feet, against the cold, against the memory? 'Your mother was brave and resourceful, Herr Ritter, but she was also young and I knew she loved him. She knew he was gone, that he was never coming back, but I was afraid that she might betray herself. She was under suspicion, they'd already questioned her but she had . . . protected him. Now she had to protect herself, Herr Ritter. She was pregnant.' Another shifting of feet, a cough in the night. 'And there was my son to think of, a boy who had already lost his mother.' He didn't mention himself, I knew he wouldn't. 'Your mother was a brave woman, that's why she never allowed herself to visit your father's grave, except once.'

The wind rose; beyond us, the trees shivered in the darkness.

'So you buried her . . . package here, beside . . .'

'I buried it, Herr Ritter, further back in the forest. It could have been suicidal to put it down here, where they had ordered him to be buried. You don't know what they were like, Herr Ritter.' A sucking sound in his breath, the swallowing noise of an old man who could see more distant shadows lurking around the grave. 'You never knew when they might come back and order this –' *this* – 'dug up again. I had other lives to consider – my son – his mother was dead, he had nobody else.'

I waited for him to continue.

'Your mother said to me that she wanted some memory to remain. Maybe someone will come, she said to me, maybe somebody will come looking for him, there ought to be some remembrance of what happened here.'

I felt the priest's grey eyes upon me: *you are that somebody*.

'I thought her words were nonsense, Herr Ritter,' a small, sad smile, 'but I didn't have enough faith, did I? Anyway, after the Wall came down – long after that – we dug up your mother's package from its hole in the ground and Thomas and I put it in this grave. And we replaced the flat stone that marked it with this little wooden cross. We couldn't do that before. We'd all suffered too much, Herr Ritter. I was afraid of what they might do to Thomas.'

I felt myself shivering. I swung my arms against my body but the shivering wouldn't stop.

'Let's go inside, Herr Ritter, some coffee will warm us. This is all a shock to you.'

If you only knew, I wanted to say. I find a dead father. I hold a slimy, plastic bag full of god knows what from my mother. And you speak of what *they* might do, how you were afraid of *them*. *They* and *them*: the officers, the guardians of my lost country.

'Come.' I felt his hand upon my arm. 'But first . . .'

I watched as he crossed himself. And I went on watching, my head unbowed, as this ancient priest murmured his prayers over the grave of my lost father.

Eight

It was a long winter. On the first day of December the snow fell thicker and heavier than even the snows of boyhood memory and blanketed the streets of Brandenburg with a morning brilliance that suggested purity and promise and a world renewed. I recall it with clarity because, when the snow began to fall, around 3 a.m., I was walking the frozen deserted streets of the town, my footsteps echoing softly between the silent shops and apartment blocks. I was on the streets that night just as I had been every night since Pastor Bruck had handed me the folded plastic bag from the grave that contained the remains of my father.

There was no doubt in my mind that this mysterious Roland was my father. *Father: Johannes Vos. Occupation: General Operative.* Thus my birth certificate. A good man, my mother had told me, a kind man. A colleague at the printing works where she stacked and folded paper for the presses. A kind man who died of cancer before I was born. A dying man, I told myself, walking the winter streets, who had perhaps lent his name to help out a young and pregnant fellow worker. He had married my mother: that certificate too was stored in the metal cabinet in the corner of our living room. My mother had never taken Johannes Vos's name. Nor had she given it to me.

But neither had she given me the name of Roland.

Odd, this *Ausländer*, this foreigner at large in our town, this foreigner with the name of Roland: Roland, who was our city's historic hero, our saviour from the Middle Ages, whose statue still guarded our city hall. In the falling snow Roland's statue stood as mute as the folded bag in the metal drawer beside my birth certificate.

Yes, a long, silent winter. They cleared the pavements and the roads of snow but the whiteness cloaked the roofs and the towers and the trees, muffling the medley of city sounds, the trundle of tyres, the clanging bells of the trams.

And muffling my heart, I thought, like a heavy scarf tied too tightly against your throat.

Of course, it wasn't the snow that was stifling me. In my heart I knew that. The snowy, night-time streets were my escape from the filing cabinet, from the plastic bag and its contents. I had never opened it. To make sure it didn't suddenly open itself I had even tied a couple of thick rubber bands around it. And the filing cabinet was locked.

Strings of coloured lights flowered between the white rooftops, beacons of Christmas consumerism above the windows of the shops. On my night-time excursions I watched the lights blink and then die, promptly, at 1 a.m. *Shopping is done for the day, rest ye now from your buying and spending until the morn.* Sometimes the dipped lights of the squad car crawling towards me along the empty street would suddenly flare full beam at me; blinking in the glare of the headlights I'd feel the eyes of the Polizei upon me as the car inched past; the eyes of outsiders, clean eyes imported from Kassel or Stuttgart, clean eyes studying this nightwalker from a failed state, a befuddled rat who didn't realize that the ship had sunk. In their green and silver car they slowed, they stared, they studied. They never bothered me. I wondered if there was a file on me in the refurbished police station.

I tried not to think about the other files but they dangled in front of me anyway, hanging between the coloured bulbs above my head. Or they invaded my broken daytime sleeping, gate-crashing the fragmented hours in my narrow bed. Brown cardboard files that bore the names of those who had fathered me. *Roland Something. Johannes Vos.* And the other one, the file with the name *Petra Ritter* on it. Buff-coloured files that had been compiled not by the lily-white hands of our invading masters but by the guardians of my own lost land.

In the wonderland of our new and united Bundesrepublik you could examine the old files of the now-disbanded Ministry of State Security. Our Ministerium für Staatssicherheit was now routinely referred to as a weapon of state oppression, its officers regarded as little more than criminals. Only once, in the staff-room at my school, had I dared to point out that the MfS had been a legitimate arm of a legitimate state and its officers had been charged with the protection of that state; the shocked, embarrassed silence among my colleagues had taught me that in our great new and uncensored state some things were more uncensored than others. And I'd been fired anyway.

Still . . .

Sometimes you had to bend the knee. Swallow your pride. Fill in the forms, say 'please' and open the files that might tell you something about your fathers. Especially about the foreigner named Roland. Whose bones had been buried at night behind an obscure chapel in Bad Saarow. Because of whom that skeletal old priest had suffered a broken back. And whose name my mother had never breathed to me until she was almost about to breathe her last.

On a dull morning in late January, when the Christmas lights of the town had been filed away for another year but the rooftops were still bright with frozen snow, I crossed the tramlined road from my apartment block to the freshly painted railway station and bought a day-return ticket to Berlin. I sat upstairs in the streamlined double-decker train and watched the wintry fields of my land speed past. It was a short trip, not much longer than half an hour, but the fleeting landscape was a slide show of the country I had grown up in and what it had become. Vast silent fields where horse and man had toiled; the brick stations of my youth shunted sideways and replaced with slicker, shinier versions. Our invaders had spent money – you couldn't deny it – but they took more than they gave. At Potsdam, on the edge of Berlin, a train from the capital was pulling in at the same time: even in late January, with snow and frost on the ground, the backpackers spilled on to the platform, headed for the palatial delights of the hitherto forbidden East. Back home in Sydney or Seattle these anoraked, cut-price travellers would be able to boast that they had trekked in the homeland of the Stasi.

And in Berlin they could even gawk and exclaim amid its plundered headquarters.

At the Zoologischer Garten I changed trains, taking the local service as far as Alexanderplatz. Amid the quietness of the elevated platform it was almost possible to forget the frantic, liberated streets below; I shut my eyes and let myself imagine for a moment that the streets were still ours and uninvaded. The U-Bahn, Line 5, took me deeper into the old city, further into streets behind the Wall they had torn down.

I climbed up the steps from the tiled station at Magdalenenstrasse. The wide thoroughfare of Frankfurter Allee throbbed with the roar of traffic. Almost a blur of speeding chrome, all the colours of the spectrum, a flashing, noisy hymn to the glory of the motor industry; slogan-splashed taxis; trucks and trailers from the four corners of Europe. I waited for the lights and fled across the road for the safety of the complex of buildings on Normannenstrasse.

I walked a narrow road between a pair of multi-storey blocks and stepped into a spacious square surrounded on all sides by a series of tall buildings. Hundreds of windows gazed down, one side lit now by a sudden blast of cold wintry sun from the west. There was neither art nor artifice in these buildings: plain, unadorned, no more than functional, these grey, multi-windowed structures reflected the state they had served.

The sometime home of the Ministry of State Security was demonized now: *here be dragons*. The mere mention of the Stasi was enough to set the grown-up children of modern Germany shivering in their beds.

Now they called it a Research and Memorial Centre. A tourist attraction. A disgorging point for coachloads of pensioners from all over the Bundesrepublik. Trek through the lair of the bogeyman and mail the postcards to your nearest and dearest.

Three coaches were already pulled up alongside Block 1. The pensioners were still easing themselves down from the last of the buses: Heritage Tours, the bus proclaimed, Hanover. *Step this way, ladies and gentlemen, and marvel at the past you have delivered us from.*

I followed the babbling herd through the front door into the reception area. I half heard the babbling Hanover guide laying down the ground rules as I looked around me. Fearful and curious about what kind of theme park they had made of the place.

It was as I remembered it. The pale tiles on the floor. The wide marble staircase. The high soaring ceiling. They'd even left our flag on show, furled, of course, in submission.

They'd added a few things. The postcard rack behind the reception desk to the right. The display stand beside it, loud with leaflets trumpeting the manifold tourist delights of Berlin. *You name it, we've got it, even a tamed and muzzled secret police service.*

The retirees from Hanover were oohing and aahing about the prison van on display near the foot of the staircase. Pale blue, box-like, barred window at the rear, a sliding side door to get the prisoner into the back.

So tiny, someone said.

But so dangerous, someone laughed.

And poisonous! from another.

Just like a Trabi! And everyone laughed.

The grey, steel-legged chairs where Dieter – *where are you now, Dieter, friend of my Rostock days?* – and I had sat in a line against the wall where the prison van now stood. The uniformed officer behind the desk inside the door had smiled at us – the black state car was outside the door, the peak-capped driver lounging beside it, and the ID shown by Dieter's father had produced a stiffening in the officer's upright stance – but I had been nervous. It wasn't every day you were driven in an official ministry car to the MfS while your friend's father delivered official (and presumably secret) papers to the Director himself. And we'd seen the reaction when the Herr Direktor's personal assistant had arrived in reception to personally guide Dieter's father upstairs.

I wondered how the widows of Hanover would react if they knew that I had sat there, unmolested, all those years ago, where the prison van was now displayed.

Privileged, they'd call us. Or worse.

And yet, in that hushed, vaguely menacing reception area we had both been nervous. Even Dieter. For him, too, it was a first time inside Normannenstrasse. I coughed, cleared my throat as if to speak and the desk officer had looked at me inquiringly. I looked away, caught Dieter's sideways glance, the almost imperceptible shake of his head.

And then footsteps on the marble staircase, the sound of approaching voices and the desk officer on his feet, standing rigidly to attention.

Dieter's father smiled across at us as the group came to the bottom of the stairs. Tall, slope-shouldered and paunchy, Dieter's father seemed almost insignificant alongside the smaller man in uniform.

Erich Mielke. In the flesh. In full MfS uniform, military ribbons emblazoned across his chest.

Alongside Dieter, I rose to my feet, hardly daring to breathe in the presence of this legend. The Director was of medium height and portly; his round face was ruddy, his greying hair plastered sideways over the beginnings of baldness.

A picture of ordinariness.

And yet . . . and yet you could sense the power of the man: his drive, his belief.

He was shaking hands with Dieter. A soft, growly kind of voice, inquiring now about Dieter's studies, his progress in economics.

'A chip off the old block?'

Dieter's father beamed at the compliment.

'And you, young man? What are you up to in Rostock, apart from swilling beer and chasing girls?'

This to me, and I could stop neither the blushing on my face and neck nor the stammering in my voice as I attempted to answer.

Dieter came to my rescue.

'Michael is a student of English, Herr Direktor – and a very good one.'

His father embellished it. 'Michael is a member of the Party – my son assures me that he is a most active member of the Friendship League for visiting students at the university.'

The Director knew what that meant. He studied me more closely now: *this one had already got Party approval, from somewhere.*

'The Party needs young men like you.' His hand on my upper arm, a smile lighting the round face.

'Yes, Herr Direktor.' Somehow, the words came out.

'And where are you from, young man?'

'Brandenburg, Herr Direktor.' I stammered again. 'Brandenburg-an-der-Havel, sir.'

'Michael Ritter.' My name on his lips told me: he knew my name, knew my seed and breed. It was his job: like the MfS itself, he was the shield and sword of the Party.

'Look to your studies, young man. I shall tell our director in Potsdam to keep an eye on your progress.' Potsdam was the regional MfS headquarters for my home area.

Abruptly, he shook hands with Dieter's father, nodded to Dieter and myself, and turned back up the marble stairs, his uniformed assistant trailing in his wake.

For a moment we stood watching their departure in silence.

Dieter broke the spell.

'You're made up, Michael!' he whispered.

His father looked sternly at me. 'I hope you appreciate the honour of this, the Direktor taking an interest in you.' I nodded. 'Direktor Mielke has a prodigious memory, Michael, he will not forget you. Work hard and you will do well.'

So here I was, doing well, half attached to a bunch of grey-haired *Wessies*, trying to ignore their chatter at this scene of my student triumph.

'My uncle was locked up in this place,' I heard. 'Only a few days, but he was a nervous wreck afterwards, even when they sent him across the Wall. He could never bring himself to tell us what they did to him here.'

Several voices cut in at once, excited, the whiff of sulphur in the crowded space. And then one voice dominant, shriller than the rest: 'You're in the right place to find out – fill in the inquiry form, that's what this place is for now, they'll have to tell you what happened to your uncle.'

My ears pricked up. This was why I had come here. I had my own questions to ask, about Roland Somebody and Johannes Vos and Petra Ritter. And maybe even about Michael Ritter.

Another babble of voices. The tour guide waited for it to die down before speaking. She was tall and spare, schoolmistressy in her calf-length, green loden overcoat.

'Not so, not here.' They quietened, schoolchildren again in the presence of teacher. 'This is not the place for making such inquiries and seeking such information. For that one must go to the Documentation Centre on Mauerstrasse.'

Four or five voices shouting *Ja!* together: everybody knew this wasn't the place to make inquiries.

I hadn't known. I gazed in dismay at the Hanover Heritage tourists and wondered what I was doing, lingering among them. I should be gone, perhaps to Mauerstrasse. I had heard of the Documentation Centre, of course, but had not paid enough attention to its purpose. But since I was here . . .

Impulsively, ignoring the ruffled looks, I made my way between the pensioners and, clutching a catalogue under my arm, made my way up the staircase that Erich Mielke had ascended all those years ago. The *Wessies* didn't own my personal history; I would walk these historic corridors alone, my ears safe from their babbling.

The displays in the first floor rooms were a shock to me: surveillance technology, a Trabi door with concealed cameras, a necktie with tiny lenses . . . More of the same: instruments for eavesdropping, watching, spying. The intestines of these machines laid bare for our awed delight.

And the workings of our dismembered country likewise laid bare for the oohs and aahs of tourists. *From this we delivered them, from themselves.* Not a word about the necessity for a beleaguered nation to defend itself by whatever means possible. *From the enemy without and the enemy within.*

I hurried up to the next floor. And paused at the door of the Minister's personal office. Stepped tentatively into the sanctum from which the Minister for State Security had organized his forces against those who would destroy us. He had failed in his struggle, *we* had failed, and victor's justice decreed a punishment of circus-like ridicule. Mielke's desk, his phone, even the tray plan of his spartan breakfast, all on display, to mock-scare, to scoff at, to remind us of the barbarian general paraded in chains in a Roman Triumph.

Into the next room, panelled with pale wood like the Minister's office, islands of coffee tables and easy chairs. Here, according to the bland catalogue, the generals of the MfS took their coffee, chatted among themselves. The catalogue didn't say if Erich Mielke moved among them, sat with them, but I imagined he did. I could see him sitting there with his generals, cigarette smoke trailing above the coffee tables, the air rich with gossip, the weekend, Dynamo's chances in next Saturday's game.

I bought a coffee from the tiny stand in the corner of the room – *you too can sip coffee where the Stasi spymasters plotted against their own people!* – and stood at the high window looking out across the city. Television dishes and aerials reached skywards and westwards for messages from the promised land. The twin spires of a church clawed at the low clouds. From below in the building came the murmur of the Hanover crocodile, winding its way through the bowels of my country's past. Behind me, in the panelled room, the ghosts of the generals inhaled on their cigarettes and talked about football.

And I knew, looking out on the unwalled, undivided streets of Berlin, that I was lost in no-man's-land. My generals were gone, their swords crushed in the *Wessie* dust beside their broken shields. No faith warmed me, neither the messages from the soaring church spires nor the siren songs of the TV antennae. Standing at that window in the general's coffee room, I felt faithless, stateless.

And orphaned. Even that unknown father, that never-known name on my birth certificate – even Johannes Vos, it seemed, had been taken from me. What remained was nebulous, a wisp of maybes and riddles. My mother's dying words. Pastor Bruck's broken back. An *Ausländer* from god knows where. The whiff of betrayal. The scent of loss, of the might-have-been, the never-to-be-any-more. The touch of plastic, sweaty and cold, taken from the earth in Bad Saarow.

In the corridor the Hanover pensioners fell silent and stood aside, as I stumbled past them, not caring what they saw, what I looked like – and anyway there was nothing I could do about the tears streaming down my face. It was the first time I had wept since my mother's death.

Nine

No patrolling of the streets of Brandenburg that night. Instead, I clung to the security of the old flat opposite the railway station. The familiar bits and pieces had never been so precious to me. Odds and sods that my mother had begged, borrowed or liberated from god knows where. The framed print of 'Starry Night' on the wall by the window. The brass tongs and poker beside the blocked-up fireplace. The dark, bow-legged sideboard that was a parade ground for a collection of framed photos of my schoolboy self. A hand-painted, scalloped plate that my mother had claimed was once the property of a local prince. I conducted my inventory of these acquisitions of an ordinary life as if I were the curator of the Hermitage or the Prado.

The sense of abandonment that had overwhelmed me in the generals' coffee room in Normannenstrasse had remained with me throughout the day; it had sat beside me on the train home from Berlin and clung to me as I crossed the wide road and climbed the stairs to my flat. To shake it off, banish it to the wintry darkness outside, I sensed that I must remind myself of who I was. And so I numbered the objects of my youth, of my mother's life, the chipped vase and the 1979 calendar with the mountain view of Austria, and found myself again. The country I had believed in was lost but my past could not be stolen from me. *You are Michael Ritter, a resident of the city of Brandenburg, the only son of Petra Ritter, a graduate of Rostock University, a teacher and scholar and storyteller.*

I knew what I was about to do. I sat in the old armchair by the window, letting my strength settle upon me, finding again the identity that was mine. The familiar noises and sights told me who I was. The whoosh of traffic on the road beyond the window. An impatient car horn. The whistle of trains. Frau Mertens moving around next door. The street lights brightening as the darkness deepened. Silence settling as the city fell asleep, or whatever it did in the midnight hours. The street lights blinked and died. Opposite, the railway station seemed to close its eyes, only the faint beam above the entrance lit to show it was there. I closed the curtains and turned on the table lamp at my elbow. It was time to have a look at whatever it was that had been sent to me from the grave by Roland Somebody.

The white plastic bag was overprinted with the green cross of a pharmacy: Apotheke Kotte, it said, with an address in Berlin. Better if all it contained were a packet of paracetamol. But there was no turning back now. I had wiped the bag clean before putting it away in the filing cabinet but a thin residue of grit still clung to its surface: tiny crumbs of clay fell soundlessly to the floor as I opened the bag.

The paper bag inside was made of coarse, brown paper, so thick that it felt almost like cardboard; it had been folded and pressed tightly together around a rectangular object: a book, I had guessed, from the moment it had been handed to me by Pastor Bruck. For just a moment I hestitated. For months I had resolutely refused to look into this memento of my own past. I had the sense that life was about to change, that the simple unfolding of this brown paper bag would alter my life in ways I could not imagine.

The crackling of the unfolding paper bag was loud in the silent flat. Whatever was inside did not slip out easily; I pushed it from the closed end of the bag, felt the paper shift and loosen, like a door reluctantly opening.

And the book on my knees, my fingers gripping its edges. A thick book with firm, dark-green covers, padded, the leather soft, unexpectedly warm after its long years in the clay. I turned the book over in my hands: nothing written on the covers, the thick spine blank. A fat book, but I could tell, even before I opened it, that it was not the number of pages that lent it bulk: it was the thickness of the pages themselves, heavy, handmade paper, the kind you might stick photographs on, the kind that a teenage girl might use as her 'secret' diary.

I eased the book open. The pages were yellow and unlined. All of them, about the size of a paperback novel, were covered in handwriting. The writing was small but I noticed that occasionally the script seemed to get bigger and then the writer seemed to force himself into the smaller pattern, as though he were more used to writing in a larger, more expansive hand. I had no doubt that these pages, fifty or so of them, had been written by a 'he': my mother's spidery German hand was utterly different from these more rounded characters. These words, I was sure, came from the hand of Roland Somebody. From my father.

Somewhere, not far away, perhaps here in Brandenburg, perhaps even in Pastor Bruck's church in Bad Saarow, my father had held the pen in his hand and written these words.

I turned the yellow pages, saw only the mass of cramped writing, tried to see the man who had done the writing. And failed.

And then, on the inside back cover of the book, a line drawing in black india ink, the ink faded now, but the sketch still vibrant, clearly drawn by my mother. She'd even signed it, *P. Ritter mit Liebe*, but I'd have known it was hers anyway; she'd drawn plenty of indignant cats and fearsome dogs, all with human faces, when I was a small boy. This face on the yellow page was neither indignant not fearsome, a handsome face, a strong chin, deep eyes, the face in three-quarters profile, the wavy, unruly hair falling over the left ear. The hint of a mischievous smile on the handsome features, as though he thought the whole thing was a nonsense. And my mother's signature, in her neat script, in the bottom right-hand corner: P. Ritter with love. Opposite the drawing his statement, his declaration: *Roland xxx Petra.* I didn't know then that Roland had never seen the drawing, that my mother had added it afterwards.

I knew I envied them, recognized the bleakness of my own life: whose name could *I* write beside my own?

At least now I knew his name. She'd written it above the sketch, *Roland Feldmann.* I rolled it on my tongue, mouthing the words, silently at first, then aloud. And wondered if it was the first time his name had been spoken aloud in that apartment. I would never know how often my mother had whispered his name to herself. I said the name aloud again. *Roland Feldmann.* A foreigner, the priest had said, but this was no *Ausländer's* name, this was a name as German as my own. And how could that be? Just one more unknown as I struggled to form a picture of my unknown father.

Two days later, seated again in the sacristy of Pastor Bruck's church, I watched his face as I showed him the sketch: the long, pale face grew even paler, for a moment he closed his eyes and, when he opened them, I could see in the pale depths the pain of sadness revisited. He said nothing, merely nodded, handing the book back to me.

'It's like him?' Stupid, unnecessary question.

The priest did not bother to reply.

'I wish . . .' I hesitated, 'I wish they'd left a photograph.'

A half smile, half grimace on the white face.

'Michael,' it was the first time he'd used my name, the first time he'd addressed me in the familiar *du*, 'what kind of country do you think we lived in? What kind of country do you think Roland came to – to visit?' A hint of exasperation in the voice. 'D'you think your mother and this young man could take photos of each other and just hand in the film to any old shop for developing? *Do you?*'

I could not meet his grey, steely gaze.

'What kind of country d'you think you grew up in, Michael?'

The words softly spoken, but they hung there, in the half-warmed air of the sacristy, like an accusation.

'When your mother was drawing this little sketch,' he went on, 'they were all over the place looking for Roland. It was a manhunt.' The eyes wide, looking past me, to some remembered horror. 'Yes, a manhunt. Like hunting an animal. You understand what I'm telling you, Michael?'

And of course I knew but what the priest was telling me was stuff I didn't want to know or understand. By then I was on my own hunt – a personal hunt, for the man who was my father, even for the person my mother had been, the young woman who seemed to have fallen in love with this *Ausländer*, Roland. *And for myself, too, although I didn't know it then.*

On the day after my visit to Normannenstrasse, I was back in Berlin, this time at the Documentation Centre in Mauerstrasse. I had been up all night, I knew I was red-eyed, unshaven and unkempt, but there was a hunger inside me that demanded immediate satisfaction. A fellow about my own age, formal in his dark suit, white shirt and sober tie, explained to me that it didn't work like that. The wheels of the Documentation Centre, he said, necessarily turned slowly: there were millions of documents to be processed; every citizen's rights had to be protected, even the rights of those who might not have respected the rights of others in the former German Democratic Republic. He adjusted his tie, leaned slightly towards me across the counter in the spacious reception area and asked if the gentleman understood.

The gentleman understood, I said, but this matter was urgent.

It was always urgent, he said.

And private, I went on, information concerning my family.

A nod, a glimmer of a smile. Information concerning any individual could not be released indiscriminately, only to an applicant who could prove a family or other significant connection to the subject of the inquiry.

My collar-and-tie-clad administrator seemed to sense my unease at this stipulation. With a glance at his colleague, a young fellow in jeans and dark sweatshirt, he came round the counter and steered me towards a wooden bench under the window.

'You have a problem with this requirement, Herr Ritter?' he asked me. 'Perhaps, if you explain the difficulty to me, I can help you.'

So I explained it to him: I wished to file an inquiry about my father but I had no documentary evidence to show that he was my father.

'He is not named on your birth certificate?'

I shook my head.

'And you have no evidence to back up your claim that he was your father?'

Only the book, I told him, showing it to him. And the words of a pastor in Bad Saarow who had known them both, my mother and my father, when they were young, before I was born.

Maybe it was a slack day at the Information and Documentation Centre, maybe Herr Gosch, as I learned his name to be, was simply intrigued by my sloppy appearance or my unusual tale, or both; whatever the reason, he listened patiently to my story and then proceeded to advise me on how best to set about my application for information about Roland Feldmann. I should submit photocopies of the most relevant pages, including the sketch, to support my application; a notarized statement from Pastor Bruck would surely lend added weight.

It was only when Herr Gosch handed me his card that I realized my good fortune in meeting him; he was, in fact, the Assistant Director of the Centre and had just happened to be checking something himself with the young receptionist when I arrived at the desk.

'In this job,' he said to me, 'I am confronted every day by impossible stories, tragic tales. Yours is by no means unusual. It might do no harm, Herr Ritter, to include a supporting reference from your employer – it might incline the Centre's Adjudication Committee to release the information you seek.'

I avoided his eyes as I told him I was unemployed.

'An unfortunate reality of our times, Herr Ritter. May I ask what your profession is?'

A teacher, I told him, a teacher of English.

How long, he asked gently, had I been unemployed.

A few months, I said, since the beginning of the school year.

Maybe he sensed my discomfort; maybe he could read the runes, but he was too well-mannered to let the silence between us drag on. He had another suggestion, he said, which might be helpful to my search.

'Complete an application for information about yourself, Herr Ritter,' he said. 'Every citizen is entitled to see any files concerning himself or herself, kept by the Stasi. It may well be that there is a Stasi file on you – and that file could contain references to this Roland Feldmann, the man you claim to be your father.'

There was no avoiding it now. I looked around the reception area, at the tall information panels that listed the Federal

Republic's version of the sins of the GDR, and saw my personal future in this united Germany laid out before me like an obstacle course – a series of traps and bunkers to be negotiated daily, always under somebody's disapproving eyes.

'I was a member of the Party, Herr Gosch,' I said, 'an active member.'

The Assistant Director seemed to move a little away from me on the bench under the window. He shrugged his suited shoulders, adjusted his striped tie.

'To have been a member of the Party, Herr Ritter, cannot be considered a crime.'

It was my turn to shrug.

'Try teaching at the gymnasium in Brandenburg,' I said.

He smiled then. 'Think about what I said, Herr Ritter.' He stood up, crossed to the reception counter and came back with a handful of A4-sized documents. 'These are the forms you must fill in to seek information from the files we hold. You should complete one form for each person you're asking about – your mother, Roland Feldmann, perhaps even the gentleman listed on your birth certificate as your father.' He held out his hand to me. 'I'll keep an eye out for your application, Herr Ritter, and,' he was holding the door open for me, 'think about what I said, about requesting information about yourself. You have nothing to fear.'

An incline of the head, the door closed, and I was alone on the steps of the Documentation Centre. Nothing to fear, Herr Gosch had said. Nothing to fear except hostile eyes searching through my past, ferreting in files and cabinets for evidence of loyalty that they would immediately brand as betrayal. In our new world, I thought grimly, night becomes day and light is turned into darkness.

And next day this old priest, in his tired voice, a voice so tired that it seems he himself is the exhausted quarry fleeing the hue and cry of chasing bloodhounds, this ancient priest is asking me if I understand.

There is much that I understand but don't wish to; there is much that I don't but hunger for.

Over the course of the next few months I will learn more. Pastor Bruck seems almost to welcome my visits, despite his son's continuing surliness; only on our walks through the Bad Saarow woodlands, when he stops unexpectedly, his face creased with pain, his hand involuntarily drawn to his back, only then am I reminded that Thomas has, after all, good reason to resent me. But the year turns, the trees put on their greenery, and each visit adds another piece to my vague jigsaw.

As do the replies from the Information and Documentation Centre. Each *Antrag auf Auskunft*, Request for Information, that I have completed brings its own shading to the picture I am trying to construct. Now I sit on a stool to eat at the worktop in the small kitchen: the table in the living room is covered with papers, maps, official stationery stamped with the eagle of the Bundesrepublik. Frau Mertens, bearing gifts of apple strudel and homemade bread, looks at the pile of papers but keeps to herself the questions I can read in her homely face. As the information grows – although the hunger in my head remains unsatisfied – I am warmed by her simple solicitude, her repeated admonitions to 'eat plenty of vegetables and make sure you get a good night's sleep'. At least the vegetables are easily acquired.

I linger longest over the request for information from the State Security files concerning myself: for weeks, perhaps months, the blank, duplicate pages of the *Antrag auf Auskunft* stare back at me from the kitchen table. I have no doubt that I feature extensively in the files of the Sozialistische Einheitspartei Deutschlands. Why should I not? Why should I not have supported the security of my homeland? The SED, the Socialist Unity Party of Germany, was the sworn 'shield and sword' of the GDR; now membership and support of that Party are deemed a retrospective crime.

And yet my unease about looking for my own files is both deeper and, at the same time, vaguer than that. As I painstakingly put the bits together about my father, I am troubled, uneasy, as though I myself had been part of what the pastor described as a manhunt. In the end I feel I have no choice but to accept Herr Gosch's advice; even so, it is with reluctance that I drop the completed form in the mailbox in Hohestrasse.

My town is dying before my eyes. Yes, the new shopfronts come with their brand names from the West, but their gaudy loudness and their windows plastered with discount posters cannot hide the continuing flight from the town. Empty houses. Windows broken, boarded up. Estate agents, the new plant in our field, sprout photos of bargains, 'ripe for redevelopment', in their polished windows, and the handful of tourists stand at the windows, their eyes shining with greed, their faces transformed by the prospect of future yields. Tomorrow is all. Who needs yesterday? Or yesterday's men?

Once in a while Frau Mertens counsels flight to the West, once in a while Steffi stops by, always without warning, and she, too, after a satisfactory workout in my narrow bed, murmurs sleepily that there is nothing to keep me in Brandenburg.

By then, as the heat of summer cools into autumn, I am past caring about my personal future. Money, for the foreseeable future, is not a problem: my substantial teaching salary, paid into my account for the rest of the school year after my dismissal, remains almost untouched – my rent is tiny, my needs basic. Besides, in the early days of that autumn, I am distracted, even excited, by something new.

It is Pastor Bruck's idea.

We are strolling on a woodland path behind his church. Early evening, the songbirds loud in the greenery, the air sweet with a kind of sadness, as though the leaves were already falling. Less than a year has passed since I first ventured here but now that chilly morning seems a lifetime ago.

I have been telling the pastor about the replies from the Documentation Centre when, suddenly, the trees are louder than ever with song, as though some unseen conductor has driven the birds of the forest to a rapturous finale. In the aftermath, in the hush, we stand wordless under the trees.

And I hear myself say, 'I don't know what to do with all this *stuff* – all this information I'm gathering.'

The priest considers the treetops, seems to hear something, his head inclined, listening.

'Write it down, Michael.' The listening pose again, the eyes narrowed. 'Yes, write it all down.'

I laugh half-heartedly, confused. I hadn't expected such a concrete response.

'But . . . I have a lot of stuff, yes, but the gaps are bigger than the information I've got.'

'Then fill the gaps in, Michael.' A hint of a smile on the pale features, a nod towards the treetops. 'Listen to the birds, listen to your heart. Your heart knows more than your head, Michael.' The smile broadens. 'That's one of the things they never learned in Normannenstrasse.' I feel his hand on my arm: the simple gesture took the sting out of his words and brought home to me how much this god-believing, ascetic priest had come to mean to me.

'You mean, make it up as I go along?' It is my turn to smile. 'Just make up a bunch of lies – the very thing you accuse the Party of having done?'

'I've come to know you in these last months, Michael, and I don't think you're capable of making up a load of lies.' No smile; just the pale eyes locked on my own. 'What I mean is this: put together all you've got – Roland's own words, the stuff from the Documentation Centre, even what I've told you myself. And if there are gaps, and if you think they must be filled, then fill them in with the truth as you feel it and as you see it.'

'I'm not sure I'm able—'

'Nonsense, Michael, you're a doctor of the University of Rostock, and you're a writer! Of course you're able to do it.' He is smiling, teasing.

'But this is different.'

'Yes, of course it's different. So what? The *world* is different now. Who knows that better than you and me?'

He makes me smile with that absurd illogical leap of his. And yet the idea intrigues me.

'It's a lot of work.'

'And work is what you need. Don't tell me that you don't miss your work.'

'No, I won't tell you that.' Sometimes I linger outside my old school, the engine clanking in the Trabi, until the might-have-been drives me away.

And yet . . .

'Who would read such a thing? I mean, apart from you and me.'

'Even you and I would be enough, Michael, but . . .' He stops on the forest trail and his words are spoken slowly, like one of his prayers. '*Someone may come. Someone who wants to know.* That's what your mother said to me.'

Something chokes in my throat. Neither of us speaks; the words that my mother spoke long ago to the pastor are vibrant in the forest air. *Someone may come:* it is reason enough.

In the weeks and months that follow I labour at Roland's story. Labour becomes habit, a kind of loving. I make notes, fill pages, scrap them, begin again. I muse by the window, I watch and listen to the whistle of the trains, I return to the table and the typewriter and my version of Roland's story. I have a few facts, a handful of files. Typed records of interrogations, rosters for a manhunt. And mostly I have gaps, the gaps I fill in when I am seated at the window, looking out at the trains. Yes, I hear the trains, but mostly I do what Pastor Bruck suggested: I listen to my heart, to a young man's song, to the cry of my own lost country.

And I read between the lines of Roland's story in the yellow pages. I know now that he had not long to live when he wrote these pages for my mother . . . and for someone who might come. Always, every time, I am struck by the first words he wrote:

> *I was born in Galway, a small town on the west coast of Ireland, on November 19th 1942 – I can't swear to the truthfulness of this – I hadn't learned to spell at the time – but my mother and father assured me that it was so.*

What manner of man could be so jaunty, with the wolves almost at his door? He had a way with him, this Roland who was my father; he could, I thought, crack a joke halfway up the steps of the gallows.

I go on writing, imagining, listening as the chill of winter comes round again. Snow blankets the streets of Brandenburg but my heart is warmed, brought home, by the story I am shaping. Only very rarely, pacing the frozen streets of my town, does the icy cold pierce me and I recall what Pastor Bruck said to me: 'Follow your heart, Michael, but have a care: *you might find a father but you might lose your faith.*'

BOOK 2

LONDON

AUTUMN 1962

Ten

September 1962, London

A sweaty Saturday night in Marylebone police station. Even sweatier in the windowless confines of Interview Room No. 2.

He can't be certain, but Roland Feldmann thinks that the small room is at the basement level. The shouted commands when the police van had pulled to a halt in the station yard had been disorientating. The night angry with barked commands. 'Move yer arse, Paddy, we haven't got all fucking night.' Feeling the fear in Terry's hand as he helped him down from the back of the van. *Touching*, the sarcastic voice of the London copper. 'A pair of holdy-handy Irish fairies.' The other bobby laughed. 'Leprechauns, you might say.' The drink-laden smells of the other prisoners, eight of them black; all of them herded together up the ramp and through the back door into the station. And the air suddenly foul inside, like a locked room that hadn't been aired for a long time: the smell of disinfectant, cigarette smoke, despair. Terry's hand tighter in his as they were herded along a stone corridor that seemed to flow down below the building, he couldn't be sure, what with the shouts of the coppers, the swelling sense of confinement and the panic in Terry's fingers clutching at his own.

A schemozzle in a larger stone-floored space at the end of the corridor. A bald, shirt-sleeved policeman behind a waist-high counter scarred with cigarette burns.

'What've you got for me, gentlemen? All drunk'n'disorderly?' His voice is high-pitched and squeaky.

'The usual bunch of clowns, Sarge.' The small one, the one who talked about leprechauns, is doing the talking. 'Pissing on the Queen's highway and taking the piss out of Her Majesty's constabulary. The usual Saturday-night shite. All except these two beauties.' The copper's baton poking in Roland's stomach. 'A pair of Paddies indulging in GBH in High Street Ken. Maybe worse than grievous. Poor bastard they laid into is gone to hospital with a busted skull, he might not make it.'

'It wasn't like that.' Terry's frightened voice. 'He was attacking a girl.'

'Shut it, Paddy.' A wolfish grin, a flash of small yellow teeth. 'Be nice, Paddy. Didn't your mummy back in Paddyland teach you to have manners, to speak when you are spoken to? Eh?'

'That'll do, Bates.' The shirt-sleeved sergeant's rebuke was offhand. 'Put them in Number Two until CID can get to them.'

Another corridor and a short flight of steps. Another short-sleeved copper joined them, took names and addresses without comment, put the contents of their pockets into separate envelopes. Issued receipts, told them to wait. And no, they could not phone home to Ireland, maybe after the detectives had had a word.

Roland looked at Terry's pale, frightened face and asked if his brother might have a cup of tea.

The policeman who was filling in the forms said this was a police station not a fucking hotel.

'Please.'

'Can't he speak for himself?'

'He's only eighteen,' Roland said. 'He's frightened.'

'He wasn't too frightened when he hit the fellow on the head.'

'It wasn't him.' Roland looked from the policeman to his brother. 'It was me . . . and we were just trying to help that girl.'

The policeman shrugged. 'Don't tell me,' he looked at the name he had just written on the form, 'Roland. Tell the detectives.'

But he got them both some tea and told them it was almost one o'clock. He watched them in silence as they drank their tea and waited for the detectives.

Two of them, ties loosened, shirt collars opened, sports jackets draped over the backs of the grey plastic chairs. Both smoking, the air thick and fuggy in the windowless room. And disbelief on both their faces as Roland recounted what had happened as they walked along Kensington High Street a couple of hours earlier.

'You're telling us *you* struck this fellow and he fell and cracked his head on the footpath?' the older of the two asked Roland.

'Yes.'

'That's not what we are hearing.' A long suck on the Senior Service cigarette. He picked a shred of yellow tobacco from his lower lip and examined it carefully. 'We're told it was your brother here that did the damage.'

'I'm telling you it was me.'

'So tell us from the start.' The two detectives exchanged a glance. 'And this time you and I will keep it between ourselves. Your brother here can keep Detective Menton company in the next room.'

'But—'

'No buts.'

A scrape of chair legs on the green lino, Terry's face white in the doorway, looking back over the detective's shoulder. The pleading in his own eyes, willing Terry to stick to the story, that it was Roland who had struck the blow. Feeling the detective's eyes upon him, forcing himself to be calm, to meet those hard eyes.

'From the top, please,' the detective said.

It was like doing an exam, Roland thought. Sift the information in your head, move the bits and pieces about to suit the pattern the examiner wanted; if you didn't have all the information, then bluff as convincingly as you could. You couldn't fabricate but you could try to paper over the cracks, you could hint that – like the examiner himself – your grasp of the basic facts was such that it wasn't necessary to write them all down. *From the top*, the detective said, but it was up to you to decide where the beginning began. And a smile never did any harm either.

So he gave the detective his widest smile, it worked with the girls at home, sometimes it even worked with his father – why not try it on with this middle-aged detective with the nicotine-stained fingers?

And could he have a cigarette? Please.

He didn't even like smoking, but the business of taking a fag from the policeman's packet, then lighting it and exhaling the first lungful of smoke – it all gave him a little more time to shape his thoughts, find his beginning. And another chance to smile at the detective while he thanked him for the cigarette.

'You need to understand that you could be in serious trouble here, Roland.' The detective's words cut across his thoughts: this was more serious than a degree exam in German. 'A man is in hospital with a serious head wound. He could die.' A pause, the policeman looking straight at him across the veneer-topped table. 'I don't want to hear any horseshit from you.'

Smiles wouldn't be much good with this fellow: he looked sterner than his father behind the counter of the jewellery store when an unwary customer ventured to ask for a discount on the gold bracelet or the silver cross he wanted to buy for his girlfriend.

'Terry and myself were coming out of the tube station on to High Street Ken when we saw the guy – he had her in a doorway and she was shouting – screaming – so . . .'

A blur in his mind, like a film rewound and then played at speed: the shouting from the darkened doorway, a glimpse of a pale frightened face, blond hair, the dark bulk of the fellow holding the girl—

'So you wade in like Sir Galahad and beat the shit out of the fellow and now he's at death's door in intensive care.'

'No, it wasn't like that.' Words were harder to find here than in an exam. 'It all happened so quickly. The girl was screaming, everybody else was ignoring it and I didn't think, I just wanted to help, it seemed the right thing to do.'

'And then your brother struck him with something, a rolled-up umbrella or a stick – we have a witness statement – and this man is on the ground with his brains hanging out.' Detective Ransom pulled heavily on his cigarette. He didn't think much of the Irish; they'd hugged the sidelines while he and his mates were fighting the Second World War. 'And our witness never mentions a girl being attacked, just your brother striking the victim and then there's blood all over the pavement.'

'The girl ran off.' He could remember the smudged mascara on the white face, the clatter of high heels on the tiles. 'I suppose she was running for the last train.'

'You suppose.'

'I'm telling you the truth.'

'You're lying.' Another drag on the cigarette. 'You and your brother were drunk and you attacked an innocent man minding his own business. Why? Was he taking the piss? Call you Paddy or something like that?'

'We weren't drunk. We had a few drinks but we weren't drunk.'

Roland tried to keep the panic out of his voice. The dirty cream-coloured walls and the green linoleum were closing in on him; the smell of cigarette smoke and stale sweat was cloying. 'I'm telling you, it was all over in a minute.'

'What did your brother strike the victim with?'

The change of tack caught him off guard.

'Terry didn't hit him, it was me.' He saw his brother's arm raised, felt the swish of air past his own face, heard the thudding noise as the other man's head was struck – and then another blow fell, the fellow's grip loosened on his own arm, there was a sharper crack as the man's head struck the pavement and blood was pooling around his shoes.

'What did your brother hit him with?'

'I told you, it was me.'

Ransom ignored his words. He glanced as his watch. Jesus, nearly two thirty. He'd had enough of this.

'What was the weapon?'

'It wasn't a weapon, it was just a newspaper. The *Mail*.'

It had been lying on the seat opposite them on the tube. A half-page photo, the man caught in the act of dying, chest out as if to breast the tape, or maybe shrink from the bullets, despairing left hand flung skyward, his peaked cap flying free above the grey wall. *Another murder at the Berlin Wall.* They both looked at the grey photo, silent in the face of death; Terry had rolled the newspaper up and stuffed it in the side pocket of his jacket.

'You did all this damage with the *Mail*?'

'I told you, he fell and hit his head.'

'After your brother struck him?'

'No, after I hit him.'

Ransom looked out over his glasses at the young fellow

opposite him. He didn't know what was going on here. He didn't even know why he was wasting his time on just one more drunken case of GBH on a Saturday night/Sunday morning. Maybe he just didn't want to go home to Hayes to Hilda's endless carping about how he should have opted for the government job after the war, like her smug fucking brother-in-law Desmond and that cow of a wife Teresa. Or maybe he was just intrigued by this lying Paddy; he was lying, Ransom just knew it. Maybe the other silly bastard *had* fallen on his stupid head but Roland what's-his-name from Paddyland was lying through his teeth.

'What's the problem with your brother?' he asked.

'What do you mean?'

'You know what I mean, you're lying to protect him. Keep this up and you'll go to jail for him. Why?'

Roland shrugged, studied a long crack near the door in the cream wall. 'Can I see my brother please?'

'Not now. What's wrong with him?'

'He gets nervous. He's only eighteen.'

Ransom's turn to shrug. 'He's old enough to go to work.'

He's just a child, Roland. He shouldn't be going with you at all. Promise me you'll take care of him. And all the rest of it, from his mother. On top of his father's more practical objections. *It's enough to have my eldest son swanning around London like a pasha, why have I to get my younger son to spend money over there as well?* His father's grasp of English failed him when he got excited, especially about spending money. *Terry should be to work going in the shop for these weeks before the university starts.* Over twenty years in Ireland and still sounding like a watchmaker who had fetched up from Berlin just the day before yesterday.

'Terry has asthma,' he said to Ransom. 'He can get an attack anytime, especially when he gets nervous. He should have his inhaler.'

'So?'

'The policeman took it.'

'I'll see that your brother gets it back.'

'Why don't you let him go? He didn't do anything.'

Ransom permitted himself a slight smile. 'We'll know that soon enough. My colleague is talking to your brother right now.'

And Terry would spill the beans, Roland thought. Terry had always been small and had always been soft. In the school playground, on the street. You'd think his size would have made him a good scrum-half or maybe a hooker, but his first school session on the rugby pitch had been his last. From then on it was his stamp album and the Hardy Boys. And the gap between them – four years – was too wide for Roland to be always at hand to take care of his kid brother.

Roland wondered if Terry had started wheezing yet. Maybe he should tell the truth, get it over with. Or maybe not. Miracles could happen; maybe Terry could keep a grip on himself and his parents wouldn't look accusingly at Roland. *Why didn't you take care of him? You promised! You promised!*

Ransom had another question for him.

'What are you and your brother doing here in London? Are you looking for work?'

'I wish.' Roland smiled wryly. 'It's just a bit of a holiday. My brother starts college next month.'

'And you?' The detective was intrigued: most of the Paddies he came across were labourers and tradesmen who excelled in boozing and brawling. 'What do you do?'

'I work in my father's jewellery shop. I finished college last year and I'd like to do something else but – you know what fathers are like.' Ransom didn't: the house in Hayes had always been too big for him and Hilda but this young Paddy wasn't to know that.

'Tell me,' he said, 'what fathers are like.'

Roland spread his hands. *They want things to stay the way they always were. They want you to spend your life selling watches and Claddagh rings and stuff in Feldmann's Jewellers on Shop Street. They want you to take care of your brother and bring him home safe, just the way you promised.*

'They don't like change,' Roland said to the detective.

'You said "you wish" about looking for work. What do you wish?' *And what the hell was keeping Menton? Surely he'd got the truth out of the younger brother by now?*

'Just something different. Maybe London, maybe America.' All that dreaming behind the counter, the tedious hours when the shop was empty. 'Maybe even Germany.'

'Germany?'

'I have a degree in German, finished last year.' He looked across at the detective. He'd heard that some of the old English had long memories about the war. 'My parents are German.'

'Refugees? They went to Ireland after the war?'

'No.' Roland smiled. 'My parents were lucky. My father went to Galway a few years before the war to train a couple of watchmakers. He liked it there and sent for my mother.' He smiled again. It was a story often told by his father when he was feeling expansive after wine. 'They weren't married so they got married in Galway.' *Our whole life of family and marriage is here,* his father would say, when he was emphasizing his 'Irish credentials'. Which didn't stop him insisting that his two sons and two daughters had private German lessons and speak the language at home. 'They were lucky,' Roland said again. 'The war started not long after that.'

Ransom could have struck him for that. The war was lucky? Try telling that to himself and his Lancaster crewmates flying bombing missions over the Ruhr; tell it to the wives and girlfriends of those who didn't make it back. Or even to those who did. Like Ransom himself. Back to what? To ration books and drudgery and the inescapable knowledge that what shaped your tomorrow was not yesterday's war service but the way you spoke and where you went to school.

And suddenly he was tired of this upstart in front of him. A half-German Paddy – with a fucking degree in Krautspeak. If he didn't get out for a moment, he really would thump the little shit.

'I'll give you a few minutes to consider your situation.' He pushed his chair back and stood up, picking up his jacket. 'When I come back, I want the truth.'

'Can I see my brother?'

'Shut it.' Ransom's ferocity startled himself no less than Roland. He forced himself to close the door quietly behind him as he stepped out into the stone-floored corridor. A lone shirt-sleeved constable sat at the end of the corridor, a runner for the half-dozen interview rooms along the passage. Only one door hung open; Ransom wondered if the cops behind the other closed doors were as pissed off at three o'clock in the morning as he was.

He nodded to the seated policeman: George of the great gut, growing bigger by the day. Put him back out on the beat and he'd die of a heart attack if he had to chase a 99-year-old granny.

'George?'

'Yes, Sarge?' The great neckless head lifted from the rounded shoulders, the great gut wobbled above the tree-trunk thighs.

'Nobody in or out of these rooms.' Ransom nodded vaguely at the door he had closed and the one beside it.

'Detective Menton is in there.'

I'm surprised you noticed, Ransom wanted to say. He could see that the *News of the World* in the pudgy hands was open at the racing page, which meant that the Sunday papers were already in. The *Mirror* lay on the floor beside George's chair; Ransom craned to read the front-page headline. 'Stand-off at Berlin Wall.' A grey photo of tanks facing each other, watched by helmeted troops. Fucking Krautland, he thought, always fucking trouble.

'Tell Detective Menton to meet me in the yard,' he said. 'And nobody goes in or out of those rooms.' He could have knocked on Menton's door himself but he wanted the satisfaction of having George lift his fat arse off the plastic chair. Even a plastic chair sometimes needed a break.

In the reception area the uniformed duty sergeant was also busy with the Sunday papers; he nodded to Ransom over the rim of his cup of tea. Endless cups of tea, Ransom thought: it was what kept you going through the endless nights of boredom, lies and then more lies. In the end, lies became your way of life; sometimes he lied to Hilda about his shifts, anything to avoid the litany of whingeing in the house in Hayes.

He stood on the steps at the back entrance to the station and listened to the night, to the absence of whingeing. Behind him, the station lights blazed but the building seemed oddly silent, like a ghost ship becalmed in a sea of darkness. Beyond the high walls of the yard, even the great city seemed subdued, as though catching its breath after the capers of another breathless Saturday night. Cars and vans crowded together against the walls of the yard, resting, until the beast of the city stirred again and summoned them to the jungle.

Ransom savoured the night, the silence, the faint hum of the city; it was the life he had lived on the edge, in the dark skies over wartime Germany. Now he had Hayes and Hilda – and a lying little fucker who didn't know when he was well off. A fucking jeweller's shop at home and a degree to his name. All of it up the

Swanee if the idiot persisted with his story. Up the Swanee for a very long time if the poor bastard in the hospital gave up the ghost.

He heard Menton's footfall on the stone steps. Tall, wiry fellow, ginger crewcut. Ransom knew by the smile on Menton's freckled face that the other Paddy, the young fellow, had given it up. He wondered if Menton had given the fellow a few slaps; he was known to use his fists in the interview room although Ransom always made sure he himself was absent when any blows were struck.

'The young fellow?' he asked.

Menton nodded. 'He just started crying. I never laid a finger on him, just looked menacing and lowered my voice a little,' he grinned, 'and he starts bawling and calling for his mummy and says he didn't mean to do it, it was an accident, you know, the usual shite.' Menton yawned, stretched his arms wide. 'I could do with a good shag now, always makes me feel like a new man. Would you mind if I took off? I've got a nice little shop girl waiting for me down in Putney.'

Menton always had a nice little somebody waiting for him somewhere. Sometimes Ransom wondered what it would be like to have a firm young body beside you in bed in place of Hilda's flowing uncorseted rump.

'It's only half three,' he said, looking at his watch, 'and anyway we've still got the paperwork.'

'Fucking paperwork.' Menton laughed. 'We'll drown in fucking paper.'

The loud voice from the doorway behind made them both turn. They looked at each other. You couldn't mistake that voice anywhere: loud, confident, laden with centuries of privilege, clipped and strangulated to the point where you wondered if the speaker was English at all.

'Evening, Mr Fitch-Bellingham. We didn't realize you'd come to visit us.'

'Evening, gentlemen.' He turned to shout goodbye and thanks to the duty sergeant, then nodded again at Menton and Ransom. 'Not huddling over a new gunpowder plot, I hope?' Fitch-Bellingham laughed at his own sally, an infectious laugh that invited you to share his amusement.

'You'll be the first to know, sir,' Ransom said, 'if we stumble across any conspirators.' Or Russian sailors or Polish seamen, Ransom thought, jumping ship for the delights of decadent England. Fitch-Bellingham never missed a locked-up Eastern European: under standing orders the spooks had to be notified even before names were written into the daybook. And Fitch-Bellingham would cruise in at the wheel of his black Jaguar, ready as always to determine whether some washed-up wretch from behind the Iron Curtain might be of some use to Her Majesty's Secret Service. Most times the frightened prisoners were charged and sent for trial in the normal way or admitted to the asylum process; the unlucky ones were returned to their communist ships or embassies – more than once, Ransom had heard some poor bugger crying and beating his fists against the side of the van ferrying him back to his waiting masters.

'Busy time for your people, I'm sure, sir.' Menton's voice oozed respect: You'd never guess, Ransom thought, that he could have the entire canteen in stitches with his mimicry of the plummy tones of Rupert Fitch-Bellingham. 'I mean,' Menton went on, 'with all this trouble about the Berlin Wall right now.'

'Indeed, the situation is fraught, gentlemen.' You never knew where you were with Fitch-Bellingham; everyone, from cleaning lady to Chief Constable, was addressed with equal gravity in the same rich tones. 'But, like yourselves and the rest of the constabulary, my colleagues and I are ever alert.'

He might be taking the piss, Ransom thought, but you could never be sure with Fitch-Bellingham; at six feet four, stick thin, impeccably turned out in pinstripes and club tie, he could be taken for some eccentric 'huntin'-shootin'-fishin' type from the shires but legendary tales abounded of his wartime exploits in the Balkans where the goat-shagging natives didn't much care if they knifed a lost Tommy or a stray Nazi. Not one to be trifled with, Ransom told himself; if Rupert told you the situation in Berlin, or anywhere else, was *fraught*, whatever the fuck that might mean, then you'd best believe him.

'Well, mustn't loiter, gentlemen,' Fitch-Bellingham flashed the two officers a smile, 'the call of duty and all that, so I'll bid you goodnight.' He was jangling the car keys – Ransom could see the old Jaguar now, tucked in between a pair of vans – as he made his way down the steps.

Ransom cleared his throat. 'Our half-Paddy, half-Jerry, sir, a pair of 'em, in fact –' Fitch-Bellingham, halfway across the station yard, swung round at Ransom's words – 'aren't you going to have a word?'

'You've got two Germans in custody?' Fitch-Bellingham came back to the steps; his voice was softer, lower. 'Nobody said anything inside.'

'Nobody knew except Menton and myself, sir.' Ransom hesitated, wondering if he should have kept his mouth shut. 'Two Paddies really, sir, picked up in High Street Ken for GBH.'

'So what's all this half-Jerry stuff?'

'Like I said, sir, a couple of young Paddies, brothers in fact, but their parents, it turns out, are both German and the older lad tells me he has a degree in German and has notions of going to work there. Anyway,' Ransom finished lamely, 'probably nothing to interest your lot, just a pair of Paddies in trouble on a Saturday night.'

'Speak German, do they?'

'So the older fellow claims, sir.' Ransom shrugged. 'Not that I'd know, sir, I just bombed the fuckers.'

Fitch-Bellingham smiled. 'Quite.' He looked from Ransom to Menton, glanced across the yard at his black Jaguar, then for a moment he looked up at the London night sky, like an old dog, Menton would say to his shop girl in Putney a few hours later, like an old dog sniffing the wind – and then, as if he had found a decision written in the distant stars, took the steps in one long-legged stride and said, 'Well, since I'm here, and you have been extraordinarily kind enough to bring this matter to my attention, perhaps I should have a word with these chaps.'

Eleven

'Sie haben ein Problem? Vielleicht kann ich Ihnen helfen?' You have a problem: perhaps I can help?

The German words startled Roland, which was exactly what Rupert Fitch-Bellingham intended.

'Wie bitte?' Who was this pinstriped stork, addressing him in impeccable German?

'I said you seem to be in shtuck,' Fitch-Bellingham went on in German, 'and that I might be able to help you out.'

'Warum Deutsch?' Ronald shook his head, looked around him at the stark surroundings of the interview room in Marylebone police station. *'Warum Deutsch hier in England? Sind Sie Deutscher?'*

'Warum nicht?' Why not, Fitch-Bellingham wanted to know, side-stepping Roland's question as to whether he was German.

He thrust his hand towards Roland, his long head inclined in the faintest of bows.

'Ich heisse Ingham,' he said, shaking Roland's hand. *'Und Sie?'*

'Feldmann,' Roland said, rising from the plastic chair, 'Roland Feldmann.' Instinctively he gave his name the German pronunciation, the very pronunciation that made him squirm when his father used it back home.

Fitch-Bellingham motioned for Roland to be seated. Scared, he thought, looking at the younger man, scared and sweaty, shirt collar open, tie askew, face white with worry and lack of sleep.

But intelligence there too, he thought. He could read it in the way he himself was being measured by the brown eyes; he could see it in the wide forehead, in the cut of the young fellow's jaw.

'They tell me you are in serious trouble.'

'That's what they tell me too, Herr Ingham.'

He remembers the name I gave him: at least he's capable of some kind of thinking under pressure.

'I hear your brother struck a man in High Street Kensington. I hear the man is in intensive care and that he may die.'

'My brother struck no one. It was me.'

And he's able to lie while looking you in the eye. At least for a while; everybody gives in, in the end.

'That's not what the detectives tell me.'

Roland shrugged. Part of his brain already knew that Terry had buckled under the younger detective's questioning but he'd play the hand as long as he could.

Watching him, Fitch-Bellingham was thinking the same thing: it was one more thing to like about this peculiar piece of flotsam washed up on his Sunday morning shore. But he wouldn't tell him yet that his kid brother had already cried for his *Mutti* and spilled the beans: that might come later.

'So tell me what happened,' Fitch-Bellingham said.

'Why should I tell you? Why are we speaking German?' Good, Fitch-Bellingham thought, staring back at Roland's defiant expression: a touch of spunk always comes in useful. 'Who are you? Are you a policeman, Herr Ingham?'

'Just tell me what happened, from the top.'

'That's what the detective said.'

'Sorry?'

'The detective used exactly the same words: from the top.'

Fitch-Bellingham permitted himself the thinnest of smiles.

'Perhaps,' he said, shifting his long frame in the plastic seat, 'perhaps the vocabulary comes with these august surroundings.'

Roland laughed. 'And then you'll let me see Terry – and phone my family – and speak to a lawyer?'

'One thing at a time, Herr Feldmann.' The smile was gone now. 'Just tell me what happened, in your own words, as clearly as you can recall.'

He watched Roland Feldmann physically gather himself together before launching himself on his lying account of the night's events; he watched the slow intake of breath, the equally slow exhalation; he watched the loosening of wide shoulders, as if in preparation for a long race; he watched the momentary closing of the eyes, as if in meditation. And he watched the half-smile on the young man's face, the silent plea for understanding, the false pitch of sincerity. Rupert Fitch-Bellingham watched it all gravely and he liked what he saw. The situation in Berlin was fraught, he had told Detective Ransom, and truthfully so, but here in this Irish-German youth, Rupert Fitch-Bellingham was beginning to discern possibilities to relieve that fraughtness.

And as he listened – without interruption – to Roland Feldmann's tale of mishap, Rupert Fitch-Bellingham could discern even greater possibilities.

He was impressed by the way this young fellow marshalled his facts – or his version of them; by the way in which he began at the beginning and told his story in a straight line through to the end. He liked the frank gaze that Roland Feldmann levelled at him while he lied through his teeth to protect his younger, weaker brother. You could do things with a fellow like this, Fitch-Bellingham told himself, especially if you knew how and where and when and just how much pressure to apply, and it was in the application of such dark arts that he himself had spent his life during and since the war.

Most of all, it was the young fellow's command of the German language that sang its siren song in Fitch-Bellingham's expert ear. Roland Feldmann spoke the language in an oddly old-fashioned way that reminded Fitch-Bellingham of the stilted, formal language he had encountered in Berlin in the immediate post-war years when he had been part of the occupying Allied intelligence service; to Fitch-Bellingham's mind, the German he was listening to had been learned in an older, stricter age, before the excesses of the contemporary economic miracle in Hamburg, Munich, Frankfurt and the other great cities of West Germany. Even the fellow's pronunciation, Fitch-Bellingham felt, was harsher than the tones of Dusseldorf, Cologne and Bonn: it sounded, to his approving ears, more like the guttural tones of the separated East, the land of fraughtness, the country behind the barbed wire and the fucking Wall.

He listened attentively, nodded approvingly, smoked languidly. He watched the boy watching him, measuring the impact of his words on this mysterious policeman type who spoke only German in Marylebone police station.

Let him go on wondering, let him go on being puzzled; a land without signposts was a land where you got lost, where – finally – you welcomed any helping hand that was extended to you. But not yet, Fitch-Bellingham thought; this youngster was not at all lost enough just yet, he still thought he held in his hands the map of his own salvation.

And, in any case, Fitch-Bellingham wasn't quite sure just how he might use this Gulliver beached on his watch; after the disaster of the last few days in Berlin, he knew the Service could find a role for Roland Feldmann but that role was still undefined in Rupert Fitch-Bellingham's inventive mind. And Yearling would torture himself, of course, no matter what inventiveness was laid before him: the unlit pipe would perform ever jerkier gyrations while its owner's Adam's apple bobbed so frantically that you feared poor old Yearling would cough it up entirely, such was his anguish over the security of the state and the disapproval of his Minister at the Service's demonstrable shortcomings. Profumo's shenanigans had got everyone's knickers in a twist; the process of untwisting them was both tedious and, to Fitch-Bellingham, a total fucking distraction from the proper concerns of the Service.

The boy was done, his story ended.

He held Fitch-Bellingham's gaze, searching for a response.

Let him wait, Fitch-Bellingham thought. It was the greatest pressure of all: waiting, not knowing, wondering what next.

'Can I see my brother now, please?' Roland asked, still in German. 'And call my parents?'

Fitch-Bellingham uncoiled himself, stood up on the stone floor.

'*Bitte warten Sie*,' he said. Maybe the waiting would be good for somebody's soul. He shut the door quietly behind him as he stepped out of the room.

The doors hung open to all but one of the other interview rooms along the narrow corridor. At the end of the corridor George was absent-mindedly stroking his great gut with one paw, the folded *News of the World* clutched in the other. This is the civilized world we are saving, Fitch-Bellingham thought: an overweight policeman with his paper of tits and horses at four o'clock on a September Sunday morning. Well, it wasn't much but it was better than slitting throats in the Balkans and watching helpless German *Frauen* being raped by the conquering heroes of the Red Army in Berlin.

George started to heave himself from his chair: there was something about Fitch-Bellingham that told you to stand in his presence.

Fitch-Bellingham waved him back to his seat.

'Never mind that.' He gestured towards the closed door. 'The younger fellow still in there?'

'Yes, sir, still there, still alive, still inclined to blubber – I checked on him a few minutes ago.'

'Nobody, but nobody, goes in or out, except with my say-so. Understand?'

'Yes, sir.'

'And the same for the older brother. Got it? I mean, *nobody*.'

'Yes, sir, I've got it, sir, nobody goes in or out of them two rooms.' George was unnerved by Fitch-Bellingham's intensity; the newspaper slid from his ample lap and spread itself in a rustling pile of pages across his polished shoes.

George's great stomach hindered his effort to stoop and gather up his newspaper; more pages came loose, in a moment the full width of the corridor was awash with the *News of the World*.

'Sorry, sir.' His face the colour of beetroot, George tried to free his feet from the sea of pages.

In a single, flowing movement Fitch-Bellingham bent, retrieved the pile of pages, somehow shook them into a semblance of order and presented the folded pages to George. His eye lingered on a photo of bare breasts, the incongruous masking black bar across the anonymous face, as the newspaper demonstrated its own peculiar modesty; at least, he thought, tits made a change from the killings at the Wall.

'Thank you, sir,' George whispered.

'Where are Detective Ransom and his colleague?'

'I think they're having a cuppa in the canteen, sir.'

'Send them to me,' Fitch-Bellingham said, pointing at the wall phone behind George's hand. 'I shall be outside. And remember—'

'Yes, sir, nobody goes in or out.'

'Well done, thank you.'

Thank God he's gone, George thought, watching Fitch-Bellingham go. Fucking lah-di-dah like Prince fucking Philip but they said he'd killed men with his bare hands in the war; they said he spoke a dozen languages, but for George's money he couldn't speak the Queen's fucking English – sometimes you'd feel inclined to send for an interpreter for old Fitch-Bellingham, like you had to do for those Russians and Poles the lanky geezer loved talking to. George wondered, as he dialled the canteen, why Rupert Fitch-Bellingham was bothering with a pair of fucking Paddies.

Dawn was breaking over London, the dark sky lightening with shades of amber and pink over the still-sleeping city. Over the good and the bad, the strong and the weak, the fabulous A-to-Z of humanity that peopled the great metropolis: banker and baker, pimp and parson, liar and lawyer. Snug in their beds, most of them, Fitch-Bellingham thought, looking up at the streaks of orange and rose lighting the sky, heedless of the spies and minders who worked through the night hours to ensure the security of their beds and boudoirs. And heedless was the way they were supposed to be; it was the business of Fitch-Bellingham and his like to make the darkness safe, to patrol the night borders of Shakespeare's sceptred isle.

Not that many of them gave a toss these days about the language of the Bard or the security of Her Majesty's kingdom. Yeah-yeah-yeah or some such American nonsense for the young ones, to go along with their so-called drainpipe trousers and their daft so-called Beatles haircuts – and tit-and-arses newspapers for the older ones like George.

And yet we do it, Fitch-Bellingham thought, sucking on the Craven A. We guard the night, we stand sentry at our frontiers, to make sure that they can make choices. Make adulterous or uxorious love. We give them the right to say yes or no.

And sometimes, when the land stands in great peril, we do *not* allow them the choice of answering *yes* or *no*. Sometimes only *one* answer is allowed.

As now, with this German-speaking youngster from Ireland, puzzled and despondent and exhausted in an interview room in the dark building at Fitch-Bellingham's back. There would be neither a phone call to Ireland nor a meeting with his asthmatic brother for Roland Feldmann, not just yet anyway, not while Rupert Fitch-Bellingham played with possibilities and permutations. The vaguest of plans was taking shape in his inventive mind, a ridiculous plan, an absurd notion, the idea quite outrageous but still . . .

He stepped on the cigarette butt, glanced at his watch. Four fifty a.m. How many cups of tea did it take to keep the ailing British Empire afloat?

He was about to go looking for them when the back door of the station opened and Ransom stood there in the rectangle of light, Menton at his shoulder.

'There you are, sir!' A forced chumminess in Menton's voice. 'You wanted to see us, sir.'

Fitch-Bellingham caught the baleful glance that Ransom threw at Menton. *Good chap, Ransom; knows when to speak and when to keep shtum.*

'Perhaps you'd be good enough,' Fitch-Bellingham said, turning to Menton, 'to phone the hospital and check on the progress of the victim of the assault,' a faint smile, 'or should I perhaps say, of the "alleged" assault?'

'We're ahead of you, sir.' Menton grinned. 'Just called them, the bugger is A-okay, just a head wound with too much bleeding, they say, and the black bugger's already been discharged.'

'Indeed.' The single word from Fitch-Bellingham seemed to silence the night.

Menton looked from Ransom to Fitch-Bellingham; he was damned if he could figure out what he'd done wrong.

Ransom cleared his throat.

'Johnny,' he said, laying his hand lightly on Menton's shoulder, 'I'm not sure if we've got everything ready for that robbery trial coming up on Monday – might be no harm in checking the file and making sure everything's absolutely shipshape. You know what a stickler the Super can be.'

Menton mumbled a goodnight and left them hurriedly. Only when the station door had closed behind him did Fitch-Bellingham speak.

'Thank you, Ransom.'

'For nothing, sir.' He looked back at the closed door. 'Menton's a good copper, sir, he's just a little ahead of himself sometimes.'

'This fellow in hospital – he's OK?'

'Like Menton said, sir, discharged and gone home – gone *somewhere*, anyway.'

'Is he likely to press charges against . . . ?' He inclined his long head, in the direction of the station.

'I shouldn't think so, sir. It seems pretty obvious that he *was* assaulting some girl when our pair of Irishmen decided to lend a hand.'

'Is there a record of this in the station daybook?'

'I'm afraid so, sir.' Ransom spread his hands apologetically. 'We just had a couple of Paddies, sir, not your Russkies or your Poles or Czechmates. The German bit only came out when I questioned the lad – I wasn't sure if I should even mention it to you, sir.'

'I'm grateful that you did, Ransom, extremely grateful.'

'Thank you, sir.'

'Here's what we're going to do, Ransom.'

Ransom nodded. Instinctively he drew himself up to his full height: somewhere in his mind he caught the echo of his commander's night-time briefing before they headed off to bomb the shit out of Dortmund or some other blot on the Jerry map.

'Firstly,' Fitch-Bellingham said, 'there will be no trace of either of these two gentlemen in this station. Neither of them was ever here. Understood?'

'Yes, sir.' A nod is as good as a wink; no order given but a sharp blade would remove the relevant page from the station daybook and allow Ransom to rewrite all of the entries. With the omission of any details of the two Paddies who had never been there.

'The hospital,' Fitch-Bellingham said. 'Can that be taken care of?' *Can we wipe all trace of one black man delivered bleeding and howling to the casualty department of the Great Western Hospital?*

'Leave it to me, sir.' Maybe, Ransom thought, I'll take Menton along with me to the hospital, introduce him to the alleyways of the dark map we share with the Service.

'And we'll be removing the two young gentlemen from your hospitality as soon as possible, Ransom, certainly before the arrival of the day shift.' Another glance at his watch. Five twenty. Just about enough time to organize transport and call Highfield to let them know a couple of unexpected guests would shortly be arriving. Yearling would have to be called; he'd bitch about being disturbed but he'd bitch twice as long and loudly if he were not kept informed. Yearling would want to know what he had in mind; he'd kick into touch on that one, promise a full outline later.

Ransom was looking expectantly at him.

'That's about it for now,' Fitch-Bellingham said. 'I need to make some phone calls. In the meantime, it might be a good idea to remove our friend,' he nodded in the direction of the station, 'from the scene of operations.'

'Of course, sir.' Ransom allowed himself a smile. 'I'll tell George to knock off early, sir.'

'It's awfully good of you, Ransom, I know it's not your job.' Fitch-Bellingham waved away Ransom's protests. 'Perhaps your colleague could keep an eye on things – you'll have other matters to attend to.'

'Menton, sir? Good idea, sir.' Let him cool his heels a while in George's chair, see what that did to his ardour for the shop girl in Putney.

'Good man, let's do it then.' Fitch-Bellingham looked at the sky. 'Be daylight soon.'

'You'll be using the station commander's office, sir?'

Fitch-Bellingham nodded.

'Top of the staircase, sir – but you know that, of course.'

'Yes, I know that,' Fitch-Bellingham said. It wouldn't be the first time he had used the station commander's secure telephone to make his urgent and secret calls.

The vans eased into the station backyard just before six thirty. Both black, both with blacked-out windows on their rear doors. They drew up together alongside the steps; almost in unison, their engines were switched off. Steam rose from their bonnets like mist in the dawn air.

Fitch-Bellingham spoke quietly and urgently to the two men who got out of the first van, then led them into the station and through the descending corridors that led to the interview rooms. Nobody saw them, nobody bumped into them in the narrow passageways, Ransom had seen to that.

When they stopped outside the first interview room, Fitch-Bellingham took from his pocket the large metal key he had been given by Ransom. He laid a finger to his lips; the driver half smiled in acknowledgement – it wasn't the first time they had played this game of pass the parcel.

Fitch-Bellingham put his ear to the closed door. Silence – or was that the sound of soft sobbing? He pushed the key into the lock, tried to turn it, gently, but the old metal grated loudly.

'Roland?' A half-whisper from within. 'Roland!' Louder now. 'Roland! Where are you?'

Fitch-Bellingham swore. Speed, not silence, would be the way now. He turned the key violently, pushed the door open and stood aside as his two parcel men rushed past him.

Terry's face, grimy with dried tears, was a mask of terror.

'Roland!' A scream now, a wound in the quietness of the station.

'Shut him up, for Christ's sake!' Fitch-Bellingham ordered.

Terry backed away from them, cowered in a corner of the small room. He opened his mouth to scream but no sound came from him.

'Terry! I'm here, answer me!' Shouting now from the interview room next door, and Fitch-Bellingham knew that Roland would not be so easy to handle.

'Quickly!' he ordered. 'We don't want a fucking circus on our hands.'

Terry managed to scream once more, no name, no word, just a long howl of fear and horror.

'Gag him. Now.' Fitch-Bellingham's voice was lower, more urgent: Roland was still calling his brother's name.

'Please, please, no.' Terry was crumpled in the corner, wide-eyed at the roll of wide tape being brandished by the driver. 'Not my mouth, no, I'll die, I can't breathe, I have asthma . . .'

Baker, the driver, dragged him to his feet, twisted the boy's arm hard behind his back.

'Gag the fucker!' he told his mate. 'What the fuck are you waiting for!'

From Terry's mouth came a stuttering series of gulping, gasping noises.

Christ, he's hyperventilating. Fitch-Bellingham was dismayed. *We could have a corpse on our hands here.*

'Wait!'

The boy's inhaler: it was in the bag of effects Ransom had handed over, the bag Fitch-Bellingham was holding in his hand.

He rummaged in the canvas bag, held out the metal inhaler to Terry.

The boy grabbed it and immediately began to suck on it. Fitch-Bellingham watched, stone-faced, as Terry slowly brought the attack under control. His thin shoulders ceased to heave, he took the inhaler from his mouth and he sat slumped in one of the room's grey, plastic chairs. His breathing was still loud, still laboured, but at least, Fitch-Bellingham thought, there seemed to be some regularity to it.

From the next room came the sound of Roland's voice once more.

'Terry! Terry! Answer me, Terry!'

Fitch-Bellingham thrust a long, bony finger under Terry's chin, tilting his head upwards.

'Another word,' he said quietly, 'just one more word and you'll be gagged. Understood?'

The boy's eyes wide, his chin nodding against the nicotine-stained finger. He started to speak but Fitch-Bellingham laid his finger across Terry's lips.

'Not a single word. Are we clear?' A faint smile on his lips as Terry nodded more vigorously. 'Now stand up and walk out of here with these two gentlemen – and not so much as a whisper out of you.' He smiled as Terry stood up, laid a bony hand on the young man's shoulder in a gesture that might have meant menace or friendship. 'There's a good chap – and take good care of that inhaler of yours, you never know when it might be taken away from you.'

Fitch-Bellingham watched thoughtfully as Terry was led away along the stone-floored corridor between the two men. How did two peas from the same pod differ so much? How could this timid, wheezing youngster be blood brother to the competent, confident young man who even now was hammering on the locked door of the interview room and demanding to see his brother at once and if he didn't somebody was going to answer personally to him, Roland Feldmann—

And yet, when Fitch-Bellingham pushed open the door of the interview room, it was in German that Roland lashed out.

'*Wo ist mein Bruder?*' he demanded angrily. '*Wo ist er?*' Where is my brother? Where is he?

The German words pleased Fitch-Bellingham but he chose to reply in English, in his most languid tones.

'Your little brother will come to no harm,' he drawled, 'provided you behave yourself.'

Roland's look was baleful; for a moment Fitch-Bellingham feared he'd have to employ a little brute force on the fellow. The young Irishman's grip upon himself was impressive, Fitch-Bellingham thought, observing the way Roland brought his breathing under control, the measured pause before he spoke again.

'Terry has his inhaler?' In English now.

'Yes.'

'And you haven't harmed him?'

'No.'

'And you want me to do something for you?'

The boy was quick, Fitch-Bellingham thought, straight to the point.

'Yes.' He permitted himself a thin smile.

'Something that involves my command of German?'

The Englishman nodded.

'Is it legal?'

'More legal than what your brother did to that fellow in Kensington High Street tonight.'

'What happened to him? I mean, is he OK?'

'He's dead,' Fitch-Bellingham said. 'He died about an hour ago.' How easily we lie, he thought, to protect our sleeping commonwealth, but the whiteness spreading across Roland's face was satisfaction enough for him.

Roland swallowed, bit his lip. When he spoke, his voice was edgy.

'It was an accident.'

'That's for a court to decide,' Fitch-Bellingham said.

The silence deepened in the small interview room as the two men stared at each other across a void. I've been here before, Fitch-Bellingham thought, in this timeless moment of decision, where a man decides his own destiny. His life was a continuum of betrayal that stretched from Britain to the Balkans and beyond. Now he waited for this young Irishman to decide his own destiny.

'And if I agree to do what you want,' Roland asked finally, 'my brother can go home?'

'Yes.' *Eventually*, Fitch-Bellingham thought, when all the dust has settled.

'I have your word on that?'

'You have my word.'

'OK, then, I'll do it, whatever it is.'

'Good man.' Fitch-Bellingham held out his hand, felt the reserve in Roland's eyes.

'I'm only doing this for my brother.'

'That's understood.' Fitch-Bellingham's hand was still outstretched.

Roland took it then and was astonished by the hint of strength in the bony, skinny hand. This Englishman, he thought, was like this peculiar night; even stranger underneath than the weird exterior suggested. At least, he told himself, Terry would get to go home and he himself would be spared the recriminations of his parents for not taking proper care of his younger brother.

There was no sign of Terry as Roland was led along the narrow corridor by Fitch-Bellingham and a pair of silent, muscular henchmen. There was no sign of anybody: the entire police station seemed deserted and Roland sensed that this, too, was a sign of the authority of the stork-like Englishman who said his name was Ingham. And my real name is Elvis Presley, Roland thought, or Donald Duck.

But at least Terry would be going home, he reminded himself, as he was shepherded into the back of the black van by Ingham's two accomplices. The door slammed shut and he was enclosed in the darkness of the windowless interior. He heard the murmur of voices from the sealed-off driving compartment; the engine purred smoothly into life and he hung on to the straps above the hard seat as the van moved off. Although he could see nothing, he could sense the great city outside, the rumble of a truck, the glassy rattling of a milk float, the sound of early-morning cars and, once, the unexpected jangle of a bicycle bell. The sounds and the stops became less frequent and he knew that they had left the city and its traffic lights behind.

Twelve

He blinked his eyes open, became aware of the cell-like room, and the horror of the night came back to him. The black man down in the station entrance, blood seeping on the tiled floor from behind his ear. 'He's dead,' Ingham had said but he wouldn't be surprised if the bastard was lying.

He took in the thin yellow curtains on the tall windows, the functional furniture – washstand with white jug and basin, chest of drawers, single wardrobe, a chair pushed under a small table up against the window. A cell for a student or a monk. Or a prisoner.

At least they'd left him his personal stuff. Ingham had placed the plastic bag from the police station on the chair beside the bed before advising him to get some sleep, that tomorrow everything would seem clearer. Roland hadn't bothered to check the door after Ingham: he'd heard the lock click as Ingham turned the key outside.

So tomorrow was here and not much, if anything, seemed clearer. Terry was somewhere else, he was sure of that. He could only hope that Ingham kept his word about getting him home safely.

MI5 or MI6 or some kind of secret service shenanigans, it had to be something like that. Ingham wanted him to do something in Germany, or maybe Austria, he could figure that much out, especially with all the newspaper headlines about Berlin.

It's more legal than what your brother did to that black in High Street Ken.

Slippery bastard, that Ingham. Well-mannered and beautifully spoken in at least two languages, the kind of customer his father would drool over if he set foot in the jewellery shop back home.

Roland looked at his watch. Handmade by his father. *House of Feldmann* it said, in tiny letters on the face. And engraved on the back by his father's hand to mark the twenty-first birthday of his eldest son, his heir apparent, Roland Feldmann, now detained in a cell-like room in an unidentified house somewhere in the south of England.

After ten, his handmade watch said. Just a few hours' sleep, then, after he'd been shepherded out of the van and into the big, silent house. Silent, but he'd sensed watching eyes as Ingham led him up the sweeping staircase and along the lino-floored corridor to the bedrooms. He wouldn't be able to sleep, he felt, not after such a strange night, but he'd fallen asleep in his underwear as soon as his head hit the hard pillow.

Gazing out over the ragged lawns he was able to admit to a deeper malaise that had been troubling him for years, standing behind the gleaming counter in his father's jewellery shop. *Smile and display, smile and clinch the sale.* Was his place behind the gleaming counter the purpose of school, of university, even of all the hours on the rugby field?

Roland was not given to bouts of fanciful introspection yet now, virtually imprisoned by a cynical manipulator who called himself Ingham, he wondered if perhaps this locked room – and what lay beyond – might not, somehow, be the destination towards which, unknowingly, he had been journeying all his life.

He looked at himself in the hinged mirror on the washstand and smiled ruefully. *You were destined for this, were you?*

Bullshit. But at the same time, who knows?

He padded to the window across the linoleum. More green stuff. Somebody in the British security service must have found a job lot at a knockdown price. Or maybe somebody in the service had a brother-in-law who produced it. Dealing with eager sales reps at Feldmann, Watchmakers and Jewellers, had made him just a little bit cynical.

The window overlooked extensive lawns which needed cutting. The surrounding hedges were also in need of a trim. Herr Feldmann, proprietor of the jeweller's which bore his name, would not approve of the unkempt appearance of such extensive premises. Roland found himself thinking that he didn't approve either.

Beyond the lawns and hedges he could see the black slated roofs and upper walls of a more modern building and, beyond it, a high wall which he took to be the boundary wall of the house. He could remember the van halting last night, the sound of voices, the hoarse noise of gates being opened and locked again behind them as they drove through. Ingham's organization didn't seem as well-versed in alarm systems as his jeweller father: even at this distance Roland could see the smashed bottle glass cemented into the top of the high perimeter wall. Maybe Ingham wanted his advice on how to secure a perimeter wall. Or how to breach one.

Hunger and the need to piss suddenly assailed him. He turned from the window and began to hammer on the door.

139

Thirteen

'And what exactly is it that you plan to do with this German-speaking Irishman?' Yearling's small head shook on the thin neck above the corpulent body. 'Or perhaps it's too much to expect that I should be kept fully informed of my organization's operations?'

'Don't be absurd, Jonathan.' Fitch-Bellingham's drawl was more mellifluous than ever. 'You know perfectly well that I wouldn't dream of mounting an operation without your approval.'

They both knew that there was a grain of truth in Fitch-Bellingham's words. Both of them also knew that Fitch-Bellingham considered it politic to keep his own left hand in ignorance of most of what the right hand was doing, or planned on doing. Yearling, although the Director of the Service, would be told as little as possible by Fitch-Bellingham. Both of them also knew that, despite Yearling's protests, this was the way the Director liked it; later, if developments proved unsatisfactory, or even disastrous (as sometimes happened), Yearling could truthfully say he had been kept in the dark by maverick subordinates.

They were sitting in the so-called boardroom of Highfield: a high-ceilinged, once-elegant room which now housed a long dining-room table and an assortment of non-matching chairs which, to Yearling's eye, looked as if they had escaped from some unruly NCO's mess. His distaste was not lessened by the remains of Fitch-Bellingham's lunch on the flower-decorated tray beside him.

'I had to hurry through a perfectly good lunch to get here,' he said, pushing away the remains of fatty chicken bones and congealed gravy. 'Couldn't they at least remove the evidence?'

'You know perfectly well, Jonathan, that there is no "they". There's just an ageing housekeeper who is visiting her equally ageing sister, and Adams, who was kind enough to prepare lunch for me and should be having a bite himself just now.'

'Ah, yes, Adams, your trusty batman of the Balkans – whatever should we do without the fellow?' Yearling made no attempt to hide his contempt.

Fitch-Bellingham let it go: Yearling's desk-bound war was an itch best left unscratched.

'Actually,' he said, 'this house would probably fall down without him. We *do* need more staff, you know we can't go on like this.'

Yearling shifted his huge weight uncomfortably on the leather seat.

'You know how it is, F-B.' The use of the initials was an intimation of collegiality. 'Budgets and ministerial cutbacks – I've protested, of course, but security is a dirty word, it seems, when it comes to spending money.'

When it comes to spending money on *us*, you mean, Fitch-Bellingham thought. MI5 and MI6 and Special Branch managed to prise funds out of Whitehall but then they had credible masters to plead their case to the politicians. Whereas we have Yearling, he thought, the kind of fellow who should be running an obscure prep school in Somerset or further afield.

'We're going to need funds to handle this operation,' he said.

'Which is exactly what? Now that we've got back to the reason for my rushing through lunch.'

'We've got to find out what happened to Imhof,' Fitch-Bellingham said. 'And maybe we can still get our hands on those maps.'

Something like a groan came from Yearling's small mouth.

'Imhof,' he said, 'is a disaster that does not need revisiting.'

'You mean we should forget that he's dead and that possibly the others are as well?'

'You know I don't mean that,' Yearling protested.

Losing Imhof had been a catastrophe, they both knew that. And not just for poor, murdered Imhof himself but for the organization too. Up-to-date maps of the entire East German terrain had been promised, together with contingency battle plans for the Warsaw Pact armies. The Minister was startled, then delighted by the prospect; the Prime Minister himself was chuffed; the Joint Intelligence Committee were agog; finally the Americans were advised of the treasures that were being spirited out of Berlin.

And then Rudi Imhof's body was washed up (or dumped) on the bank below the Adenauerstrasse bridge, with an unseemly amount of identity information in the pockets of the corpse's ill-fitting suit to make clear to the finders just who had had his neck broken before being delivered (without maps) to the watchers in West Berlin.

Cue horror in Whitehall. Fingers pointing, throats clearing, budgets under scrutiny. The JIC separately and collectively washed their hands of the whole mess. The Americans recorded it as another typical cock-up by the Brits.

The Prime Minister's personal displeasure was conveyed to Yearling. Folding up the organization's tent for good was mooted. Yearling had taken Fitch-Bellingham with him as support to a gathering of the Special Committee on Security Affairs, convened in a third-floor office in an anonymous block off the Haymarket.

Yearling and Fitch-Bellingham exited the meeting with their organization still intact. Whether the reprieve was temporary or absolute was by no means clear – but what else could you expect from politicians?

What was clear was that, in Fitch-Bellingham's words, the organization was 'in a parlous condition'. Within the month since Rudi Imhof's murder and consequent failure to deliver the Warsaw Pact battle plans, the organization had had a number of older agents permanently pensioned off. And the crew of army personnel – cooks, drivers, fitness instructors who serviced the organization – were abruptly detailed to return to their respective barracks. Fitch-Bellingham's sometime batman, Ivor Adams, together with a skeleton crew, were left to oversee the accelerating demise of Highfield. Money for the organization's operations had always been tight; now it seemed to have disappeared.

'We're falling apart,' Fitch-Bellingham said at last. 'Not just here,' his outstretched hand took in the shabby dining room and the unkempt lawns beyond the window, 'but in the field too. God knows if we have a single useful agent left in East Germany. We both know that every signal we've received since Imhof's murder has been worthless, nothing more than the kind of information you could pick up from *Time* or *Newsweek*, and that's not saying much, is it? It could be Ulbricht himself tapping out the stuff, for all we know.'

Both of them were silent awhile, imagining Walter Ulbricht, the leader of the Socialist Unity Party, at the Morse key in East Berlin.

'Or even Honecker,' Yearling said at last.

'It doesn't bear thinking about it,' Fitch-Bellingham said. 'I just hope Rudi didn't suffer at the hands of that bastard.' Erich Honecker, head of the Stasi, was, if anything, even more ruthless than Ulbricht.

'And you think,' Yearling said, 'that you can establish the truth of the matter by using this Feldmann fellow?'

'Perhaps even better than that.' This was the nub of the matter and Fitch-Bellingham leaned closer, spoke more softly to his Director. 'It may well be that our network is still intact – we simply don't know. If Rudi was held for any length of time in the "submarine", then of course he gave up everything.' Yearling nodded: in the end everybody gave everything up after a few days in the old Hohenschönhausen underground cells. 'But we don't know that. Maybe he bought it quickly – we just don't know. Maybe he was lucky to die without ever having to see the inside of the "submarine". I hope so, for the poor bastard's own sake.'

'And Feldmann?' Yearling's interruption was curt: old F-B did have an unfortunate overly sentimental attachment to long-term operatives who dated back to his time in occupied Berlin. 'What can an ignorant, untrained fellow from Ireland do about all this?'

'He might be untrained but he's not ignorant. He speaks impeccable German and he's a university graduate.'

'Of some *Irish* institution.' Yearling smiled his thin smile. 'Not exactly Cambridge, is it, or even Oxford?'

Something like exasperation shadowed Fitch-Bellingham's features. Hardly surprising the organization was a shambles when the Director was forever pining for the company of Maclean and Philby and the other nancy boys over at M15.

'The boy is clever.' Fitch-Bellingham began to tick off on his fingers. 'He's resourceful. He's a fighter. He's got guts. And, as I said, he speaks German like someone who grew up in Berlin.'

'Very well, F-B, very well.' Yearling stole a glance at his watch: best to get this business over with and get back to Marjorie and his guests. 'You have a plan?'

'I plan to insert Feldmann into East Berlin, kitted out with the best possible ID, and take it from there.'

'Take it from there?' Disbelief was evident on Yearling's face. 'That's all? *Take it from there?*'

'Jonathan, you know perfectly well that it's sometimes inadvisable for you to be involved in the minutiae of operations—'

'Minutiae, F-B, are one thing, but I've got to have some sort of broad outline if I'm to obtain ministerial approval for this undertaking.'

'It might be best, Jonathan,' Fitch-Bellingham said smoothly, 'not to seek ministerial approval on this occasion. After all, we are discussing a very low-level operation here.'

'*Low level?* Inserting an agent into East Berlin?'

'Consider, Jonathan, please consider.' Fitch-Bellingham spoke slowly, once more itemizing on his long fingers. 'One, this boy is not an agent, just a youngster doing us a favour. Two, nobody, absolutely nobody, knows he is here at Highfield. Three, if things go awry, we can have him in and out of East Berlin in a single day, just like any other tourist with his knapsack. And, four,' Fitch-Bellingham paused, 'Imhof is dead, and we have no idea how he intended to obtain those plans or how he might have conveyed them to us but we have another possibility.'

'What do you mean, "another possibility"?'

'Martin Weber is what I mean.'

'Martin Weber? He must be ninety if he's a day and what's he got to do with it?'

'He's about seventy,' Fitch-Bellingham said, 'and I know that Rudi was to get in touch with him about delivery.'

'You never told me this, F-B.'

'And if I *had* told you, Jonathan? Everybody on that damned committee of inquiry would know Martin Weber's name by now, and what would that achieve? Martin is one of the last assets we've got to ourselves, and we don't want anybody muscling in on him, do we?'

Fitch-Bellingham could read the struggle in Yearling's small, round face: a struggle between scepticism and the Director's wish for a solution to the organization's seemingly terminal woes.

'You really think it's possible to do that, F-B? Salvage everything using only an untried novice and a pensioner we haven't heard from for years?'

'Martin may be of pensionable years, Jonathan, but he is fit and well, and furthermore we have kept in touch all these years.'

Yearling looked sharply at him. 'You never said you were in touch.'

'Need to know, Jonathan, need to know.'

'You really think you can pull this off?'

Fitch-Bellingham spread his hands. 'There's always an element of risk,' he said. *And we all need to cover our tracks.* 'You're well aware of that, Jonathan.'

'The last thing we need is a propaganda coup for Ulbricht and his cronies, questions in the House and headlines in the *Mail* about operational cock-ups.'

'England expects,' Fitch-Bellingham said quietly.

'Yes, every man must do his duty.'

The Director was silent, as if savouring Nelson's call to arms. Fitch-Bellingham was amused: he wondered if Nelson would have enlisted a young Irishman and an elderly Prussian. On balance, he thought, yes.

'Do it,' Yearling said finally. 'Let me know what you need – money, passports, clothing, the usual stuff. When do we go?'

'In about a week.'

'So soon?'

'I can't keep Feldmann locked up here too long.'

'And his brother?'

'Under lock and key – and medical care. He thinks he's going to be charged with assault.'

'And the fellow here thinks his younger brother is facing a charge of murder if he doesn't cooperate?'

'He'll cooperate,' Fitch-Bellingham said. 'He *is* cooperating.'

Yearling lifted his small head, listened for a moment.

'It's so quiet,' he said. 'Where is Feldmann, by the way?'

'In the kitchen, I should think,' Fitch-Bellingham said, 'having a bite of lunch with Adams.'

'Do it, F-B,' Yearling said again. Fitch-Bellingham thought the Director looked old beyond his half-century of years, an old man hoping against hope that a last throw of the dice might win him back his budget, his organization. 'And may God help us all.'

'It's my experience, Jonathan,' Fitch-Bellingham drawled, 'that the Almighty generally helps those who help themselves.'

Fourteen

The kitchen at Highfield was in the basement. Fitch Bellingham paused at the foot of the stairs, listening to the voices coming through the open doorway of the kitchen. Adams' voice was deep but the Feldmann boy's was deeper. No quavery hint of nervousness, Fitch-Bellingham noted with satisfaction. If you didn't know the pair of speakers, you'd have no idea that one was thirty years younger than the other.

The voices drifted along the corridor in fluent German, the younger man's in fluent *Hochdeutsch*, Adams' in colloquial German picked up on the bombed-out streets of occupied Berlin. Listen with your eyes closed and you could be back in Berlin, in a bar with bare tables and a hole in the roof, listening to two fellows discussing football. Except that these two were talking about Danny Blanchflower and Tottenham Hotspur and the year was 1962.

He padded silently along the corridor but he knew it didn't matter, that Adams would sense his presence no matter how quietly he tiptoed.

For a split second Adams' eyes met his as Fitch-Bellingham stood in the doorway but he gave no indication of his presence to Feldmann, who was sitting at the kitchen table with his back to the door.

'*Alles in Ordnung?*' Fitch-Bellingham asked quietly.

'*Jawohl,*' Adams said. '*Wir unterhalten uns über Fussball.*'

'*Gut,*' Fitch-Bellingham told him in German, 'but now we must talk about work. We don't have much time to get Herr Feldmann ready.'

Roland pushed back his chair, turning to look at Fitch-Bellingham.

'Yes, Herr Ingham,' he said. 'I'm not here to talk about football. Let's do whatever you want me to do and then my brother and I can go home.'

Anger in the voice, a hint of steel. *Let's get on with it and then we can all go back to where we came from.* Fitch-Bellingham liked that, it reminded him of his own young years in Berlin. Except it hadn't quite turned out the way they'd all wanted. The bombed-out, wartime streets of the city were busy shopping thoroughfares now but the war still went on, in the darkness, out of sight, a shadow world that was real. And the Wall cast the longest shadow of all.

Fitch-Bellingham drew a chair up to the table; the metal legs squealed in a kind of agony on the tiled floor.

'If all goes to plan,' he drawled, 'you'll be going home in a week.'

'Is there a doubt about it? You said "if".'

Fitch-Bellingham gave Roland one of his thinnest smiles.

'There's always a doubt,' he said. 'There's a doubt about having your head bashed in as you're leaving High Street Ken station on a Saturday night.'

'Or being strong-armed at a police station by a fellow who gives you a false name.'

'*Touché.*' Fitch-Bellingham was no longer smiling. 'But you and I have made an agreement. Yes or no?'

Roland nodded. He looked around at the huge kitchen, the institutional cupboards, the giant range, unused now, dwarfing the electric cooker where Adams had prepared lunch. I'm like the electric cooker, he thought, at sea in an ocean that is too wide and too deep.

'Yes,' he said. 'So what do I have to do for you – or are you just going to continue feeding me lies?'

Adams stirred in his chair. 'Watch your mouth,' he said quietly, 'or else I'll have to close it for you.'

'Gentlemen.' Fitch-Bellingham looked with fondness at Adams. 'We're working together here, on the same side. No need for friends to fall out.'

Adams caught his eye, permitted himself a knowing grin. *No need for friends to fall out.* Fitch-Bellingham had said exactly the same thing to the British redcap in the flat in Wilmersdorf, just off the Ku'damm, back in the spring of 1946. He remembered the MP looking from Fitch-Bellingham to the pair of naked bodies on the bed, back to Adams, immaculate in his uniform with his corporal's stripes, still holding the gun in his hand. Adams could have vanished after shooting them but he'd waited until the military policeman arrived, then waited until Major Fitch-Bellingham arrived shortly after. Just like he'd waited until Hedwig had her Kraut boyfriend's *Schwanz* stuck inside her before he shot them both. Bitch, whispering her Kraut sweet nothings in Adams' ear, feeding his presents of food and drink to her Kraut lover, fucking him behind Adams' back. Her fucking days were over now. His own too, Adams had thought. But his major had taken care of it. *No need for friends to fall out.* Just write it all down, Corporal, Major F-B had told him, in your own words, describing as best you can exactly what happened. Two foolscap pages, complete with crossing-out and inkblots. Nobody but the major had ever read those pages. Locked in some file now, Adams thought, for the major's eyes only. Both Fitch-Bellingham and Adams knew that the foolscap pages would never have to be used as leverage. The corporal was Fitch-Bellingham's man, that was all there was to it.

'Just so he knows who's in charge, sir,' Adams said.

'I think our young friend is fully aware of who's in charge.'

Roland met his gaze, nodded. 'So let's get on with it, Herr Ingham, or whatever your name is.'

Fitch-Bellingham got on with it, in a slow, measured voice.

'I'm sending you to Germany,' he said, 'but you've probably already divined that. To Berlin, to our side naturally. You'll cross into East Berlin, visit a friend of ours, pick up a package, then deliver it to me. After that we'll fly you back to London, hand you another airline ticket to Ireland and we'll advise you to forget whatever you've done for us before we shake your hand and wave you off into the sunset – or the sunrise, as the case may be. That's it.' He spread his long bony hands above the kitchen table. 'You'll be home free in a few days.'

'If it's that simple, why involve me? I'm sure you have umpteen staff who could collect your package.' He glanced at Adams. 'My guardian here, for example. Why all the cloak-and-dagger stuff with me and my brother?'

'I told you,' Adams said quietly, 'to watch your mouth.'

The long bony hand was raised again.

'I'm accustomed to giving orders, not explanations.' Fitch-Bellingham's tone belied the severity of his words. 'But this one time – this one time only – I will explain. It's true that my colleagues here, or somebody else, could perform this errand. It's also true that this particular errand is best carried out by someone not known to our friends on the other side of the Wall. You,' he nodded at Roland, 'are such a somebody. But you are more than just anybody, which is why I am entrusting you with this task. You speak German like a native Berliner, that's important, but that alone would not be enough. You're a pretty confident young man, Roland Feldmann. You're cool under pressure. And you're trustworthy – you didn't walk away from your brother's mess. Not to mention,' Fitch-Bellingham permitted himself a smile, looking at the muscular young man beside him, 'you're in pretty good shape and you can handle yourself.'

'No doubt,' Roland said drily, 'you'll put all that in writing for me.'

'I warned you!' Adams was rising from his chair.

Fitch-Bellingham waved him back to his seat.

'This is no joking matter. Understand?'

Roland nodded. *It couldn't be as simple as this fellow was making out but he'd manage.*

'So. When do I leave for Berlin?'

'In two days.'

Fitch-Bellingham caught the look of alarm on Adams' face.

Roland shrugged. 'The sooner the better. And my brother?'

'He'll be waiting for you when you get back. You can go home together.'

'And,' a smile lighting up his face, 'I can see Terry before I go to Berlin?'

'I'm afraid that's not possible. Your brother is still in police custody and we have to sort out the paperwork.'

Another shrug, a shake of the dark head. 'But I have your word that Terry and I will go home together after Berlin?'

'Yes, you have my word.' Fitch-Bellingham stood up, stretched his long frame like a greyhound. 'I have some details to discuss with my colleague here,' he nodded towards Adams, 'so why don't you take a walk in our garden, enjoy a little of our English pastoral beauty.'

Roland looked at the two older men for a moment before turning away from them.

'I should add,' Fitch-Bellingham said to Roland's back, 'that our neighbours round here think that we run a funny farm in this place – they're always watching out for chaps climbing over the wall.'

Roland kept on walking. They heard his footsteps fading away on the basement stairs.

Adams cleared his throat, stroked his dark-shaven jaw.

'Two days, sir. What do you want me to do with him in *two days*?'

'Not a lot, Corporal.'

They heard the back door slamming; moments later they caught a glimpse of Roland's corduroy-trousered legs passing the barred kitchen window above their heads.

Fitch-Bellingham and Adams swung their gaze from the barred window and looked at each other, almost smiling. There wasn't much, legal and otherwise, that they didn't know about each other.

'Not much you *can* do in a couple of days, sir.'

'Get the maps out. Get him familiar with the city, the streets, the trams. Set him plenty of tests, the usual stuff.'

'And his cover? Student or something, visiting East Berlin?'

'He goes in as the usual day tripper.' Fitch-Bellingham fingered the salt cellar on the long table as if it were a pawn on a chessboard.

'And coming out? His pass is good for just the day.'

'I'm still working on it, Corporal.'

Adams cleared his throat again. 'And the two days, sir? I mean—'

'You mean, what's the rush? Good question, Corporal. The way I see it, Herr Feldmann senior back in the Irish Republic is liable to be asking questions soon. Right now there's a postcard view of Tower Bridge winging its way to our Irish-German jeweller explaining that the brothers Roland and Terry have decided to head for Brighton for a couple of days. In a few days' time another postcard, of Brighton Pier, will tell Mum and Dad that our boys are having fun and will be home in a few days and not to worry. All done in our best forger's own hand.' Adams nodded: James Finkelstein, forger and reformed graduate of Wormwood Scrubs, was the best in the business. 'But it seems to me that our Herr Feldmann is probably your typical German paterfamilias – he'll rant a bit at first, but no more than that. Later, when Frau Feldmann gets agitated because her boys haven't phoned, especially baby Terry with his wretched asthma, then it seems to me that our German papa will start to wonder.' Once more Fitch-Bellingham lifted the salt cellar in his long fingers. 'I daresay he'll start making phone calls, asking questions, maybe even take a trip to London. The boys have already been checked out of their hotel, very early in the morning, just the night porter on duty and he was the worse for wear. But,' he looked at Adams, 'if Herr Feldmann senior fetches up at the hotel desk, a lot of questions will inevitably be asked. And a lot of knickers will end up in a twist if we have the Ambassador of the Federal Republic asking questions.'

'Not to mention the Irish Ambassador, sir.'

They laughed together at that.

'I'll organize the passport, tickets, clothing, money, the usual stuff,' Fitch-Bellingham said. 'You'll have the boy ready for travel on Tuesday, Corporal?'

'Count on it, sir.' Adams stroked his blue-black jaw. 'Count on it. We'll get him in, no problem.'

'We need those maps,' Fitch-Bellingham said. 'We have to get the boy *out* as well.'

Fifteen

As soon as Ingham pulled away in his dark Jaguar, Adams produced the large-scale street maps of Berlin, East and West, and spread them out on the long table in the dining room. The maps pre-dated the Wall: someone had drawn a bold red line that zigzagged across the city.

Adams' finger traced the line from north to south across the map.

'On this side,' he said, pointing at the left of the map, 'you're with us, you're safe. On the other side,' his moving finger pointed to the right of the bold red line, 'we can't do much for you. Over there you're on your own. We'll tell you where to go, how to get to your contact – but you've got to be ready for the unexpected. That's when you have to use your wits. And that's when you need to know the lie of the land. The trams, the buses, the trains, the streets. So listen up and get as much of these fucking maps into your head as you can.' Adams' face was grim. 'It's your skin, Feldmann, not mine, but I don't want you to lose it. So let's get down to it.'

They got down to it.

You'll cross from the American sector, at the point they call Checkpoint Charlie.

Walk with confidence. You know where you're going.

Yes, of course somebody will be watching you. Everybody gets watched in that fucking place.

You can walk to Alexanderplatz, get on the train there.

Yes, to Prenzlauer Allee.

And from there?

Adams said he'd tell him the contact address later. It wasn't necessary to know just yet. *Your brain will be cluttered with too much information.*

It was cluttered already.

It grew dark, Adams switched the lights on in the big dining room, drew the curtains. They stopped while he fixed a saucepan of soup; he showed Roland where the bread and cold cuts of chicken and ham were to make sandwiches.

After they had eaten, Adams rigged up a projector and showed a couple of travelogues on a screen that he set up at one end of the dining room. The films showed Berlin before the Wall; the narrator had the usual fruity voice that you expected for travel documentaries: '. . . and so we take our leave of this charming city, now being restored to its former glory.'

Adams switched the lights on. Roland looked at the numbers flashing on the white screen and wondered, as the reel of film clicked on to its end, if he would manage to bid farewell to the charming German city.

Images of streets and cars and trains and trams wound their way through his tired brain as he fell asleep in the cell-like room.

Next day Adams washed and Roland dried after their breakfast of porridge and toast, tea and boiled eggs in the kitchen. Adams spread the maps across the dining room table and they started again. Memorizing streets and tramlines. Stations, cafes, bridges, bars. Questions and answers. Not so different, Roland told himself, to cramming for an exam. Except the stakes were higher.

This was not about honours or fail or pass. More than once Adams reminded him that it was *his* skin.

Lunch was served in the dining room. The middle-aged woman who placed the bowls of beef stew at the other end of the long table exchanged a brief nod with Adams but she said nothing. Nor did she speak when she came back with two mugs of tea and took away the empty dishes. Indistinct male voices came from the kitchen below them but even when Roland stood listening on the stairs, going up to the lavatory, he saw nobody. Later, during the afternoon, voices came from the hallway, footsteps on the marble floor, the sound of the front door opening and closing. He caught Adams' eye as he bent over the maps, listening, but the corporal had nothing to say. Roland and Adams were alone in their strange pursuit, plotting entry and exit from a divided city.

Around four o'clock the phone rang. The silent house seemed to shiver under the echoes of the jangling noise. Footsteps in the hall, a muffled female voice as the ringing stopped. More footsteps, the dining-room door opening. When the middle-aged woman put her dark cropped head around the door, Adams stood up without a word.

While he was gone, Roland strained to hear. The only word he could make out was 'Goodbye' as Adams hung up.

'Change of plan,' Adams said, when he returned. 'We have to move faster.'

'Why? What's up? Is Terry OK?'

'My boss will explain.'

Adams' expression made it plain that further questions were pointless.

Ingham arrived an hour later. A silk handkerchief peeked out of the breast pocket of his bottle-green corduroy jacket; brown brogues gleamed below his cavalry twill trousers. He looked, Roland thought, like some of his father's business friends at

Sunday lunch in the golf club. But fitter, leaner, harder. And they wouldn't be taking a small suitcase to lunch.

Ingham put the suitcase on the table.

He nodded at Roland, turned to Adams.

'How is our student?' In German. Roland had neither heard nor spoken English since he had arrived at Highfield.

'Making progress, sir. But now, with even less time . . .' Adams shrugged.

'But he'll do?'

'He'll have to.' Adams looked at Roland. 'He's smart and he has a good memory. But in so short a time . . .'

'War is always the same, Corporal.' Once again, the mild tone belied the implacable words. 'You can only work with what you are given. You know that.'

'Yes, sir.'

'To work.' Ingham snapped open the suitcase. 'Now,' he said to Roland, 'strip.'

Roland stared at him. 'What for?'

'Just do as the major says.'

Roland looked at Adams, at Ingham.

He shrugged and began to take off his clothes. *Fuck them, I'm younger than either of them and I'm in better shape.*

He left his shoes on the floor, piled his clothing on a chair. Naked, he stared defiantly at his minders.

'Socks,' Ingham said.

Roland removed his socks, let them fall on the floor beside his shoes. The evening was chilly in the room; he hated the goosebumps rising on his flesh. He could feel the others staring at his naked body.

'You keep yourself in good shape,' Ingham said.

'Fuck off,' Roland said.

'Watch it, pal.'

'Never mind, Corporal.' Ingham laid a bony hand on Adams' arm. Then he lifted a pair of cotton underpants and a round-necked undershirt from the open suitcase. He handed them to Roland.

Roland took the underwear. He looked at the St Michael labels before he put the clothes on.

'Now the rest.' Ingham nodded at the suitcase. All the clothes had English or UK labels – the check cotton shirt, the blue trousers, the navy donkey jacket, the black ankle-high boots with the pointy toes. Everything was clean but everything had been worn before. Roland felt strange, standing in that high-ceilinged dining room, wearing other people's clothes, as though he had stepped into another man's skin. But it was no surprise to him that everything was a perfect fit.

'You're flying to Berlin in the morning,' Ingham said.

'And my brother?'

'He's fine.'

'Can I talk to him on the phone?'

'No.'

'I'd like to phone my parents – we should be going home tomorrow.'

'They'll have a postcard in the morning to say you'll be home at the weekend.'

'You think of everything, don't you?' Roland couldn't keep the bitterness out of his voice.

'That's my job,' Ingham said.

'Blackmailing people like me and sending postcards full of lies.'

'No,' Adams butted in. 'Just trying to keep fuckers with big mouths like you alive.'

'Gentlemen.' Ingham waved a disdainful hand. 'Why don't we all calm down and have something to eat?'

Somehow it wasn't a surprise to Roland that Ingham, secret policeman and fluent linguist, was also an accomplished cook. Ingham hummed cheerfully as he busied himself at the cooker. He told Roland to set the kitchen table. He dispatched Adams to his Jaguar to bring in half a dozen bottles of German *Weissbier*. With an almost theatrical flourish, Ingham served up man-sized helpings of Wiener Schnitzel with a thick mushroom sauce and *Bratkartoffeln*, fried potatoes with chopped onions served hot off the pan.

'*Guten Appetit,*' Ingham said as they sat around the oak table in the kitchen.

The schnitzel was good, crispy on the outside, the white veal tender.

'This is good, sir,' Adams said.

'Yes,' Roland said, 'it's nearly as good as what my mother makes at home.'

Ingham's eyebrows went up. '*Nearly* as good?'

Roland smiled. The skinny old git was ruthless, no doubt about that, but he was a likeable enough old flute.

Ingham raised his glass of pale beer.

'*Prost,*' he said. 'And success.'

All of them drank to that.

After eating, it was back to the maps. They showed him the series of moves by which he would make his way from Tempelhof airport to the 'safe house', the flat, in Charlottenburg, in the Western sector of Berlin. *The U-Bahn from Tempelhof. The bus from Innsbrucker Platz to the main Zoo station. Look at the newspapers and magazines in the railway station, have a beer or a coffee. Walk along the Ku'damm, go into the store, come out this entrance here* . . . Ingham's finger pointed out the way, the twists, the turns, the doubling back; at mid-afternoon he would fetch up in the apartment in Charlottenburg.

'Got it?' Ingham asked.

'*Jawohl*,' Roland said. His mind spun between images of Terry, of his parents, of tomorrow's flight into the reality of the map on the table.

Ingham told him to go to bed, that tomorrow would be an early start.

Roland was leaden-footed climbing the staircase. In bed, sleepless, he waited for the locking of his door but nobody came. It made no difference now, whether the door was locked or unlocked; now there was no place to go, no place except where they were sending him.

He thought he wouldn't be able to sleep but he was deep in dreamless slumber when Adams hammered on his door at five thirty in the morning.

In the kitchen Ingham and Adams edged around him nervously. Like at home, Roland thought, the morning after I've been out late and my father thinks I'm too bleary- eyed to face the fabulous customers of Feldmann, Watchmakers and Jewellers. Nobody wanted to eat; they drank their tea in silence, standing up, scattered like sentinels around the big kitchen.

'Sure you won't eat something?' Ingham's face was pale under the naked light tubes.

Roland shook his head. He stared through the high uncurtained windows at the grey darkness of the early morning. He wondered if Terry was awake, staring at the same darkness.

'Your watch, Roland.'

He looked at Ingham. 'What?'

'Your watch,' Ingham repeated. 'It's not a good idea to take *that* into East Berlin.'

Roland slipped the silver bracelet off his wrist. He stared at the white face, the dark numerals, the tiny hands. He remembered his father's hands, the precise fingers manipulating the steel instruments in the workroom behind the shop. Loneliness seized him, coldness around his heart, and for the first time he wondered if he would ever live his old life again.

'Put this on.' Ingham handed him a black-strapped watch, Made in UK printed on its face. 'Time we were moving.'

The grey darkness was lightening as they pulled away from the big house. Adams drove, an old black Hillman that had been waiting at the front steps of Highfield. Fitch-Bellingham sat in the back with Roland, methodically working his way through Roland's route along the streets of Berlin to the safe house in Charlottenburg.

Surrendering his watch had disturbed Roland, as though a piece of his life had been taken from him. Sitting in the back of the Hillman he wanted to look out at the hedges flashing past, at the gathering brightness in the sky; he had the strange sensation that these, too, were being taken from him. He wanted to sit back against the shiny seat and commit to memory the shape of passing hedges and walls and clouds. And then he remembered Adams' taunt: 'It's your skin, mate, not mine.' He straightened himself in his seat and concentrated on Ingham's impeccable German words.

'Almost there, sir.'

Even without Adams' reminder, he'd have known from the increasing traffic that they were approaching Heathrow. He wondered if they would escort him to the check-in desk or if they would launch him alone.

Only Adams stepped out of the car when they pulled up at the pavement behind the line of black London cabs. Ingham handed him a shoulder bag through the open rear window. The bag was small, made of cheap imitation leather.

'It's to go with your image.' Ingham didn't smile, nor did Roland; he knew that, if asked, he was a postgrad student on a short trip to Berlin.

'Have a good trip. See you in Charlottenburg.'

The Hillman pulled away. *He could walk into the airport terminal and present himself at the Aer Lingus desk and talk someone into phoning his father.* And what would he say to his father about Terry?

He swung the bag on to his shoulder and walked into the terminal. Even if Ingham and Adams had driven off, other eyes, he knew, would be watching him.

Or watching *John Carter*. Standing in the queue at the check-in desk, he fingered the passport he had been given. His own photograph stared back at him; he remembered the flash in the police station – how long ago? Two days, three days? A flash from another life. He turned the thick pages of the passport, looked at the stamps. *John Carter* had once been to Vienna for a few days, he'd visited Paris. Now John Carter was on his way to Berlin.

He pretended to sleep on the plane but it really wasn't necessary: the pinstriped fellow beside him was engrossed in his *Times*. Or maybe he, too, was merely playing a role. Even the mirrors in Ingham's world didn't reflect a true image.

And then the stilted voice of the air hostess was announcing that they were beginning their descent and he drew his belt tighter, wondering what kind of world awaited him in Berlin.

BOOK 3

BERLIN

AUTUMN–WINTER 1962

Sixteen

He knew he was being watched as he made his way through Tempelhof terminal. Ingham wasn't the kind of fellow who would unleash you without some kind of reins; only trusting fools did that and Ingham was neither foolish nor trusting.

The terminal was a hive of busyness: passengers coming and going, ground crew bustling with baggage and tickets, everyone competing for space in the crowded confines. The noise from outside, from an aircraft taking off or landing, was overwhelming, as if you'd landed an aeroplane in a small schoolyard. Roland shouldered his way through the din, scanning the crowd. It was impossible to tell who was watching. Maybe everybody watched everybody in this heaving place.

He made his way past the cream-coloured taxis at the entrance and headed up the slope to the underground station. For now, at least, he would follow the directions he had been given in Highfield. The U-Bahn. The bus. The Zoo station was packed, the air heavy with the smell of *Wurst* and *Backfisch*, the counters and standing tables crammed with Berliners eating and drinking their way through another day. He ordered a coffee and a hot dog, found a space at a table where he could watch and listen. There was no obvious watcher among the crowd of diners. But then Ingham's watchers would not be obvious.

Roland finished his frankfurter and went into the newsagent's.

For a divided city, marooned in hostile surroundings, it seemed to him that Berlin was more than well supplied with guidebooks and maps for visitors. He picked up a streetfinder, searched quickly in the index, thumbed his way to the relevant page. He bent over the book, shielding the page from any prying eyes as he memorized the location he wanted and his route. For a few minutes, like any proper postgrad student, he lingered at the adult magazines corner. He turned the pages of tits and bums slowly, keeping an eye on both entrances to the shop, but no insight came to him. Whoever was watching him was indistinguishable among the heads bent over beers and snacks and newspapers on the tables beyond the shop windows.

So. Continue as per instructions. To the Ku'damm. The great shopping street at the heart of West Berlin. He looked in windows but found no suspicious watchers among the reflected images. He stopped to read menus beside doorposts. He waited at traffic lights. He watched and listened. And he was alone in the sea of humanity that was the pulsing heart of a great city at work and play, buying and selling, eating and drinking. *And spying*, Roland told himself.

He allowed the crowd to swing him along into a department store, the air thick with perfume, the floor bright with glass cases and costume jewellery. He followed the sign for the elevators and stood beside an elderly couple and a young mother with a baby in a pushchair. When the elevator arrived, the elderly couple politely waved the mother and child ahead of them; Roland stepped into the shiny, metal interior behind the old man and his parchment-skinned wife. The doors were closing when a brown-shoed foot was stuck between the doors, prising them apart.

'*Entschuldigung.*' Apologies. The fellow who stepped into the lift was fortyish, sandy-haired.

'*Welche Etage?*' Which floor? The old German, finger poised above the control buttons, waited politely for the newcomer's answer.

'I'm not sure.'

Roland watched the sandy-haired fellow's eyes dart towards the controls, checking to see which buttons were already lit.

'*Was suchen Sie denn?*' What are you looking for? The older German woman smiled, anxious to help.

Me, Roland thought, staring straight ahead.

'Music, records,' the fellow said

'Top floor,' the German woman told her husband. A regular, Roland thought. My father would approve of her, her understated elegance, the dark-green loden coat, the stylish hat with its peacock feather, her husband's obvious affluence.

'*Danke*,' the sandy-haired fellow said.

'Next floor, please,' Roland said.

The German woman looked at Roland, at her husband.

The elevator doors closed.

They pinged open at the next floor.

He felt the German lady's eyes upon him as he stepped out of the elevator.

Into a sea of corsets. Bras and knickers. Ladies' underwear.

He hurried between the counters, past the sales assistants with silver brooches on their ample bosoms and metallic perms above their painted faces. Ingham would never rely on just a single watcher. He made for the back of the store, pushed open double doors marked *Nur Für Personnel*. For Staff Only. But nobody stood in his way as he hurried down the tiled staircase. At the bottom of the stairs, he waited for a moment in front of an emergency exit, listening to his own heart. He held his breath as he pushed the iron bar, easing the door open, but no alarm bell sounded as he stepped out into a street of delivery bays and warehouse-style entrances. The elegance of the Ku'damm was remote from this delivery street, and so were its crowds.

There was no pavement here. Roland edged his way between a pair of trucks, skirted a couple of wheeled cages being pushed by two men in green overalls. He stood still at the corner. No sign of Herr Sandyhair, or of anybody else searching for John Carter, postgraduate student. For the next couple of hours, Ingham could piss into the wind. The street map from the station newsagent's was clear in his mind as he rounded the corner and headed towards the anonymity of the crowded streets.

The terrace of four-storey houses, almost regal with their ornamental pediments and decorative window frames, seemed familiar to him. Doors and windows on these elegant buildings were closed in the chilly afternoon but Roland was familiar also with their high-ceilinged interiors. With their dark sideboards, arrays of family photographs, tiled ovens. More than once, at home in Ireland, his father had walked him through these rooms, the third-floor home of *Familie Feldmann*. Number 31, Paulusstrasse, in the district of Neukolln. His father's voice, harsh as ever, stubbornly unsentimental as he reminded his Irish, English-speaking children of their roots in the imperial city of Berlin. Unsentimental yet determined that his sons and daughters should be aware of their origins. *But ambivalent too*. 'Why can't I go to Berlin then?' *Because you can't. Because that's the why*. And so Roland had been dispatched for a student summer to the safe confines of a middle-class family in the safe confines of boring, antiseptic Monchengladbach. His summer in the wide grey streets of anonymous houses and gardens had seemed like a sentence. *I could have been at home here*, he thought, cradling his coffee cup in the cafe opposite Number 31, committing to memory the golden image of the street, its long canyon bathed in the pale glow of a watery sun.

And yet his father had been adamant. Berlin was not where his student son would be sent to discover his Germanic roots. For all the sun-dappled glory of Paulusstrasse, he felt that now he could at last begin to fathom his father's ambivalence. Windows had smashed on these streets, red and black banners had unfurled their swastikas above pyres of burning books. It seemed to Roland, musing about the quiet street, that perhaps the jackboots still echoed on the cobbled roadway. The little corporal with his toothbrush moustache and madman's eyes was gone, but there were other corporals present, or nearly so, with their maps and instructions and reminders that life was both short and cheap.

The sense of bravado that had warmed him in Paulusstrasse was gone. He was just a little scared now: scared of Ingham's indignation and Adams' temper.

Corporal Adams could go piss against the wind along with Ingham.

He looked at his watch, the cheap replacement for the handcrafted work of the House of Feldmann. Almost two hours since he'd left Herr Sandyhair being elevated to the top floor for Music and Records. Ingham would have made music about that little excursion. As he would about Roland's excursion: Ingham didn't seem like the kind of fellow who was interested in personal pilgrimages to your personal *Heimat*.

He'd like to stay longer, sitting there in the window of the little cafe opposite the house where his father had grown up, but he had promises to keep. To himself. To Terry. To his father. 'You'll take good care of your brother, won't you?'

And to Herr fucking Ingham. He tipped the middle-aged waitress generously and stepped out into Paulusstrasse. The weak sun was low, the shadows lengthening on the narrow street. He looked across at his father's old house, wondering who would greet him if he rang the bell, introduced himself and asked to be allowed to see the apartment. There would be another day, surely, a better day, to go searching for his past.

He shrugged his shoulders in his second-hand jacket and started to make his way to the safe house.

It was part of an ugly cement-and-glass structure, north of Bismarckstrasse. The ground floor of the building was shared with a ladies' hairdressing salon to the left and, on the right, a prosthetics supplier, whose large plate-glass window displayed a range of artificial arms and legs, together with an array of rubber underpants and adult incontinence products. Roland wondered idly if he'd be needing any of these aids after facing Ingham: he was almost two hours behind schedule.

On the right of the prosthetics suppliers was a frosted-glass door, recessed from the pavement. The steel plate on one wall beside the door read OMEGA LOGISTICS. Push buttons and names for half a dozen flats faced him on the opposite wall. Roland was studying the choice of buttons when the door swung open. Adams stood there, his face dark with anger.

He yanked Roland inside and shut the door.

'Up. Now.'

He pushed Roland ahead of him up the narrow staircase. The first landing gave on to a long corridor of offices. Through a glass panel in the white door nearest to the stairs he had a glimpse of a man and a woman, about his own age, smoking and smiling at each other. It was no more than a glimpse as Adams prodded him up the next flight of stairs.

Neither glass walls nor smokers on this floor, just doors closed on a narrow corridor that reminded him of the budget-priced hotel where he'd stayed off High Street Ken with Terry. Adams knocked on the first door and, without waiting for an answer, opened it and propelled Roland ahead of him into a large featureless sitting room. The room held a couple of armchairs, a sofa and a table. It looked about as permanent as a bus shelter.

Ingham was standing with his back to them, looking out through the slats of white Venetian blinds that covered the window. Cigarette smoke curled back over his shoulder. Apart from that, the stork-like figure gave no sign of life. Roland moved towards the wall map but Adams clamped his arm in a bony grip and held him in the centre of the office.

Ingham took his time about turning round. He looked exhausted, Roland thought, drawing on the cigarette as if it might feed him. Maybe he'd walked from London, you couldn't tell with this lot.

'So you decided to show up.' Even the voice sounded knackered. 'Two hours late.'

'I'm here.'

'Why are you late?'

'Personal stuff. None of your business.'

Ingham shook his head like a disappointed headmaster facing a truculent pupil.

'*None of my business?*'

'No.'

Adams cleared his throat. 'Sir?'

'Yes, Corporal.'

'Permission to teach this little shit some manners, sir?'

The stork nodded.

He hadn't finished nodding when Adams dealt Roland a stinging back-hander across the face followed by a hard slap across the other cheek. Instinctively, Roland raised his fists to protect his face. Adams punched him viciously in his unprotected stomach. He was doubled up, gasping, when he felt another fist in his midriff.

He couldn't stop himself crumpling to the floor in agony. He lay on the dark carpet clutching his stomach, knowing that he had never been hit so hard in any rugby match.

He felt his back poked by a shoe.

'Get up.' Ingham's voice was muffled by the ringing in his ears. 'Get him a chair.'

Adams dragged him upright by the neck of his jacket and dropped him into a straight-backed chair.

Ingham tossed him a handkerchief and he coughed bile and spittle, and the coffee from Paulusstrasse, into it. He blinked and lifted his head, trying to focus. He wondered if Adams would try to hit him again.

'Everything you do here is my business. *Everything*. Understood?' Ingham was standing over him with folded arms. '*Verstanden?*'

Roland nodded, swallowing, wiping his mouth.

'Why did you go to Paulusstrasse?'

He couldn't keep the surprise, the puzzlement, out of his face.

Ingham snorted. 'Did you really think that you'd lost us after that nonsense in the elevator? This is not a game, my fine young fellow. We play with our lives over here. And better men than you have tried to lose us. Or to betray us.' Ingham paused, as if to let his words sink in. 'So. What were you doing in Paulusstrasse?'

He told them then. There was no alternative but he hated himself for doing so. It seemed like betrayal – of his father, of the Feldmanns he had never known, grandparents and uncles and aunts who had grown up under the high ceilings in Paulusstrasse and who had perished under the bombs falling from implacable skies. He felt as if he were violating their lives, as if he had invited the jackboots to stomp all over their most intimate belongings.

And in some way, Ingham appeared to sense all this. He held a hand up to stop Roland.

'Very well, it was personal. But from now on, *nothing* is personal. Tomorrow morning you're going into East Berlin and you follow instructions – nothing more, nothing less.'

He was given his *instructions*.

The hotel he would stay in that night – and he was not to leave his room.

The time he should leave in the morning to make his crossing at Checkpoint Charlie – and the route he should take to get there.

The address in Prenzlauer Berg where he should collect a package from Martin Weber and then make his way back to West Berlin.

It seemed more unreal than ever to Roland, listening to these cloak-and-dagger instructions in this unlived-in room in the city where his father had grown up.

'Won't they search me when I'm coming back?'

The package was so tiny, they had no chance of finding it, Ingham said, and anyway, Martin Weber would show him how to conceal it.

And that's another thing, Roland said. Suppose this Martin Weber wasn't there when he arrived at his door in Prenzlauer Berg?

He caught the look that Adams flashed at Ingham.

Weber would be there, Ingham said.

'But if he's not, what then?'

'Then get out, just come back.'

'And Terry and I can go home?'

Ingham nodded his long head.

It wasn't much of a guarantee but it was all he could expect.

'And I don't need a visa tomorrow?' he said.

'I told you,' a hint of impatience in Ingham's voice, 'just buy your ostmarks at Checkpoint Charlie like all the other day trippers.'

'We never did get around to finding out what John Carter does,' said Roland.

He caught a glance exchanged between Ingham and Adams.

'Time was short.' Ingham shrugged. 'John Carter is a post-grad student at Leeds. You're visiting East Berlin for a day.'

'What exactly am I studying?'

'Good manners.' Adams chuckled mirthlessly.

Ingham said, 'Romanticism in German and Irish poetry.'

'What do I know about that?'

'Make it up as you go along.'

'Like everything else in this ridiculous set-up.'

Ingham waved Adams back to his place by the door.

'I've told you – John Carter is a registered student at Leeds University.'

'Really?'

'Yes. Registered, all above board if anybody bothers to check.'

'And who *is* John Carter?'

'You are,' Ingham said, 'you and nobody else.'

Roland looked at him. Maybe it wasn't a village farce after all. Maybe he could just criss-cross this stupid Wall and then take Terry home.

Adams produced a blue holdall from under the table and opened it, taking out a navy duffel coat, a jaunty peaked cap, a scarf.

'It might rain,' Ingham said. 'You never know.'

Adams stuffed the cap and scarf back into the holdall and handed him the duffel coat.

'Good luck.' Ingham held out his hand.

'Where do we meet tomorrow night?'

'Don't worry,' Ingham said. 'We'll be watching out for you at Charlie.'

Adams led him downstairs and took him to a back door. He didn't offer to shake hands before he closed the door behind Roland.

Night had fallen and with it an autumnal chill. He put on the navy duffel coat and set out for the hotel, following the directions he had been given. The lights of the city seemed cold in the night. So did the entrance to the Morgenstern Hotel, a narrow building inserted between a kebab house and a strip joint opposite Charlottenburg S-bahn station. He registered as John Carter and paid in advance. The night clerk, fat and wheezy, took a half-hearted look at his passport. The Morgenstern Hotel seemed to be an establishment without public rooms, just a cramped check-in area and, behind it, a thinly carpeted staircase leading to the bedrooms. On the landings he could hear the sounds of voices and radios as he made his way up to his room on the fourth floor but he saw nobody. And nobody, he thought, saw him.

Seventeen

'He's on time anyway.' Fitch-Bellingham had the binoculars to his eyes, watching Roland's progress at Checkpoint Charlie from a fourth-floor window on Kochstrasse.

'So he learned something yesterday,' Adams said.

'Let's hope he's learned enough to stay alive.'

'He's a tough bastard, sir.'

Fitch-Bellingham said nothing. He watched Roland's slow progress as the line snaked forward past the sandbagged barriers in Zimmerstrasse, into the killing zone, under the gaze of the observation towers. Armed border guards shepherded the line towards the passport control huts. Uniformed Stasi, the elite officers of the Ministry for State Security, were in charge of passport control.

'He's there,' Fitch-Bellingham said, as Roland was ushered, out of sight, into one of the control cabins. There was no reason why the boy should not get through without mishap; all the same, you could never quite get rid of that lurching feeling in your stomach.

'There he is.' Adams' voice had a triumphant edge to it. 'Look.' He fingered the blind, eyes narrowed.

Fitch-Bellingham could see him now. Tall, over six feet, duffel coat swinging open as he sauntered into East Berlin. As if he were a carefree postgrad on a day excursion into an interesting city.

Young Roland Feldmann, Fitch-Bellingham told himself (not for the first time), was a serendipitous discovery. The young fellow had style, no doubt about it. He felt an odd pang of regret as Roland passed out of sight, swallowed up by the crowd on the pavements of Friedrichstrasse.

Fitch-Bellingham lowered the binoculars and gazed down, unseeing now, on the wide thoroughfare of Kochstrasse.

'I hope', he said, 'that he gets back just as easily tonight.'

The tall buildings on Friedrichstrasse had a washed-out elegance, like a ball gown that had been to the laundry too many times. You could see the outline of the shape, the design, but the style was gone. There was no style in the shop windows. A milliner's window was crowded with ladies' hats but the display contained only two colours and two designs. Next door, a ladies' outfitters displayed a range of faded squares of cloth. Only the bakery had customers, a line of women and old men waiting silently for their turn.

The bookshops surprised him, stopped him in his tracks as he strolled along the western side of the street. The windows contained a dazzling range of books, mostly hardback, politics and poetry, fiction and fable, in both German and Russian. But he was too uneasy to linger in the quiet, gloomy interior and he had Ingham's timetable to observe.

At the junction with Unter den Linden, he could see, away to his left, the half-destroyed grandeur of the Brandenburg Gate. And he could see the trucks and the tanks and the soldiers in the wide, sweeping space that faced the Wall. He swung away from it. He had a package to collect in Prenzlauer Berg. Unscheduled interviews with soldiers and border guards were the last thing he needed.

Unter den Linden took him east, over the river, to the open

space of Alexanderplatz. More tourists, more empty shops. A fellow in a raincoat bumped into him and asked him, in English, if he had dollars to sell, he'd pay top rate in marks. He shook the fellow's hand off, kept going. *Trust nobody.* One of Ingham's maxims. *And what would I do with a bundle of East German marks anyway? Buy souvenirs for my father – from Brighton?*

At Hackescher Market, he paid a few of the marks he'd been obliged to buy at Checkpoint Charlie for a coffee and a frankfurter. Two other day trippers sat at a table in the small cafe beside the station, their map and camera on the table beside their cheese rolls and coffees. They smiled at him, a young couple in bright anoraks, and he nodded in reply, but he walked past them with his coffee and frankfurter and sat with his back to them, facing the window, watching the street. Trams came and went, bells signalling their approach. A bus passed, a few box-like cars spewing black smoke. He heard the roar of motorbikes, watched as two outriders flagged a couple of cyclists aside to allow a large black saloon car with darkened windows to cruise by.

He finished quickly and left the cafe. The tram stop was just where Adams had said it would be. Adams and his fucking maps and timetables. On the other side of the Wall now, in another world. He got on the tram, paid the driver through the hatch, and took a seat at the back of the carriage. Two old women in black coats and a schoolboy with a bandage around his head shared the carriage with him. The women's murmuring voices drifted back to him, indistinct. The boy had a schoolbook open on his lap. The tram clanged its way along the middle of the broad thoroughfare of Prenzlauer Allee. There were no tourists on board. The journey seemed dreamy, otherworldly; the tram bell seemed a soundtrack to a travelogue. In another life, he thought, I'd like to come back here with Terry, maybe even with my parents. The houses on either side of the wide street seemed peaceful;

behind their silent facades lived folk who led quiet, uneventful lives which did not include passports in false names and bargains with Herr Inghams.

A pair of Volkspolizei, Vopos, were standing at the next stop. They said something to the driver when they got on and the tram stood there, its doors open. They were older than Roland, maybe thirty, jaws hard and clean-shaven under their peaked caps. He watched as the women handed over their ID cards. The Vopos nodded, handed them back. They said something to the schoolboy. He pointed to his bandage, told them he was on his way home from the hospital. The policemen smiled, came on towards Roland at the back of the carriage.

'*Pass, bitte.*'

He handed them John Carter's passport.

The smaller Vopo thumbed it, looked from the photograph to Roland.

'What are you doing here, Herr Carter, in Prenzlauer Berg?'

'I like to get off the beaten track.' He smiled. 'I like to see ordinary things – normal things.'

'Normal?'

'Like this.' He forced himself to remain calm, pointed out of the window. 'Normal life, normal streets. Not touristy stuff.'

'We're glad you find us normal, Herr Carter.'

'I'm sorry – I didn't mean – my German—'

'You speak our language very well, Herr Carter.'

The schoolboy had turned round, the two women were silent.

'I'm a student,' he said quickly.

'And you are studying?'

'Poetry,' he said. 'German poetry.'

The Vopo handed Roland the passport.

His colleague, taller, thinner, cleared his throat.

'Where are you going on this tram?'

'Just sightseeing. I'll get off somewhere to have a look around and then take the tram back.'

He felt the policeman's eyes measuring him, memorizing him.

'Enjoy your sightseeing, Herr Carter.'

They called out to the driver and stepped out on to the platform. The tram doors closed. The women glanced back at him before resuming their talk, in even quieter tones. The schoolboy stared at him from under his bandage.

Think. He almost missed his stop trying to. *Be calm. A pair of policemen have had a good look at you but you've done nothing illegal. Just get on with it.*

He felt conspicuous in the nearly deserted street when he got off the tram. A blue Trabi snorted by, labouring against the gradient. On the other side of the road, a woman freewheeled downhill on a bicycle. He crossed to the west side of the street, felt himself observed from behind sleepy shop windows. He took the peaked cap from his shoulder bag and put it on, pulling it low on his forehead. He turned left off the main drag of Prenzlauer Allee: *see, Corporal Adams, how I follow your oft-repeated instructions, to the boring letter.* He headed north in the grid of streets, away from his objective, then looped back around a couple of blocks to Martin Weber's apartment.

The apartment was on the ground floor of a large four-sided block built around a cobbled courtyard. Striding by without pause on the opposite pavement, he could see through a wide archway in the middle of the building into the open courtyard. The courtyard was deserted. Weeds sprouted between the cobbles. At the further end of the courtyard, he could see a matching archway and, beyond, a line of low sheds that might be garages.

The street seemed deserted.

Roland crossed the street and walked into a narrow alley that ran along one side of the apartment block. Like the courtyard, the alley was rich with weeds. Halfway along the alley, his way was blocked by a high wooden fence but, as he had been told, the wicket gate in the middle of the fence opened when he pushed against it. Beyond the fence, the alley seemed a dumping ground. He picked his way carefully among the rubbish. A shadow moved behind an uncovered window and he wondered how many eyes were watching him from behind blinds and curtains. He rounded the corner and found himself in an open space between the apartment block and the row of flat-roofed, shed-like garages.

There was an eeriness about the silence that enveloped the apartment block. Neither the hum of radio music nor the sound of voices. No dog barked, no bird cawed. No tram rumbled in the street. He drew back against the wall of the building, reminding himself that he was about someone else's business behind the Iron Curtain.

The black doors of the garages were closed, their cars or other contents protected by various types of heavy metal locks. Outside the furthest garage a small blue van was drawn up with its rear to the garage door. Roland waited, watching, but nobody approached the empty van.

He moved quickly then, following the instructions that Ingham and Adams had repeated ad nauseam. Under the back archway, into the cobbled courtyard. Left then, past two closed doors, push in the door in the corner.

He stood at the meeting point of two long unlit corridors. The dark stone floors gave off a faint blue glow in the gloom. He held his breath, listening, pressed against the peeling wall, but the entire building seemed to draw deeper into its own silence.

He knew that Martin Weber's apartment was the third door along to his right. He clung to the wall of the long corridor as though it might protect him. He padded on the stone floor past two closed doors. Martin Weber's was next, number 17.

The door numbered 17 was ajar.

It creaked as Roland pushed it softly. He was in a small entrance hall. A dark anorak, a raincoat and a couple of jackets dangled from hooks on the wall to his right; below them on the lino floor stood a pair of brown boots and a pair of black shoes, all carefully polished. An inner glass-panelled door was closed. He stood in the small hallway, peering through the frosted glass, listening. He could see nothing, hear nothing.

Roland tapped gently on the glass door.

He waited, tapped again.

The door was open, there must be somebody inside.

'Herr Weber?'

Nobody answered.

He took a firm grip on the door handle and pressed. The door opened into a living room that oozed brownness. Brown lino, brown table, brown chairs. The brown curtains were closed, the room drowned in a brown gloom. Roland blinked. He reached for the light switch, then thought better of it. He blinked again, his eyes growing accustomed to the gloom. Individual objects took shape: the bookcase in the corner, the sepia photographs arranged on the dark sideboard, the papers on the small table that obviously served as a desk. The heavy curtain across the opening to the kitchen area was only half-drawn: he could see that the draining board and sink were clear, uncluttered. The door into what he took to be the bedroom was slightly ajar.

'Herr Weber?'

His whisper seemed as loud as a tram bell.

He took a step into the living room. The floor creaked. The room seemed to moan.

A high wing-backed armchair stood in the centre of the room.

He reached out a hand to its ancient leather then drew back in horror.

Martin Weber stared back at him from the chair. Eyes wide in the knowledge of his own death. His mouth open in his last, silent scream. Blood and spittle had dried like scum around his mouth. His Adam's apple hung loose from the gaping wound that scarred his neck, almost severing his head from his shoulders. As if someone had pulled a cheese wire through the scrawny neck, Roland thought. The smell of blood was mixed with the smell of shit, where Martin Weber's bowels had opened in his death agony.

No flies buzzed. This shit on the carcass of Martin Weber was not ancient shit. And the dark-brown blood on the shoulders and neck was still drying.

Just get out if you have to, Ingham had said.

He was too late, too slow.

The bedroom door was flung open.

A small thin man stood in the doorway. He held his right hand extended, as though he might shake hands with Roland. Roland blinked as he realized that this weedy little fellow in a tight, zipped-up jacket was pointing a gun at him. It seemed absurd: *somebody was pointing a gun at him*.

'*Unser Freund aus England*,' the fellow said.

A part of him thought, fuck it, I'm from Ireland.

Another part of him thought, I have to get the hell out of here.

The little fellow advanced on Roland, the gun outstretched. He seemed all of a yellow piece: yellow hair plastered across a balding pate, yellow teeth like a dog's, yellow eyes to match.

Do something.

He backed away from the gun. His right hand, behind his back, searched for something, anything. Fastened on something round, heavy.

He swung his right arm. The yellow eyes seemed shocked, indignant, as the heavy glass ashtray struck him on the left ear. He howled, reaching for his ear.

Roland moved in on him, kicked upwards with his left foot. His foot connected with the gun. The weapon flew from the yellow fingers, and catapulted towards the floor.

The gun went off. The explosion filled the small room. For a frozen second, both men stared at each other. Neither was hurt. There was a fresh hole in the slumped corpse of Martin Weber, the smell of burnt clothing mixed with the stench of blood and shit.

Roland swung the ashtray once more against the fellow's wounded ear. He howled, clutched at the ear. The blood oozed through his clutching fingers. Roland struck him again, watched him sink to the floor beside the chair that held the garrotted remains of Martin Weber.

Move.

He kicked the fellow in the head and ran. He was reaching for the apartment door when he saw the key in the inside lock. He grabbed at it. He had to slow down, turn the key slowly so that he could get it out of the lock. The groaning behind him sounded like thunder in his ears. The groaning turned to blasphemies.

'Fuck! Fuck! Fuck! My fucking ear!'

Roland pulled the door shut. The key turned easily, locking the door.

Now fists pounded on the inside of the door.

'Open the door, you English fuck! Open the door!'

Roland ran. His shoes pounded on the stone floor of the corridor. The shouting stopped.

Then another gunshot: a loud, explosive noise mixed with the smashing of glass. *Yellow-eyes was out: what now?*

The last door on the corridor opened cautiously. The man in the doorway was white-haired, dressed in a grey suit that hung loosely on his spare frame.

The fellow held a hand up. Roland drew to a panting halt. Maybe, after all, this was the end of the line.

The man put a finger to his lips and stood with his head cocked, listening. Roland listened too.

The sound of an engine starting, then wheels rumbling over cobblestones. The van, he thought, there was somebody in it.

Grey-suit looked at him, his finger still to his lips. A white dog collar gleamed beneath his chin. A priest, Roland thought, a vicar.

The engine stopped. A car door opened and slammed. Voices raised in the courtyard.

'You check there, I'll take this side!' Yellow-eyes, his voice shrill.

'Quick!' The priest took him by the sleeve and pulled him inside. From behind the closed door of the apartment, they could hear the pounding on doors, the shouting.

'Engländer! Come out, you fucker!'

'You are English?' The priest spoke in a whisper.

'I'm from Ireland.' And he was shocked to realize they were speaking in English.

'Quickly now!'

The fists on the doors were coming closer.

'In here,' the priest said, leading him into a bedroom.

A yellow candle was burning on the bedside locker, beside a small crucifix. The flame flickered in the gloom, shadows danced on the old woman in the bed. Her gnarled hands were joined on the threadbare bedspread as though in prayer. Her eyes were closed.

'She died before the hullabaloo started,' the priest whispered. 'Thank God for that anyway.'

'Open up! State Security!' The hammering seemed to be next door.

Roland looked at the old woman in the bed, at the white-haired priest.

'Here, cover yourself.' The priest was drawing back the blankets on the bed. The old woman's short body was covered in a pink nightshirt that reached below her feet. 'Marta won't mind.' Something like a smile lit his features. 'Give me your coat and your bag.'

Roland handed over the holdall, tore off the duffel coat. He watched as the priest hung the coat in the wardrobe and covered it with an old dressing gown. He moved shoes in the bottom of the wardrobe, threw them on top of the bag, let a couple of old cardigans fall alongside them.

'What are you waiting for?'

Roland lay down beside the dead woman in the bed.

'Get down in the bed, I have to cover you.'

He burrowed deeper, flinched as the dead body seemed to grip him. The blankets covered him like a shroud. The sickly sweet odour of death overwhelmed him in the darkness. He wanted to sneeze.

'Open up!' Yellow-eyes shouting at the door. 'State Security!' Fists pounding on the door. 'Open up! Now!'

'Don't move, don't even breathe.' The priest's whisper muffled by the blankets.

Roland stifled his sneeze, moulded his frame as tightly as he could against the corpse's thighs.

The priest's footsteps receding.

More pounding on the door.

'*Schnell! Schnell!*' Yellow-eyes' voice angrier.

The door opened.

'Out of my way!' Footsteps hurrying towards him, into the living room. And then the bedroom door slamming against the wall.

'What is this?' The voice at the foot of the bed.

'Please, officer, please. This lady has just passed away. I was praying with her—'

'Who the fuck are you?'

'I am Pastor Bruck, officer. May I please ask you to show a little respect in the presence of the dead.'

'Shut the fuck up or you'll be dead! ID! *Schnell!*'

He could feel a hand on the bed, near his feet.

Then footsteps, the wardrobe door flung open, then slammed shut. The sound of glass splintering.

'Here, officer, my ID.'

'You are from Bad Saarow! What the fuck are you doing in Berlin?'

'She is an old friend, there was nobody else, her sister wrote to me from Cottbus. It's only by the grace of God that I was with her—'

'Priest, you are hurting my ears, so shut the fuck up. You have seen no Engländer here?'

'I have been helping this old lady to die.'

'I'll help *you* to die if you don't stop preaching your shit at me.'

'I'm sorry, officer—'

The sound of the slap sounded to him like a gunshot. Under the blankets he bit his lip.

'I warned you, priest!'

Footsteps again, hurrying away now.

He heard the door being closed. More shouting outside, fainter.

The blankets were drawn back and he looked up into the priest's face. The white skin still burned red where Yellow-eyes had struck him.

'Why?' Roland asked. 'Why are you helping me?'

'You needed help.' The priest shrugged. 'And I could give it.'

It seemed a lifetime since anybody had offered him help.

'*Vielen Dank.*' In German now. 'But why? I might be a criminal.'

'Are you?'

'No.' Roland studied his rescuer, wondering how much to say. 'I'm not a spy either but I was sent here by some sort of British spy outfit to collect a message from a man who lives here – I mean, *lived* here – he's dead—'

'Dead?'

'In his apartment. He was sitting there with his throat cut when I went in. I don't know what to do now.'

'What you do now,' Pastor Bruck said, 'is save yourself.'

From outside came the noise of shouting, the voice of Yellow-eyes, calling to his partner: *the fucking Engländer is gone, let's get out of here*. Running footsteps, car doors slamming, the engine snorting, a vehicle rattling over the cobbles.

'I saw the van this morning,' the priest said. 'I didn't see the men but you get a nose for these things.' A wintry smile lit the pale features. 'I just knew it was Stasi.'

Roland stooped in the open door of the wardrobe and retrieved his bag and coat.

'What now?' Pastor Bruck asked.

'I have to get back to West Berlin.'

'You think you can just walk back over the border? Did the policeman get a look at you?'

He nodded. Yellow-eyes had got a *very* good look at him.

'I struck him,' he said. 'With an ashtray. His ear was bleeding. I think I kicked him too. I was scared,' he finished lamely.

'You are a dangerous young man, Herr . . .'

'Feldmann,' he said. It slipped out – but it was too late now. 'It's not what's on my passport but my real name is Roland Feldmann, from Ireland.' From Galway, he wanted to say, but something choked in his throat. Feldmann, Watchmakers and Jewellers, was not even on the same planet as this dark bedroom in East Berlin.

'You've done more than enough for me,' he said to the priest. 'I'd better go or I'll be landing you in even deeper trouble.'

'Wait.' Pastor Bruck looked at Roland, then at the round white face of the old woman in the bed. 'We need to think. You can't just step out of here and then walk back across the border. The Stasi will be back – and not just a pair of them. They'll come in force and they'll scour every corner of this building. Believe me, I know they will.'

'Maybe . . .' Roland hesitated. 'Maybe if I just told them the truth? It *is* the truth. Maybe they'd believe me and just let me go?'

'Oh yes, they'd let you go – after ten or fifteen years, swapped on a bridge at midnight for some spy of their own, and your brain so full of drugs that you wouldn't even recognize your own mother.'

Roland swallowed. 'What else can I do?'

'First, we have to get you out of here. The Stasi got a good look at you?'

'Up close – as close as you and me. And a couple of policemen questioned me on the tram on my way here.'

'Marta will help us.' Pastor Bruck's eyebrows went up as he inclined his head towards the corpse in the bed. 'You and your late husband both, Marta.' He laid his own bony hand briefly on the grey knuckles on the bedcover. 'Forgive me, Marta, for my distractions on the day of your leaving.'

He turned to the wardrobe. Wire hangers rattled as his bony hands worked their way through the clothes.

'Take this.' He pulled a man's grey tweed overcoat from the wardrobe and handed it to Roland. 'Marta gave me most of her husband's clothes when he died but she told me she was keeping this to put on top of her bed on winter nights. What are you waiting for, young man? Hurry, put it on!' He turned again to the wardrobe. 'And this.' A navy corduroy cap, peaked, like a bus conductor's.

He looked at Roland, eyebrows raised again. 'It's not much of a disguise for a spy,' he smiled, 'but at least you don't look exactly like the fellow who struck a Stasi officer on the head.'

'And what now? I don't want to get you into trouble . . .'

'Marta will protect us.' The bleak smile of a frozen winter's morning. 'Even now, she is having her first private audience with our Maker. I'm sure she'll put in a word for us.'

'Pastor Bruck, I'm grateful but I'm going. Maybe if I get a move on, I can make it back through the checkpoint before the shit hits the fan – I'm sorry, I mean, before they know about me at the checkpoint—'

'Herr Feldmann, Roland, they know already at the checkpoint. They know at *all* the crossing points into West Berlin. This is the Staatssicherheitsdienst, one of the most effective security and surveillance organizations in the world. Believe me, they already know at the checkpoints about what happened here.'

Roland looked at the priest, at Marta's grey face in the bed.

'Then I should give myself up. There's no point in implicating you also, Pastor Bruck.'

'They'll be expecting you to try to cross into West Berlin.'

'But what else can I do?'

'We can try to get you out of the city.'

'Where?'

'To Bad Saarow, maybe to Brandenburg.'

'Deeper into East Germany?'

'I can't think of anything else, young man.'

'And then what?'

'Then we wait. We hide you and we wait.'

A draught stirred unexpectedly in the room and the two men turned to watch the flickering candle flame. 'We wait and try to get you out somewhere else along the border. Maybe we'll get you into Magdeburg or Leipzig and try to get you out from there.' He laid a hand on Roland's. 'At this stage, all you can do is try to be like Marta – have a little faith.'

'And wait for the mountains to move.' Roland shrugged. 'Very well. So what now? You said they'll be back.'

'We have only a few minutes so listen closely.'

Roland listened to the hoarse voice, trying to concentrate, but his mind wandered, to the old lady in the bed, to Yellow-eyes' bleeding ear, to the hammering on doors, to Ingham in the bus-shelter flat in Charlottenburg. To the Vopo on the tram.

'Now,' Pastor Bruck was saying, 'repeat it back to me.'

And somehow he was able to. It was like listening to a lecture at college and somehow the gist of the droning lecturer's words stuck while your attention drifted, to the girl at the end of the row in front, to the white-clad figures on the tennis courts, to the workshop in the House of Feldmann.

He repeated the priest's instructions. Past the row of garages, through the side streets, on to Schonhauser Allee. Walk, take the tram, take a chance. *Only luck and Marta's intercession will get you through this, young man.* East to Alexanderplatz and head south from there. Make for the Turm Cafe in a side street off Heinrich-Heine Strasse.

It sounded to Roland like a long shot and he said so.

The priest nodded. 'Like I said, with luck and a little help from Marta, you might make it.'

And then what? But he kept the thought to himself. Sometimes you just had to be satisfied with one step at a time.

'The coffee is lousy at the Turm Cafe,' the priest said, 'but it's used by students so you'll fit in.'

The priest held out his hand and Roland took it.

'Keep the heart up, Roland.'

'I will. And thank you.'

'And take this with you.' He handed Roland his duffel coat and cap. 'Dump them somewhere, maybe not all together. They'll find them, of course, unless somebody else takes them home first. 'And,' he pointed at Roland's bag, 'that should go too.'

Roland nodded. Right now this apartment, with this unlikely priest and dead woman, seemed safe; the candle at the bedside seemed like a beacon of hope. Outside, the unknown waited.

'Thank you,' he said again.

'I'll meet you at the Turm Cafe,' Pastor Bruck said. 'I have to look after Marta first.'

Roland gathered up his folded coat and cap and stepped out into the corridor. He ran lightly along the stone floor. No door opened, yet he knew that ears were listening to his fleeing footsteps. He was in the open, past the row of garages, when, in the distance, he heard the sound of sirens. He quickened his pace. Maybe Pastor Bruck was right, maybe old Marta would guide him.

Eighteen

Cigarette smoke: blue-grey tendrils lingered above the crowded tables, searching for a home. The stained walls and ceiling of the Turm Cafe looked as if they couldn't absorb any more. The cafe itself seemed the same: huddles of students on wooden chairs clustered around small wooden tables and not an empty chair in sight.

A few heads turned when Roland pushed open the door, dallied a moment to take in the late Marta's late husband's tweed overcoat and peaked cap, then turned back to more interesting fare among the clustered heads and cigarettes. A radio was playing at the innermost end of the cafe: a newsreader, Roland thought, it was that kind of self-important, official voice, but the carefully delivered words were lost among the din of competing sounds. He heard the word Cuba, then laughter drowned the radio voice.

He made his way to the counter between the crowded tables, thankful that nobody showed the slightest interest in him.

The fat fellow behind the counter did.

'Haven't seen you in here before.' There was a question in the words. Roland thought the fellow wasn't much older than himself but his hair was thinning and his huge stomach strained against the navy apron.

'Just passing, then I remembered somebody told me you had a good cup of coffee in here.'

'Typical.' The fellow grinned toothlessly. 'We get nothing in here except liars.'

Roland shrugged, wondering how to digest the words.

'Like to try it then?' The fellow was holding up an empty cup.

'*Bitte*.' He watched the coffee-making procedure: a large spoonful of powder from a bucket-sized tin produced from under the counter, add boiling water to the cup, stir vigorously.

'Enjoy.' The fat fellow managed to plonk the cup of coffee heavily on the counter without spilling a drop.

Roland paid, wondering where to sit, wondering how long before Pastor Bruck arrived, or if the Polizei might arrive first.

'There's a stool over there.' His coffee-maker was pointing at a girl sitting alone on a high stool beside a small shelf. The tooth-free gums were bared again. 'You never know, you might get lucky.'

She was sitting with her legs crossed on the stool. *Perched*, Roland thought, *perched*, the stool looks too tall for her. Her head was bent over the shelf, reading something. He could see only the back of her head, blond hair, cropped unevenly, as though it had been blindly snipped.

'*Entschuldigung. Ist hier noch frei?*' Excuse me, is this place free?

She lifted her head from the magazine and he blinked at the huge eyes, green, aquamarine, maybe turquoise, the irises dashed with tiny flecks of grey. Huge eyes, regarding him now with a hint of amusement.

'*Klar, bitte.*' She waved a hand over the empty stool as if to demonstrate beyond doubt that the stool was certifiably unoccupied.

He thanked her, put his coffee on the shelf, eased himself on to the stool, half facing her. She had a soft, wide mouth and soft, creamy skin that looked almost white above the black crew-necked sweater and the black skirt. *Idiot: in deepest shit in East Berlin and you're ready to swoon over a pair of big eyes and creamy skin.*

And yet.

And yet he couldn't help himself, side-eyeing her as she went on reading. It wasn't a magazine, he could see that now, but a folded newspaper. *Neues Deutschland*, the title clear when she spread the pages to turn them. The pages spread over his coffee cup and she hastily gathered them in again.

'I'm sorry, these pages—'

'Cuba,' he said, pointing at the headline on the front page.

She turned the paper round to read it. 'Warmonger Kennedy Accuses USSR.' A photo of Fidel Castro under the headline.

The girl shrugged. 'It's hard to know what to believe.'

Her words hung there in the smoky air, above the coffee cups, above *Neues Deutschland*, what Ingham, in the kitchen at Kingston, had termed the mouthpiece of the East German Communist Party. *Ignore her words*, the voice said in his head.

'It's always hard to know the truth,' he said.

'Like Pontius Pilate.'

He had been thinking just that.

He stared at her then. *It's as if she's inside my head.*

' "What is truth?" ' he quoted.

'You could write a letter to the editor.'

'We could write one together.'

'They'd probably put it on the front page.'

That gave him pause. *If the Polizei walk in here now, I'll be on the front page anyway.*

'You don't want to be on the front page,' she said. 'I can tell by your face.'

'Maybe it's not such a good idea.'

'OK, we'll have to settle for the back page.'

They laughed together at that. The grey flecks danced in the turquoise pools of her eyes. The cafe around them receded; they were set apart in their own bubble of time and space.

'I'm Roland,' he said. *Sod John Carter and his thesis on German poets.*

'I'm Petra.'

Their smiles were for themselves in their sound-proofed capsule. The fat fellow behind the counter saw the smiles and winked at Roland but he was unaware of it, he saw only the chopped blond fringe above the fabulous eyes and the rich wide lips smiling only at him.

And then he could think of nothing to say. *Idiot, empty-brained idiot. Not a word in his head.*

He dropped his eyes from those deep seas, saw the wide bag on the floor, beside her stool, saw the big pages of sheet music sticking out of it. And beside it, against the wall, a black violin case. Salvation for his numb brain and dumb tongue.

'You're a musician,' he said. 'You play the violin.'

Another shrug. 'I'd like to be,' she said. 'Right now they're training me to be a cartographer.'

It took him a moment to get the word.

'Maps? You make maps?'

'They're training me but I'd rather play my violin.'

It wasn't the time to say anything. He went on looking at her and he sensed a kind of uneasiness in the way her eyes looked down into her lap. She shifted on the stool, looked around the smoke-clouded cafe as if searching for something. Her eyes came back to him, stared into his. It was, he thought, as if she were trying to decide on something.

'I had an audition in the city this morning.' A decision had been made. 'To study at the conservatory here. I don't think I'm going to make it.'

'But then – you haven't been told yet. You don't know, do you? You're waiting for a decision?'

Her shrug seemed neither eloquent nor elegant now: just a tired slumping of her shoulders.

'I know,' she said, 'I just know.' Even her voice sounded tired.

'Maybe—'

'No,' she interrupted him. 'What about you? Are you a student in Berlin?'

What about you? He wanted to tell her about Ireland, about the house he lived in, about his German parents. He wanted to tell her about playing for the seconds on a wintry Sunday afternoon, about the freezing cold showers in the dump of a dressing room at the Sportsground, about how he'd like to take her for a drink with the gang after the game—

'What's so funny?' she asked.

'What – why?'

'You're smiling to yourself about something.'

'I was thinking about home.'

'Tell me – please.'

And he was about to.

Until, from the corner of his eye, he spotted Pastor Bruck entering the cafe, closing the door behind him, scanning the crowded tables.

'You've met.' Pastor Bruck's voice was low, standing beside them. 'How?'

Roland looked from the priest to the girl. He saw the same confusion in the deep blue eyes.

'I just sat beside Petra—'

She started to say something and thought better of it.

It was to her that Pastor Bruck spoke.

'I arranged to meet this young man here, Petra. I did not tell him I had already made an arrangement to meet you here.' The priest looked quickly over his shoulder towards the counter. 'I'm afraid we're a bit too noticeable like this, an older man with two young people.'

Roland glanced at the counter in time to catch the bartender staring at them.

'So we should leave,' Roland said.

'Not together,' Pastor Bruck said quietly. 'And I'm not sure if Petra will wish to travel with us.'

The girl looked at Roland, at the priest. 'There's a problem?'

'There's no need to involve you, Petra.' Urgency in the priest's voice now. 'You can get home to Bad Saarow on the train. I know I promised you a lift but – but I need to help this young man.'

'Roland.' She spoke his name softly. 'You're helping this Roland fellow?'

'It's better to stay out of it, Petra.'

'Has he murdered someone, Pastor Bruck?'

'Petra—'

'Or sold the secrets of the GDR to the Americans?'

'Petra—'

'I'll travel with you, Pastor Bruck, and with Roland. Unless you forbid me.'

The priest gave a wry smile. 'It might even look better, three of us in the car, my son, perhaps,' he looked at Roland, 'and his girlfriend. Maybe we can get out of the city.'

'With Marta's help,' Roland said.

'You know Marta?'

'Intimately.'

'I don't understand.' Petra looked at Pastor Bruck.

'I'm sorry,' Roland said quickly. 'I shouldn't have said that, it was – disrespectful.'

'Yes, it was,' the priest said, 'but Marta will forgive you.'

'How *is* your friend Marta?' Petra asked.

'She passed away while I was with her.'

'I'm glad she wasn't alone.'

'So am I,' the priest said.

'I'm sorry for what I said,' Roland repeated.

'It's all right,' Pastor Bruck said, 'it's just nerves.' Once more he glanced at the counter. 'We need to move. I'll go first with Petra, then you follow in ten minutes. The car is around the corner, Roland, at the back of this cafe, a green Trabi. We'll watch out for you. OK?'

Roland nodded. The other world was present again, his time-and-space capsule a figment of his imagination.

'You had no trouble getting here?' the priest asked.

Only frayed nerves and sweaty armpits, he wanted to say, only a lump in his stomach that made him want to vomit every time a Vopo passed or a siren blared.

'None,' he said. 'And I got rid of the stuff.' His duffel coat deep in a communal dustbin, his bag and cap in two others. 'Nobody questioned me.'

He felt Petra's eyes upon him.

'Pastor Bruck is right,' he said. 'It would be better to stay away from me.'

'It's too late now, Roland.'

She picked up the violin case and her bag of sheet music and stood beside the priest.

The priest nodded to him. 'Read your paper,' he said. 'Don't watch us go.'

He tried not to – but he did watch them, furtively, bent over the newspaper, as the priest held the door for Petra and they stepped out of sight into the street. The cafe seemed empty, menacing.

'Friends of yours?' The fat bartender was standing beside him.

'No, the girl was waiting for the old boy.'

'Her father?'

'No idea.'

'She's a nice-looking piece.'

He smiled. 'You can say that again.'

'I wouldn't mind . . .' The bartender shook his head, seemed to think better of saying aloud whatever it was he wouldn't mind. He pointed at Roland's cup. 'You haven't drunk your coffee.'

'I'll have it now,' Roland said.

The coffee was cold and it was sour but, in some peculiar way, it tasted just perfect.

Nineteen

He found the green Trabi without difficulty.

In the gloom of the unlit street, he pulled open the left hand door of the car and found himself looking at Pastor Bruck in the driver's seat.

'Careful, Roland,' the priest said softly. 'You're not in the UK now.'

Chastened, he went around to the other side of the car. Even in the fading light, the car body shone, the bumpers gleamed.

'It's new,' he said, pulling the door shut.

'Over fifteen years old,' Pastor Bruck said. 'Marta's husband looked after it like a child. Marta insisted I should have it when he passed away.'

'You wait so long to get a car here.' Petra was curled up in the back seat. Her voice sounded wistful. 'Do *you* have a car, Roland?'

'No, my father lets me drive his.' It was a running sore: *why can't I have my own car?*

'It's not a Trabant, I think.' Her voice teasing.

'No.' He felt almost ashamed but didn't want to make her ask another question. 'A Mercedes.'

Pastor Bruck laughed.

'It's an *old* Mercedes.' Roland felt sheepish, apologetic.

'We wouldn't get you out of here in an old Mercedes,' Pastor

Bruck said, 'but we just might get you away in Marta's husband's old Trabant. And a green Trabi is a lucky Trabi.'

'*Lucky?*'

'We have to believe in *something* in the GDR, Roland. So why not a *green* Trabi?'

Pastor Bruck turned the key in the ignition and the car almost purred into life.

'*Gott sei Dank,*' Pastor Bruck murmured. Thanks be to God.

'And to Marta,' Roland added.

'Amen.' Petra's voice was almost a whisper.

They pulled away into the road, past the bins at the back of the Turm Cafe.

'I've explained a little to Petra,' the priest said. 'But not enough to get her into trouble if we're stopped.'

'Would it be better if I sat in the back – or if I hid?' The car was a station wagon, with space behind the rear seat. 'You could pile papers and stuff on top of me—'

'You're a friend of Petra,' Pastor Bruck said, 'and I never met you before today. That's the truth, isn't it?'

Back to that again. Whose truth? Ingham's? John Carter's? This priest's?

It was getting dark. Street lights came on. They moved past bicycles, the occasional car. The pastor was winding his way along side streets, back roads. Sometimes, when they stopped at a junction, they could see police cars and grey military trucks hurrying along the main thoroughfare.

'There's a lot of activity,' Pastor Bruck said.

'It's dangerous, Pastor Bruck.' Roland could see the soldiers in the back of a lorry moving at speed. 'I tell you I should get out.'

The pastor eased the car across the main road into the darker sanctuary of another side street.

'It may not all be for you,' he said. 'It could be this Cuban business.'

'Cuba?'

'The American President is threatening to invade Cuba because there are Soviet missiles there. If that happens,' he went on quietly, his pale face even paler in the dashboard light, 'there's every chance that the Russians will invade West Berlin.'

'What's Berlin got to do with Cuba?'

'Not much, Roland, except that it's in the Soviets' backyard, just like Cuba is on America's doorstep.' Pastor Bruck drew the car to a halt at a corner overlooked by tall blocks of tenement buildings, then swung left into another long street canyon. 'Tit for tat, you could say.'

There were no street lights here, just a faint glow from apartment windows. There were lives behind these windows, Roland thought, lives like his parents', bound by mealtimes and work hours, birthdays, curfews, *what kept you out till three o'clock in the morning?* Lives not bordered by walls, by Cuba. Could these lorries on the streets of Berlin, the headlines in *Neues Deutschland*, threats and counter-threats from Moscow and Washington – could all this be somehow linked to Ingham's decision to blackmail him into this nightmare excursion across the Wall?

'Pastor Bruck?' It was Petra's voice, almost timid, from the back seat.

'Yes?'

'We'll have to get back on the main road to get out of the city.'

'So pray, Petra. Pray harder than you've prayed before. Pray that there's no roadblock for cars leaving the city.'

But there was. They could see the lights as soon as they swung on to the dual carriageway – lights flashing on top of police cars alongside vans and lorries pulled in on both sides of the road.

'Do *you* pray, Roland?' Pastor Bruck's face was white, skeletal.

'Stop the car and let me out.'

'It's too late for that, they can see us.' The pastor changed gears. Only three cars separated them from the roadblock.

'I never saw you people before.' Roland's voice trembled with urgency. 'I bumped into you in the Cafe Turm – I asked you for a lift – no, I threatened you, forced you to give me a lift—'

'Roland.' Her voice was soft but insistent. He felt her fingers on his lips, shushing him.

They edged forward in the roadblock queue. Only one car ahead of them now, a dark van behind them. The grey lorries on either side of the road had their headlights on, illuminating the roadblock. They could see the soldiers standing beside the lorries, the rifles in their hands. They could see the Stasi officer bent at the open window of the car in front while his partner walked purposefully round the vehicle.

'I'm praying, Pastor Bruck.' What was this, a lilt in her voice?

'So am I, Petra.'

The Stasi officer was studying the ID of the driver in front. The other officer was examining the open boot of the car.

I could strike this priest on the head, Roland thought. I could hit him hard, make his nose bleed, then run from the car. Why should he suffer for me? And this girl with the amazing eyes and the cropped hair and the violin case on the seat beside her . . .

The car in front pulled away. The Stasi officer waved them forward. He stared at the registration plate, then wrote on the wooden clipboard that he held in his left hand.

'Papers. *Schnell.*' The stink of stale garlic filled the car as the Stasi stooped at the car window.

Pastor Bruck produced his wallet, began to fumble through it.

'*Schnell! Schnell!*' From behind them came the blaring noise of police sirens; the Stasi had to shout to make himself heard.

He took the pastor's ID card and half turned to the lorry lights to read it. His leather gun holster shone in the beams. In the passenger seat, Roland forced himself to be still. He was aware of the second Stasi slowly circling the Trabi; aware, too, of the blaring sirens approaching at speed.

'You are a priest?' The Stasi was shouting now. You could hear the venom in his voice, sense it in the grimace he cast at Pastor Bruck's dog collar.

'Yes, I am Pastor Bruck.' The pastor was shouting too. The sirens were on top of them. Roland looked back, saw three flashing blue lights, felt the Trabi caught in the glare of headlights. Horns blew, brakes squealed as the convoy screamed to a halt. *Run now, save this priest and this girl from a disaster that is yours alone.*

The Stasi straightened beside the car, his partner alongside him. They both looked puzzled, even frightened, blinking in the fierce glare of the car lights.

A car door opened behind them.

A Stasi officer stood beside the open door, himself caught in the glare of lights from behind.

'Move this shit!' His roar seemed louder than the sirens. 'Now! Move it!'

For a second, the entire roadblock seemed to jump – soldiers, vehicles, Stasis.

'Now!' The newcomer stood frozen in the headlights, his arm raised, the red cuffband on his uniform sleeve like a danger signal in the night. Roland watched him get back into the car, heard the slam of the door, heard the thumping of his own heart above the revving of the car behind.

'You heard the officer!' The Stasi threw the pastor's ID card in through the open window of the Trabi. 'Move this heap of shit!'

Pastor Bruck revved the car, said something under his breath as the gears grated.

'Get this fucking thing out of here!' Both Stasi waving them frantically forward now, the soldiers at the roadside staring glumly at them.

The pastor found the gear, the car lurched forward. The Stasi officers were blowing whistles, waving the convoy onwards.

The Trabi window was still open: they could feel the surge of the convoy as it swept past them in the night. A pair of military motorcyclists, a pale blue Trabant driven by the red-cuffed officer, a black Zil, a glimpse of a red-braided peaked cap in its rear seat, a windowless Trabant van barrelling along behind.

The priest drove slowly. It seemed that nobody dared breathe until the lights of the convoy had disappeared into the darkness.

'Everyone OK?' Pastor Bruck's voice was edgy.

From the rear seat came Petra's nervous laugh. 'We're safe, Pastor.'

'For now.' He spoke to Roland. 'You?'

Roland picked up the ID card from where it had fallen on the floor.

'What was that about? The fellow with the red band on his sleeve? The officer in the back of the big car? Surely they're not out searching for me?'

'Maybe, maybe not. It's more likely to be an alert about this Cuba business. Whatever it is, it's serious. I got a glimpse of the officer in the Zil, could be a Soviet general. The Stasi officer doing all the shouting is from the Guards Regiment, so it must be serious.'

'The Guards?'

'The Felix Dzerzhinsky Guards Regiment – they're the Stasi elite, you can tell by their red cuffbands.'

Roland stared across at the pastor's reflection in the dark window, like a ghost in the night.

'You know about these elite Guards?'

'Not personally.' Pastor Bruck smiled. 'And I don't want to.'

'I want something understood, Pastor Bruck.' Roland coughed, cleared his throat. 'If we meet another roadblock, I'm going to make a run for it.'

'Let's wait and see—'

'No, I've made up my mind.'

'Very well.'

The road narrowed, became a single track without markings. Within the car, all three were silent, scratching at their own thoughts. Outside, the darkness deepened. Then the trees came, as if grown to order on the roadside, spaced at regular intervals, each marked at eye level with a painted white disc.

'It's a neat way of marking the road,' Roland said.

'Even the trees are obedient in our socialist society.' Petra's laugh didn't hide the sourness in her words, in her voice.

Pastor Bruck glanced back at her.

'Your audition?' he said. 'It didn't go well?'

'I think I played well.'

'The Beethoven piece?'

'Yes, the Beethoven piece. But I don't think it mattered what I played or how I played.'

'Baumeister?' The pastor's tone was gentle.

'Of course. The bastard – sorry, Pastor.' They could hear her swallowing, the edge of tears in her words.

'I'm sorry, Petra, truly sorry. I know how much that audition meant to you.'

She didn't answer. Roland wondered if the girl was weeping quietly to herself. He wondered who Baumeister was, wondered what he had done to balls up the girl's audition, why anyone would want to bring tears to such eyes.

He held his tongue, shifted his position to try and catch a

glimpse of her in the small rear-view mirror. They rattled over a bump in the road and for a split second he saw her in the mirror. Their eyes met and she smiled at him. *Fuck Baumeister, whoever he was.*

The poplar trees slipped by outside, painted staging posts on the road to he knew not where. For a little while, he didn't care about any of it: there was a warmth in the car, the promise of a tomorrow. His mind wandered home; he saw himself walking by the sea, the white-tops washing on the shore, this girl at his side.

The pastor's voice cut in on his daydream.

'Not far to Bad Saarow now,' he said. 'We have to decide what to do with you, Roland.'

He felt like a package. *What shall we do with Roland?*

'Maybe you could just wrap me up and post me home,' he said.

'I think the package might be delayed in transit,' Pastor Bruck said.

Petra laughed. 'You might never get delivered home.'

For a moment they all laughed together. Then, abruptly, their laughter died together and they stared out in silence at the dark empty fields around them.

'I can hide you for a couple of days in our old church, anything longer is too dangerous. They come back every now and again, just to see if there's something they forgot to smash the last time.' They were rounding a bend, the priest changed down. 'Maybe after that I can get you to Leipzig and try to get you across from there.'

'The summer houses,' Petra said. 'It's safer there than in your church.'

'The summer houses? But the men use them all the time, even now.'

'Not the old ones, Pastor.'

'Across the stream?'

'Yes, across the stream. Nobody goes there now, not since the war, they say.'

'But they're wrecks, Petra. No glass, hardly any doors, roofs gone – the lad would freeze there.'

'Not in this one, Pastor.'

The priest glanced over his shoulder at her. '*This one* – it's a safe place?'

'As safe as any place can be. I use it sometimes when I want to get away. Sometimes I even go there to play.'

'You're a strange one, Petra.' The priest smiled. 'But if *you* say it's safe . . .' He turned to Roland. 'So how do you fancy a vacation in one of our exclusive summer homes?'

'What kind of summer home?'

'I suppose you'd call them garden sheds, Roland, but here they are a place of refuge, a place where you drink beer, watch TV, talk to your garden neighbours or maybe just fall asleep on an old sofa.'

'A *sofa* in a garden shed?'

'We're a funny lot in the GDR, Roland,' Petra was half laughing, 'but you've probably noticed that already.'

Lights were glimmering in the darkness ahead.

Roland watched them grow closer, thinking about what the girl had said. His day in the life of the GDR had been dangerous and exhausting – but no weirder than life in the company of Ingham and Corporal Adams.

'Time to get you on the floor, Roland,' the priest said. 'Bad Saarow is a small place but that doesn't mean there are no watchers.'

Pastor Bruck eased the Trabi to a halt and Roland climbed out on to the dark road. The sky was starless, the air sharp with the edge of winter. He tipped the seat forward and Petra got out of the car. For a moment, standing close together in the night, it seemed like a dream.

'In you get,' she said.

He touched her hand as he stooped to get into the car and he felt the pressure of her fingers on his. The space behind the front seats was minimal but he squeezed himself in lengthways as best he could.

'I'm going to cover you with my coat,' Petra said, and he felt her hands on him through the material of the coat.

'Nobody will stop us,' Pastor Bruck said, 'but just in case . . .'

'I won't even breathe.'

But he did, inhaling from the stuff of her coat the fresh smell of her as the car moved on through the darkness.

Twenty

Her fingers still tingled from his touch. Strange: after the farce of the audition, she'd been deflated and angry; now, this foreigner hiding under her coat had her lurching towards an unfamiliar excitement.

She felt Pastor Bruck's eyes on her as he swung past the railway station, felt the question in his glance.

'You OK, Petra?'

'Yes, Pastor.' She didn't trust herself to say more.

The ticket collector standing outside the station was giving the green Trabi her full attention. Ticket collectors in Bad Saarow were not overworked; nearly everybody in the town worked locally, at the army barracks, at the Soviet military sanatorium, or, like herself, at the Cartography Institute and printing works. Visitors to the town tended to come in cars to protect their privacy.

They just didn't go as far as covering themselves with her overcoat.

The street was almost empty. Reiner, the local policeman, was standing outside the small police station, smoking. Petra could feel his eyes following their progress along the street. Beside her, Pastor Bruck swallowed noisily.

'Are we in the town yet?' Roland's voice sounded weird, muffled by her coat.

She laughed nervously.

Pastor Bruck hushed them both.

In the distance, the lights of the sanatorium were forbidding, illuminating the KEEP OUT signs. The place was avoided even by the soldiers in the local barracks, the squat building on the edge of the town.

It wasn't much of a town but it was at least an escape from the laughter-free zone of the orphanage in Karl-Marx-Stadt. In the flat in her workers' block, she had to share a kitchen and a bathroom but at least she had her own room, her private space for daydreaming and music.

And she had her own summer house. Not hers exactly but nobody else ever went there; she hoped nobody else knew about it.

They were on the long road that ran past the villas of Party members and other dignitaries. The trees were dark behind these cosseted homes; beyond the trees was the expanse of the Scharmützel Lake, the summer playground of the army brass and civilian bosses.

She wondered if the young man hiding behind her seat belonged to the class of bosses in his home town: his father drove a Mercedes.

She clasped her hands tightly together, as if to imprint his touch more deeply on her own skin. Boss class or not, she was going to help him. Maybe, just maybe, the trip to Berlin had not, after all, been a complete waste of time.

Somewhere in the town a dog barked: a casual bark, brief, exploratory, as if wondering if anybody were up and about in the darkened town. The answering growl was sustained, menacing. She turned her head and saw, behind the spear-tipped fencing around a cream-coloured villa, the muscular black and tan Dobermann pinscher observing their progress, the long head poised attentively. She shivered, reached back between the seats to touch him through the woollen coat.

'I don't dare drive as far as the allotments.' Pastor Bruck was whispering. 'Somebody might notice and wonder.'

'We'll go through the woods,' Petra said, 'from your place. I know the way.'

On her right, between the trees, she could glimpse the stuccoed village that housed the Cartography Institute; further back, unseen, was the flat-roofed printing works.

'Do they know you travelled in with me this morning?' Pastor Bruck was still whispering.

'I didn't tell them but I suppose they know. It's why people like Baumeister exist, just to *know* things.'

'He can't know *everything*, Petra.'

'Maybe nobody told him I travelled with you.' Now she was whispering too. 'I hope not. You know how much he hates what you do.'

'Maybe he's just frightened,' Pastor Bruck said. 'Like the rest of us.'

He slowed, changed down, swung on to the dirt track between the trees. They wound their way slowly along the path until they came to the church, grey and silent in the night.

Petra reached back and pulled the coat away.

'Time to move, Roland.'

'But no talking,' Pastor Bruck whispered. 'Follow me and Petra.'

The car seemed to tremble when he turned the engine off, like a dog shaking itself. The fresh smell of the wood mixed with the oily smell of the car when they stood together in the dark. Roland stretched, muscles cramped after his confinement in the car. Instinctively, all three of them were silent, listening to the small sounds of the night. Leaves stirred, a branch shook, something rustled deep among the trees.

'Let's go.' The priest led them along the wall of the unlit church. Roland wondered what kind of church it was, with a chained padlock on its front door and its windows boarded up.

'Careful.' Petra stopped in front of him, pointing at a pile of dark-green metal gun casings. 'They store some old equipment in the church.'

Pastor Bruck had his finger to his lips. He pointed to a corner at the back of the church, signalled to them to wait.

They watched him walk on alone towards a low cottage with a lighted window.

'He has a young son, Thomas.' Roland could feel the girl's breath, whispering in his ear. 'He doesn't want him mixed up in this.'

He could taste her breath on his face.

They heard the priest's approaching footsteps and drew apart.

They felt the priest's eyes upon them and looked away from his gaze, wondering if their confusion was written in their faces.

Pastor Bruck smiled at them, shook his head as if at some private joke.

'Here.' He handed Roland a small canvas sack. 'You'll be hungry.'

'We'd better move.' Petra's voice was different, nervous. 'If I get back too late, the others might start to wonder.'

'Yes.' Pastor Bruck looked at her, at her rucksack, at the violin case. 'You can manage in the dark?'

'It's not a problem.'

'I don't know when we can meet. I have to go into Berlin tomorrow to make arrangements for the funeral.'

'I know.' She turned away, spoke to Roland. 'We have to go – now.'

A quick handshake with the pastor, a whisper of thanks, and then Roland was following her along the wall of the church. She stepped in among the trees and for a second she was lost to him in the gloom. He heard her whisper and joined her in the darkness.

'Stay close,' she whispered, 'and not a sound.'

And yet the night was full of sounds. Branches stirred in the wind. A twig cracked underfoot. Night creatures scurried in the undergrowth. Dogs barked way off, lonely, lost. A car, probably a lorry, whooshed by on the road beyond the trees and they both stopped for a moment, heads poised, listening. The motor died in the distance but his heart thumped even louder.

Ahead, beyond the treeline, he glimpsed a makeshift city. Flat roofs, pitched roofs, arranged in symmetrical rows like a play town for grown-ups.

'The allotments,' Petra whispered. 'The summer houses.'

They hugged the inside of the treeline, skirting the empty town of allotments and garden sheds. Beyond the garden town, Roland could make out a high ditch, an earthen bank marking the end of the allotments.

Petra turned to him, her finger on her lips. Her face was pale, almost white; her eyes seemed deeper, larger than before.

They left the shelter of the trees, passed through a gap in the earthen ditch. A narrow stream confronted them; ahead lay another expanse of garden sheds, shabby, broken down, abandoned. A wooden footbridge led across the stream into this garden ghost town.

They were exposed here, unsheltered. Petra quickened her step. She led him among the ruins to the furthest corner.

The garden shed she stopped at seemed, at a glance, as derelict as the other buildings: a flat roof, peeling wooden walls, a sagging door. And yet, as Petra stooped, reaching behind a loose board in the front wall, Roland could see that, for all its ramshackle appearance, this garden shed – and it was no more than that –

seemed secure. The pitched roof, covered in ancient tarpaulin, was unbroken; the windows, although without glass, were carefully boarded over with weathered planks.

And the sagging door was locked: when Petra stood up, she held a large key in her hand.

'Let me,' he said.

He took the key from her and turned it in the ancient, rusty lock. The door swung open as easily as the key turned in the lock.

'I like to come here to be alone,' Petra whispered. 'I oiled the lock and the hinges.'

She eased the door shut behind them and a deeper darkness enveloped them. He sensed rather than saw her fumbling in her rucksack and heard the crack of a match. In the sizzling flame of the match, she smiled at him, then bent over a candle stub in a jam jar on an old table pushed against a wall of the shed. The cluttered interior took shape among the shadows: a table, an old car wheel, lengths of wood and rusty piping, a short ladder with missing rungs lying on the wooden floor. The rusting base of an old iron bedstead leaned against the back wall of the shed.

'No one knows I come here.' Petra was whispering. 'But I leave all this junk lying about just in case somebody gets in here.'

She saw the puzzlement in Roland's face.

'Not here.' A smile on her face. 'Back here.'

She moved the iron bedstead and a couple of planks that were propped beside it against the back wall of the shed. Behind the planks he could see a gap in the wall about a metre high.

Petra motioned for him to follow her. He pushed behind her into a space so narrow that he had to stand sideways in it. The candle flickered in the jam jar and their shadows were huge on the unpainted walls.

She stooped over the wooden floor and he drew back to give

her space. He saw her take hold of a brass ring and watched, astonished, as she lifted a wooden slab from the floor and let it rest against the wall of the narrow passage.

'Careful now.' Her voice in his ear. 'Hold the candle.'

He held the candle over the open trapdoor as she manoeuvred herself on to the ladder that was resting against the wooden lip. He held the candle lower into the space as she descended into the darkness.

'Now hand me down your stuff.'

She took the bag of food from him, then the candle and he followed her down the ladder.

The walls and floor of the underground space were lined with wood. The space seemed slightly smaller than the shed above and was just high enough for him to stand upright. A table and chair stood in a corner. Along the opposite wall a foot-high platform had been built, wide enough and long enough to lie on. After the cold of the night, the space seemed warm, even stuffy.

He held her to him, wondering who had hidden here, deep under the ground.

'It must have been the Jews.' He heard her whisper, wondered at how she could read his thoughts. 'During the war, when they were being hunted.' Her body shivered against his and he drew her closer. 'I walked in here not so long ago, the door of the shed was open, and I was rummaging about, just passing the time, when I saw the gap in the false wall.' She leaned back in his arms to look up at him. 'I felt that I had found my own secret place, where I could get away from – from things. I cleaned it out, found an old lock for the door and put some things down here.' She pointed at the box of books under the table, the big bottle of water on the wooden bed. 'I can't always get here. I don't think anyone knows but you always feel somebody is watching you.'

Baumeister. He remembered the name she had spoken to the

pastor but he said nothing. He didn't want to bring the world outside into this secret space.

She kissed him quickly on the cheek and drew away from him.

'I have to go.'

'I know.'

'I don't want to—'

'I know.'

'But they might see, they might ask questions.'

'I know.'

He climbed the ladder after her, stooped to follow her through the gap in the false wall into the main space of the shed. In the unlit gloom, she seemed smaller, slighter.

'Is it a long way home for you?' he whispered.

She shook her head. 'Not as far as for you.'

'And tomorrow?'

'I'll try. You'll need something to eat. Maybe the pastor will have news.'

'Be careful.'

'And you too. Stay out of sight. Nobody comes here in the winter and, anyway, these allotments aren't used any more, they say there are still old shells in the ground since the war. If anything *does* happen, just be quiet.'

She turned and eased the shed door open a little. The moon was brighter, bathing the ramshackle buildings in a watery light.

'Petra.'

'Yes.' She turned to him, took his hand in hers.

'I . . .' He swallowed, searching for the right words. 'I'm not sorry about today – I mean, I'm not sorry I met you.'

She giggled. 'That's some declaration.'

He felt himself blush. 'What I mean is—'

Her fingers again on his lips.

'I know what you mean, Roland.' Her fingers stroked his face and then her lips brushed his. 'Goodnight, Roland.'

He whispered goodnight but she was already moving into the shadow of the line of broken-down summer houses, her violin case swinging in her left hand, her rucksack bouncing on her back.

Long after she had gone, he was still standing there, staring out at the night through the half-open door. He couldn't be sure, but he thought he was looking west, towards the divided city and the divided land and, beyond, the unseen lights that burned in his own home, where his parents waited, anxious, perhaps even angry. Ingham was out there too, also anxious, perhaps also angry. No, he wasn't sure of the direction, he was lost. And yet he knew, staring into the shadows where she had slipped away, that in some altogether miraculous and unexpected turn, he had found his way.

Twenty-one

The working day was almost done when Baumeister sent for her.

Frau Krug, the section supervisor, was standing beside Petra's desk, her sharp features hiding nothing of her disapproval.

'The Deputy Director wishes to see you in his office.'

Petra looked from the supervisor to the unfinished work on her drawing board.

'Now?'

'Herr Baumeister does not like to be kept waiting.'

'My work, Frau Krug.' Petra gestured with her pen at the single colour map on her board. 'I haven't finished inscribing the list of names you gave me.'

Frau Krug's thin nose emitted a whistling snort of disapproval. It had a sneering edge to it that was familiar to Petra and the other half-dozen members of her section in the Cartography Institute. All of them continued to work assiduously at their tasks; all of them were listening intently to the exchange.

'Perhaps you will have time to finish it later.' Frau Krug's voice seemed to sharpen. 'Perhaps the Deputy Director will not have too much to say to the most junior and least qualified member of my section.'

'Yes, Frau Krug.' Petra stood up. She wished she could say

aloud what she was thinking: that she disliked Franz Baumeister's interest in her at least as much as Frau Krug did.

'So move – and no dilly-dallying in the toilets.'

Petra moved.

Out of the open-plan office and into the long corridor that ran the length of the building. The corridor was painted a dull green; through the small head-high windows she could see the richer green of well-tended lawns. Beyond the grassy space was the car park; further away, the road and, across the road, the line of trees.

And beyond the trees . . .

She tried not to think about him yet all day he had filled her mind. Working at her board, inscribing regimental names and troop movements, she half feared she would write his name on the military map given to her by Frau Krug. *Sixth Army*, written in looping letters around Karl-Marx-Stadt. Except that she had inked in the name *Roland Feldmann*.

Blink. Relief. She hadn't. But his name reached out to her from the drawing board, touched the fingers that held the calligraphy pen.

Don't think of him now, you're on your way to see Franz Baumeister, the Deputy Director.

Franz the Frog. All bug eyes and barrel belly.

The Deputy Director hadn't bothered to conceal his interest in her from the moment of her arrival at the Institute a few months previously. He'd left her standing at their first meeting in his office; his bug eyes had crawled like sweaty hands all over her body. *Franz the Frog gets what he wants*, one of the other girls had whispered, taking a risk.

She'd managed to keep him at bay so far, one excuse after another. The excuses were growing lamer; she knew that the Deputy Director's temper was growing shorter.

She knocked on the frosted-glass door, waited for the peremptory 'Enter' before she pushed the handle.

'Fräulein Ritter.' The round face fashioned into a smile. 'Always a pleasure to see you.'

He indicated the metal-legged chair on the opposite side of his desk. She could feel his eyes on her thighs as she settled herself, pulling her skirt tightly around her knees.

'Good afternoon, sir.'

'So, Petra, tell me how your day in the city went.' The Deputy Director had switched to the familiar *du*. 'How was your audition?'

'I don't know, Herr Deputy Director. They said they will write to let me know.'

Except we both know I won't be going to the Academy of Music, you've made sure of that.

He leaned forward on the big desk, hands together as if in prayer.

'But what was your impression, Petra?'

She hated this farce but she met his gaze.

'I don't know, sir. It was impossible to tell.'

Baumeister stood up and moved round the desk. He sat on the corner, looking down at her. He swung his leg and she swallowed as his ankle grazed her knees.

'*Entschuldigung.*' Excuse me.

He put a hand out as if to steady himself and she flinched as his hand rested on her shoulder.

'You're so nervous, Petra!' A joking tone now. 'Was the audition so awful that you still tremble?'

'No, sir—'

'I wonder, Petra,' he cut in, 'if there's anything I can do to help, anything at all?'

The way I hear you've helped so many other girls here, Herr Deputy Director.

229

'I don't understand,' she said.

Baumeister spread his hands, his foot moved beside her knee. 'I think you *do* know what I mean, Petra. As Deputy Director here, I run the Institute. A man in my position is not without influence. In fact, the Rector of the Music Academy is personally known to me. I'd be happy to have a word with him on your behalf.'

Like you've already had a word: the three assessors at the audition had barely listened to her, had hardly nodded at the end of her playing.

'It's very kind of you, sir, but maybe my playing is just not good enough.'

'Let me be the judge of that. You have only to say the word, Petra.'

Just say yes and take your clothes off.

'It's really good of you to offer, sir, but – but maybe I need to practise more. It's hard to find the time to practise, I should be practising for hours every day . . . She stopped, wondered if she had said too much.

'Exactly, Petra.'

She wondered if she had heard correctly. Time off to practise was something she had never dared to ask for.

Baumeister smiled, bent a little towards her but his great girth restricted his movement.

'You look tired, Petra. Yesterday was a stressful day for you?' He nodded, answering his own question. 'What time did you get back from Berlin? Seven? Eight?'

She hesitated. 'It was late, sir.'

He'd noticed her hesitation. 'How late? Did you come by train? I could have sent a car for you.'

She froze for a moment. She wanted to lie but he'd find out anyway and that would be even more dangerous.

'The local pastor was kind enough to give me a lift, sir. He was in Berlin to see one of his—' She stopped, frightened. 'An old lady was dying . . .'

'One of his fellow fantasists, you mean. I take it you mean Bruck. I'm told you sometimes play at his so-called services, Petra.' His voice grew harder. 'The Party is lenient with these people, but you must realize that there is only a limited future in our country for so-called believers who would undermine the authority of our state and our Party. And the same applies to their sympathizers. You *do* understand that?'

She couldn't look at him but she nodded.

'Is that a yes?'

'Yes, Herr Deputy Director.'

'Good. I'm glad we understand each other.'

'Yes, sir.'

'Good, good!' Baumeister stirred himself on the desk, reached for the telephone. 'You look a bit peaky, my dear Petra, let us put some colour into your cheeks with some fresh, hot coffee.'

When he offers you coffee, you know it's too late: words overheard, whispered in the ladies' toilet.

Nervous, shifting on the chair, watching the jelly-roll sway of his round body as he spoke into the telephone.

'We'd like some coffee in my office, yes, right now!' No please. An order, not a request.

And his eyes devouring her again, soiling her, as he went on about the merits of a career in cartography, and, even clenched in her despairing hands, her skirt seemed to grow shorter, flimsier.

'Come!' His voice boomed in answer to the knock on the door.

The secretary, grey-haired, frightened-looking, avoided Petra's eyes as she laid the tray on the desk. A cafetiere, plunger raised, two cups.

Cups with saucers and spoons.

Jammy biscuits on a matching plate.

The secretary backed out of the office apologetically. The closing click of the door behind her louder than the slamming of a prison gate.

Baumeister beamed at Petra, beamed at the biscuits. 'Foreign,' he said, 'a special treat.'

He waited, forcing her to speak.

'Thank you, Herr Deputy Director.' Her words louder than the closing door, as though the rest of the building had been evacuated and only silence remained.

Baumeister's head nodded, wobbled up and down, seemingly satisfied.

She watched him draw a chair close to hers, tried not to flinch as he settled himself beside her.

'Cosy, no?' She managed to nod as he laid his hand on her arm. *Fuck the job. If he touches me I'll kick him in the balls, I'll run away with Roland—*

He was saying something, the moist lips were moving. *Listen.*

'Petra?' A pat on her arm, pointing at the cafetiere. He was holding a cup in his other hand. 'Why don't you do the honours?'

Her legs almost buckled as she stood.

Fuck you, Baumeister.

She lifted the coffee pot, turned to Baumeister, began to pour.

She seemed to stumble, watched, ashen, grim, as the scalding coffee cascaded on to Baumeister's groin.

The cup fell from his hands, clattered on the floor.

Baumeister roared, pushed her away.

She remembered to say sorry. But she relished the sight of him, trying to bend over his belly, mopping uselessly at his sodden groin.

She hid her face, stooping, retrieving the fallen cup and saucer.

'Get the fuck out of here!'

She stood up, looked at him, his round face swollen with anger and she was afraid now, wondered at her own bloody-mindedness.

'Bitch!' The word spat at her.

'I'm sorry, sir—'

'Get out! Out! Get out of my sight!'

His tie was wet, and his shirt: he was opening buttons on the bulging belly.

Outside in the corridor she almost collided with the secretary, now looking even greyer, even more frightened.

'What . . . ?'

Petra hurried past without answering.

When he saw her hurrying across the narrow footbridge, he wanted to call out, run to her. She couldn't see him, hidden behind the garden hut, coat collar turned up against the night. The long day, the cold, the boredom of the hours in the hut, skulking among the dilapidated shells – none of it mattered now, watching her draw near, face pale beneath the woollen ski cap, the dark rucksack hugged tightly against the slim body.

'Petra.' Her name whispered in the darkness.

She came into his embrace and he felt her body tremble against him. She drew back from him, laid a finger against his lips, led him inside the hut.

In the basement she clung to him again and when they drew apart he saw the fear in the turquoise eyes.

'What?' he said. 'What's happened?'

She shook her head, started to open the rucksack.

'You must be starving. Eat.'

233

He watched her set the food on the small stool, wondered what it would be like to see her set a table at home – *their home* – on the other side of the Wall, beyond the darkness.

She poured coffee from the flask, handed him the cup. He saw her face change, the soft skin move and fold around the lovely cheekbones and he couldn't tell: a smile or a grimace – or both?

'What?'

'I poured coffee for somebody else this evening.'

He could hear the tremble in her voice, waited for her to continue.

'Eat,' she said. 'Drink your coffee while it's hot.'

He smiled. Not much to smile about but this Petra from Bad Saarow spoke when she decided to.

He ate the sandwiches, drank the coffee.

'Now,' he said. 'You poured coffee for somebody?'

She sat beside him on the narrow bed and told him, and he saw her in that metallic office, heard her grotesque boss's grotesque advances and in a way it was almost laughable, this frog with his groin scalded with steaming coffee – but it wasn't really a laughing matter, was it?

He wasn't the only one in danger.

And danger had more than one face.

He held her hand, drew the blond head on to his shoulder.

'I'm sorry, so sorry.'

On his shoulder the blond head stirred.

'No, don't talk about it.'

'But—'

'I'm OK, don't let's talk about it.' She lifted her head, turned so that her eyes looked into his. 'Tell me about your home, about your town, about your mother and father – I want to know all about you, Roland Feldmann.'

'Paulusstrasse,' Roland said. 'Paulusstrasse in Berlin.'

She said nothing but he saw the puzzlement in her expression.

'It's the street where my father lived, before the war. Sometime in the nineteen thirties he went to Ireland to work in Galway.' A shrug of his shoulders. 'I went to Paulusstrasse the day before I met you, Petra. I just stood there, looking up at number thirty-one.'

He liked her stillness, the way she didn't interrupt with questions, just waited for him to continue.

And he didn't really want to speak about Berlin; she had troubles of her own.

'My father sings the praises of Ireland so much that it's almost embarrassing – when he starts at it in front of visitors you don't know whether to hide or to laugh.' A rueful shake of the head. 'But he still made us all learn German – me, my brother, my two kid sisters.' He was going to say that it was his command of German that had got him into his predicament but he saw the complexity of it. 'Maybe I should thank him – if he hadn't pushed me at the German, I'd never have met you.'

A squeeze of his hand, a smile shared.

For a little while they were in two places: in an underground refuge where safety was questionable and in a cosy home in a faraway town on the edge of Europe where safety was as certain as his mother's patience and his father's irritability. Where his brother Terry wheezed and puffed on his inhaler; where his two kid sisters, even in puberty, behaved already like a pair of house-proud German hausfraus.

'I think,' Petra said, 'they wouldn't be impressed by the lodgings I've offered you.'

They were back in the dingy cellar, huddled together in the night like a pair of animals.

'No.' He was having none of it. 'They'd love you, I know they would.'

'I still don't know why you're here, why they're hunting you.'

He stood up, paced the cramped cellar, looked at her in anguish.

'The priest – Pastor Bruck – he kept saying that it's safer not to know too much.'

'I think we've gone beyond that, Roland, don't you?'

And he saw the rucksack on the floor, the flask on the crumb-laden stool, saw her making her way through the hostile night to his hiding place, and knew the truth of her words.

'I can never repay you for what you've done for me, Petra.'

'You're here,' she said, 'that's repayment enough.'

And he saw it then, grasped at the possibility.

'I could be happy here – I could go to them and tell them everything and you and I could be together—'

'Tell them what, Roland?'

She listened as he told her all, from the fracas in the tube station in Kensington to the police station nearby; from the stork-like Ingham to the big house in the countryside; from Heathrow to Tempelhof and Paulusstrasse.

He told her about Prenzlauer Berg, about the body in the apartment and the man with the yellow eyes.

'I was frightened,' he said, 'but –' he shivered – 'I struck the fellow so hard I could've killed him.'

She put her arms around him, held him close.

'They wouldn't listen, would they? They wouldn't let us be together.'

His words demanded no answer.

They kissed.

To Roland their kiss seemed as inevitable as everything that had happened to him since he crossed into Zimmerstrasse at

Checkpoint Charlie. And even before then: that all his life he had been moving, aware but unaware, towards this garden hut in a place he had never heard of, in the arms of a girl he had never known. And now, the apple scent of her hair, the softness of her skin, the silk of her lips – he knew now that all his life he had been waiting, searching, for this Petra from the GDR.

'I want to stay but I have to go.' Her breath whispering the words in his ear. 'I live with two others, I don't want to make them suspicious.'

He framed her face in his hands.

I'm so happy I could die.

'We'll get out together, Petra. I'll take you home with me.'

His words held her. A life beyond the Wall, beyond the reach of the groping eyes and hands of Baumeister. A life with this strong-willed, gentle fellow from a small town that he said was grey-stoned and wet and windy and friendly . . .

Go now. Before you are found out, before you betray him. Take his words to bed with you, this insane dream of escape.

'I have to go, Roland.'

They had to kiss again.

And once more inside the door of the shed.

And once more outside, in the silent night, under the white stars. A gentle kiss there, a sharing of a dream.

He watched her go, saw her slip into the shadows of the trees, followed in his mind her silent way towards the church, towards the unknown apartment block. The night was cold but his heart was warm with her touch, her memory.

Twenty-two

Time stood still the next day. Or at least the hands on the clock crawled at funeral pace on their circular journey.

She tried not to think of him in the basement: alone, cold, hungry. It made her shiver just to think of him, made the stylus tremble between her fingers as she bent over the map on her drawing board.

She could feel eyes upon her, knew that every head in the calligraphy office was inclined towards her every few minutes throughout the long day. You never knew how the information got out but somehow whatever happened within the Institute's walls seemed to become common currency. And always in distorted, counterfeit coin. Baumeister's coffee-soaked groin could easily have escalated by now into a vodka-fuelled rage.

Or worse.

Nothing was said, you read the runes of the sudden silence at the canteen lunch table, the eyes that failed to meet yours. Maybe Baumeister's secretary had said something. Maybe somebody had taken note of the Deputy Director's awkward way of walking in the car park.

She tried not to think of Roland.

Nor of Baumeister.

As the working day edged to its close, she began to think she'd escaped, that she would not be summoned to his office.

Baumeister left it till later.

'You.' Frau Krug stood beside her wearing an oddly sympathetic expression. 'Now, Herr Baumeister's office.'

Twenty minutes to day's end. *You can't scald him with coffee again.*

Her hands shook as she began to tidy her work station, a pencil fell to the floor.

'Leave it, Fräulein Ritter, I'll do it.' The supervisor's voice less harsh than usual. 'Go, I'll tidy your stuff.'

Petra thanked her, dismayed. *You're in trouble if this old battleaxe feels sorry for you.*

At least she wouldn't have to worry about her skirt; not that loose slacks over boots amounted to unsurmountable armour.

But there was determination in her step as she made her way to Baumeister's office. Somehow – maybe by a promise, a hint – *you have to keep the bastard at bay until . . .*

Until what?

Until she and Roland might, somehow, be safe together?

She knocked on Baumeister's door, waited for the command to enter.

The Deputy Director was seated on the corner of his desk, buttocks splayed across the metal surface.

He waved her to a low chair with his swinging foot.

She fixed herself in the chair, primly, thighs tight, arms held close.

'How are you, Petra?' His face screwed into a smile.

'Fine, thank you, sir.'

'Let's put that little mishap of yesterday behind us, shall we, Petra? Just an accident, it could happen to anybody.' The brown shoe, surprisingly tiny, like a child's, swung towards her knee.

'Thank you, sir.'

Baumeister shifted himself on the desk. When he spoke again, his voice was softer. 'Why don't you give up this music nonsense and concentrate on your work here?' She wasn't sure if it was his oniony breath or his very nearness that nauseated her. 'Frau Krug assures me that you have great potential in your work and, of course, I take a great personal interest in your welfare here.' He adjusted his rump on the desk; his hanging foot seemed to inch towards her thigh. 'I can assure you, Petra, that there are great prospects here for any willing worker who earns my personal interest.'

She couldn't meet his bulging gaze. She stared past the mound of his belly as though she could see her ancient violin and hear the words of Herr Lorre, one-armed survivor of the war, jack-of-all-trades teacher in the orphanage in Karl-Marx-Stadt: 'The violin is of no use to me, Petra. Learn it and love it – I notice how you love music.' And she *had* learned to play and to love playing the instrument: old Herr Lorre himself had done his utmost to teach her. And, in an odd twist of fate, it was her musicianship that had brought her to this pass, in the utilitarian office of the Deputy Director of the Institute of Cartography with those bulging eyes boring into her thighs. Frau Koch, Supervisor of the Orphanage, had happened to see Petra's transcriptions of the musical scores, had expressed admiration for the neat penmanship – and that had been that. Petra had no idea who had said what to whom but, like everyone else, she knew how the system worked: a word from one Party functionary to another, and so on up the line, and the orphan from Karl-Marx-Stadt was on her way to the Cartography Institute in Bad Saarow. 'Keep playing, I'll send your name to the conservatory in Berlin,' Herr Lorre had told her as they parted. 'You never know.'

Well, now she knew. And Herr Franz Baumeister's brown shoe was a millimetre from her thigh while he waited for her answer to his proposition.

There was a sharp knock on the glass-panelled office door.

Baumeister turned, irritated.

'Yes?'

The door opened. Baumeister's secretary, grey-haired, frightened-looking, stood in the doorway.

'I *told* you – no interruptions.'

'I'm sorry, sir. It's Berlin – it's urgent, they said.'

'Who said? What are you talking about, woman?'

To Petra, watching with a kind of shamed relief, the woman seemed visibly to draw herself together before answering.

'Herr Deputy Director, it's the Ministry of State Security on the line. Major Fuchs. He asked for you personally. He said it was urgent.'

'Major Fuchs?'

Fuchs. The fox. Although Baumeister had met the Stasi officer only a couple of times, the name alone was enough to bring to mind the narrow face with its pointed features and strange, yellow eyes.

'Yes, sir.' Relief in the woman's voice.

'You'd better put him through.'

'Thank you, sir.' The door seemed to close soundlessly behind her.

Baumeister hauled himself to his feet.

To Petra, he seemed both irritated and curious.

She stood up. 'May I go now, sir?'

Once more she felt herself undressed by the bulging eyes.

'Yes, go now.' He reached out, tilted her chin upwards with his fingers. 'You and I will finish our discussion later, Petra.'

'Yes, sir.'

She forced herself not to run from the office. The phone on Baumeister's desk was ringing as she shut the office door.

* * *

Markus Fuchs was careful not to allow the telephone to touch his good ear. The other ear was heavily taped with sticking plaster; his whole head felt as if that bastard of an Engländer had put his foot right through his brain.

The hospital doctor who'd seen to Fuchs had been lucky to escape with no more than a tongue-lashing. Fuchs had delayed going to the hospital until after midnight. Leaking blood, aching with pain and reeling with dizziness, he'd scoured the darkening streets of Berlin in the hours after the debacle In Prenzlaue Berg. The streets yielded nothing. The idiots man ning the checkpoints had clipboards covered with inky acres of nothing.

Only at midnight, driven mad with anger and frustration – and a renewed flow of blood – did Major Fuchs consent to be driven to the casualty unit of the nearest hospital.

He bellowed when the night-duty doctor touched his wounded ear.

It might have been fear of the bellowing Stasi officer that prompted the young intern to administer a heavy sedative.

It was almost ten o'clock when Fuchs came to in the hospital bed the following morning. His ear still screamed with pain and the hammering in his head was louder than ever. Worst of all, the major's wooziness made straight thinking almost impossible. *While he slept in a hospital bed, the Engländer bastard was still on the run.*

A fuck-laden tirade reduced the doctor to a trembling jelly. The major's uniform was retrieved, coffee provided, the major's car summoned. On his angry way through the hospital corridor Fuchs stumbled, was only prevented from falling by a passing porter who helped him to his waiting car.

He made it to the office, shaved in the bathroom on the second floor, drank more coffee, seated himself at his desk with a pile of reports from roadblocks across the city.

Somehow Fuchs's bandaged head didn't engage with the task in hand. He made phone calls and knew, somewhere amid his pounding pain, that the questions he asked were, somehow, off target.

He should leave Normannenstrasse, go home; he knew that his trawl through the reports was also off the mark. *Walk away from your duty when everybody in the building knows by now that you let a fucking Engländer beat the shit out of you?*

He stayed at his desk, wondered why he was not summoned to the colonel's office. He played with the papers, toyed with the phone. He nursed his anger, his venom. It was almost midnight when he fell, half clothed, into the daybed on the top floor.

And now here he was, a day later – *a day lost* – waiting for this fat fuck to come to the phone.

The painkillers spilled into his hand by the frightened doctor seemed to be working.

So did his brain. *And his nose.*

He could *smell* his prey. Could smell the foreignness of him at close quarters in the charnel room where Herr Weber sat with unseeing eyes and gutted throat. And he could smell him in the hundreds of checkpoint reports that were spread across his desk in Normannenstrasse.

Fuchs himself had checked every report from every roadblock in the city, carefully fingering his way through every line of every foolscap sheet. Every vehicle that had moved in the city was listed here under specific headings: TIME. REGISTRATION. DRIVER. NUMBER OF PASSENGERS. REASON FOR JOURNEY. The top of each report sheet carried the location of the particular roadblock.

What the hell was keeping Baumeister? Why didn't the fat sod answer the phone?

Fuchs had first directed his attention to the reports of vehicles moving towards the city centre, towards the border crossing point which the Americans had christened Checkpoint Charlie. Even to his trained eye, there seemed little suspicious in the lengthy records. Major Fuchs's nose twitched at nothing on the grubby pages that had made their way to his desk. And the trains, trams and buses had been physically searched: no fugitive Engländer there either.

What the hell was keeping Baumeister? Another minute of this waiting and *his* job might have to be reviewed.

It was when he turned to examine reports of vehicles exiting the city that Fuchs felt the familiar twitch in his nostrils. A single entry was incomplete: it was its very incompleteness that intrigued Fuchs. He'd tracked down the patrolman who had recorded only the time that the car, a green Trabant, had passed through his checkpoint. The policeman's nervousness had been evident on the phone, which was how Fuchs liked to keep it. A military convoy had been coming through, the patrolman explained, his voice edged with fear; it had been necessary to clear the way for the convoy, there hadn't been time to record all the details of the vehicle. *Hadn't been time? Couldn't the car have been pulled over? Was the officer a mongoloid idiot?* Panic in the patrolman's voice then, profuse apologies to the Herr Major but he *could* remember the occupants of the car . . . *So spit it out, man, spit it out.* A clergyman was driving the Trabi, he could remember the dog collar, from Bad Saarow, the fellow said, and there was a young girl in the passenger seat, Herr Major, he was certain of that too . . .

The coincidence was too great for Major Fuchs's twitching nostrils. Clergymen had never been so omnipresent: there was

245

that one in the apartment at Prenzlauer Berg, mouthing off so much that Fuchs had had to slap him around a bit – and now this other fellow in an incompletely checked car leaving the city. And Bad Saarow mentioned *twice*. The same fellow surely, Fuchs thought.

He decided against phoning the local police station. The usual clown on a bike wouldn't know much. Besides, Bad Saarow housed the Soviet sanatorium *and* the Institute of Cartography: a little fancy footwork never went amiss in the presence of brass and the Party's upper echelons.

So he'd called Baumeister.

And what the fuck was keeping the man?

'Herr Major, Baumeister here. How can I help you?'

'It's a matter of some urgency, Herr Baumeister, and I have been holding for quite some time.'

'Apologies, Herr Major. You will appreciate that our work here is also quite important.' *And don't you forget it, you yellow-eyed bastard.*

Fuchs took a moment before answering. Often it was the silence, the nothingness, that intimidated bureaucratic bastards like Baumeister.

'This is a matter of state security, personally authorized by the Minister.' The invocation of Erich Mielke, Minister for State Security, always worked wonders.

As it did now with Baumeister.

'I repeat, Herr Major, you have my apologies for the delay. Please, how can I help you?'

'A clergyman in Bad Saarow, tall fellow, skinny. What can you tell me about him?'

'A misguided idiot, like the rest of them. The Party is far too lenient—'

'Herr Deputy Director—'

'I think you are referring to a fellow called Bruck,' Baumeister cut in quickly. 'He is allowed the use of an old church not far from here and lives in a little cottage behind the church.'

'And he is in Berlin occasionally?'

'I have little knowledge of the pastor's activities but, yes, it so happens that I know he was in the city yesterday.'

'And how do you know that?'

'I understand that he gave a lift back from the city to a junior member of our staff here.'

In his excitement, Fuchs banged the telephone against his good ear. Baumeister could hear his exclamation of pain.

'Herr Major?'

'This member of staff – what's his name?'

'Herr Major, may I ask what this is about?'

'You may not.' *Too abrupt*, Fuchs reminded himself. Baumeister was not only the deputy head of the Institute, he was also leader of the Works Party Committee. 'Not at the moment, Herr Baumeister,' he added, more gently, 'but I will fill you in later. Now, this worker who travelled with this priest?'

'A young woman, Herr Major, name of Petra Ritter.'

Fuchs repeated the name, wrote it on the page before him, underlined it roughly with broad strokes.

'What can you tell me about this Ritter woman?'

'An unremarkable young trainee. She came here a few months ago, from Karl-Marx-Stadt, I seem to remember.'

'And politically?'

'In what way?'

'In the *only* way, Herr Baumeister.' Fuchs's voice was harsh. 'Is she a member of the Party?'

'No, Herr Major.'

'I'm surprised that you entrust such important work to non-Party members.' *Although, personally, I don't give a fuck who does your work but it's a pleasure to make your fat arse feel a little uncomfortable.*

'Fräulein Ritter,' Baumeister said, 'is merely a trainee and as such is entrusted only with the most basic work.'

'Has she displayed any reactionary tendencies? Made any anti-Party remarks?'

'Herr Major, I can assure you that, if she had, she would no longer be a member of my staff.'

'Thank you for your help, Herr Baumeister.'

'It's always a pleasure to be of assistance to a member of the State Security Service.'

Fuchs said goodbye and hung up. He turned slowly in his chair, still gentle with his throbbing head, and looked out through the plastic blinds at the neighbouring block in the Normannenstrasse complex. The entire complex belonged to the Ministry of State Security: more than a dozen grey buildings housing hundreds of tiny offices like his own, staffed by hundreds, even thousands, of operatives like himself. All of them, like himself, devoted to their cause. They were, as the Ministry itself proclaimed, 'the sword and shield of the Party'. And no Engländer, Fuchs told himself, would trifle with impunity with the bearers of that sword and shield. His nostrils were twitching like a water diviner's fork. *We're coming for you, Engländer. We're coming.*

In his office in Bad Saarow, Deputy Director Baumeister was also considering the implications of the intriguing phone call. Petra Ritter was in some kind of trouble, that was obvious. What concerned Baumeister was how to turn this trouble, whatever it was, to his personal advantage. In the end, of course, the girl would succumb; in the end, they all did. But a little caution was also advisable: Baumeister had no wish to be tainted in any way by association with anyone who, in Fuchs's words, had 'reactionary tendencies'. Caution must be his companion here, Baumeister told himself, but still, those young thighs had looked deliciously fresh and inviting . . .

Nobody knows anything, Petra Ritter told herself as she collected her coat and rucksack. And yet she couldn't quell the rising mix of fear and excitement inside her. Surely her colleagues, exchanging the usual muted farewells at the end of another silent working day, could read the nervousness in her face. *The guilt*. And yet there was just the usual softly spoken medley: *Auf Wiedersehen. Bis Morgen*. Until tomorrow.

She couldn't think that far ahead. She thought of him in the tiny cellar, wondered how long the night must have seemed, starless, in an unknown land. He'd be longing to hear a voice, as she longed to hear his.

The voice of the Deputy Director's secretary would not be quiet in her head. *The Ministry of State Security, Major Fuchs*. Whoever he was.

Nobody knows anything, she told herself again, as she left the drawing office and made her way to the exit. Old Herr Vos waved to her from behind his janitor's desk. She smiled in return. Not so old, just withered from the cancer that was killing him. *Why would I stay at home?* he'd said to her. His wife was dead, he was childless. *I might as well go to work while I can, Petra*. He'd taken a shine to her from the beginning: sometimes she went to his apartment, in the neighbouring block, to practise. It felt good to give pleasure with her playing; most of the time the girls she shared with objected to the 'noise'.

Johannes Vos waved to her again, a small guarded wave. You never knew who might be watching.

'Are you coming over to practise tonight, Petra?'

'I don't know. I'll see.'

She could see the disappointment in the faded eyes, in the faded features.

'I'll see,' she said again.

'You're always welcome, you know that.'

The exchange took only a few seconds, was spoken in little more than a whisper. You never knew who might be listening either.

She smiled at him and stepped out into the gathering dusk. The car park was almost empty. The rooks were noisy in the wood across the road, bedding down for another night. At least they could fly unhindered to another land, another resting place. *Enough*, she told herself. Get your bicycle and cycle home like anybody else at the end of a day's work. *Nobody knows anything*.

Minutes later, although she didn't know it, Franz Baumeister followed her cycling progress from behind the blinds of his office window. The Deputy Director used his binoculars to focus better on the pumping progress of her thighs, as she pedalled her way along the darkening road. He smiled to himself, adjusting the focus on the binoculars. *What goes around, comes around*.

Twenty-three

And yet, for all their longing, they circled each other warily in the windowless shed. Like coltish creatures, wanting to play, to frolic, but restrained by self-consciousness, by a kind of delicacy – perhaps even by the frightening depth of their mutual longing.

He'd been waiting for her all the day, watching the deserted garden world through the cracks in the planking. In the darkness, his heart seemed to heave when he saw her, wheeling the old-fashioned bike along the overgrown path. The dark woollen coat was buttoned up to the neck; the navy beret was jaunty over the cropped hair. He pushed the door open and she stepped inside quickly, lifting the bike so that it made no noise. He took it from her, rested it carefully against the wooden wall. She didn't quite close the door: they looked at each other in the sliver of light.

And the shyness seemed to catch at their hands, root them to the earthen floor. Their bodies bent towards each other, like saplings in a wind. His mouth brushed her cheek and they drew back from each other as though that wind had stirred again.

She took off the beret and her fingers teased at her short blond hair. For a second, her hair gleamed like pale gold in the thin shaft of light and Roland swallowed, breathless.

'Roland?'

'I was afraid you might not come.'

Outside the wind rose and a tree shook noisily. A rook cawed, hoarse, lonesome.

'Should we go down below?' Her voice was anxious like the unseen birds.

'Please,' he said, 'let's wait up here a little.'

His voice told her enough: the long day watching and listening, the minutes creeping by, the walls closing in on him.

'It must have been awful, stuck inside all night and all day.'

'It could be worse, Petra.' Her risk was as great as his – and needless.

'Is that what you say in Ireland – that it could be worse?'

'I never thought much about it.' His hands stroked her hair. 'But yes, I suppose that's what we say and think.'

'Here I think we feel the opposite.' Her voice was wistful. 'That it could be better.'

'I suppose we're both right.' Roland laughed. 'You're making me think about stuff I never thought about before.'

'I know,' she said, 'I know.'

She came to him then, release in her laugh, and his arms went round her. *Apples*, he thought. She smells of apples and flowers and if moonlight has a scent, then this is what it smells like.

'You smell like the moon,' he whispered. 'And you taste like the golden apples of the sun.'

She leaned back in his arms and swatted him gently with her beret.

'My Irish poet.'

'My German goddess.'

Her body seemed to fold itself to his and they clung to each other with a fierceness that neither had ever known.

When they parted, he fixed a plank on top of a pair of old oil drums and he brushed it with his hands. They sat together looking out through the chink in the door at the abandoned gardens, the dilapidated sheds.

'Our personal garden of Eden,' he whispered.

'It could be worse,' she told him.

Their hands met, their fingers interlocked. Their eyes sought the distant lights, a few of them, pale and dim on some faraway hill.

'Maybe we can get out together.'

His words seemed to hang above both them and the distant lights. Their fingers tightened; she leaned her head on his shoulder and he tried to draw her closer.

'Maybe,' she whispered.

She told him that she'd cycled to Pastor Bruck's cottage, that she'd spoken to his young son, Thomas. The pastor wasn't back from Berlin. She'd left no message, just that she'd called.

'I'm afraid to ask the pastor,' she said.

'Because he might refuse?'

'Because he *wouldn't* refuse.'

'But if we could both get out together?'

'Don't you see?' she said. 'If there were some way he could get both of us across the border, they'd trace it back to him, they know everything, and if they caught him . . .' He felt her tremble in his arms.

'Maybe we can find a way without him, Petra. If we had a map . . .'

She laughed. 'That's all we make in my section, nothing but maps. But they're useless, just fakes, nobody dares to say it out loud but I've heard the rumours – that they're for "disinformation", fakes that are leaked out somehow across the border.'

'But why would anybody do that?'

'Who knows what governments do or why they do it?' She

smiled at him. 'Now *you're* making *me* think of things I never thought of before.'

The lights on the distant hill blinked once and died. Maybe it was bedtime over there.

'I should be going,' she said. The other girls in the flat would be in bed by now. It wouldn't be a good idea to raise questions by going in very late.

But she didn't get up. She leaned closer to him on the plank.

'Tell me again about your home,' she said.

He laughed. 'But I told you last night.'

'I know.' She kissed him quickly. 'So tell me again – I want to know everything.'

He'd never talked so much about home. It was just the place you lived, where you slept, where meals appeared on the table. It was the place where your father showed his disappointment in you. Where Terry was forever trying to find his inhaler. Where your kid sisters were a pair of schoolgirl nuisances but you put up with them because, well, because they idolized you and didn't try to hide it.

Home was more than that when he began to tell her about it. The dark rooms and narrow staircase seemed somehow sprinkled with stardust, bathed in a soft glow and, as he whispered to her, it took him a while to figure out why. It was obvious, really: *she* was in those rooms now, he could hear her laughter in the kitchen at the end of the hallway, he could see her seated on the old leather sofa under the bay window in the sitting room, that blond head, dreaming on one of his mother's lacy antimacassars.

'You could play your violin all day,' he said, 'and I'd sit there with my eyes closed, like I was in heaven.'

'Liar!' She punched him in the ribs and they both laughed, but nervously: his words had painted a possibility.

'No,' he said at last. 'I mean it.'

'I know.'

She added that now was the first time she'd ever thought of leaving Germany.

'So many want to leave. They try to hide it from us but we see the news on West German television, we see the shootings and the killings at the Wall in Berlin.' She shook her head. 'It was never for me. I just wanted to get out of the orphanage and get the chance to study the violin. I thought maybe I'd be good enough to play with an orchestra in one of the smaller cities, nothing like Berlin or Leipzig.' She shook her head again. 'Leaving was never part of it. Why would I want to go away? I didn't know anybody anywhere else. And now . . .'

'And now,' Roland said, 'you've been fortunate enough to meet yours truly.'

'Don't laugh about it.'

'I'm sorry. I didn't mean to.' *I'm scared I'll lose you and I don't want to scare you by saying it.*

She said, 'I'm scared.'

He held her close for a while and their hearts seemed to beat together in the darkness.

He stood up. 'You *must* go, Petra.'

'I'll try to come tomorrow, maybe the pastor will have news.'

'And a map,' Roland whispered. 'We should make our own plans.'

'Yes, I'll get one somehow.' She turned to the bicycle. 'I'm a poor *Hausfrau* – I brought you a bottle of tea and some sandwiches and forgot to give them to you. I hope you like cold tea.'

'I love cold tea,' he said, putting the big glass bottle and the small brown-papered package on the plank.

'I wish I could bring you some hot food.'

He put his finger on her lips. 'Go – that's an order.'

'You sound like Herr Baumeister.' She shivered. 'I shouldn't have mentioned him.'

'But—'

'No.' It was her turn to put a finger on his mouth. 'Kiss me and send me away.'

It was a gentle kiss.

He watched from the door of the shed as she tiptoed along the path, wheeling the old Diamant bike. A cloud hid the moon and, when it had passed, she was gone.

After midnight. The complex of apartment blocks silent, shut down for another night, although lights still burned in a window here and there. Fuchs eyed these few scattered lights with professional interest. Insomniacs, he thought, night creatures like himself. Or maybe those whose troubled consciences kept them awake.

In the block outside which he had parked the unmarked blue Trabant, only a single window was illuminated – one of the guest apartments, reserved for visiting dignitaries to the Cartography Institute or, occasionally, to the Soviet sanatorium. He'd checked before leaving Normannenstrasse: no guests were expected this week in Bad Saarow. So: it had to be Baumeister. Like all the other keepers-of-the-keys to these guest apartments throughout the state, he probably used the place as his private knocking shop. With any luck, Fuchs told himself, he might occasion a case of coitus interruptus.

He closed the car door quietly and had a quick look around for any twitching blinds or curtains. For a moment he stood, head cocked, listening to the night. From the road, the coughing noise of a motorbike engine; from behind the ring of apartment blocks, the wheeze of trees in the light wind. He padded quietly towards the entrance, stopping beside the white Wartburg, parked at the front door. The registration plate was the one he'd checked at the office. *Arrogant shit: the fat frog didn't even bother to conduct his nocturnal activities with a little discretion.* Discretion perhaps was not necessary when your spouse was a cowed dumpling like Frau Baumeister. She'd been in a pale dressing gown, her greying hair tied up in some kind of net, when she'd opened the door to Fuchs, who hadn't even bothered to say who he was or to present his ID. Her husband wasn't home, she said, and, no, she didn't know where he was.

Fuchs wondered if it might be worthwhile letting the old lady know where the Herr Deputy Director was. Probably not. If he were married to the old cow, he wouldn't give a flying fuck either.

He took a ring of keys from his pocket, careful not to let them jangle, and set about opening the hall door. It didn't take long. He eased the door shut behind him and stood a moment in the dark, letting the entrance hall materialize out of the gloom. A corridor to left and right. A glass case on the wall: Rules and Regulations of Apartment House A, signed by somebody-or-other. Even in the gloom, the tiled floors shone, polished by somebody-or-other.

In front of him, the polished staircase also shone.

The apartment was on the first floor, its brown door facing the top of the staircase.

Fuchs tiptoed to the door and stood there listening. A pale crack of light escaped from under the door but Fuchs could hear nothing. Sometimes you kicked a door in but, on occasions like this, you tapped. And tapped again, just a little louder.

'Who's there?' The voice irritated.

'*Staatssicherheitsdienst.*' State Security: *give them something to be properly irritated about.*

A bolt drawn, a chain unloosed.

Baumeister stood there, squinting into the darkness.

'Major Fuchs?'

Fuchs stepped past him, into a spacious living room. Institutional furniture, brown sofa, brown wood, a silent television set in the corner. From the opposite corner, the room's only light, a small standard lamp that seemed only to lend the room a kind of semi-darkness. The door to the bedroom was closed.

'Are you alone, Baumeister?'

'Yes, I'm alone.' There was a sheen of sweat on the fellow's forehead, above the bulging eyes. 'Why? What's going on?'

Fuchs didn't answer. He swept the room again with his yellow eyes, saw the armchair drawn up beside the big window with the Venetian blinds, and understood.

'Herr Deputy Director,' he said, 'you are spying on someone. Someone in the apartments opposite us.' *And I know who, I found that out also before I left the office: your trainee who shares a flat in Block H.*

Baumeister blinked, wiped his forehead with a large white handkerchief. *What was this all about?*

'After your phone call, Major, I thought it might be a good idea to keep an eye on Fräulein Ritter, the trainee I mentioned to you. I have no idea what this is about, of course, but I'm always happy to lend my support to the security services so I've been keeping an eye on her comings and goings tonight. You never know, Major Fuchs, you never know.'

But I think we know you're interested in fucking this particular trainee, Baumeister. Aloud Fuchs said, 'And?'

'And what?'

'What *are* her comings and goings tonight?'

'She went out earlier, with her bicycle.'

'*When* earlier?'

'About eight thirty.'

'Eight thirty?'

'About—'

'But that's four hours ago.'

'Yes—'

'Is she sleeping with anybody around here?'

'Not that I know of, Major.'

Fuchs glared at him. 'She lives in that block opposite us, yes?'

'Yes.' Baumeister wiped his forehead again. He sank into the armchair under the window and looked up at Fuchs. 'I watched her wheel the bicycle out of that door across from us about eight thirty and I've been watching for her return.'

Fuchs shook his head. *Where do they grow these morons?*

'Baumeister,' he said very slowly, 'does Block H have a back door?'

'Yes, Major, but she went out of the front door.'

'Herr Deputy Director,' Fuchs said, 'you are a fucking idiot.'

Fuchs was on his way out of the apartment before Baumeister could answer. He could hear Baumeister wheezing in his wake as he hurried down the darkened stairs and out of the apartment block. Not a frog, he thought, an elephant lumbering noisily behind as he crossed the car park to Block H. He could tell the fat fuck to wait outside but Fuchs himself didn't know what this Ritter woman looked like.

'Quiet!' Fuchs was trying his keys in the front door of Block H. 'D'you want to tell the world our business?'

The keys slipped from his fingers and jangled on the stone step. As he bent to retrieve them, Fuchs fancied he heard an answering metallic echo from within. He put his hand protectively to his wounded ear. *So now you're hearing things.*

Some gentle manipulation with the next key did the trick. The entrance hall in Block H was less spacious than the one they had left: a narrower entry, an absence of marble, as befitted the lower-grade workers who shared these apartments. In the gloom, past the staircase, Fuchs could see a line of bicycles in the passageway that led to the back door.

Baumeister was reaching for the light switch when Fuchs caught his wrist.

'No lights, Baumeister. Which apartment is the girl's?'

'Number eleven, on the third floor.'

The third floor was at the top of the block. The door to number 11 was the same nondescript brown as the other three doors on the dark corridor.

'Leave the talking to me, Baumeister. Your job is just to point out this Ritter person.' *Except she's not here to point out so we'll just sit and wait until she gets back and tells us where she's been . . .*

Once more he busied himself with his all-purpose keys, more gently this time. The lock yielded first time.

Another long, gloomy hallway. A broom leaning against the wall, beside it an old-fashioned mop in a metal bucket. The lingering smell of cabbage and fried potatoes mixed with the scent of cheap perfume. The kitchen at the end of the corridor was doorless: lidded saucepans rested on top of the cooker; a couple of unwashed plates, the remains of a meal still visible, stood on the worktop beside the cooker.

The bathroom door was open. Fuchs glanced at Baumeister, saw how his bulging eyes lingered on the line of panties and bras drying above the bath. Fuchs turned away, not bothering to hide his disgust.

The apartment seemed to exhale its own silence, a kind of whispered breathing. They're awake, Fuchs thought, behind these closed bedroom doors, afraid to stir, thinking they've got an intruder on the premises.

He pushed the nearest door, reached immediately for the light switch. A fat girl in a flimsy nightdress was sitting up in the bed, staring at him, her fingers twisted in a knuckle-white grip around the thin blanket.

'Don't scream,' Fuchs said. He flashed his security ID and looked at Baumeister.

'She works in the printing area,' Baumeister said, shaking his head.

Fuchs was already pushing in the next bedroom door. The light was on here, the middle-aged woman wrapped in a thread-bare dressing gown and sitting on the bed as if nocturnal visits were part of her routine. Her features were Slav.

She spoke her name without waiting to be asked.

'I'm a cook in the hospital, sir,' she added.

'Go back to sleep,' Fuchs said. 'We are not here.'

The woman got off the bed to close her door when they stepped out into the hall. *I don't want to know you're here*.

Fuchs paused outside the last door, Baumeister breathing heavily beside him. The hallway was still unlit; already the cracks of light under the other two doors had disappeared. So, he said to himself, she is here or she is not here. *And I'm not even sure why I'm here*. But his nose had that familiar twitch.

He turned to Baumeister.

'Go,' he said. 'Wait for me outside.'

Baumeister made as if to protest, then thought better of it. He nodded and waddled his way out of the flat.

Fuchs opened the door quickly, and switched on the light.

She had short blond hair and big bluish eyes. Fuchs couldn't see anything else: she had the blankets pulled up tight against her chin. He flashed his Stasi card, flung the question at her.

'Your name?'

She told him.

'Where do you work?'

There was more of the same, a volley of short questions with short answers. She kept the big blue eyes focused on Fuchs and, the blanket pressed almost to her mouth. Fuchs saw the fear in the big eyes, wondered how to corner it. There was more than fear in the beautiful face on the pillow, an edge of resistance.

'You went out tonight, Frau Ritter?'

'For a spin, sir. I went out cycling.'

'What time did you come back?'

'A while ago, sir, I was sleeping . . .'

She was lying, holding something back.

She doesn't know how much or how little I know. Let her go on not knowing.

'Go back to sleep,' he said.

He switched the light off, closed the door, left her lying there, staring into the darkness. She heard his voice again, reedy and whiny, and then the door of the flat was pulled shut.

Her body was trembling. It had been trembling all the time the questions had been coming, the strange yellow eyes boring into her. She'd been half ready for them, she'd heard the doors opening, her flatmates' voices. The noise of the keys had alerted her, just as she'd come in the back door. She'd been leaning her bicycle against the staircase when she'd heard it, the jangling sound of metal on stone, low voices outside the front door. Her own fear told her that whatever it was, *whoever* it was, coming for her. She'd almost given herself away, the bike slipping against the wall with a grating, scraping noise. But she'd made it, up the stairs, quietly into the flat, her bedroom door closing behind her soundlessly. *Lucky*. And maybe it wasn't her they'd been searching for. *They*. She was sure the other voice had been Baumeister's. Agatha would tell her, Baumeister was often in the printing works.

She could hear sounds from the other rooms. The girls would want to talk, questions swirling in the cigarette smoke in the kitchen. She wondered if *he* was asleep yet; she'd have to get another blanket to him somehow, the nights were cold now, even chillier under the ground.

She got out of bed, took her coat off, took the dark beret from under her pillow. She moved quickly now, undressing, getting into her pyjamas, preparing herself to share in the questioning, the wondering *what was that all about?*

Twenty-four

She knew she was being watched all next day. She could feel those yellow eyes boring into the back of her neck as she bent over her drawing board, following her to the canteen, to the lavatory, wherever she moved in the Institute of Cartography.

But when she dared to turn round, there was no one there. She *knew* there was nobody there. And yet.

It was hard to explain, even to herself: to feel constantly watched and yet so utterly abandoned.

Baumeister stood a moment beside her during his customary morning tour of the Institute. It was even more chilling when he moved away without saying a word, without contriving to touch her on some pretext. It was the first time this had ever happened. Frau Krug looked across the room at her, her look inscrutable.

She was leaving the building after work when Johannes Vos fell into step beside her, breathing heavily. She slowed down as they walked together across the car park towards the bicycle shelter.

'Will you come tonight, Petra? Gladden the heart of this old wreck?'

She half turned to look at him. A perverse rosy sheen seemed to cling to Johannes' parchmenty skin.

'You should be at home, Johannes,' she said quietly.

'Don't.' He touched her arm. 'You'll come and play for me tonight?'

'Yes.'

'Good. We'll have *Reibekuchen* and apple sauce.'

Johannes turned away towards his car, an old grey Lada that shone as if it were new. He'd told her once that he was going to leave it to her and she'd blushed, told him not to be silly. 'Who else would I leave it to?' he'd said. 'Since my wife died you're the only one who comes here.' She hadn't known what to say, just tucked the violin under her jaw and started into Mozart.

The Lada was ahead of her as she exited the car park on her bicycle. She swung left, heading towards home. She ached for him, longed to go in the opposite direction, to the cell in the ground, but she couldn't risk it. Not today, with the invisible eyes following her. Even the church was out of bounds: Pastor Bruck didn't deserve any further involvement.

The apartment was empty when she got home. She tidied up, getting rid of the traces of the night before. It had been a long night, whispers, giggles, even laughter to hide the fear, the Stasi ID actually brandished in their apartment. Two saucers full of crushed cigarette butts told how long the night had been.

When she was finished in the kitchen, she lay, fully dressed, under the quilt on her bed. Her exhaustion wasn't the kind that brought sleep. She stared at the white ceiling but it was his face she saw, the dark hair, the strong jaw, stubbly now, unshaven. Until a few days ago she had not known of the existence of Roland Feldmann; now, it seemed, her world revolved around him.

Darkness seeped into the room. She got up and for a moment she watched, through the window, the darkening world outside. Involuntarily she trembled. Her flatmates were still not back, the apartment seemed empty, cheerless. She reminded herself once more that she couldn't risk going to the garden shed. *And he needs a blanket, the nights are cold now*. She closed the curtains, drew on her coat, picked up the violin. She'd eat *reibekuchen* with Johannes Vos and play for him. Maybe her playing would, somehow, ease the pain of his knowing that the cancers inside him were slowly but inexorably killing him. Maybe, just maybe, the music would ease the loneliness of Johannes Vos. And of herself.

The sound of the twig snapping under his foot was like a gunshot, like the sharp explosion of noise back in the flat in Prenzlauer Berg. He paused in mid-stride, willing himself into stillness, listening to the sounds of the wood. Darkness was falling on the trees, bare branches etched starkly against the darkening sky. He sniffed the air: woodsmoke from some unseen chimney beyond the trees, beyond the allotments.

He'd gone as far as he dared from the shed, moving deeper among the trees, away from the road. He'd stumbled on to a dirt track and had to scurry back into the undergrowth when he'd heard someone coming. He'd watched, hardly daring to breathe, as a fat figure in winter coat and boots passed within yards of his hiding place, humming to himself.

The coat reminded him of how cold he felt. The old coat that Pastor Bruck had handed to him from Martha's wardrobe was a threadbare thing. It wasn't much of a blanket either but he'd found a length of old carpet in one of the abandoned sheds and left it to air, spread out over a couple of planks in the hut that had become his home. It wasn't much but it was better than nothing: he'd wrap it round himself on the makeshift bed tonight.

Cold and hungry. Heat and food. Things you took for granted. You only missed them when you were hiding out in a strange country, waiting for a beautiful girl who was risking her life to help you. Still, he hoped she'd come. The bread and stringy chicken were long eaten, the cold tea gone too. *She'd come if she could.*

When he got back to the shed, he shook out the length of carpet, in the night air. He prowled the confines of the shed, flapping his arms to keep warm. He wrapped himself in the carpet, kept the door ajar and watched the night deepen over the broken roofs and the leafless trees. Lights twinkled on the distant hills, now and then the headlights of a car cut their way through the night, remote, unknown.

Once he heard the distant drone of a plane, to the west, perhaps over Berlin, and he remembered Pastor Bruck's words, about trouble in Cuba, about a face-off in Berlin. The drone in the sky died away. *What do I care about Cuba, about Ingham's machinations in Berlin?* After a while he knew that she wasn't coming, that she couldn't come, but he went on sitting there anyway, huddled in the length of carpet: there was nothing else he could do except go on waiting, watching the darkness.

Twenty-five

The summons was as abrupt as usual.

'Major Fuchs? In my office in five minutes.'

Colonel Gunter Neiber didn't wait, ever, for his subordinates to reply when he phoned. Orders were for obeying, not for discussion.

Within a minute Fuchs was crossing the open space from Block 7, where he had his office, to the HQ Block. His uniform made no difference here: he still had to produce his ID and wait for the sergeant on duty to get telephone clearance before he was permitted to mount the stairs to the second floor, from where Colonel Neiber controlled his Special Investigations (Counter-Espionage, Internal) Unit.

Fuchs's attitude to the HQ Block was ambivalent. Like every ambitious officer he longed for a desk here, close to the centre of power; and, like most officers, a summons here was a call he dreaded. His ear was playing up again, his headache was worse.

And Neiber left him standing in the corridor outside his office, like he always did. Neiber's assistant, an owlish, bespectacled fellow, told him curtly to wait before going back to his typewriter. A fucking cissy, Fuchs decided; put him in the field and he'd be looking for his *mutti*, no chance he'd survive an ashtray against his ear.

He heard voices from the inner office, the doorknob stirred

from within. The owlish assistant looked at the door, a hint of panic on his face, and leapt to his feet as the door swung open.

Erich Mielke, Minister of State Security, stood in the doorway, Colonel Neiber beside him.

Fuchs watched, breathless, as the two men shook hands.

'I'll take care of it, sir.' Neiber's tone had none of its usual barked arrogance.

Mielke nodded and turned away. He nodded again at the owlish lieutenant but said nothing as he stepped out into the corridor. Fuchs was standing rigidly at attention, his gaze firmly fixed on some invisible spot on the opposite wall.

'Major Fuchs, I think?'

'Yes, sir.'

Mielke stepped closer. Fuchs could smell the cigarettes on his breath, mixed with a sweetish aftershave.

'That's an ugly-looking wound on your ear.'

'It's – it's nothing, sir, nothing at all.'

'I hope the other fellow came off worse, Major Fuchs.'

He felt the blush spreading right up past his fucking ear.

'Yes, sir.' It came out in a croak.

Mielke grunted then turned away.

Fuchs was still standing to attention, still studying his point on the corridor wall, when he heard Neiber's voice.

'Come on, Fuchs, we haven't got all day!' The colonel was again his commanding self.

Fuchs followed the colonel into his office. He had no doubt that his name had come up between Neiber and Mielke; he was certain, too, that Mielke would by now have read his report of the incident in Prenzlauer Berg.

Neiber motioned for him to sit.

'A disgrace,' Neiber said without preamble. 'One of our officers assaulted by a foreigner in this very city! And then the bastard gets away! What kind of officer permits this to happen?'

Neiber had chosen to remain on his feet, perhaps the better to hurl his fury down at his subordinate. Fuchs couldn't meet the colonel's furious glare and found himself studying Neiber's substantial uniformed midriff.

'We have an emergency on our hands, on our doorstep. The Americans have backed down in Cuba but Berlin has not seen so many of their tanks since the war. And right here in our midst we have some fucking British agent running loose because you let him go!' Colonel Neiber paused in his tirade. His great stomach seemed to swell before Fuchs's yellow eyes. 'Well, what have you to say for yourself?'

'He took me unawares, sir—'

'Unawares! You are an officer of the *Staatssicherheit*, Fuchs, you are not there to be taken *unafuckingwares*!'

'I am following a line of inquiry, sir.' Before his eyes the belly expanded, seemed to drop, then moved away.

'Tell me.'

At least the fat fucker is in his chair, behind his desk.

Fuchs told him.

Neiber stared across the desk at him. The colonel's head was bald; the entire shiny crown of his head seemed to move as his thin eyebrows went up.

'A priest in Bad Saarow,' he said sceptically, 'a trainee map-maker who wishes to be a violinist – this is your line of inquiry?'

'I just have a feeling, sir. Some things fit. And Bad Saarow . . .' He paused, uncertain.

'Bad Saarow, what?'

'The Cartography Institute, sir, maybe . . .'

'Maps.' Neiber was thoughtful, fingering his jowls. 'We still don't know what this fellow Weber was trying to hand over to the British?'

'No, sir.'

'And that's another thing, Fuchs, why did you have to kill the fucker before he talked?'

'He came at me with a knife, sir.'

'And I suppose you were taken unawares again,' Neiber said drily. 'I'll give you a couple of days to follow up your line of inquiry. Half of our units are looking for this bloody Engländer, Fuchs, but I hope you understand that there's a good chance you'll soon be chasing reactionary adolescents.'

'Yes, sir.' The message was clear: come up with something or you'll be reduced to hunting pimpled students who listen to fucking Western pop music.

The colonel waved him away. He didn't even look as Fuchs backed out of his office.

Twenty-six

'You!' She was in the middle of an after work crowd, almost at the main exit, when she heard the voice, recognized it from the rapid-fire questions in her bedroom.

The group of women paused to look at the man standing outside the door but it was at her alone that the strange eyes were staring. The others glanced at her, then with obvious relief turned away and hurried out into the evening.

She moved to the side of the corridor. Workers streamed past, heads studiously averted from the Stasi ID card that Fuchs was holding up. He closed it slowly, reluctantly, then pointed a finger back along the green corridor. He said nothing but she could feel his footsteps at her heels. In an instant the whole building seemed to have emptied: just two pairs of footsteps echoed in the silence.

She felt his hand on her elbow and tried not to shiver. He steered her down the metal staircase, to the basement. Their footsteps were louder on the stone floor. The ceiling was lower here, the walls blank. This was where the maintenance staff kept their tools, behind the closed doors. The stinging smell of cleaning chemicals clung to the walls, the sour tang of old mops and buckets. And the silence of the building seemed deeper than ever.

His fingers were on her elbow again, forceful this time, halting her at a door almost at the end of the corridor.

Fuchs pushed open the door. A feeble bulb inside a metal cage on the ceiling lent a dim light to the small room. An old printing press had been pushed against one wall, its entrails still dark with congealed ink. Trays of faded metal print slugs were stacked haphazardly alongside. A metal-legged table filled the corner, a chair with three legs upended on top. The room smelled musty, as though it had not been opened for a long time.

The air of abandonment pleased Fuchs. It was a forgotten place. A place for the forgotten.

But not a place that would be forgotten. Least of all by this piece with the blue eyes and the cropped blond hair and the violin case swinging in her hand as if she were a schoolgirl heading off to a lesson.

She'd learn a different lesson here.

'Sit.' Petra felt herself pushed into the chair.

The discovery of the old easy chair had also pleased Fuchs. Its high seat of worn leather and its pair of flat wooden arms seemed almost to have been specially designed for his purposes.

'Now, Fräulein Ritter, we will conduct an experiment, you and I.' He noted the look of alarm on her face with satisfaction. 'You and I will perform our very own lie-detector test, under the strictest laboratory conditions.'

The nicotine-stained teeth he flashed at her seemed of a piece with his strange eyes; when she flinched in the chair, he nodded in approval.

'There is nothing to fear, Fräulein Ritter.' His voice was a whisper. 'The truth will set you free, as they say. Untruths alone will keep you chained – and worse.'

As he spoke, Fuchs was securing her left arm to the arm of the chair with two short straps that he had taken from his black briefcase. He buckled two more straps round her right forearm. He eased the straps so that the buckles did not touch her skin.

'Comfy, Fräulein Ritter? We don't want you hurt – at least not unnecessarily.'

Another flash of the stained teeth, another mouthful of sour breath in her face.

'Your legs,' he said, and she flinched again, drawing them tightly together.

Fuchs nodded. 'Whatever is between your legs, Fräulein Ritter, is of no interest to me. I just want you firmly settled in your seat so that we can proceed with our lie-detector test.' His hand moved, drew the hem of her skirt further down over her knees. 'Better?'

She tried to swallow, nodded at him. *Humour him. Think of Roland. No, think of something else, of music, get Roland out of your mind. Lest you betray him.*

Fuchs pushed a small table against the left arm of her chair and drew her hand towards him. He looked at her slowly, deliberately, then splayed her fingers flat on the tabletop.

'For the detection of lies, Fräulein Ritter. Ready?'

She nodded.

'It is necessary that your answers are spoken aloud.' With his foot he drew his briefcase closer to his own chair, facing her. 'Do you understand?'

'Yes. Yes, sir.'

'Your name is Petra Ritter?'

'Yes.'

'Your job is?'

'A trainee cartographer, sir.'

'You like this job to which you have been assigned by the state?'

'Yes, sir.'

275

'Yes – but you were in Berlin for a test, an audition, is that not so, three days ago?'

She stammered, looked at Fuchs, at her fingers splayed on the dirty tabletop.

'I can't hear you, Fräulein Ritter.'

'Yes, sir.' A whisper.

'I can't hear you!'

'Yes, sir!'

'You are raised by our state in an orphanage, you are assigned to useful work, and you are ungrateful for this?'

'No.'

'But you sought an audition in Berlin – to do what?'

She looked away from the yellow eyes, saw only the discarded machinery, the abandoned tools.

'To study the violin, sir.'

'Ah, the violin.' Leaning back in his chair now, arms folded, shaking his head. 'The state assigns you to valuable work but *you* know better, Fräulein Ritter.' Another shake of the head, mournful, disappointed with this ungrateful child. 'Is that not so?'

'No, sir, it's just . . .' She couldn't go on.

'It's just that you are lying to me, Fräulein Ritter, and this is a lie-detector test.'

She bit her lip. She had never been in a place so remote, so empty, so full of menace.

'You like the violin?'

'Yes, sir.'

'This is your violin?' He picked up the case, laid it across his knees, his thumbs on the metal catches.

'Yes, sir.'

'You bought it?' He snapped the catches open.

'No, sir. A teacher at the orphanage gave it to me, he taught me to play.'

'You fucked him, Fräulein Ritter?' Fuchs lifted the instrument from the case, gripped it by the neck. 'You fucked this reactionary teacher and he gave you this violin because he liked the way you fucked him?'

'No, sir.'

'No? No? You lie to my face, Fräulein Ritter?'

'No—'

Fuchs swung the violin by the neck and smashed it against the edge of the table.

She screamed.

She went on screaming until Fuchs struck her across the face with his open palm.

At her feet lay the shattered violin, its torn strings like severed arteries above a gutted carcass. She struggled against the straps around her arms, opened her mouth as if to scream again.

Fuchs struck her once more, harder. Her nose hurt. She tasted blood on her lips.

'We understand each other, Fräulein Ritter?'

'Yes, sir.' Spitting blood through her words.

Fuchs leaned over her, wiped her mouth with a dirty handkerchief.

'Who did you meet in Berlin?'

'Sir, the teachers at the Academy, the examiners.'

'Who else?'

'Pastor Bruck, sir, he gave me a lift to the city.'

'The priest?'

'Yes, sir.'

'And coming home?'

'Yes, sir, I came home with him too.' *It's coming now, the question. Think about music, about your unbroken violin.*

'Who else was in the car?'

'Nobody, sir, just myself and Pastor Bruck.'

Fuchs had his briefcase on his knees. Slowly he drew from it a short-handled hammer and laid it on the table beside her hand. She could feel the coldness of the grey metal hammerhead against her little finger.

'Fräulein Ritter, who else was in the car with you and the priest?'

'Just me and the Pastor—'

The hammer was in his grip, was swinging downwards in a blur of slow-motion speed, and her fingers seemed smashed like sausages on the tabletop. For a split second her brain refused to countenance what her eyes saw: her hand melded to the table, shattered, mushy, blood seeping from under her nails and spreading around her flesh, the white flesh and slender bones now blue fading to black.

She didn't know she was screaming.

And then she knew, when Fuchs struck her across the face.

She went on screaming anyway, even when he struck her again. She struggled with her right arm against the strap, bellowed in her pain. Fuchs was roaring at her but the pain screaming in her brain was louder and that pain was shrilling out of her open mouth.

She tried to stand. The chair turned over and she went with it, tumbling to the floor, the armchair strapped to her arms like a carapace. The broken violin was at her face on the stone floor, Fuchs's brown shoes were at her head and his voice was still shouting, distant, angry, invading her pain.

Now there was another voice.

'What's this about?' She knew the shoes, knew the voice.

'Herr Deputy Director, this is a security matter. Stay out of it.'

'Major Fuchs –' She strained to hear Baumeister's words, low, diffident. 'Major, I would never interfere in security matters but please, consider, I mean, the girl will scream the building down, everyone will hear, and anyway she looks half dead . . .'

She knew they were looking down at her, on her knees, her head bent to the stone floor. The chair astride her back.

'Herr Deputy Director, you are right.' *You don't need Colonel Neiber asking you once more, why did you have to kill the fucker anyway?* 'You're right,' Fuchs said again. 'We can continue our examination of this suspect in Normannenstrasse.'

The brown shoes and the black shoes stayed beside her head, beside her wounded hand, while the discussion went on. Remote, in the far distance above her.

'You wish to take her to Berlin now, Herr Major?'

'Perhaps not.' *This is your line of inquiry, Major Fuchs? A screaming girl, who needs a fucking doctor?* 'No,' Fuchs went on. 'Not today. Just get the bitch out of here.'

She heard Baumeister's grunting, smelled his face beside her own. She heard him say that he was going to loosen the belts and help her to her feet. She shut her eyes, let him do it, was even grateful for his pudgy-fingered touch.

When she was on her feet she saw that the man with the yellow eyes was gone. Major Fuchs, Baumeister had called him. His black briefcase was gone, so were the belts and the metal hammer.

The pain in her battered hand was not gone.

'Here.' Baumeister was holding out a faded white handkerchief to her. 'Wrap it round your hand.'

She took the handkerchief in her right hand, tried to shake it open. Baumeister took it, unfolded it. Petra held her hand out to him and she saw him flinch before the pulped mess of flesh.

'Wrap it tight,' she said. 'Please.'

His own fat hands trembled as he wound the white cloth round the bloody mess.

'Thank you, Herr Baumeister.'

'You're welcome.' He didn't look at her. *I don't need this kind of shit in my Institute, not even if it is Stasi shit; you never know how it can come back to haunt you.* 'Let's go.'

'In a moment,' she said.

What was the bitch doing, back down on her knees?

'My violin.'

Christ.

He got down beside her, gathered up the broken bits of the fucking violin and managed to squeeze them into the case. *She'll be playing fuck-all violins with that hand.* He snapped the case shut, hauled himself to his feet.

'Thank you,' she said again. Her right hand was wrapped round her left, blood already darkening the white handkerchief.

He turned away and she followed him out of the room, along the corridor and up the stairs.

He held the main door open for her. The night was black, starless. Footsteps came hurrying towards them across the deserted car park. Johannes Vos came out of the gloom, his doomed face paler than usual.

'Vos! What are you doing here?'

The caretaker ignored Baumeister. He was looking at Petra, at the way she was cradling her left hand, at the blood seeping through the twisted cloth.

She leaned towards him, almost fell into the arm he reached around her. With his other hand he took the violin case from Baumeister.

'I've got her, sir,' he said. 'I'll deal with it.'

Baumeister looked at them both, wondering. He shrugged, turned back inside the building. He didn't need this shit. He didn't look back at Vos and the girl making their way across the car park to the ancient, shiny Lada.

'Johannes,' she said, 'what are you doing here?'

'I saw that weird-looking fellow taking you downstairs and I just thought I should wait around for you.'

She started to weep, her body trembling.

'Let it out, Petra,' Johannes Vos said, 'let it out, it'll do you good.'

Twenty-seven

Slowly her eyes became accustomed to the darkness, to the shapes and shadows in Johannes' living room. She didn't want to switch on the light. The door to Johannes' bedroom was half-open: she could imagine him resisting sleep, listening, in case she needed him. He'd wanted her to take the bedroom but she'd insisted: he'd done enough, more than enough; the sofa was fine. He'd fussed gently. He made tea, produced a flannel nightdress that had belonged to his wife, plumped the pillows on the sofa, tucked the blankets around her. He'd kissed her on the forehead. 'Call me if you need anything.' She'd never had a father. Roland had a father who didn't know where he was. And Johannes and his dead wife had shared a childless life. *Life.*

She eased herself into a sitting position on the sofa. She could just make out the clock on the old sideboard: ten past one. So she'd slept a while, despite the throbbing pain, the smashed fingers. And she'd woken, despite the sleeping tablet.

'Painkillers,' Johannes had told the doctor. 'And something to help her sleep.'

The doctor's fear had been evident. *What kind of workplace accident left a hand shattered like this? And brought an elderly cancer patient to your private apartment after hours?* The old man had been insistent, as though his own mortal illness had lent him authority.

So the doctor had cleaned the wound, injected the mangled flesh, handed over aspirin and a couple of sleeping tablets, dressed and strapped the useless fingers. Only the thumb and the index finger of the left hand had escaped the alleged 'workplace accident'; the other digits would be crippled for life. He'd caught his wife at the study door, saw the alarm on her thin features and shooed her away. Better not to know some things. And he wanted neither thanks nor payment: just get this doomed old man and this wounded young creature out of his home so he could get on with his life of not knowing things that were best not known.

She was dressed when she heard Johannes stirring in the bedroom. He padded into the living room and switched on a small lamp. The bedroom slippers and the striped dressing gown made him look older, closer to death.

'It's late.' His voice seemed hoarse. 'You don't have to leave, Petra.'

'I have to go somewhere, Johannes.'

'You're not going to your apartment?'

'No.'

'It's after one o'clock in the morning, Petra. It's not good to be out.'

'I know.' *He needs a blanket, food.*

'Maybe you should wait until morning.'

'The dark is better.' *And I need him.*

Johannes' pale, rheumy eyes met hers. He smiled.

'Do what you have to do.' He hadn't asked about what had happened in the basement. 'Just be careful.'

'I need some things, Johannes, a blanket—'

'Don't.' He raised a hand. 'You're welcome to take whatever you need, Petra, but it's better to tell me nothing.'

'A blanket, some food, tea.'

'Whatever you need, just take it.'

'And I'd like to come back here, I don't want to go back to my apartment yet.'

'You know you can stay as long as you like.' Another ghostly smile, his face like faded paper in the half-light. 'I'll put the kettle on for the tea.'

He made the tea while she rolled a thin blanket up tight enough to fit into her rucksack. He added sugar and a little milk, poured it into a thick bottle and plugged it with a strong cork. He handed her a second container, of metal, sealed with a screw-on cap.

'Maybe this will help. I heated some soup.'

'I've taken some of your bread and cheese.'

Johannes smiled his wan smile. 'Whatever I have is yours.'

'I'm putting you in danger, I think.'

'What's danger to me, Petra?'

He eased the straps of the rucksack over her wounded hand, settled the rucksack on her back.

'I can come with you if you like.'

'No, Johannes, I have to do this alone.'

'Yes, some things must be done alone.'

He turned the light off before he eased the door of the flat open. He checked the dark corridor before motioning for her to go.

'Be careful. Come back safe.'

She felt his fingers on her hair as she stepped past him and tiptoed down the stairs and out into the night.

A night still starless, the sky heavy with low-hanging clouds. Afterwards, when it was all over, when she was almost alone again, her trek along the path and through the trees would seem to her like a dimly remembered magical odyssey. She made no conscious attempt at caution yet she seemed to glide silently along the dirt track. No twig cracked underfoot. No branch snapped against her. The cloudy night lent her a cloak of blackness. Her own eager heart lent her speed. Snatches of music hummed in her head: Beethoven's *Romance*, Mendelssohn's *Wedding March*. Petra knew, instinctively, that she would never trip a bridal progress along any church aisle but, in some strange way, this journey along a wooded path was her own wedding march, the only one she would ever have. The organ played in her head, the choir sang in the night branches.

She tiptoed across the wooden footbridge. The disused allotment sheds looked like abandoned kayaks upturned on a desolate shore. Her own breathing sounded loud in the silent night. She tapped lightly on the door of the shed, whispered his name.

When the door creaked open, they stared at each other. He drank in the turquoise eyes, the blond hair, the bandaged hand. She saw the gauntness of him, the hunted look behind the unshaven face.

They whispered names and she stepped inside the shed and Roland pushed the door shut and they clung to each other. They parted and he lifted her hand gently, and she led him deeper into the shed, down the ladder. She saw the strip of carpet spread on the bed, the emptiness of the dungeon-like space, and she shushed him.

'Eat,' she said, opening the container of soup, 'eat, you look famished.'

He sipped it first, still hot from the can, and then he drank it down in noisy mouthfuls. The can was almost empty when he saw the spoon in her hand.

'I'm sorry,' he said. 'My mother would kill me for eating like that.'

'You're not to do it again,' she said with mock sternness.

'Only when I'm starving,' he told her. 'And only when I haven't seen you for an eternity.'

'You have to go.' Her eyes filled up. 'You have to try to get out, Roland.'

He took her hand, lightly kissed the bandaged fingers. 'Tell me what happened.'

She left out the worst of it but he seemed to feel it anyway: in the flat in Prenzlauer Berg he had seen and felt for himself the fury of the man with the yellow eyes. The fellow had a name now: *Major Fuchs*. He shivered, imagining the so-called 'lie-detector test'.

'You must go,' she said again. 'I can't trust myself the next time.'

'There shouldn't be a next time. We should go together.'

'How could we go? I'm being watched.' She leaned into him. 'Hold me, Roland.' Her voice was muffled against his chest.

She raised her head to be kissed. Their hunger took them. Hours of loneliness and years of waiting fell on the floor with their discarded clothing. Under Johannes Vos's blanket, they found in each other a respite from the nightmare into which they had stumbled together. He told her he loved her; she told him that she loved him, too. She held him tight and he held her tighter. It was a time out of time, a place beyond the world, beyond the allotment shed, beyond all frontiers, where neither Wall nor passport control existed.

When they were done, they lay beside each other and he drew the thin blanket closer around their naked bodies.

'I'll come back for you,' he whispered. 'Maybe they'll let you out to get married.'

'Who?' She kissed him on the nose. 'Who am I going to marry?'

He made a face. 'On the other hand, my mother and father might not approve of a daughter-in-law from East Germany.'

She slapped him on the rump. 'A workers' paradise and don't you forget it.'

They went on teasing each other, touching each other. For a little while, they could keep the world beyond their underground bed at bay, they could hold back the sunrise.

But only for a while.

'I should go,' she said. 'I need to get into Johannes' flat before light.'

They loved each other again, fiercely, hurriedly. In the end you knew that tomorrow was coming anyway.

In the darkness he panicked, wondered how long they'd slept, if light was already fingering its way across the eastern land.

He heard her shallow breathing, felt her hair like lace on his face, the heat of her buttocks nestled against his groin. Desire trembled in him.

Move. They might be at her door now. Fuchs or the frog fellow, hammers at the ready, voices raised in the icy air of morning. Send her away, save her from yourself, from your doomed love.

Move: she doesn't need to be doomed.

He eased himself away from her, shivered with the winter air on his skin when he lifted the thin grey blanket she'd brought from Johannes' apartment. He folded the grey stuff around her pale shoulder, watched it rise and fall with her breathing.

Move. The cheap watch that Ingham had given him said three forty-five, so they'd slept only for a few minutes, a few breaths shared under the scratchy blanket on the narrow platform.

Petra stirred, muttered something in her sleep.

In the half-lit gloom he watched her waken to the world, to the dawn. Watched her body turn, her arm stretch out from under the blanket. She turned her head and in her fabulous waking eyes he saw the tears glisten, knew that – even in her brief sleep – she had wept.

'I'm sorry.' He remembered his roughness, the urgency. 'I hurt you – I didn't mean to—'

Her finger stopped his lip. 'Nothing you could say or do could hurt me, Roland.' Her fingers played on his mouth. 'It's this.' Her other hand, bandaged, was raised a little. 'I guess the painkillers are wearing off.'

He took her wounded hand in his own, bent to kiss the wrist above the bandage.

'Your violin,' Roland said, 'your playing . . .'

She shook her head. 'Maybe some things are not meant to be.' He felt himself drawn into the turquoise pool of her eyes. 'And maybe some things *are*.' She drew him down to her, kissed him on the mouth.

'But it's something you loved.' His voice was a whisper.

'Sometimes you have to give up what you love, Roland.'

In her words he heard the echoes of a world not his: a world of war, of fathers lost, of invasion, a world hidden behind a prison wall.

And he had strayed into this world where you gave up what you loved.

'I will love you always,' he said, 'no matter what happens.'

'What could happen?' Petra laughed. 'We're here in the lap of luxury in our very own country estate.'

He loved her laughing face, her dancing eyes. Forced himself to laugh with her.

Maybe she knows, maybe she, too, is putting on a brave front.

'*Ich liebe dich*,' he said again.

'*Ich dich auch.*'

Move, Roland reminded himself.

'It's almost light,' he whispered. 'We *must* move.'

'I know,' she said. 'It's not so bad, is it?' Her glance took in the dark cellar, the flickering candle, the shadows dancing on the walls. 'Even here I could be happy with you.'

He bent to kiss her. He didn't trust himself to speak.

In the candlelight they dressed quickly. From a small compartment of her rucksack she took a folded map of East Germany and opened it out on the bed.

'It's Johannes', he doesn't know I tore it from his atlas.' She gave a wry smile. 'He's like the rest of us, better off not knowing things.'

They were kneeling side by side on the floor, bent over the map.

'We're so small we're not even on the map but we're close to here.' Her finger rested beside the town of Fürstenwalde. 'Berlin is here.' Pointing again. 'It's safer, I think, if you go east, through Fürstenwalde, on to Frankfurt an der Oder and then take a train south, to Karl-Marx-Stadt and Leipzig. I don't know how, but try to make your way to the border from there. Maybe this is stupid, I just think they might not be watching so closely for you down there. Maybe they don't even know about you.'

'It's not a bad plan.' *But I'll have no part of it: it leaves you exposed here for too long, while I traipse across half of East Germany.*

'I'll try to see Pastor Bruck tomorrow,' Petra said. 'Maybe he knows somebody in Leipzig who can help you.'

He didn't answer, just leaned across and kissed her hair.

'I'm scared, Roland.' Her voice edged with tears.

'It'll be OK.' *If they have me, they'll leave you alone.*

'If Pastor Bruck can help, I'll get here somehow in the afternoon. Your best bet is to take the train after four o'clock, when the early shifts from the sanatorium leave. You won't be so noticeable then.'

'And you? You can't work with your hand.'

'It doesn't hurt so much when I'm with you.' She smiled as he lifted her bandaged hand, laid it against his cheek. 'But it's better if I go into the Institute and get the nurse to look at it – she'll send me home and then I'll be free to help.'

'You've done too much already.'

'I've never loved anyone before.'

'You didn't know me when you got into the car with me.'

'A girl like me knows what she wants.' She tried to smile but her eyes were filling up. 'Even if all she wants is an unshaven fellow who needs a bath.'

'My God.' He wrinkled his nose. 'I suppose I stink.'

'Like rotten fish.'

'That's a nice thing to say to your future husband.'

'Future wives are allowed to say what they like.' She was weeping now. 'Just you wait till we're married, see what I'll say to you then.'

He couldn't answer her, his own heart was too full. He wiped her tears with his hand. Got to his feet and drew her up alongside him. The flickering light from the candle stub on the floor threw their shadows on to the wooden ceiling, dark, even menacing.

'Go,' he said. 'It'll be light soon.'

'Wait.' She opened her rucksack, took out her purse. 'You'll need this for the trains.' She gave him a handful of folded notes.

'They gave me some money.' *They*. Ingham and his accomplices, creatures now even more insubstantial than the shadowy images on the ceiling.

'You'll need it.' She folded his hand around the money. 'God knows how long it'll be before you get home.'

'You *must* go, Petra.' He picked up her rucksack and started to zip it shut. The small notebook inside the bag stared up at him. He took the notebook out, looked at Petra.

'I write shopping lists in it.' She smiled. 'Not that there's ever much in the shops to buy.'

'If you don't need it—'

'It's yours,' she said, smiling now. 'What're you going to do, write your life story?'

'Something like that. I'll have time to kill before I go to the station; I thought I might write down a few bits and bobs about me and where I come from.' He took her face between his hands. 'Something to remind you of the Irish fellow who tried to make a mess of your untroubled life. It could be a long time before I get back for you.'

She stood on tiptoe, kissed him quickly on the lips.

'You make sure you don't forget me, Roland Feldmann, and get yourself back here as soon as you can.' On tiptoe again, kissing him again. 'I'll be waiting for you.'

They climbed the ladder and stood at the door of the shed, looking out at the night. The clouds had lifted, stars sequinned the dark sky. The abandoned sheds were ghostly in the starlight. The world was silent, asleep, waiting.

'I love you,' she whispered.

'And I love you.'

He watched her slip away between the sheds. One last time she turned and waved and blew him a kiss and he waved back at her and she was gone. For a long while he stood there, his hand raised in farewell, looking at the spot where she had stood, as though her image were imprinted on the night. She was imprinted on his heart, he knew that. He knew, too, that he would never see her again.

Twenty-eight

The ticket clerk hardly lifted his head as he sold him the ticket to Berlin. It was after three o'clock, the afternoon chilly. At the far end of the platform, a tall, thin commuter with a briefcase was stamping his feet to keep warm. In the wooden shelter a woman with a canvas sack at her feet sat chomping on an apple.

Bad Saarow in mid-afternoon. The kind of place where nothing happened twice. Every day. The kind of place where you waited for a train that would take you away from the girl you loved. Where you left her just a notebook with pages filled with jottings of your life in another land.

He placed himself midway along the station platform, drawing the navy-blue cap down tighter on his head. The cap, folded in on itself, had been stuffed into the pocket of the coat from Prenzlauer Berg. It looked like a sailor's cap, with a small peak. There were two buttons under the crown that might have held a strip of braid, maybe printed with a name. Maybe the late Marta's late husband had owned a boat, pottered about on the river on a Sunday afternoon.

They could hear the train now, could see the plume of black smoke above the engine. The woman with the canvas sack stood up, positioned herself in front of the shelter, wiping her mouth with her sleeve. She glanced at Roland and he looked beyond her at the approaching train, refusing to catch her eye. The fellow with the briefcase was probably staring at him too: he knew he looked trampish, dirty, in need of a shave. He didn't look like the guy who had clobbered Major Fuchs with an ashtray.

Which was good if it got him out of Bad Saarow unrecognized.

Which was useless if, when they found him, they didn't recognize him.

Which was why he'd written the Prenzlauer Berg address on a page torn from Petra's notebook and folded it over and over until it was no bigger than a postage stamp and stuffed it into his trouser pocket. They weren't stupid, he knew that now, but maybe they were too clever. It was something his father often said, considering the failings and failures of shopkeeping rivals: 'He's not stupid, just too clever for his own good.'

The train belched to a halt. It was almost empty: he had the pick of empty compartments. A whistle, a green flag from the ticket clerk in his other role, and they were clanking west, towards Berlin.

Ingham was likely gone now, him and Corporal Adams. He wondered if other eyes had watched his stumbling progress in East Berlin, had reported back. It didn't matter now, he was out of time.

It was what had driven him to cover the pages after Petra had left the shed: his time was running out and he wanted her to know him after he was gone. Especially after he was gone. And so he had begun: 'I was born in Galway, a small town on the west coast of Ireland, on November 19th 1942 . . .'

He'd gone on writing in the cellar until the candle guttered and then he'd climbed the ladder and, sitting on the plank, gone on filling the yellow pages. Dawn had broken, light filtered through the cracks in the wooden walls. Somewhere a bird warbled, the trees stirred in the new day. He'd have liked to savour it, this last sweet day, but he wanted to leave his story behind. Sentences were reduced to phrases, glimpses of the life he had known. When he'd finished, the watery sun was high. He left the notebook on the chair in the cellar, words of love for the time when he was gone. On the last page, like a schoolboy, he'd signed off: 'Roland xxx Petra.' He looked at it one last time, smiling before wrapping himself in Johannes Vos's blanket on the wooden bed. He'd give himself an hour, maybe he'd sleep. He was exhausted but he needed to be gone before Petra returned, even if she had some word of help from Pastor Bruck. He knew now what needed to be done. And he hoped he could do it.

The train steamed on across the flat landscape. The wind caught the plume of smoke, blew it freakishly low alongside the train. For a few moments the land was hidden in the pall of smoke and then they were out of it, clanking, cruising towards the city. He was out of the gloom now, could see his way to the end. It had always been his strength, what set him apart from Terry: this ability to unknot the problem and then tie it up the way it should be tied.

Sometimes he wished it were not so. Sometimes he'd have enjoyed being helpless, even feckless, on the receiving end of mollycoddling in the house back in Ireland.

It was too late now. They were entering the city. Apartment blocks, factories and embankment walls lined the route. And to his left, as they entered a delta of tracks, a high mesh fence topped with razor wire. The Wall on the railway, it *must* be. And then they were past, sliding once more between embankments.

He got off the train at Alexanderplatz, one among a couple of dozen passengers. On the adjoining platform another train was disgorging a heavier load of travellers and he angled his way until he was in their midst, making for the exit gate. It was almost five o'clock, the station busy with commuters. Volkspolizei patrolled in pairs but Roland saw nobody being cut out for questioning. He stayed with the flow of the crowd, not knowing where they were going. They entered a tunnelled walkway, went down stone steps, signs overhead. U-Bahn. The tube to High Street Kensington flashed into his mind, the blood on the tiled floor, Terry wheezing, panicking. *Which is what you can't do right now, so concentrate.*

He concentrated, moved halfway along the underground platform. There were Vopos here too, just standing, watching. There were trains arriving on both sides of the platform. *Eeny, meeny, miney, mo.* Take the train on the left. He tried to picture in his mind the street-maps that Adams had quizzed him on in the down-at-heel dining room in Highfield. *Think.* He found a seat next to a pair of schoolgirls, their hair blond as Petra's. He looked at their hands, resting on their schoolbags, saw their fingers were whole, unbandaged. *For Christ's sake, think.* The train slowed to a halt, some of the passengers stood up, moved to the doors. He saw the name on the platform: Jannowitzbrucke. *Think.* The doors were sliding open. It came to him in a flash, this route, Adams forcing him to recite the litany of stops. *Get out here.*

He felt the girls' eyes on him as he stood up. Their noses wrinkled as they looked at each other, smiling.

At least he knew he was headed in the direction of the Wall. Beyond the Jannowitz bridge stretched Brückenstrasse. Straight on lay Heine Street. And the Wall. Traffic was light on the bridge; he felt exposed, vulnerable above the dark waters of the Spree.

And the wind cut him; the old overcoat might as well have been made of paper. He turned into a side street, away from the traffic. A church tower rose out of the quietness. Opposite the church he saw the lighted window of an Imbiss and he was reminded of his hunger. He was out of time but he might as well eat, get warm.

The heat inside the small snack bar was muggy. Two young men were eating *Wurst* at a high table beside the sweaty window; they looked at him for a moment, then went back to their beer and sausage, their complaints about the Dynamo striker. The middle-aged woman behind the zinc counter said, 'Good evening,' in an accent that might have been Polish. She hardly looked at him as she began to prepare his portion of *Currywurst;* she lifted her eyes to his only when he asked for tea. She seemed about to say no, then looked again at his unshaven face, his flimsy coat, and went back through a hanging plastic curtain into the kitchen. He wondered if she might be phoning, perhaps the Vopos; he thought about walking out of the Imbiss. Then she was back and he cupped his hands gratefully around the steaming glass of black tea. He paid her, took the tea and plate of sausage to the chest-high shelf on the wall beside the door.

There was an old copy of *Junge Welt* strung on a nail above the shelf. He turned the pages of the magazine as he ate: keen young Party workers beamed out at him, hiking, swimming, playing football. They didn't seem any different from schoolboys and schoolgirls back home. He wondered if Petra read *Junge Welt*. Strange, how you could love someone more than yourself, more than your life, and still know so little about them.

The woman behind the counter thanked him when he returned the empty glass and plate. She didn't smile as one of the counter-staff in Feldmann, Watchmakers and Jewellers would have done but her eyes met his, took in his unkempt appearance, his need of a shave. It occurred to Roland, meeting her frank gaze, that hers might be the last human face he would look upon close up. She was about his mother's age, her round face maternal, a small mole below her left eye. It might not be the face you'd choose to look your last upon but it wasn't a bad face either. He thanked her, gave her a smile and was rewarded with a softening in the brown eyes.

It was a softening that he took with him out of the snack bar into the night.

It had begun to snow, the first fall of the year. Instinctively he drew the collar of the old coat tighter. It didn't make any difference but that didn't matter any more. The snow fell in large, soft flakes; when they melted on his face they felt soothing. He padded along the deserted street, remembering his mother's hands, taping a wounded knee. He wondered if they'd have snow back home; it didn't fall often in the west of Ireland. Maybe Petra was out in the snow, feeling its softness, wondering if he was feeling it too.

Enough. A last look at the silent church tower, like something on a snowy Christmas card; a last wry reminder to himself that he would not be seeing Pastor Bruck's old grey church in the snow. He bore south along the deserted street, towards the Wall.

They went to bed early in the GDR, he thought. Or maybe they were all playing chess behind the shuttered windows. Listening to West German radio, Ingham would say. *Maybe they'd report tonight's incident at the Wall.*

He hurried on, his shoes plopping on the damp pavement. A car squished past on the snow-wet road; he watched it swing left at the corner, in the direction of Heine Strasse.

Roland turned right. He knew the kind of quietness he sought; he could only hope it existed. There was a park to his left, bare trees gaunt inside iron railings, the undisturbed snow carpeting the grass with a fine whiteness. He hurried away from it, exposed against the white backdrop.

He turned into a narrow street of two-storey houses, small, intimate, the kind you'd find in the back streets behind Feldmann, Watchmakers and Jewellers. For a moment he paused, taken back, taken aback by the unexpected streetscape. He gasped, breathless, like Terry without his inhaler.

Move. Not far to go now, time and space running out. He gulped at the air, felt the snow on his tongue, savoured the wet freshness of it. Goodnight, Terry, *auf wiedersehen*.

He tiptoed into a passageway between two blocks of houses, past dustbins slick with snow. Behind him he heard a door opening and he hurried around the corner of the house, leaning backwards into the wall. The noises carried in the night: a lid raised, rubbish dumped, the lid banged down. A man's cough, a door closing.

His own heart thumping.

When he lifted his eyes, his heart thumped even louder.

The Wall reared above the small back gardens of the houses. The grey slab of it glistened in the falling snow, a dark menace that the night had spawned. Over ten feet high, and not a hand grip in sight.

For a moment longer he hugged the shadows of the house. *Move*, he told himself. This is journey's end. Put your money where your mouth is. Put your life where all those noble thoughts of protecting her have been admiring their own wonderfulness. *Move*.

The short back gardens were an unfenced continuum, with an evenly spaced line of wooden sheds. One after another he tried the sheds; one after another he found them locked. He was contemplating forcing open a door when he saw the ladder, lying on the snowy ground, resting lengthways against the base of the shed. It was a homemade structure, the wooden rungs of uneven thickness, but it seemed solid enough. And it had to bear his weight only once: there would be no return ticket.

He lifted the ladder from the ground, manoeuvred it into the space between the wooden sheds and the Wall. He stood the ladder upright, then let it fall cautiously towards the Wall. It hit the cement top with a soft clunk and Roland stood, listening, waiting for alarms. Nothing stirred except the softly falling snow. He found two stones, wedged them under the feet of the ladder and started to climb up. The ladder creaked under his weight. At any moment he expected to hear shouted commands.

Yet within seconds he found himself lying on top of the wide structure. He gathered his breath and his strength and began to haul the ladder upwards. He tried to lift it clear of the Wall but it moaned against the stone. Still no alarms, no shouts in the night. He lowered the ladder on the other side, pushed downwards on it, trying to secure it.

And when it was done he lifted his head to look at Berlin. Behind him, to the east, scattered lights glimmered above the dark streets. Ahead, to the west, stretched the brighter night, a panoply of orange and sodium lights, the roar of traffic.

And he was on top of the fabled, demonic Wall. Did Ingham realize you could raise a borrowed ladder and just climb over the damn thing?

'The Wall isn't just a wall.' Corporal Adams' words came back to him. 'It's a complete fucking obstacle course.' Those obstacles stretched ahead of him now, all the way to West Berlin: the tank barriers, the alarmed fence, the anti-vehicle trench. He could see them now, spaced out in the dim light of no-man's-land. A hundred yards to his right rose an observation tower, with its circling beacon light; just one of a series that ran the length of the Wall.

'A killing zone,' Adams had said.

He shivered, hugging the top of the Wall.

Move. You're not here to make it. You're here because you love those wounded fingers, those mysterious turquoise eyes.

He waited, counted the seconds between the circuits of the watchtower light. *Now.* He inched his way down the ladder, drew his breath as he stood on the wet surface of no-man's-land. Hurriedly he pulled the ladder down, laid it against the foot of the Wall.

He knew that he had never been so alert, so *alive*, as in these last moments. His hands tingled from the snow, the ladder, the Wall. His nostrils twitched, filled with the metallic smell of cement, of steel. And something else: *dog shit*. He'd forgotten about the dogs, about Adams' warning: 'They're trained to kill.'

Not that way, not the dogs.

He began to crawl towards the tank barriers. The search-light swung round and he froze, waited for the shout, the gunfire.

The light swept over him in silence and he crawled on, hugging the frozen ground. He was under the line of tank barriers, past them. He drew level with the observation tower, was beyond it. He could see the pathway used by the patrolling guards, slick and shiny under the snow and the lights. And beyond, within reach, the last barrier, the final frontier. He could see the lights beyond the Wall, could taste them, almost touch them. He could make it if he tried.

Don't move. You are here in no-man's-land so that she can live. In the precious metal of your father's shop you found nothing of value; on the dark side of the Wall you discovered the treasure of love and loving. Now guard that love with your life.

The circling searchlight swept towards him. He felt in his pocket for the carefully folded paper with the Prenzlauer Berg address. He pushed the paper deeper into his pocket, reassured. Its discovery would be her passport to life.

He waited for the searchlight, rose to his knees to meet it. The light blinded him, swept past him. From the watchtower a shout, then another, the light swung back. For a second he was splayed in its yellow beam. *Move. If you don't they'll take you alive.*

He ran from the light, from the shouts, but no-man's-land was floodlit now, a noonday blaze with nowhere to hide.

The first bullet caught him high on the shoulder, spun him round, facing the east. He knew her face, saw her huge eyes open, waiting for him. He called her name, reached out beyond the blazing lights to where she smiled at him from behind the stars. And then it was neither night nor day, neither dark nor light, just a white stillness falling around him. Just for a second his broken body burned with the searing metal but then the snow entered him and he knew that he was falling into her arms.

Twenty-nine

On a bitter Tuesday in January 1963, Petra Ritter married Johannes Vos in the Rathaus of Fürstenwalde. Their marriage was witnessed by the Deputy Mayor and a clerk from the Accounts Section. Petra was showing by then, the lilac linen dress stretched taut across the incipient bulge of her stomach. Johannes was showing too, but in his case it was the cancer that was becoming more evident: his sunken cheeks were the colour of wax; more than once, during the brief ceremony in the Deputy Mayor's office, Petra had seen his features crease and flinch with pain.

The marriage was Johannes' idea. He'd said nothing at first when she'd been sick in his flat; in those dark nights he could see the strain in her pale face but he hadn't asked, was fearful of intruding.

She had longed to tell Johannes. The not knowing was hell, the wondering where he was, whether Roland was even alive. She knew the contents of the notebook by heart, treasured the words like a much-loved melody. And as each day passed and still the Stasi did not come for her, she tried to convince herself that he had got away.

And that he would come back for her, take her to that life, that world, that he had crammed into the small pages of the notebook in the cellar of the allotment shed. It was a hope she had nursed through the nights after his leaving, after she found the notebook in the cellar.

The hammering on her door early on that Saturday morning had murdered that hope. Pastor Bruck's young son stood there, sobbing, incoherent, incomprehensible, until at last she managed to calm the boy enough to learn that his father had been taken to the hospital.

She found the pastor in a corner bed in a ward filled with old men, reeking of disinfectant and piss. He hadn't wanted to meet her eyes and that frightened her more than the bandages, more than the traction pulleys that held the pastor's legs raised above the bed. She knew the pastor for a man of courage, a man unafraid to face pain, to tell it like it was.

When he finally looked at her, he told it in a rush, as if it were something evil that he wanted rid of. How the Stasi with the yellow eyes had descended upon his church at dead of night, roaring drunk, the truck engine revving, the church door battered and kicked. Two others with him, sober, obedient, menacing. They were the ones who'd slid the long wooden box off the back of the truck; it was they who, under Major Fuchs's barked orders, had crowbarred the lid off the cheap coffin. The light of the moon was enough to let Pastor Bruck see the decaying face of the young man he'd first encountered in Marta's flat in Prenzlauer Berg. When he was finished retching on the grass, they'd handed him a spade, another to his son, Thomas, and shown him where to dig the grave in a quiet place behind the church cottage. 'I know you had something to do with this fucker,' Major Fuchs had snarled, 'and now my boss wants him disappeared, so bury the fucker.' They'd watched him sweat, swore at his progress. When he'd finished, when the earth had been heaved back on top of the coffin, Major Fuchs took the spade from him and swung it once against the priest's back. And as he buckled slowly to the ground,

Fuchs raised the iron spade above his head and caught the pastor with a downward blow across the base of his spine. 'Something to remember me by,' Major Fuchs said. They drove off noisily but Pastor Bruck had passed out by then on the frozen ground.

'My son got the doctor.' He met Petra's eyes then. 'The doctor came and brought me here.' He touched the white neck brace. 'They tell me I'll walk but I have broken discs at the top and bottom of my spine.'

She'd started to cry, sitting there on the metal-framed chair in the ward, but Pastor Bruck reached for her hand and spoke urgently to her.

'You must be strong now and keep these things locked in your heart. The man who came last night is a mad dog but he knows nothing, he has only his suspicions and anyway he has suspicions of the whole world.' He looked shrewdly at her, his voice a whisper. 'Are you pregnant, Petra?'

She nodded, still weeping.

'Then you must be very careful indeed,' he said.

Johannes Vos said the same thing when, finally, she told him what had happened. 'We must get married,' Johannes had said. He saw the puzzlement, even alarm, on her face and said hurriedly, 'Don't worry, Petra, not like that, but your baby needs a father – you need a father for your baby. It will stop the questions, they won't come bothering you again with their questions.'

It wasn't hard to see the sense in what he said.

Johannes put on his best suit and a yellow tie to drive them to Fürstenwalde. He had to stop once on the way to be sick at the side of the road. On the way home to Bad Saarow after the ceremony, he had to make two stops. He smiled at Petra, wiping the sweat from his face in the car. 'What a man you've got for a husband.'

She took the handkerchief from him, patted his face gently. 'You *are* a man,' she told him.

She nursed him in the apartment until he died, in his sleep, two weeks later. She sat beside him for a long while before she sent for the doctor. His death was another grief that had to be acknowledged, taken into her heart.

It would have been easy to feel that there was room in her heart for nothing but grief but her growing belly told her otherwise. There was a baby to think about.

When she applied for a new work assignment, she was surprised by the speedy, positive response. Maybe, she thought, the Deputy Director wanted rid of her, the way you wanted to get rid of a bad smell. She didn't care where she was sent; one place was as good as another now. Brandenburg-an-der-Havel, the notice of assignment from the district office said: at least it wasn't a long journey.

A young colleague from the Institute helped her to load Johannes' few bits of furniture on to a borrowed truck on a Saturday in April. He drove the truck to Brandenburg; Petra followed behind in Johannes' Lada, glad that she had learned to drive, however erratically. The sun shone palely; the savings that Johannes had left her were reassuring in her purse. When they drew up outside the flat she'd been allocated, opposite the railway station in Brandenburg, a little more of the grief softened inside her. The place needed a thorough cleaning, she thought, surveying the empty rooms, and the whole thing could do with a coat of paint (wherever that might come from) but for the first time she began to feel that she might be able to survive all that had gone before and whatever else might be thrown at her in the years to come.

Her hand still pained her but she nursed it in silence, careful to make no complaint stacking and carrying reams of paper at the mill. She understood that from now on the only work she would be offered would be unskilled labour – and that, too, was unimportant to her. She never again touched her broken violin, never lifted it from Johannes' old trunk, locked, stowed under her bed. The very mindlessness of her new work soothed her; she worked at it until the day before her son was born.

Petra had never realized, until she was handed her wet, still-bloodied infant, just how much you could read in the features of a newborn baby. The midwife assured her that the baby looked like his mother, but his mother knew better: in those calm eyes, in that stubborn chin and unyielding jaw, Petra saw clearly that this bawling boy was the spit of his Irish father. The crown of dark thatch was merely confirmation.

She'd like to have called the boy Roland but to do so would, perhaps, have invited disaster and made a mockery of Johannes' marriage to her. At the same time, Johannes was *not* the boy's father, so that name would not do either. She didn't know how or why she chose the name Michael. She was groggy, half-asleep, when the hospital secretary came round to take particulars for the birth certificate. 'Michael,' she said, and Michael it was. It was as good a name as any.

What she feared most was that they would take the boy from her. Too much had been taken from her; she wasn't sure that she could survive another loss, another parting. To this end she became, as much as possible, an exemplary worker. She kept her house clean and her opinions to herself. She went to services in the small Lutheran church near her flat but never referred at work to her attendance.

She didn't have the boy baptized. It was, she told Pastor Bruck when she visited him that autumn in Bad Saarow, too much of a risk. 'I can't afford to antagonize them,' she said. 'He's all I've got, all I have left.' The pastor looked at his own son, thickset, muscular, absent-mindedly whittling a lump of wood, and nodded: you did what you had to do.

Petra never visited Pastor Bruck again. They both understood that to do so might alert the ever-watching eyes, the always-listening ears.

She devoted herself to her work and to the boy. Whatever misgivings she had about Michael's developing interests were kept to herself. She said nothing about his Boys Brigade uniform, his devotion to his GDR homeland. His progress at school, his accomplishments on the athletics field pleased her and she showed pride and pleasure in him. He took her pride as his due. Even so, the depth and extent of her pride when he was selected – when he was *allowed* – to study English at the University of Rostock was a puzzle to Michael himself. 'What's the big deal, Mutti?' he asked, as she read the letter of acceptance for the umpteenth time. 'It's just English at Rostock.' She didn't answer but he could see tears in her eyes and he was too young to guess that there might be more than normal parental pride on display.

She was pleased, too, that he chose to live at home when he came back, *Herr Doktor Ritter*, to teach in his home town. 'Where else would I live, Mutti?' He was fascinated by her reaction to his book, *Workers' Dawn*, a collection of short stories published while he was teaching. Sometimes, at night, he'd lift his head from the essays he was correcting and he'd look over at her, seated on the ancient sofa, turning the pages of his book, rapt. Petra was wearing glasses by then, there was grey in her hair, but even Michael knew that his mother was still a beautiful woman. 'You must know *Workers' Dawn* by heart, Mutti,' he said to her once. 'Maybe you should write your own story.'

She lifted her head, the amazing eyes smiled at him over the glasses. 'It's not finished yet, Michael,' she said.

Maybe she was thinking of Roland's story, hurriedly written in the hours after they had loved each other in the cellar. She no longer had the small notebook. She had no need of it, could still remember it line for line, word for word. She'd given the book to Pastor Bruck on that last visit, all those years ago. 'It might be safer,' Pastor Bruck had said, 'to destroy it.'

A shake of the blond head, the rich blue eyes looking into some private future.

'Someone,' Petra said, 'might come.'

BOOK 4

HOMELANDS

1994

Thirty

It was, at first sight anyway, something less than impressive, this town that my father had written about in the hasty pages of that old notebook. A straggly square of patchy grass looked up at you as you made your way downhill from the railway station; a nondescript hotel building flanked the bottom end of the square, while the top end offered all the usual glories of a car park. A steady flow of traffic puffed and panted around the perimeter of the square. In his hurried, scribbled words Roland Feldmann had invested this Irish backwater with a touch of romance, but even eyes as sympathetic as mine could see only a run of the mill provincial town that couldn't hold a candle to the derelict beauty of Brandenburg.

Stop it, I told myself. You're not here to study architecture or compare streetscapes.

You're on the last leg of a journey that has taken you from Bad Saarow to Berlin to London to the west of Ireland, in search of some kind of truth.

Closure, the psychologists would say. They'd be wrong. I wanted an opening, daybreak on a new day that would offer me some replacement for my lost country, my aborted life. Or maybe I was searching for the father I never had, for the mother I had lost.

The voice in my head said: your country was your father, your mother. Now you're a 31-year-old orphan on a wild-goose chase in a remote corner of Europe.

Shut it. Truth was, I didn't know what I wanted, not beyond finishing what I'd started.

What had started in Brandenburg, with my dying mother's words about Roland, had to end somewhere. It might as well be here. The public records I'd scoured in Berlin and London had yielded dates, information. What I was seeking in this obscure town was a touch of reality: flesh and blood and a human voice.

And there it was, opposite me, a few steps from the square, on what seemed to be the town's main street: Feldmann, Watchmakers and Jewellers. There was a cafe to the left, a clothing store to the right, but the Feldmann sign and window lorded it over the entire block. Looking across the street at the shop I was, for a few moments, unaware of pedestrians pushing past me on the pavement or of the traffic going up and down on the busy road. For those moments it seemed as if the words in the cellar notebook had come to life. Sometimes, wading through records in Berlin and Kew, it had almost seemed that what I was engaged in was no more than a post-doctoral research project. Now, looking across the street at this jeweller's shop in Galway, words had leapt into life. I had to shake my head, clear it, before crossing the road to stand in front of the shop.

The long, plate-glass window gleamed in the August sunshine. Rings and watches, bracelets and brooches, necklaces and crosses – they shone in clearly defined sections of the long window. Everything sparkled, gold and silver and diamonds, on backgrounds of glass, mirrors and velvet. Feldmann, Watchmakers and Jewellers, was no common-or-garden emporium: this establishment reeked of money.

The door stood open. The cool interior offered more lights, more glitter, more velvet displays. The marble floor of the doorway was decorated with the name 'Feldmann' in a heraldic-style scroll. I stepped over it gingerly, reluctant to tread on it.

The long L-shaped counter was a series of display cases, the facing wall a bank of more display cabinets. The air was rich, self-satisfied, like the voice of the assistant showing diamond rings to a young couple at the counter. Another assistant was displaying watches to a middle-aged fellow in a suit; a third was winding a grandfather clock that stood in a corner of the shop. All of the assistants were young women; all of them wore white blouses and black skirts – nothing so tacky as a uniform, the outfits seemed to say, just something refined, classy, like the elegant House of Feldmann itself.

The whole place was an affront to me. While my mother had eked out a living for both of us in our spartan flat opposite Brandenburg railway station, the House of Feldmann had preened and purred its comfortable way through a shopkeeper's life. I stared unseeing into a glass wall cabinet and told myself to get a grip, that I hadn't come all this way simply to lose my rag over the injustices of twentieth-century capitalism.

'Can I help you?'

The grandfather clock lady was smiling at me.

'I'm – I'm just looking.' *At tanned skin, even teeth, shoulder-length dark hair.*

'Let me show them to you.' In her hands she held a long silver chain, at the end of it a cluster of small, shiny keys.

'But it's not – I mean, I'm just—'

'It's no problem.' She turned a key in the lock, slid the door sideways. 'Anything in particular you'd like to look at?'

I realized I was looking at a display of fine chains and small crosses.

I shrugged. 'I really am just having a look around,' I said. 'I've only just arrived in town.'

'Your first time here?' Another smile; a barely discernible perfume.

'Yes, first day in Ireland, first day in Galway.'

'We get a lot of tourists in here; they've read about our handmade stuff.' She looked straight at me then. 'Was that it? You heard about us before you came?'

'I suppose you could say that.'

Another turn of the small silver key, chains and crosses safely locked up again. Now that she seemed about to go back to her grandfather-clock duties, I wanted her to stay: her and her faint perfume and her creamy skin.

'The name,' I said. 'It's from Germany, like myself.'

'Sorry?'

'Feldmann, it's a German name.'

'Oh.' A flash of the even teeth. 'Yes, old Mr Feldmann. I suppose that was a long time ago. Feldmann's is part of the furniture here now.'

Old Mr Feldmann. It wasn't possible, was it? A hint of interest now in her smile. 'Which part of Germany are you from?'

'Brandenburg. It's a small place, not too far from Berlin.'

Over her shoulder I could see a door opening at the back of the store, a glimpse of carpeted stairs before the door swung shut again. The man who had entered the shop from the stairway had an obvious proprietary air about him: white shirt, silver tie with a gold clip, dark grey suit.

He seemed to know the customer looking at watches: heads nodded, greetings were exchanged.

He looked across to where we were standing in front of the cabinet of crosses.

'Jennifer?' From such a short, paunchy body the voice was oddly high-pitched, wheezy. 'Excuse me.' A nod directed at me. 'When you're free, could you pop up to see me for a moment?' A flash of stiff white cuff and gold cufflink as he raised his hand, pointing at the ceiling.

'Be right with you, Terry.'

'Good.' Another managerial smile at me. 'Sorry to interrupt. You're in good hands with Jennifer.'

Terry. Hard to believe that this sleek, suited fellow was the same person as the whingeing teenager of the handwritten statement in the reading room at Kew, the tearful asthmatic who had injudiciously swung a rolled-up newspaper in the tube station at High Street Kensington.

I needed to make sure

'Is that "old Mr Feldmann"?'

She grinned, amused. 'No, that's Terry, Mr Feldmann's son. Terry is the manager but Mr Feldmann himself still comes in once or twice a week. He likes to keep his hand in, you know.'

'Old Mr Feldmann is still alive?'

The look she gave me was sharp. 'Are you *sure* you've never been here before?'

'No, never.' I fumbled for words, embarrassed, as though I'd lied and been caught out. 'I guess I just like stories.'

'Stories?' Sceptical, immaculate eyebrows raised.

'Yes, stories.' Somehow her good opinion was necessary now. 'I write stories . . .' I shrugged, knew I was blushing. 'I've had one book published.' *Shut up, you sound like a boastful kid seeking approval*.

'So we have a distinguished author on the premises.'

I searched for sarcasm but her smile was open, kind.

'It's in German,' I said lamely.

'I think that's why Mr Feldmann hired me – *old* Mr Feldmann.'

'Sorry?'

'German was one of my subjects – I think Mr Feldmann liked

that.' She fiddled with the ring of keys. 'Ireland is booming now, Mr . . . ?'

'Ritter, Michael Ritter.'

'The economy is booming here, they're talking about something called a "Celtic tiger", but when I graduated seven or eight years ago, jobs were scarce and I was glad when Mr Feldmann offered me the job here.'

I nodded, flattered by the confidence, unable to come up with anything to keep the conversation going. The young couple at the engagement rings were saying they'd go and have a think about it over a coffee, the fellow with the watches was handing over his credit card. In a moment my lady with the keys would also be gone.

'You could read my book, I mean, if you wanted to.'

'That would be lovely, thank you.'

'It's in my bag, at the station.' Her eyes were grey, flecked with amber. 'It's in German.' I was repeating myself.

'Well, it would be, wouldn't it?'

I laughed sheepishly. 'Yes, it would be.'

'So you'll drop it in to me here?'

'Tomorrow, when I get it from my bag.'

'At the station.'

'Yes, at the station.'

'What's it called?'

'The station – the railway station.'

'I mean the book.'

I had to think. *'Workers' Dawn.'*

'It comes every day.'

'Sorry?'

'Dawn comes every morning for workers, when you have to get up and face the day.'

'Yes, of course.'

'I look forward to reading your book, Michael Ritter.' Another smile. 'I'd better go, Terry will be thinking I've got lost.'

I watched her as she high-heeled her way across the carpet. I hadn't touched a woman in almost a year; Steffi had stopped coming round to the flat after I'd said I was too tired.

The door at the back of the shop closed behind Jennifer of the grey eyes and the white teeth. The faint trace of perfume lingered where she had stood beside me.

Not to mention Terry and 'old Mr Feldmann'. I stepped out of the shop, telling myself that I had just seen my uncle for the first time.

It was after five. The street outside was busier now with traffic, the pavement more crowded with what I took to be office workers released from their pens. Like the lady had said, workers' dawn was an experience that had to be endured daily.

I shouldered my rucksack, making my way along the busy street. I needed to find a place to stay, then locate 'old Mr Feldmann'. I wondered if my first sighting of my grandfather would seem as unremarkable as my first glimpse of my Uncle Terry.

Thirty-one

The house stood on a busy road not far from the town centre. A few trees, guarded by shoulder-high metal cages, tried unsuccessfully to take the bare look off the place. I wondered, looking across at the Feldmanns' flat-roofed house, what it must be like to have a permanent view of the stone wall behind me and, beyond that, the forbidding bulk of what looked like a barracks but was probably a school.

Flat roofs seemed to be the style here: the school was also flat-roofed, as were several of the houses on either side of the Feldmanns'. I hoped the fashion in roofs didn't extend to brains and outlook: the story I planned to tell 'old Mr Feldmann' wouldn't find much of a welcome from someone who harboured a flat-earth view of the world.

Although I really didn't care very much if Herr Klaus Feldmann believed me or not. For me, standing here outside the house of Roland Feldmann, this was just the end of a journey. What it might mean for the old fellow inside this pebble-dashed, flat-roofed house was not my concern.

It had been easier than I'd expected to find out where Roland's family lived. In the bed-and-breakfast I'd booked into near the docks I'd asked for the local phone directory and there it was, *Feldmann Klaus*, staring back at me.

And here I was, within touching distance of words scribbled on small pages over thirty years before.

You tell yourself you don't care but there's an unexpected dryness in your throat as you cross the road and open the garden gate. The wrought-iron gate is freshly done in silver paint; it swings easily on well-oiled hinges. The long narrow lawn that fronts the house is smooth as a golf green; roses bloom along the edges. The gardeners at work in the newly liberated mansions of Bad Saarow do not seem so distant.

The white bell in the frame of the pale blue door has PRESS printed on it. I am trying to distract myself by wondering what else you could do with this bell, apart from pressing it, when the door opens.

The woman looking out of the doorway at me is of medium height, bespectacled, her short hair the colour of straw.

'Yes?' In the gloom of the doorway it is hard to see her features but the single word is enough to let you know that this woman dislikes answering the door at eleven o'clock on a mid-week morning. Perhaps she dislikes opening the door at any time.

I have my own plan: I speak in German.

'I'm from Germany. I wonder if I might see Herr Klaus Feldmann, please?'

'Pardon?' In English. Her eyes narrowing behind the thick lenses.

I offer a smile but repeat myself in German.

'Don't you speak English?' Then louder, with a gesture of red-varnished fingernails for extra clarity. 'English!'

'*Ein bisschen*, just a little.' And then I launch into a rapid flow of German.

She blinks at me, exasperation written all over her sharp features. I am in full flow, merely repeating that I would like to see Herr Klaus Feldmann, when something stirs in the dark hallway behind her.

'Dolly? What's up?'

Dolly?

'Dolly? Who's there?' The voice coming closer. The words English but the accent unmistakably German.

The woman stands to one side and, in the doorway of a flat-roofed house in the west of Ireland, I am looking at Roland Feldmann's father. At my grandfather.

'Herr Feldmann?'

'*Ja.*' Sharp blue eyes look me up and down.

'My name is Michael Ritter, I'm from Germany.'

'It's a good place to be from.' Amusement in the pale blue eyes. 'What can I do for you, Herr Ritter?'

'May I speak with you?'

He shifts on his walking stick; I notice he is wearing green corduroy bedroom slippers. He looks from Dolly to me.

'What about?'

'About Roland Feldmann.'

Dolly's expression has shown she does not understand our exchange in German; now, at the mention of Roland's name, a kind of gasp escapes her. Klaus Feldmann's soft pudgy face pales; he leans on the hooked top of his stick with both hands.

'What about Roland Feldmann?'

'He was your son, sir.'

'I know he was my son. What's that to you?'

I'm not sure if I'm hearing anger or resentment in the old man's voice but I can see his double-handed grip tightening on his stick. It wasn't supposed to be like this, blurting out my truth on a doorstep while traffic whooshed past behind me.

'Please, Herr Feldmann,' I say, 'let me talk to you inside.'

The blue eyes rake me again, taking in the white T-shirt, the faded jeans, the old trainers, and inwardly I curse myself for not dressing more formally.

'Dolly,' he says in English, 'I want you to phone the police and tell them we have a nuisance on our doorstep.'

A look of malice behind the glasses, a toss of the straw-coloured hair. She is turning away when I blurt it out.

'Roland Feldmann was my father.'

I see him swallow, see the Adam's apple bob in the soft folds of his turkey neck. The pale blue eyes blink; he raises one hand as if to ward off a blow then brushes it aimlessly through his white hair as if he has forgotten what he meant to do with it. The Adam's apple trembles again; the blue eyes look up at me, then skywards, as if the summer sky might offer answers. And then I realize that Klaus Feldmann's eyes are vacant, that whatever he sees is in some other place, some other time.

'Klaus?' Another voice, a woman's, from further back in the dark hall. The faint hum of rubber tyres on the parquet flooring, the wheelchair pushing past Dolly until Frau Feldmann draws it to a stop beside her husband.

'Klaus.' She ignores me, reaches out her hand to touch her husband on the arm. 'Are you OK, Papa?'

My grandfather goes on looking up at the summer sky. His voice seems to come from a great distance. 'This young fellow says he's Roland's son.'

Frau Inga Feldmann adjusts her wheelchair to get a better look at me. She is very old now, but there is something girlish about her face, about the way she looks up at me.

'In that case,' my grandmother says, 'you'd better come in.'

We sit around a pale oak table in the large kitchen-cum-living room. My grandmother has positioned herself with her back to the stainless steel double sink, the long kitchen window. I am placed opposite her; behind her I have a view of tall green trees. My grandfather and the woman called Dolly are seated one on either side of me at the rectangular table. Apart from indicating where I should sit, not a word has been spoken since the hall door was closed and we followed my grandmother's wheelchair along the L-shaped hallway.

Roland's father looks at the two women, at me. In the brighter light of this room his eyes are bluer but his face is paler, the loose skin more parchmenty.

'Speak English,' he says. 'Dolly is my son Terry's wife. She never learned German.' He doesn't bother to conceal his disapproval of this failure of character.

'I live in Ireland,' Dolly says waspishly. 'We don't speak German here.'

'Papa.' There is a hint of a smile on my grandmother's face. 'I'm sure Mr Ritter is not interested in a replay of old family squabbles.'

The old man shrugs, fiddles with his stick. 'If we are to believe Mr Ritter, then he's a part of this family himself. Although I have to say,' looking straight into my eyes, 'it all sounds like a cow-and-bull story to me.'

'A cock-and-bull story,' Dolly says.

'What?'

'You said a *cow*-and-bull story. It's a *cock*-and bull story.'

'English!' My grandfather grins and I half-suspect his mistake has been deliberate. 'It's not logical – cows go with bulls, not cocks.'

'Papa!' My grandmother sounds exasperated, as if this is not the first time she's witnessed these antics.

I sit straighter on the kitchen chair and fiddle with the straps of my rucksack, wondering what kind of family I have stumbled upon.

He grins again but, when he catches my eye, there is nothing softer than steel in the look he gives me.

'So, Mr Ritter,' he says, 'you've come all the way from Germany to tell us a story.' He taps with his stick on the kitchen floor, like a concert MC. 'We are all ears.'

'Paulusstrasse,' I say. 'Number thirty-one, a third-floor apartment in the district of Neukolln, in Berlin.'

The gnarled hands, pocked with dark-brown liver spots, clench and unclench around the crook of the stick.

'What did you say?' A croaky whisper.

'It's where you lived before you came to Ireland.' I have rehearsed these words, as an opening gambit. 'I know because Roland mentioned it in an account he wrote for my mother.' *And I know because I found Familie Feldmann listed in an old street directory for 1931 that the librarian in Neukölln dug out for me.* 'Roland himself went to see the street when they sent him to Berlin.'

The two old people look at each other, then at me. Then I see their gaze switch to something behind me. When I swing round I see what they are looking at: a framed black and white photo of a young man smiling at the camera, at the world, from his perch on the wall above the fridge. I don't need to ask.

The stick falls with a bang from the old man's hands and slides across the floor beside my feet. I stoop to retrieve it; as I hand it to him, I see that his eyes are wet. The Adam's apple bobs, the flesh around it wobbles.

Dolly stands up.

'This is bullshit,' she says, 'absolute bullshit.'

'Shut up, Dolly,' my grandfather tells her.

The kitchen door slams behind her.

The air in the kitchen seems to tremble in her wake, or maybe it is the aftershock of my words.

'You'd better start at the beginning,' my grandfather says. He reaches for his wife's hand. 'Tell it to us slowly. I don't care if you tell it in English or German but it better not be a cock-and-bull story.'

My telling is not impromptu. I am, after all, both a storyteller and a teacher. And of course I am German, which means, according to how others see us, that I am methodical, even plodding. So I know where I will begin my account of the meeting of Roland Feldmann and Petra Ritter: I have made notes, organized them, as if I were indeed writing a story or teaching a lesson.

I begin at the end: my mother's dying, her last words about my father, about a priest in Bad Saarow. My grandfather and my grandmother listen without interrupting; sometimes they exchange a glance or their eyes move to the photo over the fridge. I tell them about Pastor Bruck, about the abandoned sheds and allotments, about Johannes Vos.

I see the question in their eyes, am about to explain to them how I trawled through old Stasi records in Berlin, when we hear the hall door opening and closing. There are voices and footsteps along the hallway, the kitchen door is flung noisily open.

'What's going on here?' Terry Feldmann's soft, round face is flushed. 'Dolly called me with some bullshit story about some fellow claiming to be Roland's son.'

There is a triumphant look on Dolly's face. Both she and Terry are staring at me.

'Who the fuck are you?' Recognition dawns. 'You were in the shop yesterday! What the fuck are you up to?'

'Terry.' His father's voice is low. 'That's no way to speak to a visitor in this house.'

'A visitor? A chancer, more like!'

'Herr Feldmann, this is my son, Terry, who seems to have forgotten his manners.'

I stand up, reach out my hand. Terry ignores it.

'Terry, this is Michael Ritter, from Brandenburg. He's telling us how his mother met your brother, Roland, all those years ago.'

'I suppose his mother was visiting London—'

'Terry!' Whiplash in the voice now. 'You will either leave the room or sit down and listen.'

Terry snorts, looks at his wife. Her face is white with fury but she nods and they both seat themselves on the opposite side of the oak table. I look across at Terry, puffing at his inhaler, and remind myself that it was for this brother that Roland elected to go to East Germany.

'You were telling us about the Stasi records office in Berlin.' My grandmother smiles at me, then leans across and pats Terry on the knee.

I begin again: the comprehensive Stasi records, the incident in the flat at Prenzlauer Berg, the manhunt across the city, the interrogation at Bad Saarow. It was as if those record-keepers didn't know how to leave anything out. But for the cross-referencing in the files to Pastor Bruck and Petra Ritter I should never have found the border guard's report of the killing of Roland Feldmann at the Wall. For all their resources and expertise, the State Security Services had never discovered the true identity of the youngster who had died that night in 1962. The file held a sequence of photographs of his bullet-shattered body: the close-up of his face, oddly unmarked, was unmistakably the same as the picture of the young man on the kitchen wall.

I don't give them the details of the killing. I gloss over it: 'He died.' I take from my wallet a copy of the close-up of his face, hand it to his mother. Roland's eyes are unclosed in the photo, his mouth half-open, as if smiling. For a long moment there is silence in the kitchen as the two old people fondle the picture.

Terry takes the photograph from his mother's fingers. He looks at it for the briefest of moments before tossing it carelessly on the table.

'I tell you this is crap,' he says. 'Roland disappeared in London, the last time I saw him was going into that police station in London. What would he be doing in Berlin?'

All eyes are on me.

I tell them about the Public Records Office at Kew, in south-west London. I tell them about the thirty-years rule, under which thirty-year-old files can be seen by the public. But you have to ask. Sometimes you have to keep asking. I tell them how the Cultural Attaché at the German Embassy in London applied a little pressure on my behalf: I am, after all, a published German author. I don't tell the Feldmann family of the Cultural Attaché's reluctance to help me: I am, after all, a published author of the failed GDR and my favourable reviews were all in publications of that failed, unlamented state.

I tell them about the tiny, almost absurd security fiefdom run by some maniac called Fitch-Bellingham, a war hero who afterwards seemed not to realize that the war was over. I describe the events of that Saturday night in west London, from the alter-cation at High Street Kensington to Roland's trip in the blacked-out van to some unnamed destination in the English countryside. I watch Terry straighten in his chair; I watch him fumble repeatedly for his inhaler. I don't spare him with my words: the account at the PRO in Kew was graphic about Terry's fear, about his weeping.

'There's no need for this.'

His mother's words startle me; she is holding Terry's hand in her own.

'No,' I say. 'I apologize.'

'But how do you know all this?' the old man asks. 'They wouldn't write it in such detail.'

329

'It's very detailed,' I tell him. 'Written by some detective called Ransom. The way he wrote it, he seemed to me like a disillusioned kind of fellow, maybe fed up because he was passed over for promotion, something like that.' I shrug. 'Believe me, it's detailed.'

'I wrote,' the old man says. 'I telephoned and I wrote letters. I wrote letters to the government in Dublin, I wrote to the government in London. I even wrote to the Prime Minister at Ten Downing Street. They just wrote back to say there was no record of my son being in the United Kingdom.'

I don't tell Klaus Feldmann that I have seen his letters in the file at Kew. Old wounds are sometimes best left alone.

Instead, diversion. I tell them that in 1964 the matter of Roland Feldmann somehow came to the attention of the newly elected Labour government: maybe it was chance, maybe an anonymous tip from a disappointed detective. Within months, according to a note initialled by an anonymous civil servant, Fitch-Bellingham was summarily pensioned off and his little fiefdom put out of existence.

A silence settles over the table when I finish my story. A fragile silence: tectonic plates shift, an entire world is being disturbed here. Somehow these people learned to live with Roland Feldmann's disappearance; now his ghost is sitting at their kitchen table.

It is, inevitably, Terry who punctures the silence.

'I tell you, this fellow is a chancer, peddling a yarn that nobody can verify. OK, he's got a photo that looks like Roland but what else has he got? Smoke and mirrors, that's all, nothing else.'

'There's this,' I say, taking the notebook from my rucksack and placing it on the table.

My grandfather reaches for it, turns the pages. I sense that he is seeing only the writing, that he is not reading the words. His wife takes the notebook, looks at a page, turns another. She hands the notebook to Terry.

'It's Roland's writing,' she says. 'I'd know it anywhere.'

'So what!' Terry glares at his parents, at me. 'This guy could have found it or stolen it! We don't know anything about him!'

My own anger is colder. I have no wish to be related to this wheezing, round-shouldered uncle of mine but neither will I allow him to take away from me this personal past that I have spent so long excavating. I realize, looking across the table at Terry, that this past is important to me, that it is not lightly to be taken from me.

'Roland Feldmann,' I say quietly, 'was my father. A friend at the Humboldt did the DNA test.' It would be too painful for them to hear that I sent a fragment from the remains in the ground behind Pastor Bruck's church for testing, along with a swab from my mouth. 'You can see the results if you like.'

'At the Humboldt University?' A strange mixture of reverence and longing in the old man's voice, in his face. 'In Berlin?' He looks across at his son. 'That's good enough for anybody, Terry.' His voice gentle, even pleading.

'So why are you here?' Terry demands. 'What do you want?'

'It's hard to explain. I never knew my father – it's difficult even to call him that. I thought I should meet Roland's family.' It sounds inadequate and I know it. 'I didn't expect . . .' I look at my grandparents.

'You didn't expect to find two old relics still alive,' my grandfather says.

'I'm sorry, I didn't mean—'

'Yes, you did.' The pale blue eyes are twinkling. 'Tell the truth.'

I can only shrug.

Terry won't let it go.

'So you want nothing from us, right? So tell us who you are, what you do. How d'you earn a living?'

'I write.' Again I look in my rucksack, place *Workers' Dawn* on the table. The full-colour portrait of a shirt-sleeved, muscular factory operative stares up at us from the dust jacket.

Terry handles the book as if it were radioactive. He gingerly turns it over, looks at my author picture on the back cover with its thumbnail biography.

'You're telling us you make a living from this stuff?'

'I also teach.'

'Where?'

'I'm unemployed at the moment.'

Terry guffaws. 'An unemployed scribbler lands on our doorstep but tells us he wants nothing from us! Tell that to the marines!'

His father has my book in his hands. He touches my grandmother's arm, points at the back cover biography.

'It says here you have a PhD from Rostock University, yes?' I nod. 'So we must call you Dr Ritter.'

'I've been called worse in recent times.'

'I'll bet you have.' Terry has taken back the book from his father and is studying the imprint page. 'This thing was published in nineteen eighty-nine in Leipzig.' He looks almost happy. 'You're a fucking communist, aren't you, all the way from good old East Germany, the home of democracy and freedom?'

'Yes.' Defiance stirs in me. 'I was a member of the Party.'

'The same fucking Party that shot our Roland?'

'The Party didn't—'

'Yes, the Party didn't shoot anybody; they just gave the fucking orders, right?'

I have no answer for him. I am not about to try to explain to this choleric fellow that this paradox keeps me awake at night; that the country I loved had killed the father I never knew.

'Cat got your tongue?' Terry slams the book down on the table, leans back in his chair, work well done. His wife is nodding sagely at his side.

My grandfather clears his throat; we wait for him to speak.

'Your Aunt Rosa was a communist,' he says, 'your mother's sister. The Nazis got rid of her.'

I almost smile.

'It wasn't the Nazis who killed my brother,' Terry says. 'Not if we're to believe this fellow.'

'This "fellow" is your nephew, Terry.' My grandfather's voice is even. 'At least I believe he is.'

'We'll see about that,' Terry says.

'What we'll see about right now,' my grandmother says, 'is a bite of lunch.'

'Some of us have work to do.' Terry pushes back his chair, gets to his feet. 'I'm going back to the shop.'

His wife leaves the kitchen with him. We hear their voices, indistinct, in the hall.

'You'll stay for lunch?' My grandmother looks at me. 'Won't you, Michael?'

It's the first time she has called me by name.

'Yes, thank you.' I don't know, yet, what to call her.

'And we'll be seeing you again? You'll be staying for a few days?'

'Yes, I'll be staying for a few days.'

Thirty-two

The few days became a few weeks, stretched to a few months. The premises of Feldmann, Watchmakers and Jewellers, contained a one-bedroom apartment on the upper floor, behind the workshop and the office areas. My grandfather took me to see the flat that first Sunday afternoon. The entrance was from an unpaved yard at the back of the store, just one of a number of service entrances and delivery bays. The back door of Feldmann's was as nondescript as its neighbours' but it was steel-plated and carried three locks. The old man locked it again from the inside before we climbed the bare, narrow stairs to the first floor.

Another door, another pair of locks. The old man never fumbled, just drew the right key from the heavy ring each time. Inside, my grandfather pointed to yet another steel door at the end of the corridor.

'That's the shop,' he said, 'the workshops and offices.' He was opening the other door in the corridor. 'This is what I want to show you.'

The flat inside smelled musty, as if it hadn't been used in a long time. It was furnished but the rooms echoed emptily to the pock-pock of the old man's stick as he limp-marched through the rooms. Living room, bedroom, kitchen, and bathroom. A faded magnolia on the walls, a sense of abandonment in the stale air.

'We used to have staff living here,' he said. 'Now they want mod cons, new kitchens, shiny shower units. It's been empty for years.'

I didn't tell him that it felt familiar, would not have been out of place in any of the old apartment blocks back home. I knew why I'd been invited to this viewing.

'It's fine,' I said.

He looked at me, smiled.

'You'll stay a while then?'

It was as simple as that. No deal, no agreement as to how long I'd stay. We both knew it couldn't be any other way. We knew next to nothing about each other yet we shared a long history.

My Uncle Terry wasn't interested in exploring any shared history. Creating any kind of friendship didn't interest him either. When my grandfather suggested that, in the interests of added security, I should be given keys to the steel door that separated the flat from the shop, he simply said, 'No.' He gave the same answer to the suggestion that I might pick up the mail from the shop's private box at the post office, or even make hand deliveries (there weren't many) to customers in the town. I didn't care, although I'd have been glad to do something to please the old fellow. I understood why my grandfather didn't contest Terry's imperious refusals: to have lost one son was enough . . .

Roland Feldmann had two younger sisters, both primary school teachers, both married with kids and living in Dublin. On a weekend in September both sisters arrived in Galway, minus husbands and broods, to conduct their personal investigation of this unexpected nephew from Germany. Lunch in my grandparents' house, where these heavily made-up aunts had grown up, was a strained affair. Politeness, extreme civility, was the essential accompaniment of the food but I had a sense, through it all, of husbands waiting in Dublin for a full report of how their inheritance might be affected by my arrival. I chewed and swallowed and sipped and went through my story yet again, handing around the postcard-size photos of my mother.

'You can see why our Roland fell for her,' my grandfather said.

His daughters nodded politely but offered no comment. *An uneducated floozy who seduced our impressionable brother*: say it, I thought. Like me, they held their tongues. I wanted to stand up, declare that I had come only to find out what kind of place and people had produced the man my mother had fallen in love with, that I had no interest in their present or future wealth. For all that, I was warmed by my grandparents' acceptance of me; if they had misgivings about their son's brief and impetuous affair with my mother, such misgivings were never voiced.

It was partly the old folks who kept me there. Finding living grandparents was at first a novelty; as the weeks passed and we became easier with one another, we became, also, something like family. Sometimes one or other of them would say something about settling in Galway; more than once my grandfather made noises about redecorating the flat behind the shop and putting in new furniture. I made non-committal replies. My grandfather, especially, knew that I couldn't go on simply living rent-free in his flat and doing nothing productive. 'You're a Doctor of Literature,' he told me, 'you could get work in the university here.' I walked through the campus, through the odd mix of grandiose Victorian and ugly modern architecture, and I went out the back gate on to a traffic-clogged road. I never went back.

I had the time – and the new trainers – to walk the rest of the town. Around the rabbit warren of inner-city streets. East along the busy Dublin road, forever choked and choking with traffic.

West by the sea; even here it was traffic, not the Atlantic Ocean, that ruled the waves of the town's daily life.

I didn't care much for the place. It seemed to count cars and punts, the local currency. Looking at the bill for a coffee and cake could give you vertigo. And still, as in a mania, the town went on reproducing itself: the skyline was scarred with the steel of cranes, the air barked with the growl of diggers and drills. Housing estates were mushrooming like a virus, the shop tills went on ringing. *Another new Berlin.*

I called at my grandparents' house most days. Coffee and talk, turning the pages of photo albums, picking a slow way through the biscuit tin of snapshots that had never made it to the albums. Trawling the years, discovering and exploring a world that I had never known but which was growing into me like a transplanted organ. Sitting in that big kitchen at the back of the flat-roofed house we gave a simple, existential joy to one another, those two old folks and myself.

'You'll be staying for Christmas, Michael.' My grandmother slipped it in, innocently, as she was pouring me a fresh cup of coffee. She had her back to the window, her face in shadow; beyond the window the November day was dark, grey-skied.

'But of course he'll be staying for Christmas.' My grandfather was seated in characteristic pose: short body ramrod straight, leathery hands clutching the knobbed head of his cane, the cane planted firmly on the floor between his small, slippered feet.

'I don't know,' I said. Their friendship – their *love* – was seductive but I was tired of my aimless walking, weary of the view from the flat behind the shop.

'Terry will come round, don't worry.' My grandfather tried to smile.

'It's not that, I just feel I should be *doing* something.' Now it was my turn to try to smile. 'Don't ask me what. Just *something*, anything.' I swallowed. 'Back home.'

'And what about Jennifer?' My grandfather now trying *not* to smile, an innocent cat among the pigeons.

I laughed. My grandfather didn't miss much on his forays into the House of Feldmann. Maybe, I figured, you had to be like that to establish a successful business in an alien land, to become, yourself, a part of that landscape.

'What about Jennifer?'

'She's a lovely girl, Michael. You're not just going to walk away from her, are you?'

I'd have stayed there all that time anyway but knowing Jennifer made it easier.

We'd become lovers a few weeks after I'd given her my book. Not wanting another face-off with Terry, I'd waited outside the shop for her; the eyebrows went up in mock surprise when she stepped out on to the street a little after six o'clock and saw me standing there, rucksack hanging from my left shoulder. She took the book, she took my arm and we went for a drink in a pub around the corner.

It was probably in the same pub, a couple of weeks later, that she broached, with gentleness, the subject of Terry.

'He's a nice man, a good boss and now he's worried.'

I sipped the black beer, waited for her to go on.

'C'mon, Michael,' a gentle dig in the ribs, 'you know what's worrying him.'

'I know,' I said. 'He thinks this East German has arrived on his doorstep looking for his share of the loot.' Another sip of the bitter stout. 'What do you think, Jennifer?'

'If I thought you were a gold-digger, Herr Michael Ritter, I wouldn't be sitting here with you.'

'I came,' I said, 'just searching for a little information, maybe even some answers. Instead a miracle, I find a grandfather, a grandmother.'

Another dig in my ribs; the young barman looked away, laughing to himself.

'And?'

'OK,' I said, 'I found you too.'

We slipped into an indulgent daily routine: a walk together after work through the emptying streets, a drink and a bite to eat, a stroll to her flat in an old three-storey building beside the river. It was easy to fall in love with her; it was not so easy just to say goodnight outside her door. 'It won't hurt to wait,' she'd say, kissing me and pushing me away at the same time. She was wrong about that but at the same time I knew the truth of her words.

It was in the flat behind Feldmann, Watchmakers and Jewellers that we made love for the first time. She'd been quieter than usual in the cafe but by then I knew what to expect: she was always like that on Saturday evening, the busiest day of the week, as if she'd been forced to give away too much of herself over the glass-topped counter. She picked at her meal. No, she didn't want to go for a walk. Not the cinema either. 'Let's go home, Michael.' She looked at me. 'To your place.' She was even quieter in the flat. It was her first time there but she made no comment. 'Just hold me,' she said. We lay beside each other on top of the bed and she fell asleep in my arms. I was still awake, my arms around her, when she stirred a couple of hours later. She kissed me, nestled her body into mine. Making love to her was like finding myself, like coming home after a long journey.

'You have a good name,' she whispered. 'A good, strong name. *Michael Ritter*. Michael the knight.' A kiss, a sigh in the darkness of the unlit bedroom. 'Sir Michael, *my* knight.'

'I never thought of that.' Why were we whispering? *'Ritter*, yes, the knight.'

'Men!' She was giggling like a small girl. 'They can't even see what's in front of their eyes.'

Desire stirred in me. 'I hope you can see what's in front of you now, Lady Jennifer.'

It was a long, dreamy night. The curtains were open, the red neon of a nightclub across the road pulsed like a silent heartbeat on the wall opposite the bed. Sometimes the whoosh of a late-night car came in from the night, the pounding bass of a car stereo. Her nearness made magic in the night, lent enchantment to it all – every flash of light or shadow, every stir and silence in the darkness. I knew, holding her in my arms, that my life was forever changed.

Afterwards, looking back on those first weeks and months with Jennifer, I could not distinguish one day from another, one loving from another. It's like holding a book you have read and loved but the pages are stuck together, cannot be separated, leaf by leaf, page from page. Still, it's in your hands. The love, too.

And she could read me like a book. I was wondering how to tell her when she saved me the trouble.

'You're going back, aren't you?' We were walking by the sea, collars turned up against November and the wind.

'Yes.' I looked away from her, out at the white-topped waves rumbling in the darkness. 'I have to.'

'Back to your workers' dawn.'

'That sort of thing isn't allowed in the great new reunified Bundesrepublik.' I felt her hand squeeze mine. 'Or at least it's frowned upon by the new powers that be.'

'But you're going back anyway. *Mein Ritter ohne Furcht und Tadel.*' She said it in German. My knight in shining armour.

'Maybe I'm the wrong kind of knight for today's Germany.'

'You don't really believe that.'

'I think maybe Roland Feldmann was the *real* knight.' We stopped on the dark prom, hand in hand, facing the sea. 'Look at it, a quiet place on the edge of nowhere, my father comes out of it like Sir Lancelot and gives his life for – for love.'

Jennifer leaned against me, her fingers tightening around mine.

'All of that's true.' She knew the story, had listened to my words about it all more than once. 'But maybe your mother is the real knight – a "lady knight" – of it all. She *lived* a life for you. It can't have been easy, and that's putting it mildly. She had only a memory to keep her going and that was a memory she could never talk about. It was all she had. That,' fingers tightening again, 'and you.'

My mother's face came at me out of the darkness above the Atlantic waves. The penny-pinching in the flat opposite the railway station, the mend-and-make-do philosophy.

'You're right, Jen.' I kissed her lightly. 'As usual.'

'So.' She didn't look at me now, just stared out at the dark expanse of sand, at the unseen waves. 'When are you leaving?'

'In a few days.'

'Christmas is only a few weeks away.'

'I can't explain it, I just want to be home.'

'And us? You and me?'

'I love you.' The words seemed inadequate but I said them again anyway. 'I love you. Come with me.'

'You think I'd let you waltz out of here without me?'

'So you'll come.'

'It's only a few weeks to Christmas, Michael.' She reached up to muss my hair. 'Some of us are working folk. I can't just walk out on them at the busiest time of the year.'

'Then come for Silvester,' I said, 'for New Year's Eve.'

'Michael, after Christmas the whole country goes mad on Sales.' She said it with a capital S. 'They'll need me in the shop until January.'

'Money!' I snorted. 'Always money!'

'Don't knock it, my Teutonic knight. You're going to need some loot to support this Irish colleen in your Bundesrepublik.'

A car cruised by, headlights sweeping the darkness, somebody bound for home, perhaps late after a long day in some shop or factory. A small dog yapped past, dragging its owners on the lead, a young couple out for their constitutional from their mortgaged semi-detached. Who was I to take this gorgeous creature from such domesticity to such uncertainty?

'Maybe you should wait until I've found a job.'

'What happened to my knight in shining armour?'

'I've told you I was fired—'

'Michael! *I'm* a worker too. I don't expect someone else to hand me my dawn or my anything else.' She put her finger to my lips. 'No more daft talk. You just have that flat sparkling for me when I arrive in January. I always did want to visit the ancient city of Brandenburg-on-the-Havel!'

I had to run to catch up with her, skipping along the prom. Her face shone in the light of the street lamps, laughing and unafraid.

Thirty-three

December 1994, Berlin

I left the train from Schönefeld airport at Hackescher Market. Below the elevated railway tracks the marketplace was stirring to morning life. Cafe waiters fiddled at positioning tables, chairs, plastic menus. Stall operators played dominoes on their trestle tables with their cartons of bric-a-brac, books, records, bits and pieces of forgotten, discarded lives.

I made my way down the station steps and under the railway arch. The nearest cafe looked no different from the rest and the Turkish waiter was quick with the coffee. I could have gone inside but I sat under the striped awning and turned my collar up against the December bite and let the hot coffee and the *Bauernfrühstück* – fried potatoes and eggs – warm me, ease the tiredness out of me. I hadn't slept on the night bus from Galway to Dublin, or on the dawn flight to Berlin: the heady love-making with Jennifer before the frantic dash for the bus was too much with me on the long haul over land and sea.

And there was something about the Hackescher Market which made sleep seem absurd: the energy of these unfettered capitalists, with their shops and stalls and cafes, was as palpable as the rumble of the trains above our heads. The Holy Grail they sought was nothing more exalted than bankable currency but they were, nevertheless, full of religious zeal in their commercial crusade.

Enough. Who was I, unemployed teacher-cum-scribbler, to look down my sometime Party member's nose at their buying and selling? My Uncle Terry had been blunt in reminding me of my economic status. Although he'd overlooked my lowly status the day before I left, when he'd told me he'd been looking at the Berlin property market, that perhaps I'd like to locate some suitable letting properties for him in what he felt sure was 'a rising market'. I would be paid a percentage of the rents I collected: 'You can't lose, Michael.' I told him I'd think about it. I had, for about a second.

Terry wasn't an easy man for me to like. In a way, he'd cost my father his life, condemned my mother to an existence founded on loneliness. It had been – as usual – Jennifer who reminded me that, without Terry, Roland Feldmann and Petra Ritter would never have met in that cafe in East Berlin.

I paid the Turkish waiter, shouldered my rucksack. I was travelling light. It didn't take much to keep you going for six months – a couple of weeks in the London hostel, the rest of the time in Ireland – although the traders in the Hackescher Market probably wouldn't like to hear that.

Trains ran about once an hour from the Zoogarten station to Brandenburg but first I had unfinished business to attend to. I went back under the arch and across to the tram stop.

Third time lucky. I'd tried twice, during the months I'd commuted to Mauerstrasse, excavating the old Stasi files. The staff got to know me; in the mornings my files were waiting for me. It had been the cross-referencing that led me to him; finding his name in Berlin's new and improved telephone directory had been a surprise.

But two trips on the tram had led only to a locked door on the second floor of a shabby apartment block in Pankow. On the second occasion the next-door occupant – an elderly woman in hairnet, housecoat and slippers – had peeped out into the corridor for just long enough to let me know that her absent-silent neighbour had a fondness for the drink. I'd hammered again on the door but it had remained unopened.

The mid-morning tram was almost empty. A couple of women with plastic shopping bags, an old man reading a newspaper. Tram passengers who seemed not to have caught the city's tide of prosperity. Maybe they were too slow. Or maybe they had old Party cards hidden in their inside pockets.

The tram rattled north through the wide streets. The tram stops had been upgraded to include full-colour advertisements for beer and cigarettes; the peeling apartment blocks on either side remained as they had been when my father had made his own journey north through neighbouring streets. Only a few streets separated our journeys yet we travelled on different planets.

Maybe the travellers hadn't changed.

I got off at the town hall in Pankow. The few shops on the street had cabbages and potatoes on display in boxes, brushes and plastic buckets hanging from wall hooks. There wasn't much evidence of any commercial tigers out here, Celtic or German.

I waited at the traffic lights beside the supermarket, crossed the street, and swung left. Our new masters hadn't got around to fixing pavements or applying any paint in these side streets. *Sauerkohl und Diverse*, the wall beside a boarded-up street-level window proclaimed, 'Sauerkraut and Miscellaneous', the words painted directly on to the crumbling wall in the world that was gone. I wondered what 'miscellaneous' items had been sold or bartered through that window, what lives had been lived behind it. And where those lives were now being lived.

The block I sought was one of a group of six. All six blocks looked the same, varying only in degrees of undernourishment, abandonment. Windows broken, a few boarded up. Metal rails on tiny balconies rusted, bent or just missing. A few windows gleamed, polished by hardy owners who had decided to tough it out among the graffiti and the spilled garbage. Or maybe they simply had no choice.

I figured that the occupant with the drink problem in the second-floor apartment definitely had no choice. His CV included more baggage than a Party member's card.

When I knocked on the door of his apartment, it was, again, the neighbouring door that opened. The old lady seemed to be wearing the same slippers and housecoat. It was over six months since she'd seen me but I could see the recognition dawning in her eyes.

'He's in there, definitely.' In a whisper. 'I can hear him.' Her door closed as silently as it had been opened.

I hammered on the door, then again. And again. Three times was enough. More than enough.

From behind the door came a soft, shuffling noise. I stood in front of the peephole.

The door opened, the length of a security chain.

'Yes?' A chain smoker's hoarseness in the single word.

And for a moment I was speechless, struck dumb by this voice from a lost world.

'Yes?' he said again. 'What d'you want?'

'I want to talk to you, Major Fuchs.'

I could hear the gulping noise in his throat.

'There's no one here of that name.'

The door began to close.

I stuck my foot in the opening and pushed. I had journeyed too far, through too much pain, to be fobbed off now by a flimsy door chain.

'Open the fucking door, Fuchs, or I'll break it down.' I kept my voice low. 'Or maybe I'll start shouting that you're Major Fuchs from the Stasi.'

'What do you want? Who are you?'

'You knew my parents, Major Fuchs.'

'Go away. I'm going to phone the police.'

'Do that, they might like to hear from an old comrade.' This time I kicked the door. 'Now open up before I lose my temper with you.'

'Who—'

'Now!'

I let him close the door, heard the chain rasp along its metal slide.

The door opened and Major Fuchs, late of the Stasi, stood in the doorway looking up at me.

And I was looking down into those yellow eyes that my father's scribbled words had described, that Pastor Bruck had spoken of. The strange yellow was faded now, the eyes rheumy with age, perhaps with drink.

'What d'you want from me?' He was small, shrunken, the strands of greasy hair drawn flat across a balding pate, but he stood defiantly in front of me in the doorway.

I pushed past him, shoved the door shut behind me with the sole of my shoe.

A staleness filled the small living room, as though the windows were never opened. A stack of old newspapers rested on the floor beside a button-back armchair. The sink in the recessed kitchen area was almost clean; judging by the single cup and plate on the draining board, Major Fuchs didn't do much entertaining.

'Tell me what you want.'

'Why don't you sit down, Major Fuchs.'

'Don't call me that!'

'Sit.'

He looked even more shrunken in the old armchair. I noticed his freckled hands, the odd way he held them, the knuckles like huge, misshapen knobs.

'Arthritis.' He caught me looking. 'The doctors say they can do nothing. Lying bastards.' He drew the frayed cuffs of the brown cardigan down until they covered the twisted hands. 'Tell me what you want or get out and leave me alone.'

'You knew my mother and father.' It was hard to believe that this gnomish creature, cornered in an armchair, could have inspired fear, inflicted pain.

'Big deal,' he said. 'I knew lots of people.'

'You broke my mother's fingers.' I tried to keep my voice steady. 'With a hammer. In a printing works in Bad Saarow. Over thirty years ago.'

The eyes blinked. I saw the hands fidget under the frayed sleeve ends.

'I don't know what you're talking about.'

'I can beat it out of you, if you like.'

'Why don't you go to the fucking truth commission, or whatever the fucking *Wessies* call it? They'll write it all down, check the records – whatever the Americans didn't bother to steal – and they'll declare that Major Fuchs was a very naughty boy.' He stirred in the chair, clenched and unclenched his hands. 'D'you think I give a shit? Look at this dump.' One deformed hand emerged from its covering, gestured at the flat. 'I found it empty when I came back from Erfurt, I didn't even have to break in, the door was open, everyone gone fucking west. Now they won't give me my pension! All I did was serve my country! And for doing my duty, I'm rewarded with this shithole!'

The outburst exhausted him. He slumped back in the chair, smaller than ever. He took a cigarette from the packet on the table beside him, put it between his thin lips. I watched his swollen fingers fumble with the matches and took the box from him. He didn't look at me as I struck the match and held it to his cigarette. His breath came loud, hollow, as he sucked in the nicotine.

He twisted in the chair, looked out through the uncurtained window at the sky like someone searching for answers, explanations, a lost world. The thin shoulders shrugged and then, as though something had been decided, the yellow eyes came back to mine.

'A tough little piece of stuff.' I realized he was talking about my mother. 'I only meant to scare her but it got out of hand.' He sucked on the cigarette. 'I only meant to smash the fucking violin.' Another suck, the smoke exhaled in a thin plume. 'I forget her name.'

'Her name was Petra Ritter.' *And you took a hammer to her fingers.*

He nodded. Another case, another name.

'The British had sent in a spy, the bastard nearly killed me over in Prenzlauer Berg.' He touched his left ear. 'Ear still hurts in the cold.' Another desperate drag on the cigarette, the yellow eyes narrowing at me through the smoke. 'Your mother had something to do with it, I was sure of it, but the powers that be got cold feet or just lost interest, they wouldn't let me get on with it. End it, they said. *End it!* So I delivered a body to some priest out in Bad Saarow, let him take care of it.' Another pull, another plume of smoke. 'And then they sent me to fucking Erfurt to take charge of records. Me, a fucking clerk!'

'You broke that priest's back, Major Fuchs.'

'I told you, it's *Herr* Fuchs now.'

'He's still bent, still in pain.'

'The old fella is still alive?' He looked vaguely interested, surprised.

'My father's not alive. It was my father's body you delivered to the priest.'

Fuchs straightened in the chair. 'So I *was* right all along! That little blonde piece *was* working with the Engländer!'

'That's all you've got to say? That you were right all along?'

Fuchs lit a fresh cigarette from the stub of the old one. He pushed the dead butt into the overflowing ashtray.

'What d'you want me to say? That I did what I thought was wrong? We did what we thought was right, Herr . . . ?'

'Ritter, Michael Ritter.'

'We were a country under siege, Herr Ritter, our way of life constantly under attack in newspapers, television, radio. And spies, they kept sending spies. Why couldn't they leave us alone? And I had a job to do, I was an officer of the security forces. Why shouldn't I defend my country the way I was trained to defend it?'

His question hung in the cigarette smoke in the dingy flat. All through my own journey of discovery I'd been pondering the same question.

'D'you ever think that maybe we were wrong, Herr Fuchs?'

'We?' He hadn't been a policeman for nothing.

Anyway, I had nothing to gain by not telling him.

'I was a member of the Party too.'

'But . . . your mother . . .'

'She never spoke of it, not until last year. She was dying. I knew nothing about my father before that.'

'I interviewed the border guards who were on duty that night,' Fuchs said. 'One of them said the damnedest thing, so odd I still remember it. He said the Engländer was almost away, that it looked like he stood up deliberately, as if he wanted – you know, as if he didn't want to get away.'

'Maybe he wanted to draw your attention away from my mother.'

'Maybe, but why was he here at all?'

I didn't answer Fuchs. That part of it wasn't his business. Maybe none of it was.

Snow was falling, soft flakes melting, dying, on the window-panes. I stood up, picked up my rucksack.

'May I ask, Herr Ritter, what you do?'

I laughed. 'I'm a teacher, Herr Fuchs, and a bit of a writer, but now I share your fate.'

'You've been sent to Erfurt?' Something like a grin opened his features.

'Not yet,' I said. 'They fired me from my school in Brandenburg.'

He looked at my rucksack. 'So you're leaving?'

'I'm on my way back there.'

He was silent a while, looking over his shoulder at the softly falling snow.

'It can't last for ever.' For a moment I thought he was talking about the snow. 'In the end there's always a thaw, no matter how long it takes. They can't go on forever punishing fellows like me – even fellows like you, Herr Ritter. When the Wall came down, they could've left us alone, let us try to work out something for ourselves but, no, they had to take us over and teach us their way. They forget, Herr Ritter, that it's still our country as well, yours and mine.'

He levered himself out of the armchair. When he stood close to me I could smell the cigarettes, the sweet cologne. Fuchs wasn't an easy man to like but what he said bore the tang of truth.

When he offered his hand at the door, I accepted it.

'Herr Ritter,' he said, 'will you come again?'

'I don't know.' The past stared up at me from the faded yellow eyes. My father dying in the snow. My mother living on with her silent grief, her shattered violin. I struggled, but maybe I had to begin forgiving this ruined husk of a creature for what he had done to them.

And yourself, Michael Ritter. You need also to begin forgiving yourself.

'Yes,' I said, 'I probably will.'

Outside, the snow was still falling, large soft flakes carpeting the roofs of cars and houses. I left my head uncovered, opened my mouth to taste the falling sweetness. Above the rooftops a giant crane swung through the December sky, quarrying the last working hours from the fading light. The hammering, the drilling echoed across the streets, man and machine reshaping the city.

Our city. It's still our country, yours and mine.

I had to believe the old fox was right. The thaw would come, it always did.

In the end, if I kept knocking, they'd let me into *some* classroom. And if I kept the faith – in what I had been taught and in what I had discovered – my words would find a home on *some* printed page.

I looked at my watch. It was still on Irish time: half past one. Jennifer would be waiting beside the phone in the small staffroom of Feldmann, Watchmakers and Jewellers. My grandfather and grandmother would be at their lunch of soup and sandwiches in their big kitchen. Them I would call tomorrow after I'd handed over their cheque to Pastor Bruck. 'We're too old for the trip,' my grandfather had said. 'This is a small thanks for what he did for our Roland, it will help with his church.'

There was another cheque in my pocket, for me. We'd almost argued about it. 'You're a member of this family,' he'd said, pressing the cheque on me. I knew that my uncle and my aunts didn't welcome my appearance but I didn't care; the old man's words were enough, like a fire blazing in a house that had grown cold.

When I reached the crossroads I could see the tram coming through the snow, the bell ringing like a song. The lights were red but I sauntered across the road anyway to the tram stop: you had to start somewhere at learning to break the old rules.

THE BERLIN CROSSING

Bonus Material

Author's Note

Q & A with Kevin Brophy

Reading Group Questions

Author's Note

In the 1990s, after the fall of the German Democratic Republic (GDR), there was an understandable reluctance among many who had been Party members to wear their past on their sleeve. In my work as an English-language teacher in Germany I was fortunate enough to meet a few such individuals who took me into their confidence. These very different individuals, regardless of where they lived in the GDR, shared a common sense of grievance: in the 'new' Germany their accomplishments and experience were spurned and, secondly, many of the 'Wessies' who had come east were, to them, just a bunch of carpetbaggers.

It was from the personal stories of these disenchanted former citizens of the GDR that the idea for this book emerged.

During various trips, teaching and otherwise, to the former GDR, many people helped with information and anecdotes. These included not only students, as I have said, but also teaching colleagues, tourist office personnel in the city of Brandenburg, railway staff in Berlin, hotel staff in many cities. And the man (or woman) in the street in umpteen towns and cities who was ready to help with some snippet or opinion. The office worker returning to work after lunch just off Friedrichstrasse was typical: I wanted to know how the U-Bahn functioned in the divided city; what I got was a personal history of a GDR adolescence. To my shame, I neglected to record my informant's name.

I do recall that on that occasion I was on my way to the Research Centre and Memorial Site in Mauerstrasse, Berlin. And I well recall that my inquiries there were answered with unfailing grace and patience by the staff.

I dipped into a lot of books about the Berlin Wall and the GDR. I am indebted especially to *Stasiland* by Anna Funder for its account of a failed escape attempt; *The Stasi Files* by Anthony Glees gave valuable information about GDR activities in the UK. Detailed information on the Berlin Wall is taken from the map pamphlet *Walk The Wall*, published by the Museum at Checkpoint Charlie.

I have taken liberties with the little town of Bad Saarow: the town, as far as I know, had no Institute of Cartography and Pastor Bruck's church is entirely a figment of my loving imagination. I chose the town simply because I liked the place and the people.

And I can say the same for the city of Brandenburg-on-the-Havel. The city, like many others in the old GDR, has suffered in the wake of reunification – it's a bit down-at-heel and its population is declining – but, for its faded elegance and its unstinting friendliness, it is very dear to me.

Finally, the usual caveat: any errors in the book are mine and mine alone.

Q & A with Kevin Brophy

1) Did you always want to be a writer? What inspired you to start writing?

I *always* wanted to be a writer. I can remember, aged nine or ten, telling my mother, in the kitchen of our military barracks married quarters, that I was going to write books when I grew up. Ever practical, she asked if I thought I could earn a living that way.

As a boy I read comics and later the usual fare: Franklin W Dixon, *Bomba the Jungle Boy*, *The Hardy Boys*, *Jennings*.

2) What is the structure of your writing day?

When I'm working on a book I try to get in a few hours at the kitchen table five days a week, if I skimp during the week I try to make up for it by working Saturday or Sunday. I have a handsome leather-tooled desk in a dedicated office but somehow nothing happens except bill-paying and other nuisances. The kitchen inspires – perhaps because the kettle is to hand for frequent brew-ups.

3) Who are the writers you most admire, and who are your biggest influences?

John le Carré is the master – not just of a genre but of the novel. The sustained quality of his work over a long life of writing is staggering. I admire the novels of Alan Furst; also the East European sequence of novels by Olen Steinhauer. And how can you beat Graham Greene for storytelling with a bleak heart? And for its kind, even sentimental heart – as well as its storytelling – my favourite book is *David Copperfield*.

4) What advice would you give to aspiring novelists?

Keep reading and keep writing. And ask yourself: for whom am I writing? After all, it is the reader who pays for your scintillating output . . .

5) What is the inspiration for your characters, and how do they evolve?

The idea for the disenchanted character of Michael Ritter came to me from listening to former card-carrying members of the Socialist Party in the German Democratic Republic: these were folk I met as a teacher of English in the reunified Germany. Their discomfort – even distress – in the Federal Republic was as real as their confusion; they could enjoy the benefits of the new Germany but they were also deeply aware of what they had lost.

Dissent, of a limited and controlled variety, was allowed in the GDR, which is why the startling revelations about his real father are made to Michael Ritter by none other than an evangelical priest. Even dyed-in-the-wool party members like Michael would recognise the integrity of 'mistaken' enthusiasts who persisted with their 'faith' under the most difficult conditions.

6) A large part of *The Berlin Crossing* is set in 1960s Germany. Do you enjoy writing about different countries and time periods?

Writing about another country and its history has to be considered a presumptuous activity. My only defence is that, over many years and many visits, I have come to love Germany and her people as much as my own country.

7) Did the story ever take a direction which surprised you? If so, how?

I don't write a plot outline before starting a novel, but with *The Berlin Crossing*, I had the story fairly clear in my mind before I put pen to paper. The 'surprises' came for me in smaller ways: I started a scene knowing what needed to be forwarded in the plot or what theme(s) needed highlighting and then some minor detail/character opened up from God-knows-where and lended life to it all.

8) Were there any characters in the novel you particularly enjoyed writing about, or any you found it difficult to sympathise with?

It would be impossible for me to carry on with a character if I couldn't be in sympathy with him or her. Even the 'bad guys' are your creation and must have your respect. At the beginning of *The Berlin Crossing* Michael Ritter is a sad, bitter young man without a future but in that very sadness, that very bitterness, I can feel for him.

Frau Mertens is one of those respected characters that ramble in from nowhere: you see her (or rather I do!) first as a neighbour-cypher in Michael Ritter's apartment block and then she assumes a fullness, insists on your writing more 'roundly' about her to show her goodness as well as her limitations.

Before I started the last section of the novel I had no notion of what kind of people Michael Ritter's grandparents were. When the door of the house in Galway opened, there surfaced in my mind an old man in Germany whom I have come to know and admire and – bingo! – I was off . . .

9) How challenging did you find it writing about such a conflicted spell in Germany's history?

Berlin is for me the most evocative of all cities. I walk its streets and I am negotiating a fault-line in history. I hear the tramp of marching boots, the boom of artillery, the raised voices of hate, of insanity. But I hear also the insistent song of survival, of love. I suppose what my imagination is hearing is the anthem of a people and a country which lived and almost died but learned and goes on learning.

As I said earlier, I love the place and for my love I hope my writing will be understood . . .

10) What are you writing next?

My next novel is another incursion into Germany, a love-story-cum-spy-story spanning the sixties, seventies and eighties and culminating in the fall of the Berlin Wall.

Reading Group Questions

1. *The Berlin Crossing* deals with several different themes. What are these and which resonated the most with you?

2. The reunification of Germany left those who had previously supported the GDR feeling bewildered and displaced. Discuss the novel's portrayal of the after-effects of reunification.

3. What purpose does the split time chronology serve in bringing the novel's main themes to the fore?

4. 'We did what we thought was right. Why shouldn't I defend my country in the way I was trained to defend it?' (Major Fuchs). 'It was the business of Fitch-Bellingham and his like to make the darkness safe, to patrol the night borders of Shakespeare's sceptred isle.' Discuss the novel's depiction of agents in both the east and west. How far do you think the individuals are driven by ideology, patriotism or their own personal agenda?

5. 'This paradox keeps me awake at night; that the country I loved had killed the father I never knew.' Can Michael ever reconcile himself to this knowledge? Discuss Michael's conflicted loyalties.

6. How do you think Michael changes over the course of the novel? Does finding out about his past set him at ease with his present?

7. What do you think of the depiction of Stasi Germany in the novel?

8. Which character did you find the most sympathetic, and why?

9. What are the similarities and differences between Roland's relationship with Petra, and Michael's with Jennifer?

10. The novel is about one man's search for his roots. Discuss how themes of identity are portrayed within the novel.

ALISON PICK

Far to Go

'*Mamenka and I send you a hug and a snuggle. We look at your photograph every day and pray to God for your safekeeping . . .*'

Czechoslovakia, 1939.

Pavel and Anneliese Bauer dote on their six-year-old son, Pepik, and enjoy a life of domestic comfort. But as rumours of the Nazi threat, and then German troops, reach the Sudetenland, this charmed existence is turned on its head: for all that the Bauers barely consider themselves Jewish, their lives are now in danger.

Far to Go plunges us into the hearts of a family fleeing for their lives, and offered a desperate chance to save their child. Above all, it is a story about love, the painful choices it demands of us, and the way it endures.

'Emotionally powerful . . . Full of foreboding, Pick's book is never less than psychologically convincing: it deftly conveys both the sense of gathering storm and the denial and self deceit of those facing it' *Financial Times*

'Resolutely compassionate and unflinchingly honest . . . [an] extraordinary story' *Daily Mail*

978 0 7553 7943 9

headline
review

EMYLIA HALL

The Book of Summers

Beth Lowe has been sent a parcel.

Inside is a letter informing her that Marika, her long-estranged mother, has died. There is also a scrapbook Beth has never seen before. Entitled The Book of Summers, it's stuffed with photographs and mementos compiled by her mother to record the seven glorious childhood summers Beth spent in rural Hungary. It was a time when she trod the tightrope between separated parents and two very different countries. And it was a time that came to the most brutal of ends the year Beth turned sixteen.

Since then, Beth hasn't allowed herself to think about those years of her childhood. But the arrival of The Book of Summers brings the past tumbling back into the present; as vivid, painful and vital as ever.

978 0 7553 9085 4

headline
review

SARAH WINMAN

When God
Was A Rabbit

This is a book about a brother and a sister.

It's a book about childhood and growing up,
friendships and families, triumph and tragedy
and everything in between.

More than anything, it's a book about love
in all its forms.

'Captivating . . . rendered with an appealing frank-
ness, precision and emotional acuity' *Observer*

'Beguiling . . . you can't quite get the voice out of your
head' *Daily Mail*

'Mesmerising' *Good Housekeeping*

'Sharply funny, whimsical and innovative' *Guardian*

978 0 7553 7930 9

headline
review

Now you can buy any of these other bestselling titles from your bookshop or *direct from the publisher*.

FREE P&P AND UK DELIVERY
(Overseas and Ireland £3.50 per book)

Far to Go	Alison Pick	£7.99
The Book of Summers	Emylia Hall	£7.99
When God Was a Rabbit	Sarah Winman	£7.99
Rue Thérèse	Elena Mauli Shapiro	£7.99
The Long Song	Andrea levy	£7.99
The Hand That First Held Mine	Maggie O'Farrell	£7.99
My Last Duchess	Daisy Goodwin	£7.99
The Butterfly Cabinet	Bernie McGill	£7.99
The Death Instinct	Jed Rubenfeld	£7.99
Of Bees and Mist	Eric Setiawan	£7.99
The Secret Life of Bees	Sue Monk Kidd	£7.99

TO ORDER SIMPLY CALL THIS NUMBER

01235 400 414

or visit our website: www.headline.co.uk

Prices and availability subject to change without notice